The Hardy B

CRIMINAL OPERATIONS

Brother Against Brother
Perfect Getaway
The Borgia Dagger

Franklin W. Dixon

AN ARCHWAY PAPERBACK
Published by SIMON & SCHUSTER
New York   London   Toronto   Sydney   Tokyo   Singapore

BROTHER AGAINST BROTHER, PERFECT GETAWAY and
THE BORGIA DAGGER were first published in Great Britain by
Simon & Schuster Ltd, 1992
A Paramount Communications Company

Simon & Schuster Ltd
West Garden Place
Kendal Street
London W2 2AQ

Simon & Schuster of Australia Pty Ltd
Sydney

A CIP catalogue record for this book is
available from the British Library

ISBN 0-671-85475-5

Printed and bound in Great Britain by
HarperCollins*Manufacturing*

Brother Against Brother

Chapter

1

"SURPRISE!" JOE HARDY shouted, whipping an Uzi submachine gun from the cart he was pushing.

The two hijackers froze in the middle of the airplane aisle. A moment before they had thought he was one of them—a terrorist sneaking aboard the plane disguised as a food handler.

Now Joe and his brother, Frank, had dropped their disguises. They were really there to stop the hijacking and rescue Frank Hardy's girlfriend, Callie Shaw.

"We're all going to die!" a terrified passenger screamed.

"Not if I can help it," Joe Hardy said. "Drop those guns, you two."

But the terrorists didn't throw down their weapons. The dark-haired terrorist curled his lip, raised his Uzi, and began shooting. His blond comrade followed suit.

Screams rose, echoing wildly in the confined space of the plane.

Bullets came flying past Joe. It seemed as though an army was shooting. There were more bullets than two machine guns could fire. Miraculously, nothing hit him—in spite of the fact that he was right out in the open.

Joe knew he had to stop these guys. He leveled his gun in a firing position. But when he pulled the trigger, nothing happened. The Uzi was jammed!

More bullets tore past him—a storm of lead. Joe could hear screaming behind him—people were being hit. "Somebody help us!" a woman shouted. "Please!"

Joe couldn't help, though. He stood facing the terrorists, desperately trying to get his gun to work.

But his fingers were clumsy. He fumbled with the bolt of the gun, watching it slip out of his sweaty grasp.

Then a familiar voice cried out behind him. Joe did turn for a second and saw Callie Shaw staggering in the aisle. She had one hand over her shoulder—small streams of red ran between her fingers.

Joe stared at her dumbly, while his brother Frank was yelling, "Callie! You're hit!"

Frank jumped to help her as the storm of bullets increased. Both Callie and Frank fell to the floor, chopped down by the enemy's fire.

"No!" The word was torn from Joe's throat. *"NO!"*

He threw away his useless gun, balled his hands into fists, and charged at the terrorists.

They were still shooting, foot-long flames jetting from the muzzles of their Uzis. Yet none of their bullets touched Joe.

Just as he was almost on top of them, the terrorists stepped aside, revealing a third man.

He was middle-aged, with thinning hair and a pudgy face. Joe recognized him—the leader of the gang. The man grinned an evil smile and held out his right hand.

In it was a bomb detonator!

Joe leapt at him, but the head terrorist pressed the firing button.

"Fool!" was the last word Joe heard before the plane exploded. It all made a terrible sort of sense to Joe. Frank and Callie were gone. And now he was going up in a ball of flame, just as his girlfriend Iola had when a terrorist car bomb had exploded.

Joe stiffened and felt himself being flung into the air. And then . . .

"Sir, sir, wake up."

Joe's eyes opened to meet those of a young woman in uniform.

"Sir, please. We're about to land."

Joe realized that every muscle in his body was

3

rigid. His blond hair was damp with sweat. He forced himself to relax, shaking his head. "What's going on?"

"Sorry to bother you. You must have dozed off. Please bring your seat to an upright position. We're about to land in Denver."

Joe looked down at his hands. They were still gripping the armrests. "Right," he said, pushing the button to adjust the seat.

The flight attendant walked away. Joe shook his head again and yawned. What a weird dream! he thought. I wonder if the airline food brought it on.

He tried one last time to shake the nightmare away. It was like a horror-show version of their rescue of Callie from hijackers in a recent case, *Hostages of Hate*. So much could have gone wrong. . . . Joe shuddered. He hoped the dream wasn't a bad omen for his present mission.

"That movie put you to sleep?" his neighbor, an overweight businessman, asked.

"Guess so," Joe said. "How did it turn out?"

"Typical Hollywood ending. The guy killed about three thousand bad guys, then rescued a pretty girl from hideous aliens just before the spaceship crashed into San Francisco Bay. The special effects were awful, just awful. The head alien looked like a bicycle covered with carpet."

The businessman put a small calculator and note pad into his briefcase.

"What time is it?" Joe asked.

4

The man showed Joe an expensive Swiss watch. "Remember, though, we've traveled across two time zones. Denver's on Mountain Time, two hours earlier than this." The businessman straightened his tie. "You have family here?"

"No," Joe told him.

"Out here on business then?"

Joe eyed the man. Was he being friendly—or maybe a little too nosy? "It's mostly a pleasure trip," he finally said.

"Well, the mountains are beautiful, that's for sure."

Joe glanced out the window and saw beyond Denver to the blue foothills, and beyond them, the white peaks of the majestic Rockies filling the horizon.

"I couldn't help but hear you mutter in your sleep," the businessman told Joe.

"Is that right?"

The heavyset man nodded. "I couldn't make out what you were saying. But it sounded like a girl's name. Ilene. Elaine. Olive. Something like that."

Joe's breath came in with a little hiss. "Iola?" he said.

"Yeah, that sounds right. She your sweetheart?" the businessman asked with a nudge and a wink.

Again, the image of a ball of fire flashed through Joe's mind. This wasn't a nightmare,

5

though. Iola had really disappeared when the Hardys' car exploded—and Joe had been helpless to save her. "Iola was—special," Joe answered, almost in a whisper. "But she's no longer in my life."

"Well, girls are like buses," the man said, not understanding. "If you miss one, another will be along in a few minutes."

Not willing to set the guy straight, Joe tightened his seat belt, and as the plane began its gentle descent, leaned back in his seat.

He turned his head toward the window, trying not to think about Iola. About what a dangerous place the world had become. The skyscrapers of downtown Denver, surrounded by miles of streets and houses, filled his view. For a moment, as the plane descended, the mountains disappeared behind buildings and the horizon.

The mountains. What a perfect place to hide. He turned his head away from the window and thought about his mission. Later that day he'd be in the Rockies, searching for a man on the run.

The man had been in a witness protection program. But his cover was broken, and he had been running from hit men ever since. His only contact was Fenton Hardy, Joe's private investigator father.

The witness trusted only Fenton Hardy. They maintained a thin line of contact—one that Fenton had to use right then. Apparently, the underworld killers were getting very close to their target. Joe's job was to deliver a coded warning to the witness while Fenton pursued the killers.

The jet's wheels touched down, screeching as rubber hit the concrete runway. Joe felt himself lurch forward slightly. The engines roared as they were reversed to slow the jet. Then the airplane began to taxi toward its gate.

"Ladies and gentlemen," a flight attendant said over the P.A. "Welcome to Denver's Stapleton International Airport. We hope you've had a comfortable flight. And we wish you a pleasant stay here in Denver or wherever your eventual destination will be. Think of us the next time you need air travel, and have a good day."

The airplane rolled to a stop. Passengers leapt to their feet, scrambling to reclaim coats or luggage from overhead compartments. Several people, late for connecting flights, pushed toward the exit.

Joe waited for the bulk of the people to clear out, quietly tapping a finger against the rubber heel of his hiking boot. Hidden inside it was a small plastic capsule housing the message he had to deliver.

The plan was not without danger. Joe was to drive to a remote spot in the Rockies to meet the witness, a man he had never seen. What if Joe did his part, only to be met by hit men?

Maybe it was a hangover from his nightmare, but Joe suddenly felt anxious. He glanced around the cabin. Could the hit man possibly be on board? Could he be one of the flight attendants, even the guy sitting beside him?

"After you," the overweight businessman said, stepping back to make room for Joe in the aisle.

Joe moved in front of the man, almost expecting a weapon to be stuck into his back.

"You take care, now," the businessman said, gently nudging Joe toward the exit. His words sounded like a grim joke. "Take *good* care."

Chapter

2

AT THE AIRPORT Joe picked up a rental car, which Fenton had reserved. "Typical," Joe grumbled as he revved the motor. "They stick me with the least expensive—and least powerful—car in the lot. I'll probably have to *push* this thing uphill!"

Still, it was a beautiful, clear afternoon, a perfect day for cruising toward the Rockies.

The air was dry and a bit thin. Joe noticed that he had the slightest bit of difficulty in breathing because he was almost a mile above sea level. He remembered reading a newspaper article on how more and more athletes were coming to Colorado to train their bodies—and lungs—for the Olympics and other events.

Leaving the airport, Joe got on the interstate heading west and drove past Denver's downtown area. Not as impressive as New York or Chicago, he decided. Still, a dozen or so skyscrapers glistened in the sun.

West of the city limits, the flat plains crowded with suburban houses gave way to rolling hills. As he drove on, the road gradually inclined. Heavy trucks had to downshift to maintain their speed, and Joe passed them, pressing the accelerator pedal to the floor.

Joe noticed a sign for a point of interest just ahead. He checked the car clock—he was ahead of schedule, so he decided to pull off and see it.

Apparently, to build the highway, a large hill had been blasted. The remaining slopes on either side of the road were laid bare as if a piece had been sliced out of a cake.

His car rolled to a stop, and Joe looked up at the impressive road cut. Layer upon layer of geologic history lay exposed. A section of sandy-colored rock was wedged up against a black coal vein, which was wedged up against a thick level of brown stone.

A display explained that the site was an excellent example of the upturning of sedimentary layers, which happened some sixty-five million years before, when the present Rockies were formed.

In the background Joe could see Red Rocks Park. It was composed of gigantic monoliths that looked like ancient, landlocked ships, sandy red and eroded.

Just looking at them Joe knew they were old.

But the display told him they were part of the Ancestral Rockies, the first mountains in the area. And they had been formed three hundred million years ago!

Joe shook his head and returned to the highway, which wound through the foothills, gaining altitude quickly. The car began to lose momentum, and Joe had to move to the slow lane as more powerful cars whizzed by.

As he traveled farther and farther into the high country, the car radio picked up more and more static, eventually losing the local stations altogether. Joe shrugged. Guess the signals can't penetrate these hills, he thought.

Ahead of him, he saw a tourist shop shaped like an Indian tepee. Joe pulled off the highway, deciding to get a snack.

After he walked past shelves of Indian pottery and jewelry, candy bars and peanuts, polished rocks and souvenirs, Joe came to a rack of postcards.

A grin lit up his face. I'll send one to Frank, he decided. A little reminder of who's stuck at home in Bayport and who's in the Rockies.

Joe looked through the postcards, staring at one that had a strange-looking creature on it. It had the body and head of a jackrabbit but the antlers of an antelope. He turned the card over and read the inscription.

"The jackalope is a very shy animal found in the high mountains. Hunters covet its beautiful

11

antlers, but the jackalope hops so quickly that it is nearly impossible to trap.''

"Sell you that, son?''

Joe looked up to see an older man wearing a cowboy hat and western shirt grinning at him—obviously, the owner of the shop.

Joe grinned back. "Nice piece of trick photography on this card," he said. "Did you ever see one of these?"

The shop owner broke into laughter. "Well, most flatlanders, knowing no better, swear that they've seen jackalopes crossing the highway."

"Maybe I'll send this to my brother Frank," Joe said.

"Hold on—you may find a better card. We have lots of strange critters running around." The owner chuckled again.

Joe checked out some more postcards and found a whole weird menagerie. One card touted the "Rocky Mountain Furry Trout," a thick-haired fish that survived in the coldest mountain lakes. Another told about the "Gargantuan Grasshopper," which was larger than the two humans posed beside it. Colorado's a strange place, Joe concluded.

He bought the postcard of the jackalope and a stamp. On the back of the card he wrote:

Dear Frank,
Having the best time ever! Wish you were here! The sights are beautiful, and the girls

love to party! How are things at home? Having a good time with Dad and Mom?

> Your brother,
> Joe

"The postman is outside," the owner told Joe. "Catch him now, and that card will be on a plane tonight."

"Thanks." Sure enough, Joe found a postman emptying a mailbox near the road and handed him the postcard.

Although there were a few hours of light left, the sun had already set behind the western hills. Joe quickly paid for a cold drink and some snacks, then returned to the car.

Through a tunnel, around a hairpin curve, and Joe glimpsed the real mountains. Bluish, tree-bare summits rising some fourteen thousand feet above sea level filled the horizon.

Joe drove on, but as the sky continued to darken, the scenery faded into shadow. Joe had to concentrate on his driving. The road had become steep and curvy and ran along the edge of a ravine. On his left was a slope of loose boulders and rock. On his right a river roared through a mountain valley. The sound of the rushing water filled the air.

After coming out of a curve in the late twilight, Joe was heading down a deserted stretch of road. In the hazy, dark distance, something—one of those strange picture-postcard animals?—was standing in the middle of the road.

As Joe drew closer, the figure bounded directly into the path of his car. It was a man! Joe had to slam on the brakes and swerve to avoid hitting him.

He brought the car to a stop and jumped out, asking the man if he was all right.

The elderly-looking man had a hat pulled down low on his head with just a fringe of red hair hanging below. He was getting to his feet, dusting himself off.

"I'm okay, sonny," the man called as Joe walked back to him. "But my car is having a problem. I have a flat tire."

"I didn't even see you until the last possible moment," Joe said.

"No need to explain," the man said. "I'm just glad that someone was on this road. Thought I might have to spend the night out here by myself. You don't know what may happen in the wilderness once the sun goes down."

"Well, let me help you," Joe said, following the man to the edge of the road to where an old car was parked.

Joe walked around the vehicle. Its front left tire was flat.

"Problem is, I can't find my jack," the man explained.

"Hard to change a tire without one," Joe said

with a grin. "I bet there's one in my car. Wait here. I'll be right back."

Joe headed back to the rental car, took the keys from the ignition and opened the trunk. He pulled aside the spare tire and found a jack, which he began to loosen from its mount.

Then he heard a soft sound behind him—a foot scraping on the road surface. Joe started to turn, to tell the old man that he'd found the jack.

That's when he saw the tire iron swinging at his head.

Joe tried to spin away, but he was just a second too late. There was an explosion of light behind his eyes as the metal hit his skull. Then everything went black.

Everything was still dark when Joe came around—dark and stuffy. He had no idea where he was or how long he'd been unconscious. Gingerly, he touched the back of his head. He winced as his fingers probed a large welt—swollen, tender, and wet. He was probably bleeding.

After a moment, as his eyes adjusted to the darkness, he realized that he was in the trunk of a car. A tire lay beside him, and the jack ground into his back. It had to be the jack he was just removing. He was in the trunk of his own car! He tried pushing against the hood, then pounding on it. "Of all the times to get nailed," he muttered.

Joe tried to twist his body so he could push the lid with both legs, but he was too groggy to make much of an effort.

"Hey!" he shouted.

He waited for a response, but heard only the wind rustling through pine trees and the sound of the river roaring below.

"Hey!"

He rested for a moment, trying to gather his strength. Then he heard something stirring outside.

With renewed effort, Joe pounded on the lid. "Open up!" he yelled. "In the trunk!" He kicked at the metal.

He stopped, waiting for a response. Instead, he heard footsteps move away, toward the front of the car. He felt the car shift slightly as someone climbed into it. Then, after a moment, the weight shifted again, as whoever it was got out.

"Hey! Back here!"

Suddenly the car moved. The brakes were off! Someone was pushing the car from the front!

"Stop it! I'm trapped back here!"

Slowly at first, the car slid backward. Then, gaining momentum, it moved faster.

Joe could hear the pavement under the car and knew when it hit gravel. Then he heard the car brush through weeds and bounce over rocks. The roar of the river became louder. He was heading for the lip of the ravine!

He started fighting with all his strength to open the trunk. But the hood didn't budge.

Then the car tipped as the rear wheels rolled

free of the ground. Joe was thrown against the hood as the car teetered. . . .

"No! No!" he yelled.

Joe bounced around helplessly in the trunk as the car tumbled down the slopes of the canyon. He heard the windshield shatter, and a crunch of metal as the roof caved in.

Then the car backed into something large, springing the trunk lock. The lid swung up as the car bounced off a huge rock and flew high into the air. Joe had a look at where he was heading—into the boulder-strewn river of roaring white water!

Chapter

3

"ANY WORD YET?" Frank Hardy couldn't keep the anxiety out of his voice. "Has Joe called?"

His mother shook her head. "No word. This isn't like Joe. It's been two whole days."

"Where's Dad?" Frank asked, sitting down at the kitchen table in their Bayport home.

"Notifying the authorities of Joe's disappearance." Laura Hardy stared at her son for a long moment. "Frank, what's going on?"

Frank avoided her eyes. "Where's Aunt Gertrude?"

"Don't change the subject. I'm worried about Joe." Laura Hardy said sharply. She sighed and rubbed the back of her neck. "I'm sorry, Frank. I guess we're all wound up a bit too tight over this."

"It's all right, Mom," Frank said. "I'm worried about Joe, too.'' He reached across the table and took an apple from a bowl of fruit. But he wasn't really hungry. ''I think I'll go for a run,'' he finally said.

The morning air was salty as Frank ran along the beach of Barmet Bay. Most mornings, before breakfast, Frank and Joe would run together to the beach and back. And, most mornings, Joe won.

Frank hated to admit it, but it drove him crazy. He spent his mornings exercising, doing weight training and karate workouts. Joe rolled out of bed an hour after him, and did nothing but play a little football or baseball. He was as good an athlete—or better—than Frank.

Joe jokingly referred to Frank as the brains of their operation and himself as the brawn. He was slightly shorter than Frank but stockier and more muscular. They made an excellent team. Frank sometimes wondered if the underlying competition between them was what made their team so successful.

Frank smiled, pushing himself to run faster. No, that wasn't it. They worked together so well because their abilities meshed perfectly. Because they were brothers. He'd hate to see what would happen if they ever found themselves on opposite sides.

Just as Frank returned home from his run,

Fenton Hardy walked into the kitchen, where his wife was sipping coffee.

Frank poured himself a glass of juice and joined his parents at the table.

"Is there any news?" Laura finally asked.

Fenton Hardy shook his head.

Laura Hardy shrank in her chair. "In that case, I think I'll go for a walk. I could use a little fresh air, too," she told Frank.

Frank waited for his mother to leave before he asked his father, "Nothing at all?"

"No word from Joe," Fenton said. "And no word about the hit man, either." At a look from Frank, Fenton added, "I'm doing everything I can."

Frank gripped the edge of the table, trying to stay calm. "I should have gone with Joe. It wasn't a good idea to send him alone."

Fenton Hardy shook his head. "Two people traveling together might have attracted attention. We agreed on that. And Joe won the draw to go," Fenton reminded Frank. "If we're going to play might-have-been, *I* should have gone."

"Come on, Dad. Any hood would be sure to know you. They'd follow you straight to the witness. That's why it had to be either Joe or me." He shook his head. "Joe is just too hotheaded. If he got himself into something . . ."

Fenton's eyes drifted toward the phone. "I hope not, Frank. The hoods on this case are very dangerous. Organized crime types."

21

"Are we going to sit here and do nothing?" Frank asked.

"I'll be in my study," Fenton said, abruptly rising to his feet. "Leave the phone line open, in case Joe calls."

The next hours were the longest in Frank's life. The kitchen phone never rang. All day Fenton shut himself up in his study. Frank could hear him talking over the private line, phone call after phone call. Laura Hardy came home and disappeared upstairs. Frank tried watching TV, then listening to music, but he couldn't get his mind off Joe.

When Fenton didn't show up for supper, Frank went to his study and knocked on the door. "I'm going after Joe," he told his father.

"I'm not sending another son out," Fenton Hardy told him firmly.

"Come on, Dad," Frank begged. "The only word we received today was some silly postcard that Joe sent two days ago! Besides, someone still has to deliver the warning to the witness."

The door opened. Fenton Hardy stared at his son. "I don't like your idea one bit," he said quietly. "But I will think about it." With that, he disappeared back into his study.

"Well, I'm not hanging around here," Frank said to himself.

He drove his van around aimlessly, up and down the streets of Bayport. All he wanted to do was help Joe. But he had to respect his father's wishes. At a train crossing, the barriers came down, lights flashing, bells clanging. Frank braked and watched the New York City express barrel past on the tracks. At least it was going someplace! He slammed the steering wheel in frustration. I'm beginning to act just like Joe, he thought.

As he was driving past the mall, Frank saw Callie Shaw, Chet Morton, and Liz Webling leaving the movies. Frank pulled up and waved to them.

"What do you say we go over to Mr. Pizza?" Chet suggested. "I'm feeling a little hungry."

"You're *always* hungry," Callie kidded him.

"That's how I maintain my figure." Chet chuckled, grabbing his middle. "Hey, Frank, why don't you come along?"

Frank shook his head. "Actually, I was hoping to take Callie away from all this."

Liz grinned and took Chet's arm. "I can take a hint," she said. "Come on, pal, lead me to that pizza."

Callie climbed in, and the van took off. The breeze from the window ruffled her blond hair as she looked at Frank. "Something's bothering you. What is it?" she asked.

Frank told her about Joe. "I want to go after him," he said.

"Sounds dangerous." Callie frowned. "Besides, you don't know for sure what happened to Joe. Maybe he's out of touch to *avoid* trouble.

You should have an idea of what you'll be fighting before you jump in the middle of it.''

"I guess you're right,'' Frank said, reaching over to squeeze her hand.

She shuddered a little. "I always get a bad feeling in this place.'' She looked out across the parking lot. "It's where your car blew up—with Iola.'' Her voice was very quiet. "I hope Joe's all right.''

Frank sat quietly for a moment, his face set. I can't stand by and do nothing, he decided.

Callie was studying him. "Frank? Are you okay?'' she asked quietly. But lost in his troubled thoughts, Frank didn't answer.

It was like a nightmare playing over and over in his mind. Joe saw himself trapped in the car trunk, tumbling down the canyon wall again and again. He tried to open his eyes to stop the dreaming, but he couldn't. No, he could do nothing but live through the confusion and fear again and again.

How long ago had it *actually* happened? It could have been hours, days, or weeks. Joe had lost all notion of time. All he remembered was trying frantically to get out of the open trunk as the car tumbled toward the river. He was right above the gas tank. If it hit a boulder and exploded, he'd be splattered all over the landscape.

He'd made one desperate jump, hitting his shoulder as the lid swung closed. But he'd gotten free of the car, even if he plummeted down the slope helplessly. The last thing he saw was the blunt edge of a boulder, flying up to meet him. He twisted desperately in midair, but all that followed was this dark trance.

He had clawed his way back to consciousness. Sharp, piercing pain held him paralyzed. His body and limbs were bruised and bloody. His head throbbed in time with his heartbeat. Instinct alone got him to his feet and forced him to hobble away. Whoever had pushed him down would come to check the accident site—and maybe finish the job.

Staggering drunkenly, Joe forced his battered body along the riverbank. Stopping by a still pool of water, he looked at his reflection. It looked like something out of a splatter movie. A deep cut in his scalp had left a mask of blood over half his face, making it completely unrecognizable.

He stared at the frightening stranger in the water, then stumbled on. The river flattened and slowed. Joe stopped. Maybe he could enter the water. Perhaps its coolness would soothe his aching hurts. Moving like an old man, he gingerly climbed over some boulders lining the shore. Then he heard something duck underwater.

Leaning against a boulder, Joe blinked, trying to focus his eyes. Concentric ripples in the water marked the spot where whatever it was had disappeared. Would it surface again?

It did—and Joe gasped in amazement as a

human head broke through the water, tossing long, water-soaked hair over tanned shoulders. A girl, and a pretty one! Then she saw him and crouched in the water up to her chin!

Reeling forward, he stretched his hands toward the girl.

She reacted as if he were the star of a horror movie, moving quickly to grab for a towel lying on a boulder. Covering herself with the cloth, she climbed out of the water.

"Please," Joe tried to say, but it just came out as a moan. Then a golden retriever, teeth bared, came splashing through the water, snarling at him.

Joe tried to pull himself together, to defend himself, but everything was swirling around him. He looked at the girl and heard a voice—his own? hers?—whispering, "Help me!"

Then he collapsed, helplessly crumpling into darkness.

Chapter

4

"CAN YOU TELL me anything more? Please try to remember," Frank Hardy said. "It's really important." He leaned across the rental car counter at Stapleton Airport. In his hand was his one slim lead to Joe, the jackalope postcard which Joe had sent him.

The clerk, a young woman with a stiff blond hairdo, thought for a moment, then said, "I'm sorry. There's a few conventions in town, plus the usual tourists. I showed you our records, so you know what kind of car he rented. But I just don't remember anything else about him."

"He may have asked directions to the mountains. Does that help?" Frank asked.

"I just can't remember your brother," the clerk said. "I mean, I remember helping someone who looks like that picture you showed me. But that was a few days ago. If he was headed for the mountains, you've got a big job ahead of you."

Frank glanced over the clerk's shoulder. On the wall was tacked a road map of Colorado and the surrounding states. And the mountains filled an enormous part of the map. If Joe were lost up there, it would take a miracle to find him, Frank thought to himself. But he knew the route Joe was supposed to follow, and now he knew what Joe was driving. That was a start.

It had taken some doing to convince his father to let him try this mission—they had argued well into the night. Finally, as much because of exhaustion as discussion, Fenton Hardy agreed to let Frank go. If they waited much longer, Joe's trail might be too cold to follow.

"We can only hope Joe's alive," Fenton finally said. "And you'll have to find our witness—and that hit man."

Frank barely had time to pack a bag before his father was hurrying him to the airport.

"I'm giving you twenty-four hours," Fenton had warned Frank. "If there's no sign of Joe or the hit man, I want you home. Understand?"

"Okay, Dad." Frank looked up at his father's pale, drawn face. "Everything will turn out all right. I promise."

The rental car clerk's voice cut through his thoughts. "Sorry I couldn't be of more help. Good luck in finding your brother."

"Thanks, anyway," Frank said, flipping the

postcard against his palm. Suddenly an idea came to him.

"Can I bother you one more second?" he said to the clerk.

"No bother."

"Have you ever seen one of these?" Frank asked, showing her the postcard.

The clerk studied the postcard, then grinned. "Well, it's not too easy to see a jackalope—since it doesn't exist. It's only a gag postcard, understand. Tourists buy them by the gross."

"Where are they sold?" Frank asked.

"All over the state," the clerk said. "May I see it?"

"There's no clue on it," Frank said. "Just a joke message from Joe."

"But there's also a postmark," said the clerk. "Maybe I'll recognize where it's from."

Frank handed over the postcard, and she examined the inky postmark which had cancelled the stamp. "Summit County," she said. "I know where that is. Up in the mountains, about sixty miles due west of here. And I bet that I know exactly where your brother bought this."

"Really? Where?"

"There's a tourist shop right off the highway. It's built to look like an Indian tent. The owner loves this sort of junk."

Frank took back the postcard. "Thanks. At least it's a start."

In a rental car of his own, Frank began to trace

29

Joe's tracks from the Denver airport. On the highway, heading west, Frank turned on the radio. It was too much to hope for news about Joe, but he wanted a weather report. Already his mind was working, trying to estimate the driving time to the mountains, taking into consideration the weather and amount of traffic.

Most of the time these mental exercises were just games. Frank knew this, but he tried to keep his mind sharp with constant practice.

At first Frank felt confident that he could find Joe. Call it a hunch, but it would not be the first time that Frank got his younger brother out of a tight spot. All too often, Joe's hot head got him into trouble, charging into situations without thinking things through. *Caution* was not to be found in Joe Hardy's vocabulary.

Frank smiled to himself. What dumb thing had Joe done this time? Run out of gas on a deserted mountain road? Completed his mission and then run into a few girls, forgetting altogether to call home?

The car began to lose its momentum as the incline of the road became steeper. Frank hit the accelerator, wanting to maintain a speed just below the legal limit. Ahead he saw the Rocky Mountains. Massive, imposing, endless. And Frank's optimism began to fade.

How could one person search a whole mountain range? he asked himself. It could take weeks, even months, to track Joe down. He could already be dead—or dying—before Frank reached the foothills.

Still, he couldn't turn back.

Joe, sweaty, breathing heavily, fought against delirium. His mind, like some video machine gone berserk, kept flashing brief, violent scenes —confused memories. Voices, momentary images of faces and scenes turned over and over. The people and places were both incredibly familiar and frighteningly alien.

Tumbling in and out of darkness, Joe found himself struggling again with Al-Rousasa, the terrorist who had killed Iola Morton.

He and Joe were fighting again not far from where Iola had been murdered.

"Wait a second, this has to be a dream," Joe told himself. "This can't be happening again. Or is it happening for the very first time?"

Joe didn't have any more time to wonder. Al-Rousasa hurled him against a concrete bench. The impact left Joe seeing stars as the terrorist knelt over him, raising his knife for the kill. Joe, cut and bleeding, got off a perfect roundhouse right straight into Al-Rousasa's face.

The punch knocked the terrorist backward and over a safety rail, where he could drop sixty feet to the mall below. But no. Al-Rousasa had the agility of a cat. He twisted himself around in midair, snatching at the rail and catching onto the edge of the floor.

31

Joe stood, glaring down at those white-knuckled hands and the dark eyes burning with hatred. A quick stomp on those hands, a kick into that despised face, and Iola's killer would be gone. . . .

Suddenly the dream shifted, and the terrorist dissolved into a cloud of fog. Out of the haze appeared the laughing face of a beautiful girl with pixielike features.

"Iola!" Joe heard himself call. "Iola, please forgive me!"

She turned and ran away. Joe tried to follow, but it was as if his feet were fixed in concrete. "Iola! Wait."

Suddenly Joe felt himself swept up. He was swooping along a cliff, flying over sharp-edged rocks. He could feel the wind whipping past him, blowing the mane against his face—the mane? Now he was on a horse, galloping madly.

Joe gripped the horse tightly with his knees and with his arms wrapped around the animal's neck. Then the gunshots came streaking past.

The horse raced across a pasture, then down a moonlit asphalt road. Hoofbeats thundered so loudly that Joe had to yell to make himself heard.

"We've done it! We've shaken them!" he shouted triumphantly, looking over his shoulder—at what? Where were the others?

Only an empty highway stretched behind him.

He faced front again, to see a huge mountain of a man preparing to shoot a girl. The girl charged him, moving without a word, a knife held tightly in her hand. She would never reach the man in time. "No!" Joe screamed, but he was too late.

The Super Blackhawk came up, fired. The bullet caught the girl in the chest, whipping her about violently. She hit the ground and lay motionless.

Not caring if the guy shot him, too, Joe jumped for him. But the man dissolved, and Joe found himself landing on hard concrete.

"Joe!"

He scrambled to his knees, to find Iola standing where the girl had gone down. She was surrounded by flames, and calling his name.

"You've got to save me, Joe! You can't let me die!"

Joe hurled himself forward, but never made it to that ring of fire. Someone was in his way—a tall, dark-haired guy about his own age. He looked so familiar, but Joe didn't recognize him.

But that didn't matter then. Joe tried to shove his way past him, to get to Iola. But the dark stranger didn't move. He held Joe back.

The next thing Joe knew, he was throwing a punch. It didn't land. The dark-haired stranger ducked. But when Joe tried to dart past again, the stranger grabbed him.

It was like wrestling with an octopus. Joe couldn't get loose. And all the time he fought, he could hear Iola in the background, screaming.

He looked into his captor's face, and the

33

THE HARDY BOYS CASEFILES

stranger began laughing. Sometimes it sounded as if he were just kidding. Other times his laughter was mocking—threatening.

The laughter became louder and louder, mingling with and drowning out Iola's screams. Then Joe was screaming, too. "Iola! It's not my fault! Stop it. *Stop it!*"

His body arched with pain as someone shook him violently. Then he realized his swollen eyes were open. This was no dream!

Squinting, he couldn't make out who was looming over him. Was it a friend or enemy? Was it the dark-haired stranger?

Still groggy, he struck out and his hand clamped around a neck. He heard a gasp as the stranger fell to the floor.

"I'll get you!" Joe screamed. "I'll kill you with my bare hands!"

Chapter

5

FRANK'S SHOULDERS SLUMPED in defeat. For hours, well into a long, long night, he had searched for Joe. But there wasn't even one solid clue as to where Joe was. Joe had started off on the route his father had given him, and then it seemed as if he had disappeared.

The owner of the tepee tourist shop had remembered Joe, but he had provided no concrete leads.

"Sorry," he'd said. "I can't keep track of every lowlander coming this way. Sure I can't interest you in a nice silver bracelet for your girlfriend?"

"Girlfriend? What makes you think I have a girlfriend?"

That got a chuckle from the owner. "Fella like you would be sure to have a girlfriend."

All Frank had wanted was a phone. He had called back to Bayport from the shop. His parents had nothing to report. But Fenton Hardy had reminded him that his twenty-four hours would be up the next afternoon.

Frank had answered that he wasn't going to leave Colorado without some information about Joe's fate.

After leaving the tourist shop, Frank had covered the main roads of Summit County until well past sundown. He'd stopped at gas stations and truck stops, at restaurants and motels, describing Joe's car, showing Joe's photo. He had talked with the local law, asking if anything unusual—an accident, a rock slide, a shooting—had been reported. He checked with the local hospitals. But everywhere he went, Frank had come up empty.

Finally, he couldn't drive any farther and pulled into a rest area. Under better circumstances the place would have been very restful. It was off the main road and had several picnic tables surrounded by tall, thin pines and aspens. Nearby, a stream ran downhill through a canyon.

But Frank found little rest. When his eyes closed, all he could envision were horrible scenes. Joe hurt and lost. Joe attacked by the very hit man he was trying to stop. Joe dazed and wandering. Joe . . . Joe . . . Joe . . .

Frank napped for a little while, then shook himself awake, his eyes and mouth feeling gummy. He started the car and looked for a place to eat.

Now he was sitting in a truck stop. It was late, closer to sunrise than midnight. The only other customers, truck drivers.

Frank sat at the counter, sipping a large glass of soda, barely touching the hamburger and fries in front of him. His place mat was a map of Colorado, the kind with facts about tourist attractions.

Frank pushed his food away and unfolded a road map. With a pen he marked the places he had already visited.

"Looking for a place to bed down for the night?" the waitress asked. "There's a decent motel about three miles down the road."

"No," Frank told her. "I've got to keep moving. May I have my check, please?"

The waitress totaled up Frank's bill and left it on the counter. "You look pretty tired," she said. "I hope that you're not planning to do much more driving. The roads around here can be dangerous in the dark."

Frank put some money on the counter. He shook his head, trying to come up with a new course of action. The waitress marched over to freshen the coffee for two truckers sharing a booth.

"How are you guys tonight?" she asked.

"Stuck here," one trucker said with a grin.

37

"How about two slices of your famous apple pie?"

"And keep the coffee coming," said the other trucker. "Might as well stay put till they get that accident cleaned up."

"Accident?" the waitress asked.

"Heard it over my CB," he said. "Road's closed up near Cripple Mine. They found some car went off the road, and they've closed it till a tow truck can pull the car up from the river. Decided to do it now, so they wouldn't block the road during the day."

Frank spun around on his stool, giving the truckers his full attention.

"Was it a bad crash?" the waitress asked.

"Yeah. But they think it happened a while ago. Some guy just reported it today, though. A buddy of mine was the last truck they let through. He was passing by just after the police had arrived. Told me about it over the CB. Strangest thing, he said the car had been picked clean of any ID. The glove compartment was stripped. No registration. Even the license plates were missing."

"Well, who was driving?" the waitress asked.

"No sign of anyone." The trucker shrugged. "I can't figure it."

The truckers and waitress continued to talk, but Frank turned back to the road map before him.

"Cripple Mine," he whispered to himself, tracing over his map. His finger had strayed across the border into Utah before he shook his head, realizing he was too tired to use common sense.

He turned the map around to check the directory of places listed on the back. Sure enough, there was a Cripple Mine.

Using the location code, Frank first circled the general area, then, peering closer he zeroed in on Cripple Mine. He circled it with a pen. Using the mileage legend he figured that he could reach Cripple Mine by sunrise.

Frank quietly folded the map and left. He was feeling some hope, even though that accident sounded bad. What if he finally found Joe's car, only to learn that something horrible had happened to his brother?

Joe Hardy had tumbled to the floor, a cold grip around his enemy's throat. Hands were feebly beating against his wrists, but they couldn't break his hold. The dark-haired stranger wasn't so strong now! He'd kill him!

He stared at his enemy—and leapt back, blinking. "Am I dreaming?" he whispered to himself. The stranger had disappeared. Instead, his hands were locked on the throat of an auburn-haired girl with lovely green eyes—apprehensive eyes at that moment, as she huddled on the floor, arms raised to protect herself.

He reached up and felt a bandage wrapped around his head. "Wha-what's going on?" he asked, his voice thin and reedy.

"You began shouting and tossing around on the bed," the girl said. "I tried to shake you awake—and you started strangling me!" She looked at him nervously. "Do you always wake up like that?"

Joe leaned back against the bed, his head spinning. Little by little, he took in his surroundings. A rustic cabin with log walls. A small, single room equipped with a wooden table and chairs, one bed and several folding cots, and a cast iron wood-burning stove.

"I'm sorry if I scared you," he finally said.

The girl dropped her defensive pose. "You could make a career out of scaring people—like when you came up to the river."

Joe rubbed his head. "You—you were the girl in the water!"

Her face went red. "I was—um—skinny-dipping, and then you came lurching out of the rocks at me like some kind of monster. My dog, Lucky, ran at you—he's a good watchdog. I thought he'd have to attack you. But you just fell on your face."

The girl helped Joe back onto the bed. "I could see that you were pretty badly banged up, especially when I couldn't revive you. I heard later about a car half-buried in the river. Was that yours?"

For an instant Joe remembered tumbling through the air. "Yeah," he muttered.

"You were lucky you survived." Joe nodded.

"Anyway, I dragged you back here. It took a while, because you were bleeding pretty badly, and you weighed a ton! I was afraid you wouldn't make it." She smiled sweetly and began readjusting Joe's bandage.

"Once I got you here," she continued, "my Uncle Delbert helped me get you into bed and worked on your wounds. We didn't dare move you. The closest hospital is miles and miles away."

"I owe you and your uncle a lot," Joe said. "Thanks."

The girl smiled at him. "My name is Rita, by the way. My uncle's not here right now. He went out for, uh, supplies."

"I don't know how I can thank you." Joe tried to sit up. Pain brought his hands to his temples and forehead.

"You kept muttering in your sleep. I thought that maybe we should take our chances and move you to a hospital—even with the long drive."

"Long drive? We must really be isolated," Joe said.

Rita nodded. "Uncle Delbert likes the quiet." She dampened a cloth and lightly ran it over Joe's face. "You're looking a lot better. How do you feel?"

"Like I was hit with a ton of bricks," Joe said. He attempted a smile, but a sudden pain in his head made him groan instead.

"Well, you'll need a lot more rest. Your body

will need time to heal," Rita said. She collected the cloth and bowl of water and began to move away. "You know," she said, stopping, "you haven't told me your name."

"I'm—I'm—" Joe began to say, expecting his name to naturally follow. He rubbed his head. "I can't remember!"

"What?" Rita said. "Are you joking?"

"I can't remember!" Joe rose up in panic.

"Now, lie back and try to rest. Remember, you took an awful thump on the head." She covered him with a quilt and then pulled a chair beside the bed and held his hand. "Just take it easy," she said. "Don't try to force anything. It'll all come back to you."

"I can't remember my own name!" Joe began to push himself off the bed.

Rita gently pushed him back. "Where do you think you're going? You can't travel."

"You don't understand," Joe's voice rose. "There's something I have to do!"

"What's that?" Rita asked.

"I—can't remember!" Joe said.

"Then you can't do it, can you?" Rita said, trying to calm him. "First you have to remember your name."

"But I can't!" Joe's whole body was quivering.

"Calm down!" she said gently. "I'm here to help you. Just close your eyes. Relax, and tell me what comes into your mind."

Joe closed his eyes and sank back into the soft

pillow. At first his mind was a clean slate—then a hazy image appeared. Slowly it became clearer—a girl seated in a sedan. "Iola," he whispered sadly.

"Iola?" Rita said. "That's an interesting name. Is that the name of your hometown or something?"

"No, no. It's the name of a girl," he said.

"Your sister?" Rita asked. "Your girlfriend, perhaps?"

Then he saw the flames, and the dark stranger's face, just like in his dream. "Iola, I-I've got to help her," Joe stammered. "He's stopping me!"

"He?" Rita echoed. "Who is 'he'?"

"There's danger. Awful danger!" Joe opened his eyes and sat up. "Something evil is outside."

"Please, please calm down," Rita said. "That's only the wind moving through the trees. Believe me, we're miles from the nearest neighbors."

"No!" Joe told her. "You've got to believe me. It's lurking outside, ready to hurt us!" He lurched up from the bed and stumbled to the door, pulling on the handle.

The heavy wooden door swung open—to reveal a man standing on the porch, a rifle in his hands.

"Hold it right there, buddy," the man said. "You make a move and I'll use this thing!"

Chapter

6

FRANK HARDY DROVE frantically through the Rocky Mountain dawn. Sunlight was a long time coming to the low canyons where his route took him. The sun had been up for an hour before it was high enough in the sky to climb over the craggy mountaintops.

Till then, Frank had driven through a faint glow. Little by little, though, the glow increased, bringing a pink tone to the rocks around him. Then, as more light hit the rocks, the pink intensified into reddish brown.

The air began to warm, and Frank realized he no longer needed the car heater. He turned it off and opened a window. Cool, dry breezes filled the car, bringing with them a scent of pine.

It was a beautiful spectacle—but Frank hardly noticed. Except for a brief nap, he had been up all night. His whole body ached from lack of sleep. His stomach rumbled, his neck and back were shot through with pain. His mind buzzed with a series of unanswerable "what ifs."

"What if I can't locate Cripple Mine?"

"What if the cops don't let me through?"

"What if the car's already been towed away?"

"What if I'm forced to return to Bayport without Joe?"

"What if I find Joe dead?"

"What if the hit man is lying in wait for *me*?" The road passed through some woods. For just a moment Frank thought about stopping the car, walking through the woods, kneeling beside a brook, and rubbing some of its icy water over his tired face. But he drove on.

"Hang on, Joe," Frank whispered. "I'm coming. I'm coming, brother."

He curved around a bend in the highway to find a patrolman removing a wooden barricade, to open the road to traffic again.

Frank slowed, checking out the scene. Through the open window he heard the roar of a raging river. Beside him he saw the steel guardrail smashed apart, with tire tracks rolling off the road's edge and disappearing into the ravine.

Just ahead of this, parked at the side of the ravine, were a tow truck carrying a wreck and a highway patrol car. An officer was jotting notes down, while the tow truck operator waited.

Frank stopped and shouted out the window, "Excuse me. Is this near Cripple Mine?"

"Yes, it is. But just keep moving, son," the officer said. "Got to keep the road clear."

"Looks like some accident," Frank said. "How did the guy who was driving come out?"

"We found nothing but the wreck itself," the officer said. "No body, no identification."

"Well, thank you," Frank said. He accelerated slightly, moving past the tow truck.

He nearly slammed to a stop as he studied the wrecked car—the same make and model that Joe had rented. "No one could have survived in that," he whispered to himself. The windshield and all the windows of the car had been shattered. The roof was flattened against the body. The engine was in the backseat. The sides had been punched in like a collapsed milk carton.

Frank's face was grim as he drove away. If Joe had been in there . . .

He drove a mile or so, then finding a place to pull off, he hid his car among some trees. Then he walked back along the road toward the accident site.

Seeing the approaching roof lights of the tow truck and patrol car, Frank ducked for cover. He crouched low in some bushes while the procession passed by. Then he jogged along the asphalt road.

He followed the guardrail until its violent break. Glancing down the rocky ravine Frank

47

could see the tracks the wreck had made as it was winched up from the river. Gingerly Frank stepped off the edge and started down the ravine.

He picked his way carefully. One false step and he'd be unable to regain his balance. He'd tumble out of control over sharp boulders to the wild river below. He leaned into the hill, until he reached the bottom.

The sun was high over the pines now. It gave perfect light for Frank's search. His eyes focused on the ground, looking for anything the highway patrol might have missed.

Paint on some boulders and a deep indentation at the river's edge indicated to Frank where the wreck had landed. He remembered how the wreck had looked. About the only part of the car not severely damaged had been the trunk. Maybe, if Joe had survived, he might have gotten out through there.

Moving farther downstream Frank spied a tire iron among some rocks. It couldn't have been there long—no cobwebs, moss, or rust. Frank picked up the steel bar and inspected it closely. Near the top he found what looked like a cluster of hairs glued to the iron with dried blood.

The muscles in Frank's jaw tensed as he took this in. The crash looked very little like an accident now. Whoever had stripped the car had a purpose—a deadly one.

Hefting the tire iron like a club, Frank moved on. He stopped to examine a flat boulder—and the sticky, reddish stain on it. A smear of dry blood, as if someone had stopped to rest—or die.

Frank looked downstream. Someone could have followed a narrow trail up the rocky slope toward the trees. Or, someone could have walked along the rocks lining the river edge.

But, Frank deduced, if someone was injured and bleeding, he would follow the river trail, since it would be easier.

So Frank began to follow the river. His tiredness fell away from him now; every sense was awake and alert. He cast back and forth over the soft mud, finding one print and then another. The pattern they made looked like a drunken—or injured—stumble. Then a new set of prints were introduced—not human. Frank knelt to examine them. They looked like the prints of a large dog.

Frank continued on and spied a new set of human prints. Small bare footprints, most likely a woman's or boy's. And, off to the side, caught in some brambles, was a white bath towel!

Climbing onto a boulder, Frank tried to get an aerial view of the three sets of prints. Yes, it all made sense. It looked as if the small prints had come from the water. Then whoever made those prints dragged the person who made the larger prints away. The larger person was probably injured. Frank crossed his fingers and barely allowed himself to hope it was Joe.

But who were they for sure? And where did they go?

Frank followed the prints until he was confronted by a massive boulder blocking the river path. The ground all around it was rocky, and the prints disappeared.

"Just my luck," Frank said. He ran across the rocky ground, which led to the edge of some woods. Casting around, Frank inspected the area, looking for any sign—a broken branch or scuffed pine needles—anything that would indicate that somebody had been dragged that way.

For the first time he felt a faint glimmer of hope. Perhaps Joe had survived the wreck and somehow had found help. Maybe Frank could find him.

But one disturbing question remained. Who had used the bloody tire iron? And if he used it once against Joe, would he be satisfied that he had done his job? Or would he try to kill Joe again?

Chapter

7

JOE WAS VERY much alive and trying to stay that way. "Now, hold on, mister," he said taking a step forward.

"No, *you* hold on," said the man, thrusting his rifle at Joe. "I've got a lot of questions I want answered." The rifle was pointed straight at Joe's chest.

"Anything you say," Joe said soothingly. He managed another step forward, then swung his arm quickly, batting the rifle aside. After a quick scuffle, he had the weapon in his hands, a little amazed that he had won in his weakened condition.

But the man before him was even more feeble. He could have been anywhere between forty and fifty. But he looked wasted. His face and neck were gaunt. His skin had a pale, pasty quality, and his eyes showed both fear and sleeplessness.

"Go ahead," the man said, his face stony. "Shoot me. End it!"

But Rita screamed. "Don't! It's my uncle!"

Joe glanced from the man to Rita, then lowered the weapon. "Do you always carry a rifle when you go out for supplies?" he asked suspiciously.

"Uncle Delbert and I are down here for a hunting trip," Rita explained. "We're from Wyoming."

"Right," Delbert said. "Whenever I go out, I carry the gun. I might get a lucky shot at something."

Or *someone,* Joe thought. He looked back into the cabin. Plenty of wood had been cut and was stacked near the stove. Provisions lined the kitchen shelves. These people weren't there for a simple vacation, and it didn't look as if they needed supplies.

"How long have you been here?" Joe asked.

"A couple of days," Rita said quickly.

"Shot anything?"

"Nope. All I've seen so far were a couple of jackalopes," Rita answered, smiling slightly.

"Jackalopes?" Joe echoed. An image flickered through his mind. "Knock if off, Rita. Anyone who spends time in the Rockies knows jackalopes don't exist. I sent a gag postcard with a jackalope to my brother."

"Your brother," Rita said. "Then your memory is coming back." Eager to change the subject, she explained about Joe's memory loss to her uncle.

Joe stood very still, trying to recall more images. A mall—a sporting goods store, where he had bought a pair of— "My boots," Joe whispered. "My hiking boots."

Rita stared at him. "What's that?"

"There's something hidden in one of my boots," Joe told her.

Uncle Delbert raised his head. "Hidden?" he repeated.

The three of them went back into the cabin, and Joe found his hiking boots by the door. Rita had cleaned and polished them. He picked up the right boot, feeling along the sole. Then he twisted the heel—it swung out!

Nestled inside the hollow heel was a small capsule.

Joe pulled the capsule open, and a scrap of paper dropped into his hand.

Eagerly, he unrolled the paper. He smoothed it against his palm and stared at it in frustration.

"What does it say?" Rita asked.

"It's just a line of letters." Joe tried to pronounce them. " 'On-ot-ow-at-ish-ik-a.' "

"May I try?" Rita asked. Joe handed her the message. " 'O-no-to-wa-*tish*-i-ka?' Maybe it's an Indian name?"

"It's a code," Joe said. "And I don't have the

key!'' He paused for a second. How had he known that?

Delbert snatched the paper from his niece's hand. "Where did you get this?" he demanded.

"I can't remember," Joe said miserably. "I can't even read what it says!"

Delbert's face was hard and suspicious as he looked at Joe. He had just opened his mouth to say something, when frenzied snarling and barking rang out from outside the cabin.

"Lucky!" Rita moved to a window.

But Delbert grabbed her arm. "Stay low," he said, stretching his hand out to Joe. "I need that rifle, youngster."

Joe handed it over, and Delbert jacked a round into the chamber. He threw open the door and dove outside. After rolling across the porch, he came up in a crouch.

Lucky gave a yelp of pain and ran to the door.

Both Joe and Delbert scanned the area, looking along Lucky's line of flight. No one was there. Delbert backed through the door, his finger still on the trigger.

Rita was kneeling on the floor, checking Lucky. "His whole side is sore. I think someone hit him or kicked him!"

Delbert ran from window to window, pulling the curtains tight, blocking the view from anyone watching outside. Then he sat down by the stove and looked at Joe's coded message. "This has gone far enough," he said. "You kids have to get out of here!"

Moving methodically, his senses alert and supercharged, Frank bushwhacked his way through the woods. The floor of pine needles had been disturbed, here and there, giving him a path to follow. He stopped to check out a muddy patch. Footprints—the same footprints he had seen near the river. Farther on, losing the trail again, he found some white strands caught on a branch. Clothing threads, he thought.

He continued on, but stopped when he came to a steep rocky slope. No one could drag another person up there—but which way had they gone around?

Frank decided to give ten minutes to the right-hand trail. If I don't find anything by then, I'll turn back and try the other side.

He pushed on, finding no hint of a trail. At a gap in the rocks where a small stream trickled downhill, he stopped to look for tracks. There was something in the soft mud. He leaned down for a closer look. A large animal had passed by there, its paw pads shaped like a cat's. "Great," Frank muttered. "That's all I'd need to do—meet a mountain lion."

He turned around and slowly retraced his steps, keeping an eye out for anything he might have missed. Returning to the place where he had turned, he headed left. The way was smoother. Yes, it was the trail to try.

A few minutes on he stopped and inspected a blurred footprint. With renewed confidence, he quickened his pace, thinking that *something* must lie ahead!

In the cabin, Rita stared at her uncle. "What do you mean, you want us to get out of here!"

Delbert glanced at Joe. "I think you should get him and his message to the law as soon as possible. That means the county sheriff in Corralville."

"But that's so far away!" Rita objected.

"Then you'd best be going," Delbert said. "That message may be important."

"I'm not leaving you alone here," Rita told her uncle.

"Well, I'm not leaving the cabin empty with some prowler out there," Delbert answered. This time, both of them gave Joe a look.

Joe felt as if he'd come in at the middle of a movie. The whole conversation didn't make any sense.

Delbert dug into his pocket. "Here're the keys to the Jeep. I want both of you out of here. *Now!*"

He moved to a small pantry off the kitchen and took out a box.

"What are you doing?" Rita stared at the box.

"I just want my old things nearby," Delbert

said, setting the box on the table before him. "You two had best be going while you still can."

Rita seemed on the verge of tears. Joe walked to Delbert's Jeep, wondering what was going on.

"Do you feel well enough to drive?" Delbert asked Joe.

"Yes." Joe got behind the wheel. His head was still a bit foggy, but Rita was visibly upset and in no condition to drive.

"Stick to the main roads—Rita will give you directions," Delbert said. "You take good care of her," he added in a softer voice.

Joe was completely baffled. Until then Rita had been taking care of *him*. He started the Jeep and pulled away from the cabin. They headed up an old logging road, bumping over half-buried rocks.

When they were out of sight of the cabin, Joe stopped the Jeep and turned to Rita. "You're not from Wyoming. Right?"

"Right. We're from the East Coast. And I didn't want to come here. The idea of living out in the wilderness scared me. But I've gotten to like the quiet. The chance to see nature."

Joe was getting tired of not understanding. "Rita, what's going on here?"

Tears began to stream down her face. "I—I can't tell you."

"What's so important about that box your uncle took from the pantry?" Joe pressed.

"Please!" Fear filled her eyes.

"We're not moving until you tell me why that

57

box is so important." Joe stared at her, waiting for an answer.

"All right." Rita seemed to shrink in her seat. "I never even knew that he'd brought that box along. But I know what he keeps inside it. A pistol—and plenty of ammunition."

"A pistol," Joe repeated. Suddenly an image popped into his head. It was the dark-haired stranger from his dreams, a gun in his hands.

And two words swam up to his conscious-ness—*hit man!*

Joe grabbed Rita's wrist. "Your uncle—he's afraid for his life, isn't he?"

He swung the Jeep around and headed back down toward the cabin.

"What are you doing?" Rita demanded. "You're going the wrong way."

"We've got to stop him!" Joe shouted above the roar of the Jeep.

The Jeep bounced along the road, throwing up a trail of dust. Joe held on to the steering wheel, and Rita gripped the seat beneath her.

"Stop who?" she shouted.

The Jeep reached the clearing where the cabin stood, and Joe leapt out. The Jeep sputtered and died in its tracks. Rita jumped out and tried to stop Joe, but she couldn't catch him.

He was running flat out when a pistol shot rang out!

Chapter

8

FRANK HALTED AT the edge of a clearing and saw a cabin. He stepped back into the bushes, out of sight of any watchful eyes peering from the windows. Crawling on hands and knees, he eased forward to scout the place out. It looked deserted. No smoke rose from the stone chimney. There were no cars parked in front. The windows and the door were closed.

Frank, resting his hand on the ground as he crouched, felt something beneath his fingertips. He held up a small shred of thin paper—the kind used to wrap cigarettes. The paper was still white, so it hadn't been there very long. Frank smelled it—there was still a hint of smoke.

Someone had been watching the cabin just as he was. But the person had smoked a cigarette, then field-stripped it to hide the fact. It was dumb luck that Frank had found the paper. Why such secrecy—unless the other person was up to something unpleasant!

Frank was about to start circling the cabin when he heard a dog bark. He stayed crouched in the brush as the barking and snarling continued.

Then Frank heard a car engine and an instant later saw a Jeep roar into view and stop. Someone vaulted out and ran for the cabin. Frank squinted, trying to identify the person. Could it be Joe? No. It looked as though this guy was wearing a turban.

Frank blinked. But that made no sense. He strained for a better view. The figure was too far away for Frank to see him clearly.

Then the sound of gunshots exploded just above his head. Frank dove for cover. He had been spotted!

After staying quiet for a minute, he crept back to the edge of the clearing to a new observation site. But when he got there, the turbaned person had disappeared.

Frank waited a moment or two. Part of him wanted to throw caution aside and rush the cabin, settling this thing right away. But the person he saw didn't look exactly like Joe. And someone inside that cabin had a gun and was willing to use it. No point in taking foolish risks.

So Frank crept deep into the woods. He would eventually make his way to the cabin.

* * *

At the first pistol shot, Joe whirled and tackled Rita, dragging her to cover behind the Jeep as two more shots sounded.

"Wait here," he told her.

"No! I'm going with you," she said through gritted teeth.

"Rita, I'm just going to check out the cabin. If Delbert is all right, I'll signal for you. But if I'm not back in a few minutes, you have to take the Jeep and get the sheriff."

Rita gave him a mutinous glare but said nothing.

Joe, crouching low, faded back, and used the trees for cover as he sneaked behind the cabin. He crept up to a window, and slowly rose to his full height and peered through the glass.

Inside, Delbert appeared to be alone. Frightened and agitated, he darted back and forth at the front windows, looking out. He held the rifle in one hand and a pistol in the other. The dog stood guard near the door, barking furiously.

Delbert sure has a nervous trigger finger, Joe thought. What's he afraid of?

The words *hit man* went through his mind again.

Joe shrugged. Whatever was going on, one thing was certain. When they left, he and Rita would take Delbert with them. He was in too much danger, alone in the woods. Of course, there was still the job of getting inside to tell Delbert without getting shot.

Gingerly, Joe unwrapped the bandage around

his head, planning to wave it as a flag of truce. Then he heard Rita shouting, "Don't shoot! It's me, Rita!"

Frank, hearing the girl's voice, peered out of the brush. A young woman came running from the Jeep toward the cabin.

Then another figure came to join her from the far side of the cabin. Frank gasped. It was Joe! His younger brother looked much the worse for wear—but he was alive and apparently all right!

Frank was about to shout to him when a man waving a pistol stepped from the cabin door. Frank remained down as the man motioned Joe and the girl inside.

Still hiding, Frank tried to make sense of the situation. A cabin in the mountains, Joe hurt, a man with a gun—Wait a minute! Joe was heading for a cabin in the first place! Could it be this place?

He shut his eyes, trying to trace the route Joe was supposed to follow. Of course, that route would have followed roads. Frank had cut cross-country on foot. Without a good map, he couldn't be sure. Still, it made a reasonable theory.

But the guy with the gun? Was he the fugitive witness? Or could Joe have walked into the arms of the hit man? Frank was determined to find out as he moved deeper into the woods so he could use its cover to circle to the rear of the cabin.

* * *

Behind the log walls, Rita's Uncle Delbert shouted, "Why'd you come back?"

"Who were you shooting at?" Rita asked.

"I saw someone moving outside. At least I thought I did—now I'm not sure. No one returned my fire. Must have been my nerves making me see things."

"You don't understand," Joe cut in. "Someone *is* trying to kill you!"

Delbert seemed to sag. "I understand plenty," he said quietly, dropping into one of the kitchen chairs. Rita stepped behind him and began to rub his shoulders and neck.

"Try to relax," she told him. "It makes no sense for you to stay here. Come with us. *Please* come with us."

"I can't!" Delbert moaned. He looked up at Joe. "Why did you come back? Did you start remembering?"

Joe reached into his pocket and took out the undecipherable message. He held it out to Delbert. "Was this meant for you?"

Delbert gave him a calculating stare. "If I say yes, you'll stay and try to help me. So I'll just tell you to get it to the sheriff—along with Rita."

"I'm not leaving you," Rita insisted. "We'll see this through together." She was shaking with tears.

"No, we won't," Delbert said. "I'll end it here. See, honey, I don't have much time left for run-

63

ning, anyway. I'm terminally ill. The doctor in Corralville told me months ago. There's no hope for me."

He picked up the box on the kitchen table and reloaded his pistol, looking totally drained. Then he slumped down in his chair, facing the door. The golden retriever came over and lay down at his feet.

"There's only one thing I want," Delbert said. "And that's seeing Rita safe." He stared at Joe. "I can't escape. And I'd just as soon die here. Maybe I can take out the guy who's chasing us."

"You don't have to die," Joe said.

"All three of us may die if you two insist on staying here," Delbert said. "Now go, and that's an order. Take the Jeep and clear out."

"Let *him* go," Rita said, motioning at Joe. "I'm staying."

Delbert pushed himself to his feet. For a moment it looked as though he were about to lose his temper, then his expression softened. "Rita, girl, you are my life. Please. If you won't leave because I order you, leave because I'm begging you. You must go on without me."

Rita ran into Delbert's arms. They embraced each other fiercely—as if they knew it was their last goodbye.

After a moment Rita reluctantly pulled away. "Come on," she said to Joe. "We'd better get going."

Delbert tried to give Joe the pistol. "Here," he said, "you may need this."

Joe shook his head.

Delbert gave him the ghost of a smile as he saw them out the door, but his face was set and pale. All he could manage was a wave of his hand as Joe led Rita from the cabin.

They got into the Jeep, threw it into first, and climbed the ridge behind the cabin. The road was steep and loaded with hairpin turns, so the cabin was in and out of view, getting smaller and smaller with every turn.

Rita, her eyes swollen and teary, stared over her shoulder at her home.

Joe wanted to console her, but didn't know what to say. Instead, he concentrated on his driving. It was so weird. How could he remember how to drive a Jeep—yet not remember his own name?

The Jeep came around a sharp hairpin turn, and, below, the cabin came back into view. It looked so peaceful down in the clearing, like something in an enchanted forest.

And then it exploded! A star of brightness appeared on one wall, and chunks of wood and stone shot high into the air. Flames blossomed in the wreckage.

As smoke and ash filled the air, Joe braked to a stop, staring in disbelief. For a moment, he wasn't seeing the cabin anymore. He was seeing a car exploding in a mall parking lot, the girl he loved vanishing in a ball of flame.

"Iola," he heard himself whisper.

Rita's screaming brought him back to the present. She had vaulted out of her seat and was running blindly back along the road to the cabin.

He gave chase, running in front of her to get her to stop.

It was as though he were invisible. Rita rammed right into him, and tried to keep going.

Joe wrapped his arms around her as she tried to pull free. Now he could hear what she was yelling. "No, no, no! Dad! *Dad!*"

"Dad?" Joe's grip slackened as he stared at Rita in amazement.

But Rita stayed where she was, sobbing wildly. "He wasn't my uncle," she choked. "That was my father down there—and now he's dead!"

Chapter

9

FRANK HARDY HAD just circled his way through the woods so he would come out behind the cabin.

It was dead ahead, masked only by a few trees. He had just started for it, when he heard a twig snap nearby. To his strained nerves, the sound was as loud as a gunshot. Frank froze behind a tree. Twigs didn't break by themselves. They snapped when something—or *someone*—stepped on them.

Then came the explosion!

It blasted Frank like a rag doll, tossing him off his feet and back against the trunk of a tree.

Later he groggily opened his eyes. The last thing he remembered was the blast. He must have been knocked out. The question was, for how long? He rubbed the back of his skull. His whole body was sore, covered with pine needles and debris from the explosion. He lay still, checking his arms, legs, and ribs for broken bones.

At last, he hobbled to his feet. Everything was quiet, except for the wind moving through the treetops.

He steadied himself, then moved ahead. Reaching the clearing, he saw that the cabin had been totally destroyed. Little remained but some shattered timber and stone, some bent and charred tin cans—and no signs of life.

"Too late—just a few minutes too late," Frank said to himself, not having heard the Jeep pull away. "I came so close to catching up with Joe, and now he's gone. No one could have survived this."

His hands were clenched so tightly, his fingernails dug into the flesh of his palms.

Joe led a shocked Rita back to the Jeep, which sat on the top of a hill. Below, smoke still hovered over the area where the cabin had been.

She tried to pull free, and he had to restrain her.

"I can't leave him there!" she said, her voice shaken.

"He's gone," Joe said roughly. "Dead, just like Iola," he added under his breath.

But Rita heard. "Who's she?"

Joe lowered his eyes. "A girl I loved. She was killed in a car bombing." He helped Rita into the

Jeep. Then he got behind the wheel. "I couldn't help her. But I can help you, Rita," he said quietly. "I can get you out of here, to safety."

She covered her face with her hands and began to sob. Her body heaved with each surge of grief. Joe leaned over and took her in his arms.

"We can't stay here," he told her gently. "Whoever set that explosion probably saw us leave and will come looking for us."

Afraid to make any noise, Joe released the brake and clutch, so the Jeep would roll silently down the hill. As it gained some speed, Joe nudged the brake pedal so it wouldn't go too fast.

He glanced at Rita. Her head was thrown back, tears streaming down her cheeks.

Joe steered the Jeep around some curves as it descended the hill. Reaching a flat stretch of road, Joe pushed in the clutch, threw the Jeep into second, and allowed the engine to drop-start and ignite.

Rita gained control of herself, taking deep breaths and wiping her eyes.

"There are some things you should know," she said in a choked voice.

"A whole lot of things, I bet."

She sighed. "It's true. Well, you know that Uncle Delbert is—was my father."

"Why all the secrecy?" Joe asked.

"Because there was a contract out on his life, that's why," Rita explained.

"Who was your dad, really?" Joe asked.

"My father's name was Mark Tabor," Rita said. "He was a businessman who was approached by some organized crime types. They wanted him to go along with a construction scheme to defraud the government out of a lot of money."

"Nice," Joe said sarcastically.

"Dad had a building supply business. Concrete and steel. The mobsters wanted him to overprice the cost of supplies needed for some big public building. Then the mobsters were going to charge the government for the inflated costs and pocket the difference. It would've meant millions and millions in illegal profits."

"But your dad wouldn't go along with it," Joe suggested.

"Well, actually," Rita said, "he did go along with the scheme. But only after he had notified the authorities. They asked him to help gather evidence."

"You mean, he was sort of a double agent," Joe said.

Rita nodded. "Right. After the mobsters were arrested, they figured that they'd get off, since there was no hard evidence against them. But they didn't know about my dad. He testified at the trial, and the mobsters were convicted and sent to prison."

"Which put your dad's life in jeopardy," Joe said.

"Yes. During the trial, right before Dad was

70

set to testify, my mother disappeared. Kidnapped." Her voice shook. "Murdered. When Dad hired a detective and found out that my mother was already dead, he went ahead." Rita began to weep again. "And now both of my parents are dead. And I hate the people who did it!"

Joe brought the Jeep to a stop. He held Rita, trying to console her, until she calmed down.

"I'm sorry," she said.

"You have nothing to apologize for," Joe told her.

"After the trial the authorities knew that his life and mine were in danger," Rita explained. "So, as part of the witness protection program, they gave us new identities. But the mobsters maneuvered for a new trial on a technicality, and started tracking us down so we couldn't testify. We ran—until we finally settled here."

"But someone just found your dad," Joe said.

"It won't do them any good," Rita said. "I know as much about the scheme as he did."

"I think they know that, too. That bomb was meant to kill both you and your dad."

Rita nodded grimly. "Well, they missed me. And I'll have my chance to convict them."

"Right," Joe agreed, starting the Jeep again. "But they'll have checked and know that you got away. And that makes *you* the new target!"

Back at the cabin, Frank Hardy prowled

around the smoking remains. There was little that hadn't been destroyed. He found the twisted remains of a pistol and rifle and the charred bones of only one body! The skeleton was too small to be Joe's—Joe must have survived! There was no sign whatsoever that his brother had been in the blast.

Joe had to be alive! And the girl with him.

Frank turned again to the remains of the cabin for a closer look. Bending down, sorting through the rubble with a stick, he found the remains of a thrown satchel charge—an old-fashioned kind of bomb, but a professional one.

Frank looked out on the road. The Jeep was gone! That was how they got away, he decided. But why didn't I hear the Jeep? Then he remembered—he had been deep in the woods then, circling around to the cabin. Frank quickly retraced his path through the woods. If Joe had gotten away in the Jeep, Frank had to get back to his car—and fast. He burst out of the woods, and climbed his way up to the highway above. There he flagged down a passing car.

"Can you give me a lift to Cripple Mine?" he asked. "I was hiking, and got turned around."

"Hop in," said the driver, a middle-aged man with a grizzled beard. "Folks get lost around here all the time," he said. "They wander off in the trees and lose their bearings."

"Yeah," Frank said. "That's what happened to me."

72

"Well, you be careful next time," the driver warned Frank. "Most anything can happen here in the high country if you don't know what you're doing."

Frank nodded silently. Up ahead he saw the spot where he'd hidden his rental car. "This will be fine," he told the man.

The driver laughed. "Don't want to admit somebody brought you back, huh?" But he good-naturedly pulled off the road. Frank thanked him and got out. "Would you know where I can find a phone?" he asked, leaning back into the car.

"There's a general store, oh, six miles up the road. It'll be on your right, on the river side," the driver said. "You can't miss it."

"And the sheriff," Frank added. "Where is his headquarters?"

"Well," the driver said, "that would be in Corralville. As the crow flies, it's not too far. But it's quite a drive from here—the mountains get in the way."

"I understand. Thanks again," Frank said.

Frank waited for the motorist to drive away, then he climbed in the rental car. It was time, he realized, to report to his father what had happened.

He drove to the general store, which looked like an old fishing lodge. Pulling into the parking lot, Frank went inside.

A couple of old-timers were standing around, talking about the weather and trout fishing. They were dressed in plaid flannel shirts and corduroy trousers. Each wore a battered fishing hat complete with hooks and lures. Frank got a sandwich and a soda, then found a pay phone in the back.

He called home collect. His father accepted the call and immediately began to yell at him.

"Your twenty-four hours ran out this afternoon," Fenton Hardy growled. "You should have been home already. Now we're stuck here worrying about you, as well as your brother."

"Dad, I'm sorry, but there was no time to call. I had a lead on Joe and took off after him. I did see him and nearly caught up with him," Frank told his father.

"Where is he? And where exactly are you?" Fenton Hardy demanded.

"I'm in a general store in the mountains," Frank said. "I wish I could give you good news about Joe. But I just don't know for sure. Something terrible did happen. I found a cabin where, I believe, Joe was staying. Just as I was about to reach it, it was blown sky-high."

"*What?*"

"It was awful," Frank said. "I searched thoroughly and I'm almost positive he wasn't in it. But I think your witness might be dead. Did he live in a cabin?"

"He lived in a cabin about a mile from a place called Cripple Mine. And there should have been another person there—he had a daughter."

74

"Would the hit man have wanted to kill the daughter, too?" Frank asked.

"I would assume so, but let's not rush to conclusions," his father said worriedly. "A stove or gas leak might have caused that explosion."

"Dad, that explosion was no accident!"

"We can't know for sure," Fenton said. "I've just gotten word from a pretty good source that the hit man I sent Joe to warn the witness about is off the case. My source says it was just a wild-goose chase."

Frank shook his head. "Dad, I really think the man may have gotten to the witness. The explosion in that cabin was made by a satchel charge—very professional."

The silence that followed was so long, Frank thought he'd lost his connection. But Fenton Hardy finally spoke again. "In that case, we have no choice about keeping this secret. His daughter is in grave danger. I'm calling in the local police and the FBI right now!"

"Great," said Frank. "I'll get off the line." But even as he hung up, his brief flash of optimism faded.

There would be a lot of lawmen out looking for the hit man. But could they find him before he found the girl—and Joe?

Chapter
10

IT WAS LATE afternoon when Frank headed off toward Corralville, speeding along a steep and curving mountain road.

The sheriff was the nearest local law, and Joe would probably go there to report the blast at the cabin. It might be a slim hope, but it was the best one that Frank had.

As Frank drove, he weighed his evidence again. He was certain he had seen Joe going into the cabin. After the blast, he had found no traces of Joe in the rubble and debris. And the Jeep had disappeared.

Therefore, Joe couldn't be dead. He just couldn't be! Frank tried to shake that possibility from his mind, but it lingered like a bitter aftertaste.

Frank pushed on a little faster into the now deepening twilight. The mountain road was unlit—a series of unending, twisting curves. Still, Frank kept his foot on the gas. When he finally hit a short stretch of straight road, he pushed the accelerator to the floor.

That was when his headlights caught something dead ahead in the road. Frank stared. A Jeep! It looked like the Jeep from the cabin!

He slammed on his brakes too late—surprise had slowed his reflexes. His car rammed into the rear of the Jeep, and Frank went bouncing against the steering wheel. Only his seat belt kept him from sailing through the windshield.

Frank tore loose from his belt and tried to open his door as the Jeep slowly rolled off the road, tumbling into a dry canyon floor below!

"No!" Frank shouted, struggling with his door to get out. He shouldered the door again and again, throwing himself at it until it finally gave way.

Frank slid out of the car and dashed to the trunk. Unlocking the lid, he rummaged for a flashlight. Badly shaken and aching from the crash, he limped to where the Jeep had rolled off.

"Hey! Anybody down there?" he shouted.

There was no response.

Frank flashed the flashlight beam down at the Jeep, which was turned over on its side. He played the light around, looking for any movement. But he saw nothing except the wreck itself.

Finding a sketchy path, he started down the steep hillside. The slope was slippery with gravel and bits of rock, and Frank nearly lost his footing more than once. For one horrible moment, his feet started sliding, and he had to grab a boulder to break his fall. The flashlight nearly went flying.

Finally hitting bottom, he found himself in a sandy ravine, perhaps a dried riverbed. Flashing the light back up at the road he inspected the steep, treacherous hill he had come down.

Then he limped toward the Jeep. "Joe?" He looked hard where the flashlight cast its beam, but saw nothing move.

He was almost afraid of what he'd find at the half-overturned jeep. But when he reached it, he found the Jeep empty. "This is weird," he said to himself. "If he's not here, where is he?" Frank swept the area with the flashlight again, but saw nothing but sand and brush.

The hood of the Jeep was loose, and Frank peeked in. "What's going on?" he muttered, staring at the place where the ignition wires had been torn out. That had to have been done by hand—the rest of the engine hadn't been damaged by the fall.

Leaning over the engine, Frank heard some

noise from the road above. He turned the flashlight upward—but again saw nothing.

He turned back to the Jeep. Nothing.

On the road above Frank, two figures moved out from behind the large boulder where they'd been hiding.

"I still don't understand how we ran out of gas," Rita said to Joe.

"Ask him." Joe pointed to the dark-haired scavenger below in the ravine.

"We could've driven over a rock or something that punctured the tank," Rita suggested.

"Up to a couple of minutes ago, I would have agreed," Joe whispered. "Now I think we're dealing with a professional killer—a guy who wanted us dead back at the cabin. But he couldn't stop us because his car was up on the road. So he punctured our gas tank, so we would be stranded in the middle of nowhere. Then he just drives up and finishes us off. You saw the way he hit the Jeep at a perfect angle, so it would roll into the canyon. And now he's down there, searching for our bodies!"

Rita crouched very still, watching the man climbing over the Jeep. "You mean that's the guy who murdered my father?" she asked.

Joe nodded. "He's a real pro. Look how easily he found us! He knew we'd run out of gas. What he didn't count on was our leaving the Jeep." Joe waved the ignition wires at Rita. "I took these out just so no one could steal the car. But he moved it right off the road.''

"What should we do?'' Rita asked. "He probably has a gun.''

"You can bet on that,'' Joe said grimly. "I've been trying to figure some way to capture him. But I'm not going to get myself shot trying it.''

Rita motioned toward the "killer's'' car, resting against the rocky wall. "We could hide in the back and ambush him when he returns.''

"We could,'' Joe agreed. "But we'd have to move pretty fast to nail him before he got a shot off.''

"What are we going to do?'' she asked.

"I don't know—and we don't have much time to come up with anything. I figure he'll look around for a few minutes more. Then he'll decide that we got away somehow and come after us again.'' Joe looked at her desperately. "It's a case of him or us, Rita!''

"But if we can't capture him, how can we''— she faltered on the word—"kill him?''

"Look,'' Joe said, pointing just up the road.

"What am I supposed to see?'' Rita asked.

"That big boulder right on the lip of the canyon,'' Joe told her. "I bet I can start it down the hill.''

"You mean a rock slide?'' Rita asked.

Joe nodded. "Granted, a rock slide may not be fair, but it is effective.''

Rita stared up at the night sky, struggling with

the idea. "My father always tried to play by the rules, and look where it got him. Chased down and hounded into the wilderness. His wife and finally himself killed," she said quietly.

"You said this wouldn't be very fair. Well, neither was throwing a bomb in our cabin." She looked Joe in the eye. "Let's do it!"

Rita and Joe rested against the big boulder and dug in with their feet. Then with all their strength they leaned back into it. It started to wobble.

Below, Frank stopped his search when he heard a low grinding noise. He looked up at the noise. It grew louder and louder, until a deafening rumble filled the air.

Frank lifted his flashlight—and shrank back. The gigantic boulder rolling down the side of the ravine was picking up speed and loosening other rocks. He was in a direct path with it.

He jumped back. A shower of gravel and pebbles pelted him on the head and chest. One rock struck his arm with stunning force and his hand went numb, forcing him to drop the flashlight. It hit against the ground with a thud, and the beam died.

Frank turned around and ran. How could he escape this trap?

Joe and Rita followed the boulder as it tumbled toward the Jeep.

Rita hid her head against Joe's chest as the deafening noise increased.

Joe rubbed her back, trying to calm her. He could feel her heaving with fear. "That should take care of him!" he said.

His words were nearly drowned out by the sound of boulders crashing against the canyon floor.

Chapter

11

FRANTICALLY TRYING TO outrace the thundering rock slide, Frank dashed for the far wall of the canyon. He scrambled up the steep rocky face on his hands and knees, trying to secure toeholds and handholds. His numb arm slowed him as he dragged himself up.

Now I know how a target in a shooting gallery feels, he thought as rock fragments *pinged* off the canyon wall. He tried to pull himself up with his bad arm, but it betrayed him. Frank slipped down. He yanked with his good arm and just cleared the spot where a stone smashed against the wall.

Frank struggled upward as the rock slide buried the Jeep. Vibrations brought more rocks down—on both sides of the canyon. As he clawed his way to safety, Frank had to hug the wall, covering his head and neck. Minislides rattled over him. Stones tore at his handholds, bashing his body with the force of punches. Rock dust choked him.

Then, as suddenly as the slide had begun—it stopped. A cloud of dust settled on Frank as he clung precariously to a ledge, waiting for aftershocks. But, after a moment, the night was eerily still.

Frank dragged himself to his feet, fighting to catch his breath. "*That* was no accident," he muttered to himself.

As if to confirm Frank's suspicions, a mechanical noise came from the road above him. A car engine. Frank's rental car? He lay low, just in case a light might pan the ravine below. Instead he heard someone gas the car, rev the motor, and drive away.

Frank groaned. He was much too far away to make any effective objection to the theft.

He sat up and started scouting his surroundings. The Jeep at the bottom of the ravine had disappeared, buried under tons of boulders and rocks.

But Frank now had a suspicion as to why he had found the Jeep empty. Imagine the nerve of that killer, he thought. He's done something to Joe and the girl and driven off in their Jeep!

Then when the Jeep stalled, he set up a trap, sure to lure any motorist to certain death in the ravine.

Frank's face went grim as he realized what he had just thought. Joe could be dead!

But Frank had survived and that gave him a temporary edge over the man.

"Some edge." Frank snorted. "No flashlight. No map. No car. But I'll have the advantage of surprise if I can run fast enough to catch up with him," he said ironically.

The killer hadn't even bothered coming down for a closer look. He'd just assumed that the rockslide had done Frank in.

Frank wished he hadn't dropped the flashlight because the darkness made for a slow climb. Only the dimmest starlight penetrated the deep ravine.

Carefully, Frank stepped across the still-shifting boulders, which now filled the canyon floor. "This could have been my grave," he muttered. Another climb up the opposite wall brought him to the deserted road above.

He started walking down the road. In his mind he recreated the map he had left in the car. As far as he could remember, the road got narrower and more winding, until it curved around a flat stretch of private land.

Concluding that he could save time by cutting across the land, Frank ducked under barbed wire and set off across a patch of grassy flatland. It was relatively easy for him to find his way.

About halfway across, he heard something large stirring nearby. The rising moon threw light on the scene. He laughed to find himself in the midst of a herd of cows. Apparently he was crossing private grazing land.

Quietly he moved past the herd, trying not to disturb the beasts. Up ahead he saw some lights. A ranch house? No, the lights were moving. A car. His calculations had been right! By going cross-country he had saved himself miles of walking.

Frank broke into a trot, then a run, trying to reach the road before the car passed. He ducked under another barbed wire fence and hid himself in some tall grass by the roadside.

The car approached, its headlights on bright. Frank squinted, so the glare wouldn't destroy his night vision. The car was almost on top of him before he recognized it. It was his own rental car!

Frank strained to see the driver, wanting to be able to identify the hit man. The face behind the wheel was revealed by the moonlight—his brother!

"Hey!" Frank shouted, getting to his feet and running into the road. "Stop! Joe! Stop! Stop!"

The car's brakes screeched as the wheels locked. It slowed to a stop.

"Joe! It's me, Frank!" he called, running toward the car.

The car did a three-point turn and slowly returned to Frank like a lumbering beast. Frank was engulfed by the headlights. The car stopped, but the engine was left to idle.

Joe warily got out and planted his feet. Instinctively, his hands rose to a defensive position. The face approaching him looked familiar.

Joe tensed, trying to place the face of the stranger walking toward him. He knew he had seen it often—but where? Those confusing dreams flashed again. The dark-haired guy who struggled against him. That grim face, aiming a gun!

"I was afraid you'd gotten away from me—that I'd never catch up with you," Frank said, smiling.

That was all Joe needed to hear. He rushed like a charging bull, tackling his enemy before he could pull his gun. Both of them went spilling into a dry gully off the road.

Joe rode his enemy down, keeping him on the bottom as they slid, choking in the dust. Maybe he'd be able to overpower this hit man, bring him in to justice. . . .

But when they jolted to the bottom, Frank Hardy managed to twist free. "What are you doing?" he yelled. "Don't you—"

His words were cut off when Joe threw a handful of dust into his face. Frank clawed at his eyes, and Joe tackled him again.

Joe knocked his blinded adversary flat. As long as he couldn't draw a weapon, they could fight on fairly even terms.

But even blinded, this guy was dangerous. Before Joe could pin his arms, his enemy lashed out with a karate blow and knocked Joe flat.

Joe shook his head once quickly, as another flash of memory came to him. He remembered another blow like that, one that knocked him out as he had tried to run to the burning car where Iola was trapped.

Joe threw himself at his adversary. He didn't care anymore about hidden weapons. He just wanted to smash that face!

Frank scrambled backward, trying to block his brother's wild onslaught. Fists, elbows, and knees pounded at him in a whirlwind attack. Frank ducked as a knockout blow grazed his ear instead of connecting with the side of his head. "Have you gone crazy?" he gasped.

But Joe just kept swinging with lunatic strength.

"Okay, you asked for it." Frank swept his leg around, catching Joe behind the knees. Joe dropped to the ground, just barely bracing himself on his hands. Frank fell on him and his hands darted to the pressure points on the neck. First he'd get Joe calmed down. Then he'd ask him what was going on.

But Joe wasn't finished yet. When he felt the fingers clamping down on him, he twisted with all his might, unleashing a right-handed haymaker from the ground up.

Frank saw the blow coming and tried to block it. But he used the arm that had been injured in the rockslide—the arm that had gone numb. It was still weak, and Joe's punch brushed by it to land right on the point of Frank's chin.

Joe grinned in triumph as he watched his enemy's head snap back, his legs go limp, his entire body slump bonelessly to the ground. "Get up!" Joe shouted, grabbing his enemy's shirt. "You killed Iola. You killed Rita's father! Get up and fight!"

He tried to lift his adversary to his feet but the dark-haired guy was dead weight. Joe let him fall hard against the ground.

He'd beaten him! All he had to do was tie him up, and bring him to the sheriff. . . .

But yet another memory was triggered—Joe charging out of some woods, pistol in hand, stopping when he saw the dark-haired guy sprawled motionless on the rocks, a big red stain on his shirt. Joe remembered how he had felt then—how upset he had been.

Upset? Over an enemy being shot? How could that be? This guy was a filthy murderer, a killer for hire! In a flash Joe decided there was only one way to stop him from ever killing again.

Joe picked up a large, flat rock, raising it over his head.

"This is it!" he snarled. "This time I'll finish you!"

Chapter

12

"WHAT'S GOING ON?" a voice called down from the road. "Wait! What are you doing? Stop!"

It was Rita. Joe heard her slide frantically down the gully, rush to him, and grab his arm. Joe let her pull the rock away, somehow glad for the interruption. His arms dropped to his sides.

Rita stooped and looked at the dark-haired guy passed out cold. She checked his pulse, shaking her head when she saw the blood on his face.

"What are you doing?" Joe asked.

"What does it look like?" Rita snapped. "He's got a split lip and a bloody nose. And I'm trying to help him!"

"I wouldn't get too close to him, Rita. He could be faking. We know he's a killer!"

"*Maybe* he's a killer. We don't know for sure,"

she said. "And he's still a human being. We can't just let him bleed."

"I go with 'An eye for an eye.' " Joe wiped the sweat and dust from his forehead with the back of his hand.

"Look at him lying there," Rita protested. "He's young. He could be your brother. Why, he even looks like you."

Joe stumbled back a few steps, confused. His mind was a jumble. What was going on here? Why was he relieved that Rita had stopped him from killing the dark-haired guy? Was he losing his mind?

Rita took a clean tissue from her pocket. She gently dabbed at the guy's mouth and nose, cleaning him as well as she could, making his breathing easier. "We can't leave him here," she said quietly. "He's badly hurt."

Joe stared at her. "You're not thinking of taking him with us, are you?"

"Why not?"

"I'll tell you straight out, Rita, I wouldn't want him behind me in the car while I was driving. He wants to *kill* us."

"We could tie him up," Rita suggested.

"We don't have anything to tie him with." Joe turned and climbed up toward the road. After a moment he turned and saw that Rita had not moved.

"We're going to leave him," he said. "By the

94

time he comes around, we'll be safely out of here." With that, Joe continued on his way.

Climbing up from the gully, he reached Frank's rental car and climbed in. He sat, waiting for Rita.

After a minute Rita silently slid into the car. "Are you really going to leave him down there?" she asked.

Joe's answer was to turn over the engine, put the car into gear, and drive off.

When Frank came around it took him a moment to realize where he was. He lay on his back, his body aching. Above him, the sky was radiant with the full moon shining. He tried to sit up but slipped back, feeling ill. The memory of his recent fight rose before him, and he felt sicker.

What happened to Joe? Frank wondered. He tried to kill me! Has he been brainwashed? He didn't even know who I was. I was fighting a robot!

Gingerly, Frank forced himself to sit up, waiting for the cobwebs to clear from his head. "What a mess!" he muttered. "The good news is that Joe is alive. But the bad news is that Joe must think that I'm the hit man!"

Swaying to his feet, Frank took a few wobbly steps, testing his ankles and knees. They still worked. He climbed up to the road again and set off.

To take his mind off his pains, Frank concen-

trated on inventing a new plan for finding and
saving Joe. But he had no edge, nothing to work
with. Alone in the Rocky Mountains at night, he
had only his wits to help him. This was a time
when he really could use Joe's help—but Joe,
apparently, was on the other side.

The road began to slope up, and Frank walked
for what seemed like hours. He was making some
progress, but could never catch Joe on foot. No
cars passed for Frank to flag down. No, he was
on his own—on foot—whether he liked it or not.

The road forked, and Frank stopped to decide
which way to go. He couldn't remember his map
this far along. The left-hand route remained
paved and appeared to snake up into the mountains, the right-hand route was dirt-covered,
heading down into a large valley.

From his vantage point, Frank saw a small pool
of light on the valley floor—not large enough to
indicate a town, but light nonetheless.

It could be a place where he could find help.
Besides, he had to take the easier route. So Frank
took the road down into the valley.

As Frank approached the lights, they became
brighter and more distinct. They were from some
kind of building off the road in the near distance.

Frank quickened his pace, breaking into a hob-
bling run.

Just before he finally arrived, he stopped and
leaned against an old fence to catch his breath.

He was at an old truck stop, left over from the days when this road had been the only one.

"I can't go in there looking like this," Frank said to himself. So he took a moment to comb through his hair with his fingers, then dusted and smoothed out his clothing. He wiped the blood off his face. Even with this effort, he still felt like the Wild Man of the Mountains.

Walking past a couple of antique gas pumps, he headed into a beat-up diner with flickering neon lights. There were no trailer trucks in the gravel parking lot, just an old pickup and a Highway Patrol car.

Frank entered the diner and smiled in surprise. The place was spotlessly clean. The linoleum floor shone with wax. The counter and stools were polished. Tubes of neon lights raced across the ceiling. Along the window wall were several booths. An old jukebox stood in one corner. Near it was a pool table and a rack of cue sticks.

The counterman, tall and skinny, with thin hair slicked back, wiped his hands on an apron, eyeing Frank. "Howdy, stranger," he said with a western twang.

He reached behind the counter for a coffee pot, and freshened the cup for a heavyset highway cop sitting on a far stool. As he leaned forward, he muttered something to the cop, who turned around and looked at Frank.

Obviously, the patrolman was not impressed by Frank's bedraggled condition. The lips went thin on his heavy face, and he crossed his arms across his chest. A metal bar pinned below his badge indicated that the cop's name was Higgins.

Patrolman Higgins didn't say a word. He merely glared at Frank as if he suspected Frank were an escaped convict or something.

Frank was so distracted that he nearly jumped when the counterman appeared before him.

"Sit anywhere you want," the man said, handing Frank a menu.

Frank took a seat in a vinyl-covered booth.

"You just take your time," the counterman said with a grin. "As you can see, the kitchen isn't exactly swamped with orders." With that, he returned to Higgins.

"You wouldn't believe my night so far," Higgins said. "Just before I pulled in here, I got an all-points bulletin over the radio. Dispatch said keep an eye out for a young guy with blond hair traveling with a girl. And get this—they said there was a hit man, some professional trigger-puller, loose in the area."

Higgins twisted his stool and gave Frank another hard look. "Didn't hear you come driving in, son," he said.

"No. My car broke down up the road," Frank said. "I think the clutch went out—the old wreck just died on a hill. So I left it and walked here."

"Is that right?" Higgins said.

"Is there a bus coming by?" Frank asked. "I need to get to the county seat."

"Bus service was stopped on this route months ago," the counterman broke in. "No profit left. Too bad about your car."

"What about that pickup out front?" Frank asked. "Could I rent it for a day or two?"

"Sorry," the counterman said. "That's mine, and I need it to get home.

"I really have to get somewhere—fast. It's a matter of life and death." Frank looked hopefully at the highway patrolman. "Do you think—"

"Sorry, son." Higgins didn't sound very sorry at all. "My patrol takes me in the opposite direction. You'll just have to sit tight till morning when a wrecker can help you."

From the look on Higgins's face, Frank wondered if he might be seeing a posse of local lawmen, first. He didn't dare tell the cop about Joe for fear Joe had really flipped out. Joe could attack this guy, as he had Frank, and be killed. No, Frank decided. I'll just cool it and find Joe on my own.

Then he looked up again. "I guess you're right," Frank told Higgins and the counterman. "My old wreck isn't going anywhere." He grinned. "So I might as well eat. How about a steak, baked potato, the works?"

The counterman went into the kitchen, and Higgins returned to his coffee. Frank stared out the window anxiously.

A big plate of food soon appeared on the table. Frank tore into the steak. He hadn't realized how hungry he was. "Delicious," he told the counterman. "Mind if I take this outside? I'd like to eat under the stars."

"Suit yourself," the counterman said with a chuckle.

Frank picked up the plate and went outside. Glancing back inside, he noticed that the counterman and Higgins were paying no attention to him. There was no place for him to go, anyway.

Frank strolled past Higgins's car, number twenty-eight, and dropped to one knee, glancing nervously to see if either man was looking out. They weren't. He shoved the baked potato into the cruiser's exhaust pipe. Then, putting the plate on the ground, he walked over to the pickup and climbed inside.

Ducking low, he yanked at the ignition wires. It was a nerve-racking job, hot-wiring a truck in full view of the owner. If either of the two inside glanced his way—

The motor caught, backfired, and finally turned over. Frank leapt behind the wheel. He pushed in the clutch and punched the stick on the floor into reverse.

The noise caught the attention of the two men inside the diner.

Just as Frank was backing away, Patrolman Higgins burst from the door, hauling his service revolver from its holster.

"Hold it!" Higgins yelled, dropping into the classic marksman's firing-line position.

The gun in his hand looked about the size of a cannon, and it was aimed straight at Frank's head.

"Stop!" Higgins yelled again. "Or I shoot!"

Chapter
13

"COME ON, YOU old piece of junk!" Frank shouted, stomping on the pickup's gas pedal. He spun the wheel and the truck squealed out of the parking lot. A storm of gravel flew from under the tires. Frank hoped the gravel might block Patrolman Higgins's aim.

He glanced back for a second, expecting to see a bullet with his name on it. Instead, he saw the counterman shove Higgins's arm up. Frank gave a sigh of relief. Apparently, the counterman didn't want any bullet holes in his precious pickup.

Frank pushed the steering wheel, as if that would somehow make the pickup gain some speed. "Come on, you old clunker! We can make it."

In the rearview mirror, Frank saw Officer Higgins making for the highway patrol car. The counterman stood by the diner, waving his hands, jumping up and down.

"With my luck," Frank muttered, "I'll be arrested for stealing this hunk of junk *and* not paying for that steak."

The pickup groaned its way up a hill as the lights on Patrol Car 28 went on. In the mirror, Frank saw it roar out of the parking lot, spinning clouds of dust.

If I had to steal something, Frank thought, I should've stolen the patrol car, instead. At least it has some power.

He grinned at the image of Officer Higgins trying to chase him in the wheezing pickup. But his grin disappeared at the first scream of the siren behind him. Of course, he realized, stealing a patrol car would have landed me in jail.

Then he caught a glimpse of the revolving red lights on top of the cop-car closing the distance between them. Of course, if Higgins catches up with me, I'll *still* be in a ton of trouble!

Frank checked the rearview mirror again. The patrol car was gaining on him. Not too difficult, since the pickup speedometer was indicating a mere forty-five miles per hour. Higgins flashed his lights at Frank, insistently pointing to the side of the road.

The patrol car came so close that Frank could hear its roaring engine. Then Higgins's voice came blaring over the rooftop speaker:

"Okay, son, just pull over. Your little prank is finished. Pull over and there won't be any problem. Come on, kid, give yourself up and the judge might be more lenient."

"Oh, thanks a lot!" Frank said. His eyes desperately scanned the landscape ahead. If he could just make it to the top of the rise, he might be all right.

"Pull over right now!" Higgins barked. "I'm warning you, son. Right now! I'm counting to five, then I'll shoot your tires out! One, two, three—"

Frank pressed the accelerator pedal again, and the truck spurted over the rise. The patrol car did the same. By now, it was so close, it nudged the pickup on the rear bumper.

"I'm not going to pull this off," Frank said to himself, despairing. "Well, I gave it my best shot—"

Suddenly car 28 sputtered. Hearing the sound, Frank watched the scene in the rearview mirror. The patrol car jumped ahead, stopped, sputtered, jumped ahead again, and then died. Stone cold dead in the middle of the road!

Inside the patrol car, Higgins kicked the transmission back into park and turned over the ignition. The engine wouldn't catch. Over and over Higgins tried to start it—with no success. He slammed his hands against the dashboard in frustration, then picked up the mike.

"I'll get you, kid!" he roared after Frank.

Up ahead, putting some distance between Higgins and the pickup, Frank grinned with relief. The potato *had* blocked the patrol car's exhaust pipe. And the exhaust gases, with nowhere else to go, had damped down the engine.

"All *right!*" Frank whispered, congratulating himself.

But his grin soon faded. He'd lost a lot of time. And he wasn't going to make any of it up, chugging along in this heap. Joe would be long past the county seat before Frank even got there—unless the hit man caught him first.

That thought set Frank to work like a madman, squeezing every bit of speed from the pickup. The road began to rise and fall like a roller coaster. At the top of an especially high hill, Frank pushed in the clutch and slipped the gears into neutral. Using the weight of the truck and the steep decline, he soon had the pickup rolling along faster than sixty miles an hour.

Cruising well ahead on the road, Joe glanced over at Rita. She was curled asleep, her body turned toward the seat. Joe's jacket covered her.

Joe tried to hold his eyes open. A few times he had found himself nodding out over the wheel. But he had forced himself to sit back and stare ahead. Joe wasn't sure how much longer that would work. He was exhausted.

Nudging Rita with his elbow, he asked, "Any idea how much farther to Corralville?"

She yawned and stretched. "How long have I been sleeping?"

"An hour and a half," Joe told her.

"We should be pretty close," she said. "Want me to drive?"

"Maybe so," Joe said. "I can't stay awake. But you know, maybe it's a good idea to enter Corralville in the morning, when the sheriff will be at his office."

"So what do you want to do?" Rita asked.

"Let's pull over and knock off a few Zs," Joe suggested. "We can hide the car off the road."

"All right," Rita said.

Joe slowed the car, then pulled off the highway onto a narrow dirt road. He followed the road as it passed some rangeland protected by barbed wire fences.

Figuring that they were safely out of sight, Joe pulled off the road into a patch of buffalo grass.

"Well, good night then," Joe said, turning off the engine.

Rita mumbled, already half-asleep.

Joe leaned against the driver's door and closed his eyes. His body was exhausted—but his mind wouldn't give up. The pictures in it weren't making a whole lot of sense, but they kept flashing.

If these are my memories, Joe thought, I must lead a pretty violent life. Faces kept appearing— a big, beefy blond guy, smiling. A heavyset guy who grinned a lot. An older man and woman—

his parents? And, of course, the dark-haired guy, laughing at him.

Joe forced himself to relax, closing his eyes. His breathing became more regular, his head tilted to one side. . . .

And then the dark-haired guy was leaping across the hood of the car. He pinned Joe with a cold stare as he coolly drew his pistol. He was every inch the pro. The gun was aimed right at Joe's head, the bullet tearing through the windshield.

Joe grabbed at the handle and rammed into the door. He had actually fallen out onto the grassy margin at the roadside before his eyes opened! Still shaken, he stared around the empty field, almost positive the hit man was still there.

"A dream," he whispered to himself. He glanced up into the car at Rita, who was still fast asleep.

"Boy," he muttered, "this girl could sleep through a hurricane."

He stood up and checked the dashboard clock. Apparently he had dropped off for an hour's rest, though it didn't feel like it.

Time to find the sheriff, Joe thought, and finally put an end to this nightmare.

Without waking Rita, he turned the key, started the engine, and began to follow the road back toward the highway.

Frank couldn't believe his luck. No one had

found him yet. Higgins had to have called the highway patrol. They were probably searching the major highways. No one would believe he'd stay in the area on a small road.

Frank was pretty tired though. He'd spent the past hour playing any game to stay awake. He did complicated math problems. He named, in order, every element in the periodic table. He sang the lyrics to every song he could remember. He tried to recall the name of every kid in his classes from elementary school. He began to recite the fifty states: Alabama, Alaska, Arizona, Arkansas, California, Colorado—Colorado!''

Frank couldn't believe his eyes. Pulling into the highway just ahead of him was a familiar car. His rental model—with Joe in the driver's seat!

No one would believe him, Frank thought to himself.

He slowed the pickup—not a difficult task—and allowed the rental car to gather some speed. The big problem was figuring out a way to approach Joe without turning him into a madman again.

I'll never catch up to him if he tries to pull away, Frank thought. My one advantage is that he won't recognize this truck. Maybe I can lure him back.

With that, Frank honked the horn a few times, drawing Joe's attention. When the rental car's brake lights went on, Frank whipped the pickup's steering wheel to the right. His idea was to fake a blowout and hope Joe would respond.

Frank held on, as the pickup skidded off the road. Quickly he looked up. Joe had gone for the bait! The rental car was turning around and approaching the pickup.

Frank opened the door and climbed out. Ready to take on Joe, if necessary.

The rental car stopped, catching Frank in its headlights.

Frank took a few steps toward the car. Good, it looked as if Joe would be reasonable.

Joe's suspicion turned to horror as he stared at the dark-haired guy appearing out of the predawn mist. "Oh, no!" he shouted, waking Rita.

He spun the steering wheel and floored the accelerator.

Frank leapt aside as the car swerved right through the area where he'd been standing. "Not *this* again!" he groaned, pulling himself up and rushing back to the pickup.

His tires screamed as he threw the truck into motion. The chase was on!

Chapter

14

BY THE TIME Frank had his pickup back on the road, the rental car had zoomed ahead. Frank chugged slowly behind.

"I'll never catch him," Frank told himself miserably. Still, what choice did he have?

Frank watched the taillights of the rental car disappear over a hill. All the tiredness that his momentary excitement had burnt away fell back onto him. What had gotten into Joe? he wondered.

If he were trying to warn Frank off, that rockslide was far too deadly. Maybe Joe was somehow being forced to act hostile. But the beating he'd given Frank hadn't been acting. And he could have whispered an explanation during one of the clinches.

The pickup plowed along following the cloud of

dust raised by Joe's car. Frank was determined to make some sense out of his brother's weird behavior.

What would make Joe act this way? Frank asked himself.

Brainwashing? But Joe had only disappeared a couple of days. Frank couldn't believe he could have been brainwashed in such a short time.

Hypnotism? That might explain why Joe was so unexpectedly hostile. And it would explain why Joe might attack him but not finish him off. People under hypnosis couldn't be ordered to do things that they believed to be wrong. Frank shook his head. A hit man using hypnosis? That was just too bizarre.

Frank laughed at the image of a thug with a gun in one hand, saying, "You are in my power." He would wear a black mask, and a magician's turban—*turban!*

Frank's hands clenched the wheel as he remembered creeping up on the cabin in the woods. He'd seen a distant figure walking from the Jeep—a figure that had turned out to be Joe. But the first time he'd seen him, Frank thought the guy was wearing a turban. What if it wasn't a turban—but some kind of bandage on his head?

"Amnesia." Frank exhaled loudly. It made sense. Joe had looked pretty battered. He must have been bumped around a lot when his car was wrecked. What if Joe had bumped his head? Then Frank remembered the bloody tire iron, with the hairs caught on it. What if Joe had been *hit* on the head? What if he lost his memory?

What if he thinks I'm the hit man who's after him?

Frank gripped the wheel. He *had* to catch up with Joe.

"Slow down!" Rita shouted, pulling at Joe's arms. "We've lost him! He can't hurt us now!"

Joe glanced in his rearview mirror. She was right. The dark-haired killer and his pickup had fallen far behind. But Joe still kept the gas pedal down low. It might be irrational, but he swore to himself that he'd take no chances with that guy.

"Slow down! Please!" Rita pleaded as the car screeched around a sharp curve. "Do you want us to go off the road?"

Joe didn't answer her. And he didn't slow down.

"What's the matter with you?" Rita's voice rose. "Have you gone out of your mind?"

Joe twisted around to glare at her, wild-eyed.

"Look out!" Rita screamed.

He turned forward again. He was approaching a hairpin turn that was upon him right then. Slamming on the brakes, Joe twisted the wheel into the turn. The car screeched along a steel guardrail, which alone kept it from spilling down the steep rocky slope.

Joe fought to regain control of the car—and

himself. "I—I think we left some of our paint on that railing," he finally gasped.

They slowed down, then stopped.

Rita pried his hands off the steering wheel. "What happened back there?" she asked.

"Please, Rita," Joe begged, "don't tell me I've gone crazy. I saw him back there. The dark-haired guy. The hit man. He came walking right into our headlights. Smiling. *Smiling*. I couldn't take it. I had to get away."

He shook his head. "I guess I did go crazy, for a while. That was a foolish stunt I pulled. I could have gotten us killed."

"All the time, I keep getting flashes—pictures of that guy fighting with me, laughing at me. He stopped me from saving Iola. . . ." Joe's voice broke off.

Then he turned to Rita, whispering fiercely, "But he's not going to keep me from saving you!"

He shook his head. "I haven't been able to stop him yet. But I've just got to outplan him. Every time he's turned up, he's caught us by surprise. So this time we'll have to surprise him. *Really* surprise him.

"Let's take a look at the map."

Rita spread it out. "I know this stretch of road," she said, pointing at a line snaking through the mountains. "A few more miles and we'll clear these mountains. From there on it's a flat five-mile stretch into Corralville."

Joe examined the map very carefully. "What's this line here?" he asked suddenly, stabbing at the map with his finger.

Rita squinted, then nodded. "That's an old logging road, just at the edge of the mountains," she said. "I don't know if anyone even drives there. You can't really see it, it's hidden by some aspen trees."

"Perfect," said Joe. He started up the engine again and drove off.

Frank, making the best time he could, came wheezing downhill in his stolen pickup. Long before he had lost sight of the rental car.

"At the speed he took off, Joe will be in California before I make it to Corralville," he said, fuming.

"I hope somebody nails that hit man. Because *I* want first crack at my baby brother. I'll pound some sense into that thick skull of his." That got a laugh out of Frank. "Dr. Hardy's Amnesia Cure."

He eased the truck around a last curve, which provided a fine view of the valley below. Some six or seven miles off were the lights of Corralville.

Frank anxiously scanned the flat expanse of roadway. "Empty," he said. "Not a car out there. Joe must be in the town already—unless he went another way or just passed through."

Then he remembered the all-points bulletin that

had been posted for Joe. He also thought that there must be one out for him, too. "There's a sheriff in Corralville. Maybe *he* got hold of Joe."

Frank tromped the accelerator again, eager to reach Corralville.

The pickup whipped through the final turn, and the road began to flatten.

All of Frank's attention was on the road before him, so he barely noticed a churning sound erupting from a stand of aspens off to one side.

He turned when the sound got louder and saw a car come barreling into view—flashing straight at the pickup!

Frank tried to brake, tried to turn aside. But the onrushing car caught him broadside, smashing him off the road, into the ditch.

The last thing Frank remembered was his own brother, grim-faced at the wheel, ramming him!

Chapter

15

JOE HARDY BROUGHT his car out of the crash and fishtailed back onto the highway. He didn't even look back at the pickup he'd sent hurtling off the road. He was just happy that his car wasn't so badly damaged that it couldn't be driven. The door on Joe's side was sprung, and the whole front end was bashed in—but still the car drove.

Rita stared out the rear window as the truck landed on its side. "The gas tank didn't explode," she said. "I guess he'll be all right in there."

Joe nodded. "One thing's for sure. He's not going anywhere. The sheriff can pick him up."

Billboards advertising restaurants and motels clustered along the roadside, announcing that they were approaching Corralville. Then came signs announcing a decrease in the speed limit and a school crossing warning. A few minutes later they were stopped by a true sign of civilization—a traffic light.

Joe brought the car to a stop, steam billowing out of the engine, then he turned to Rita.

"So what's our plan?" she asked.

Joe peered through the spider's web of a windshield to see that night had given way to dawn. Daylight illuminated the road ahead. "The sheriff should be getting to headquarters soon," he said.

Rita nodded. "Right. Our best hope is to get the coded message to the authorities."

Joe patted his breast pocket, feeling the paper inside. "Yes."

Rita leaned back. "Thank goodness. Imagine, before long I'll be able to stop running. I'll be safe and free." She turned her head toward the window. "I'll look for the sheriff's office," she said.

But before Joe could get the car in gear, he had another memory flashes—a crooked sheriff aiming a gun at Joe's nose. "They pay me good money to take care of problems like you," the sheriff said. He remembered his muscles tensing for a hopeless spring—and the dark-haired guy warning him back. Then the two of them together had overpowered the corrupt lawman.

"The dark-haired guy *helped* me!" Joe muttered to himself.

"What?" Rita said. "Did you say something to me?"

Joe shook his head. "No, I was just thinking out loud."

"What about?" Rita asked with concern.

"Maybe going to the sheriff isn't such a good idea," Joe told her. "Maybe the right thing to do is turn back and see if that guy in the pickup is okay."

"Don't start acting crazy again!" Rita warned Joe. "We're so close—can't we just finish this thing and get on with our lives? Please? The sheriff isn't going to hurt us."

Joe forced the disturbing memory into the back of his brain.

"Okay," he said. "We'll go to the law."

Rita nodded in approval.

They topped a rise, and sprawling out before them in the sunrise was the town they'd been struggling to reach. Corralville, the county seat.

Rita looked around the dusty main street. "It's hard to believe Corralville was once one of the richest towns in the world," she said.

"This place?" Joe said in disbelief.

"They found silver in these hills," Rita said. "The whole town sprang up overnight. Hotels and gambling houses, fancy shops and saloons."

Joe looked at a sagging wooden building. "Didn't last, I guess."

Rita nodded. "The mines dried up, and most of the people left. Nobody comes here now— except people who get lost looking for the ski resorts."

"It is almost like a ghost town—especially at dawn," Joe said as they silently rolled along the empty streets.

They passed a few old wooden houses that lined both sides of the road. Then they reached the tiny downtown section. A school filled much of one block, and churches were set on various corners. They passed a gas station and a general store, a coffee shop and a garage. In the middle of the block Joe slowed the car to a crawl.

On one side was an old red brick county courthouse. And, across the street, next to the post office, was an unassuming one-story, yellow brick building with the words County Sheriff stenciled on the window.

Joe rolled to a stop and parked the car outside the sheriff's office. A light inside indicated that someone was on duty. He turned off the engine and glanced at Rita.

"Well," he said, "here we are."

Dawn found Frank stumbling over his own feet as he staggered along the road. He was moving as much to stay warm as to find Joe. The second task was surely hopeless—his brother was long gone.

Bruised and bone-weary, Frank challenged himself to keep his feet moving. He was shaken—not just by the physical batterings he had sustained, but by the realization that his brother could attack him so savagely in cold blood. Frank couldn't erase the memory of the look on his brother's face as his car rammed into him. He didn't even check to see what happened to me, Frank thought. It's got to be amnesia. But who does he think I am?

But that didn't matter right then. Joe was in trouble, and somehow, Frank had to catch up with him. He glanced at his watch. Twenty minutes since he'd pulled himself out of the wreck, and he'd gone only about a mile. At that rate, Frank could expect to hit Corralville in about an hour and a half. Maybe Joe would be there, with the sheriff. Or maybe by then, Joe would be ninety miles away.

Frank forced his legs to move faster, stumbling into an ungainly jog-trot. When he got to the sheriff's he could report what had happened and he could call his dad and maybe get some help for his brother.

He had reached the first set of billboards announcing Corralville when he heard the siren screaming behind him.

Frank dove off the road and lay low in some buffalo grass, out of sight. This is a great time for the Highway Patrol to catch up with me, Frank thought.

Well-hidden, he crawled to a spot which allowed him a clear view of the highway.

Barreling down the road was Highway Patrol Car 28, the one he had sabotaged at the truck stop.

Frank rose up at the exact moment the cruiser came rushing by. What he saw gave him a very bad feeling indeed.

That can't be, Frank thought. The man at the patrol car's wheel did not look like Officer Higgins. This cop had red hair and a sharp, needle-like nose. What was this guy doing in Higgins's car? And why was he breaking the speed limit to get to the county seat?

The image of the driving officer's red hair returned to Frank's mind. What if the guy in the car was an impostor?

Then whatever business he had in Corralville, he couldn't be up to any good.

Frank jumped back on the road, redoubling his pace. Trying to take his mind off the pain in his legs and the burning in his lungs, he tried to imagine how someone else could have ended up in Higgins's car. It was all too simple.

The redhead must have found Higgins right after his cruiser conked out. Catching the cop by surprise, he overpowered Higgins. Then, with the officer either stunned or dead, the guy must have figured out that something was blocking the car's exhaust system.

"Nice work," Frank told himself sarcastically. "I stopped Higgins all right. And in doing it, I may have given the hit man a perfect cover for his next killing."

Yes, the hit man! If his impostor theory were right, who else would be masquerading as a lawman? Frank almost stumbled again as that thought hit him. "If he gets to Joe and murders him, there will be only one person to blame. *Me!*"

Frank pushed back his horror. He lowered his head and forced more speed out of his oxygen-starved legs. Joe was *really* in danger now. He had to make Corralville, and right away. He *had* to!

Chapter

16

HALF AN HOUR later Frank Hardy was still stumbling along the road, wondering if he were running in place. Corralville seemed to be as far away as ever. Although his worry for Joe kept him plodding onward, he could feel his body betraying him. He was limping even more, and a catch in his side sent pain screaming through him with every step.

If Joe had stopped in Corralville, Frank was almost afraid of what he would find there. He might arrive to discover he had a score to settle with Joe's killer, Joe having died without even knowing who he was—

That nightmare vision spurred Frank into a slow-motion parody of a run. His body was just too wasted, too battered, too *tired* to perform the way Frank wanted it to.

Frank's feet hit a patch of loose gravel, and he lost his balance. He nearly fell flat on his face, but at the last instant he broke his fall, scraping his palms raw. "Great," he muttered, wincing at his new injury. "Can't I do *anything* right anymore?"

Pulling himself wearily to his feet, Frank spotted a vehicle on the road. It was coming toward him from Corralville. Frank tensed. Was it the highway patrol cruiser? Was the impostor making his getaway, heading back after finishing his job?

Frank thought he saw lights mounted on the top of the car. He glanced around desperately for some sort of weapon, even a rock to throw. He couldn't let this guy escape. But as the vehicle drew closer, he recognized the outlines of a tow truck.

Jumping up and down, waving his arms, Frank flagged it down. The tow truck rolled to a stop ahead of him, and Frank ran to it. He hopped onto the running board, leaning in the window. "Boy, am I glad to see you."

"What are you doing out here?" The driver's big, beefy face had a look that fell somewhere between scorn and suspicion. "You look like vulture meat, friend."

Frank ignored the sarcasm. "I really need a lift into Corralville," he said.

The man's eyes narrowed. "I tow cars. I'm not a taxi service."

But Frank knew that if this guy—Bert was

printed on his coverall—saw the wrecked pickup, his problems would only be starting. Bert would be sure to recognize a local truck—and he'd have to know that Frank had stolen it.

"Hey, give me a break," Frank said. "It's very important I get there as soon as possible. A matter of life and death."

"Look, kid," Bert said coldly. "If you're so eager to get to town, you can walk from here."

"You don't understand!" Desperate to convince the man, Frank reached through the window, grabbing Bert by the arm. Bert yanked himself loose and thrust open the door, knocking Frank off the running board and onto the ground.

Frank landed heavily. By the time he scrambled to his feet, Bert had jumped out of the truck. In his hand was a large, heavy wrench.

"I thought you looked suspicious," Bert growled, hefting the wrench. "Weird things going on. Sheriff tells me we got a hit man creeping around somewhere. And I bet he's you!"

Bert moved fast for a beefy guy. He charged Frank, swinging the wrench overhand, straight for Frank's head.

Frank threw his arms over his head, crossing them and locking the forearms together.

Bert's wrist smashed into Frank's block. He grunted in surprise and pain. Frank grabbed Bert's wrist and attempted to disarm him.

But the scrapes on his palms let him down, and Frank couldn't get a good grip. Bert tore loose.

"Smart boy, huh?" Bert stepped back and swung the wrench sidearm, aiming for Frank's shoulder.

He had expected Frank to back-pedal—but instead, Frank attacked! He rammed his forearms down, moving not for the wrench but for the arm that swung it.

Bert stared in surprise as his blow was again slowed. But this time, Frank clamped down on the arm with the wrench, capturing it between his left arm and his body. His right hand rammed up heel first into Bert's chin.

Bert's head snapped back, and his whole body followed, helped along by Frank's right foot behind his ankles. Bert hit the ground with a thud, and Frank leapt on him, his hands darting for pressure spots in his neck—

A moment later Frank was dragging the unconscious truck jockey to the side of the road. "So much for famous western hospitality," he said. "Sorry, Bert."

Dumping Bert in a safe spot, Frank dashed back to the tow truck and climbed in. The engine started on the first try, and soon Frank was whipping the truck in a tight U-turn. Pressing the accelerator to the floor, Frank quickly worked his way through the gears, speeding toward Corralville.

"I only hope that I'm not too late," he said to himself.

* * *

The county sheriff, a short bald man with a pot belly, kicked his cowboy boots up on the desk. He leaned forward and took a sip of coffee, eyeing Joe and Rita, who were seated across the desk.

"Now, let me see if I've got your stories straight," the sheriff said. He pointed at Rita. "You're telling me that you survived the explosion that wiped out the log cabin."

"That's right," Rita said. "The explosion that killed Mark Tabor, my father."

The sheriff ran a hand along his chin. "The papers on that cabin don't say anything about a Mark Tabor."

Joe interrupted impatiently. "She explained about all that. They're under the witness protection program."

That got him a dirty look from the sheriff. The lawman studied Joe slowly.

"You have to believe us!" Rita said. "We told you exactly what happened at the cabin. Doesn't that prove anything?"

"It shows you knew a lot more about the explosion than we told the press. More than any innocent person should know." The sheriff removed his feet from the desk, then he leaned forward, thrusting his face into Joe's. "Now you tell me you survived a car wreck near Cripple Mine, escaped the explosion, fought with the hit man, and brought this girl to me. Quite a story."

He leaned back in his chair again, trying to

look casual. "Now, what did you say your name was?"

"I'm telling you, I can't remember!" Joe said.

"How about some ID then?" The lawman's voice got harder.

"I must have lost it," Joe told him.

"Mighty convenient, not being able to tell me your name." The sheriff looked more suspicious now. "You have nothing you can show me?"

Joe then remembered the coded message in his pocket. "I've got something which may convince you," he said, reaching into his pocket. Mark Tabor had told him to bring it to the sheriff. Maybe the lawman could figure it out.

But Joe's pocket had not been the safest place to be during this adventure. To his horror, the paper came out as a crumpled mass, almost torn in two pieces. Joe tried to straighten it out, but the paper looked like a torn mess, its message illegible.

The lawman squinted at the paper, then looked at Joe. "This is all you've got to show?" he asked, trying hard not to smile.

"What about the hit man?" Joe said desperately. "He might still be out where we rammed his car. Can't you go and look around?"

"I will—soon as my deputy gets here." The sheriff glanced at his watch. "That'll be about an hour and a half. We'll check out your story."

"And what are we supposed to do in the meantime?" Joe asked.

"You may be important witnesses—or suspects—in a murder. I think you should stick around." He pointed to a door at the rear of his office, and fished out some keys with one hand.

Rita and Joe both leapt from their seats.

"You're going to lock us up?" Hands clenched, Joe took one step forward.

The lawman quickly unholstered his service revolver, pointing it at Joe. "I don't want any trouble," he said. "Now stand where you are, and keep your hands where I can see them."

Having no choice, Rita and Joe did as the sheriff instructed.

The lawman motioned them around the desk, keeping the pistol pointed at Joe. He unlocked the door he'd pointed at. "Okay, you two," he said. "Come this way."

Rita and Joe moved into the back and saw two separate holding cells. The lawman unlocked one cell and told Rita, "Make yourself comfortable, little lady. I've got a few phone calls to make."

Rita walked into the cell and the lawman closed and locked the door behind her. He then unlocked the neighboring cell and motioned Joe inside. "Remember," the lawman said, "no funny stuff."

Steaming with frustration, Joe entered the cell, standing with his back toward the lawman until the door closed and he heard the lock tumble shut.

The sheriff returned to his office, tossing the

keys on the desk before him. He tried to decipher the coded message again, but even an expert could make no sense of it now.

He reached out to pick up the telephone when he heard someone step up on the outside stoop. The front door opened, and a tall, thin, redheaded older man dressed in an ill-fitting highway patrol uniform entered. The man had a shotgun slung over his shoulder.

"Morning," the stranger said.

"I don't know you," the sheriff said, giving him a hard look.

"Nope. I'm the new man on the force," the stranger said. "Just dropped by to get acquainted."

"Then what's with the shotgun?" the sheriff asked, surprised at how old the stranger was.

"We're taking no chances, what with all the troubles around here lately," the redhead said, setting the weapon against a chair. "A scattergun might be just the thing to take care of some big-city hit man."

The sheriff grinned at that. "Yep," he said. "My little town isn't used to such a ruckus. And isn't it just like headquarters not to bother telling me about any extra patrols."

The stranger grinned back and chuckled. "Hey, sheriff, I noticed the rental car parked outside. You wouldn't happen to know where the occupants are?"

"Well, I have them under lock and key in the back," the sheriff boasted.

"You don't say," the stranger said with a nod. "Good work. I'll be sure to tell headquarters about you. I've been tracking those fugitives all night. How about a look?"

"Okay." The sheriff turned and unlocked the rear door. He swung it open. "See? They aren't going anywhere."

The stranger stood behind the sheriff, taking in the sight of Joe and Rita, locked in separate cells.

The sheriff was enjoying his moment of triumph. "See?" he said, gesturing at his prisoners. "All tight."

"Yup," the stranger echoed. "All tight." He swung the shotgun in a vicious arc, until the butt caught the sheriff in the back of the head.

Joe, Rita, and the stranger watched the sheriff topple to the floor.

Then the stranger brought the shotgun up to firing position.

"Now that the local law is asleep," the phony patrolman said, "I can finish up my real business!"

Chapter
17

Frank roared along the last mile to Corralville, maintaining the truck's speed as he raced down Main Street. The town was deserted so early in the morning, as if everything and everyone were in storage.

Like a movie set for a western, Frank thought. The final showdown.

Frank caught a glimpse of himself in the rearview mirror. He looked about as hard-faced and dangerous as any cowboy heading for a shootout.

His face only got harder as he sped along, searching for the sheriff's office. There it was, dead ahead and parked in front was patrol car 28. Right in front of that was the rental Joe had stolen from him. The bright morning sunlight reflected off the sheriff's office windows, denying Frank a look inside.

Frank continued past, pulling the tow truck around the corner and parking. He had to plan his next step very carefully. If the guy in the patrol car was an impostor, that meant the hit man was already in the sheriff's office. Wearing Higgins's uniform—even if it didn't fit—he could convince the sheriff that he was a legitimate lawman.

If Frank went storming in with accusations, the hit man would start shooting. Could he phone a warning in? No, the hit man might answer the phone.

Frank just didn't know what was going on inside the office. So he'd have to get the lawmen *out*, before he could go in. He needed some kind of diversion. But what?

All Frank had was whatever he could find in the tow truck he'd "borrowed" from Bert. He opened the glove compartment, but found nothing but papers and maps. Checking under the seat yielded a tool kit and a few spools of wire.

Frank climbed down from the cab and searched the back. He found only a set of jumper cables, some old oily rags, and a gasoline can. Shaking the can, he heard the gasoline slosh around inside. Instantly, his mind started planning.

"Hmmmm," he said. Not much to work with but— He had the glimmering of an idea. It was the best plan Frank could come up with in a hurry. And it *would* make a pretty spectacular diversion.

He removed the cap of the gasoline can and stuffed the oily rags inside, leaving only a tip of cloth to serve as a fuse. To this makeshift fuse he wrapped some wire, which he then attached to one end of the jumper cables. Before leaving the truck, Frank dug out a tire iron. Then, with his homemade bomb in one hand and the steel rod in the other, he approached the sheriff's office.

Frank crept up on the stoop. Straining his ears, he could hear nothing inside. So he took a chance and peeked through the window. The front office was empty, but there was an open doorway— where Frank could see the back of a tall, red-headed man in an ill-fitting police uniform. He stood over the body of another man in uniform, and he was holding a gun!

That did it. Frank knew his adversary was in there. And he had little time to spare. He would have one chance, and only one chance, to make good.

Sneaking behind the cruiser, Frank placed his economy-size Molotov cocktail on the ground. Then he jimmied open the trunk with the tire iron.

"Well, well," Frank said in surprise. The trunk wasn't empty as he'd expected. In fact, it was quite full—of a furious, squirming Officer Higgins! The highway patrolman was in his underwear, his arms and legs bound together, his mouth gagged. He looked like a trussed-up turkey, ready for the oven.

Higgins twisted and turned, trying to say something through the gag.

"It hasn't been your day, has it?" Frank said, reaching for him.

Frank lifted the heavy officer from the trunk and eased him to the ground.

Higgins began to roll in the dirt, emphatically demanding that Frank untie him. It was just as well the gag reduced his shouts to mere mumbles. Frank didn't want the hit man getting any warning.

Instead, he quickly pulled Higgins well clear of the car and left him leaning against the side of the building.

"Sorry about this, officer," Frank said, dashing back to the police cruiser. He placed his homemade bomb in the recently vacated trunk, on top of the car's gas tank. Then he ran to the front of the car, where he opened the hood and quickly removed the battery.

Placing the battery near the front stoop, he knelt down with the contacts for the jumper cables in his hands. "Not much of a detonator," he whispered. "I just hope it works."

Inside the small cell block, the hit man couldn't resist gloating over his triumph.

"You led me on a merry chase," he told Joe

and Rita. "But it's over. I've finally caught up with you."

Joe's face was a study in anger. He gripped the bars that held him in, yelling, "You dirty—"

"Call me Skell, kid." The hit man's thin lips creased in a smile. "It's just a nickname—but in my line of business, you don't give your real name away." The smile broadened. "Even if you make sure no witnesses will be left."

"I don't believe you," Joe said. "You're going to kill us—in a sheriff's office? Every lawman in Colorado will be after you."

The hit man shrugged. "By the time I finish, it will look accidental. Maybe a fire." He glanced around. "Or maybe something more artistic."

"You'll never get away with it."

"Famous last words, kid. Tomorrow, I'll be on a beach somewhere, relaxing in the sun." Skell smiled down at the fallen sheriff. "Yes, sir, everything's here in a neat package. All tight, just as he said."

Rita stood with her hands clenched around the strong iron bars of her cell. "*You* killed my father?" she whispered.

"That's my job. I'm the best." Skell tapped a finger to his skinny chest. "My employers knew when they hired me that the job was guaranteed." He looked at the two prisoners. "Even if the clean-up meant a lot of work."

Joe threw himself against his cell door—but it held without budging. "Come on," he taunted the hit man. "Make it a fair fight. How about you and me going hand to hand? No weapons, no tricks. And let the better man walk away!"

"Hey, I'm no hero," Skell said with a smirk. "I'm a businessman. Give it up, kid. You're history. I'm just enjoying a few minutes before I'm rid of you forever."

He checked the magazine of his riot gun. "Eight shells," he said. "Way more than I need. One shot for the brave fool. One for the little lady. A quick job. But you've made me a rich man, kids." His smile was knife thin, now.

"Yeah?" Joe countered. "How much are they paying you?"

"Good work doesn't come cheap," the hit man said. "But my employers knew that I'd make good on the contract. You," he added, pointing the shotgun at Joe, "will have to be a freebie."

"Quit torturing us," Joe said quietly. "If you're going to do it, then get it over with."

"I'm in no hurry," Skell said, throwing the shotgun over his shoulder. "You know what your problem is, kid? You've got a thick head. You don't know when to die. You should have bought it in the trunk of your car, back at Cripple Mine. Either you were lucky, or I was sloppy. Either way, I'll clean it up now. But I'll try to make it quick. After all, I owe you some thanks on this job."

"You owe *me* some thanks?" Joe echoed.

The hit man nodded. "Sure do. You see, I

didn't know exactly where to find Tabor. But when I tracked you and Rita back to the cabin and saw 'Uncle Delbert,' well, I knew I'd found the right cabin. Sorry I couldn't get you there, but my gun was in my car up on the road. I knew I'd catch up with you, though.''

Joe glanced over at Rita. "I'm sorry," he said miserably. "I blew it. I blew everything."

Rita took his hand through the bars and squeezed it. "It's all right," she whispered. "It wasn't your fault. You tried to help."

"Hey, I hate to cut this touching scene short, but, well, business is business," Skell cut in. He pulled a knife from his belt. "What do you think of this plan?" he asked Joe and Rita. "After I shoot you two, I'll get the boy's prints on this knife and then stick it into the sheriff."

He nodded happily. "When they find you, they'll piece together what must have happened. A tragic story. A punk stabbed the sheriff who, dying, somehow managed to shoot his attackers. Artistic, huh?"

Rita lost all control. "Your bosses may kill me, but they're all still in jail," she snapped. "And I'm glad of it."

"Yeah, well, they're in jail now," Skell admitted. "But there is the new trial. And without the star witnesses, my bosses can buy their way out of it. What do you think about that?"

"I think you're a real sick piece of work," Joe said.

THE HARDY BOYS CASEFILES

Skell brought up his shotgun, his eyes cold as ice. "I was going to kill the little lady first, just so you could watch," he told Joe. "But I'm tired of your lip. You go first!"

Joe drew himself up as straight as he could, as did Rita in her cell.

"How pretty," the killer snarled. "Just like Romeo and Juliet. Okay, kids, the party's over!"

Skell's finger tightened on the trigger—and the whole room shook with a tremendous force!

Chapter
18

INSTINCTIVELY JOE HARDY closed his eyes. Then he opened them in surprise. He wasn't dead! What had happened?

He looked first at Rita, then at Skell. The explosion had thrown Skell against Joe's cell and he stood staring through the doorway into the front of the sheriff's office.

The place was destroyed. The explosion had shattered the windows, sending glass and debris sailing. Smoke was pouring in, and they could all hear the crackle of flames outside.

Joe tried to take advantage of the moment, grabbing for the barrel of the shotgun. But before he could get a solid grasp, Skell snarled and yanked the weapon away.

"I'll deal with you two later!" the hit man shouted, running to investigate the blast.

Skell charged into the office and went into a crouch behind the sheriff's desk. But it took him a moment to realize that the explosion had come from *outside* the building. Holding the shotgun in one hand and Higgins's stolen service revolver in his other hand, he crept to the window for a view.

Even in the back room, Joe could hear Skell cursing.

Quickly the hit man moved to the front door, kicking it open. Smoke came billowing into the office, carrying the stench of burning gasoline. Firing the revolver, Skell plunged into the smoke, toward the spot where he'd left the patrol car.

Crouched low on the porch beside the front steps, Frank watched the hit man rush past him. As soon as he saw the hit man disappear into the billowing cloud of smoke, Frank dashed inside the sheriff's office.

There was no time to congratulate himself, even though it seemed that the diversion had worked. Frank grabbed the sheriff's keys from the desk and ran to the cells in the back. He had a suspicion who he'd find there.

Holding a finger to his lips, Frank leapt over the prone sheriff and quickly unlocked the door to Joe's cell.

"The hit man will be back in a moment," Frank whispered. "Stay where you are. We'll get the drop on him together."

Joe stared in amazement. Maybe the shock of almost dying had cut through the tangle of half

144

memories in his head. Now he realized who this dark-haired guy was. "Frank," Joe whispered. "You're my brother, Frank."

Frank glanced up and grinned. "Well, it's about time! I was getting pretty tired of being the Hardy Boy. Let's put an end to this whole mess."

"And how!" Joe said.

Frank was just about to unlock Rita's cell when he heard the hit man returning. He had only a moment to dive back into the front room and under the sheriff's desk.

Skell holstered the pistol and used his free hand to clear the smoke from in front of him. Frank held his breath, as he watched Skell's boots move past him, marching toward the cells.

"I don't have time to fool around now!" Skell's face was twisted in a snarl. "Somehow, the patrol car has exploded. I'm finishing this job and getting out of here!"

The hit man took a step toward Joe's cell and leveled the shotgun. "So long, kid."

Joe's foot shot out, kicking his cell door open right in Skell's face! A shotgun blast ripped into the ceiling as the hit man staggered back.

Frank scrambled free from the desk and jumped Skell from behind. But even though Skell was skinny, he had wiry strength and agility. As soon as he felt Frank's weight, he ducked and sent Frank spilling over him. Skell reared back, ready to club Frank with the butt of the shotgun.

145

But Joe came charging out of his cell, plowing into Skell's belly.

The tackle sent the hit man tumbling backward.

Joe followed up, lifting the hit man to his feet. He swung both fists into Skell's chest. Then he grabbed for the shotgun, trying to wrestle it from the killer's grasp.

But Skell wasn't finished yet. He smashed the gun down on his knee, breaking Joe's hold. Then he threw a solid punch to Joe's jaw, sending him whirling back until he crashed against Rita's cell.

Rita helped the cause by pushing Joe back toward the action.

Both Hardys came at Skell from different directions—Frank in a classic karate stance, Joe with his fists up.

But the killer still had the upper hand—he still had the shotgun. Ramming the butt into Joe's stomach, he swung the barrel wildly, clearing some room for himself. Joe and Frank had to jump back.

"Cute. But not cute enough." Skell's lips were a thin, angry line.

"It's two against one," Frank told him. "Put the gun down."

"Two against one doesn't count—not when I can blow you away!" Skell swung the shotgun again at Joe, who ducked from the blow, moving toward Frank.

"Don't get too close to me," Frank hissed. "We can't let him take us out with one shot!"

Skell twisted around, aiming the gun at Frank. His face registered surprise as Frank's foot lashed out at his chest. But the hit man met the threat, clubbing Frank's leg with the shotgun barrel. Joe circled round, trying for another attack.

Working as a team, the Hardys closed in on Skell. He began to back-pedal, bringing up the gun again. "Okay, who wants it first?" the hit man said, quickly shifting his aim from Frank to Joe, then back to Frank.

His eyes were locked on the brothers now. If Frank or Joe took a step forward, Skell was ready to shoot.

He stepped back to get a little more distance from his attackers—and crashed into Rita's cell.

Rita's hand darted through the bars to snatch the service revolver from his holster, jabbing it into Skell's back.

"Hold it right there," she warned.

The hit man was taken by surprise. He stiffened, half turning his head. Frank was ready to take advantage of that lapse. He clubbed both fists down on the shotgun, knocking it from Skell's hands.

Even as Frank was attacking, Joe unleashed an uppercut that sent the killer's skull crashing against the iron bars, knocking him out.

Skell slumped to the floor, and Joe drew back for another punch. Frank grabbed Joe's arm and felt the muscles tensing under his fingers.

"Stop it!" Frank shouted. "That's enough!"

"No, it isn't!" Joe shouted, trying to pull free. "This guy's a killer, Frank!"

"Then he'll face charges in a proper court of law," Frank insisted, barely holding Joe back.

Joe's fury began to ease. "You're right," he told Frank. "I guess I just forgot who I was for a moment."

"For a moment?" Frank said with a grin. He released Joe's arm and patted his brother on the back. "It's good to have you back, Joe."

Joe found the keys and unlocked the door to Rita's cell. She stepped out, and began to break down, her body shaking and tears falling freely down her face.

"It's over. It's all over now, Rita," Joe said softly. He removed the pistol from her hand and drew her close.

She leaned against him and wiped her eyes. "Yes. You even know who you really are, now."

Frank stepped forward and smiled. "This may seem like a weird time for introductions—but I'm Frank Hardy." Gesturing toward Joe, he added, "This is my younger brother, Joe."

By the time the sheriff finally came to, he thought he was still dreaming. Hovering over him were Frank, Joe, and Rita. Officer Higgins, back in his uniform, was on the telephone, calling his headquarters. And behind bars was Skell, handcuffed to the steel frame of a cell cot.

The sheriff jumped up with a fierce look. "Someone had better have a good explanation for all this!"

Frank and Joe chuckled.

Officer Higgins hung up the phone. "Well, sheriff, it's this way." He quickly brought the local lawman up to date, carefully avoiding some of the more humiliating things that had happened to him in the course of the adventure. "These kids cut a lot of corners," he finally finished. "Blowing up my patrol car is a serious offense." He grudgingly continued. "But they did pull the fat out of the fire. For *all* of us."

The sheriff still looked pretty embarrassed. "That guy sure got the jump on me. But then, I usually think a man in uniform is on my side." He shook hands with Frank. "Thanks for coming along when you did."

Then he turned to Joe and Rita. "Guess I owe you two more than thanks—you deserve an apology."

Joe nodded. "At least it's all over now."

"Pretty soon, you'll be heading home," Higgins cut in. "Headquarters told me that your dad is in Denver, hopping a helicopter to get here."

"Dad!" said Joe. "I forgot about him!"

"You forgot about a lot of stuff," Frank said with a laugh. "But I think Dad will be glad to find you all in one piece."

Joe went over to Rita, who was standing outside the door to the office, staring at the wreckage of patrol car 28. He understood her silence. The terror would not be over for her. Skell was in custody. But she'd lost her father, and her hiding place. The criminals would be after her until she testified—and maybe afterward for revenge.

"Come with us," Joe told her. "You'll be safe in Bayport."

"I'd like to think so," Rita said, sadly shaking her head. "I'd enjoy getting to know you better. But I can't."

She took a long, deep breath. "I'm going back into the witness protection program." She clasped Joe's hand. "Not because I want to go. Because I *have* to go."

Joe nodded numbly. "So this is goodbye, then. I'll never see you again."

She kissed him, her eyes shining with tears. "Never say never, Joe."

As they drew apart, Joe could hear the clattering sound of a helicopter approaching. "Hey, Frank," he called inside. "I think our ride is coming."

"Great," said Frank, coming to the door. "Just promise me one thing."

Joe looked puzzled. "What?"

Frank grinned. "Whatever you do, don't hit your head climbing aboard. You can be a dangerous enemy—and I don't want you trying to push me out of that chopper at two thousand feet!"

Perfect Getaway

Chapter

1

"DECK THE HALLS with boughs of holly," Frank Hardy chanted ironically, looking around at the palm trees fringing the deserted white beach on which he and his brother, Joe, stood.

"Fa-la-la-la-la-la Flor-i-da!" Joe joined in as he pushed sweat-dampened blond hair off his forehead. The sun was hot on his face. The jeans and sweatshirt he had put on in Bayport that morning were threatening to cook him. But then, when the two boys had left the North for Miami, they had taken off in a blizzard.

Frank was dressed like his younger brother, except that his sweatshirt bore two Chinese characters—his karate dojo's logo—instead of an orange varsity football letter. Frank's martial arts specialty wasn't a school sport at Bayport High, but he was very proud of his brown belt.

"This sure won't be a white Christmas for us unless we get this case wrapped up fast," said Frank. He, too, was sweating after the five miles they had walked on this beach to leave swimmers and sunbathers far behind.

"I'm asking Santa for a swimsuit—delivered early," said Joe. He looked up at the clear southern sky and stretched his arms wide, trying to unkink muscles still stiff from the air trip. "Are you sure we don't have time for a swim?"

"Forget it," said Frank. "This isn't a vacation."

"Don't remind me. We never take vacations. That trip to Colorado was the closest we've come in at least a year, and *that* was certainly no joyride," Joe said. The Hardys' last case had led them deep into the Colorado Rockies in pursuit of a hit man.

"You know, we *could* actually make this a vacation if we wanted," Joe continued, his blue eyes twinkling. "We could definitely afford a beach house if you'd just shake loose a little of that cash—"

"Get serious, Joe," said Frank.

"That's the problem with you, Frank," Joe said. "You're always serious. If you'd go with the flow—"

"We'd both have gone down the drain long ago," Frank said, cutting him off. "One of us has to take care of business, and it sure isn't you."

"Yeah," said Joe. "I saw the way you were

holding that bag on the flight down here." He looked down at the expensive leather attaché case that was lying on the sand next to their duffel bags. "Were you afraid I'd grab it and go on a shopping spree when we hit the Gold Coast?"

"No sense tempting you." Frank grinned. "One of the local girls might want a night on the town."

"You're right." Joe grinned back at his older brother. "But just let me take one more look inside. That's the stuff that dreams are made of."

Frank hesitated, then shrugged. "Okay," he said. "But just for a second." He squatted next to Joe in front of the case, clicked open both locks, and lifted the lid.

For a few seconds both Hardys stared at the bundles of bills neatly stacked in the case.

"Enough," said Frank, abruptly snapping it shut.

Joe was about to protest when he heard a car horn blare from behind the palm trees: once, twice, three times.

Frank looked at his watch. "Right on time," he said, his brown eyes suddenly wary.

He took a whistle from his pocket and gave three shrill blasts. The two Hardys waited. Silent. Still. A minute later a small man in a tan chauffeur's uniform appeared among the palms. With one hand he motioned for Frank and Joe to approach. In his other hand was something that turned his gesture into an absolute command: a

3

large nickel-plated automatic, glinting in the bright afternoon sun, pointed straight at them.

When the Hardys reached him, the man with the gun spoke in a clipped British accent. "Joe and Frank, I presume."

"That's right," Frank said.

"I apologize for the informality of addressing you gentlemen by your first names, but it's company policy," the man said.

"And what's your name?" Frank asked.

The man smiled, his lips a straight, tight line. "You may call me Jeeves." He motioned them closer with his gun. "Now, if I may see your tickets, we can move on."

"Our tickets?" asked Frank.

The gun gestured toward the attaché case.

"Oh, I get it," said Frank and snapped it open.

Jeeves glanced at the contents, then nodded. "Very good, sir," he said. "We may proceed with our journey."

"Just out of curiosity," said Joe, trying not to watch the gun pointing at him, "what would have happened if we didn't have our, er, tickets? The, uh, train would have left without us?"

"Not at all, sir," Jeeves replied. "But your final destination would not have been the one you originally intended."

"I get it," Joe said, managing a grin. "A one-way trip, huh?"

"An elegant way of putting it, if I may say so, sir," said Jeeves. "And now, if there are no more

4

questions—'' He motioned for them to walk ahead of him through the palm trees.

Beyond the palms ran a blacktop road. Parked beside it was an enormous gray stretch limo. Its chrome was beautifully polished, and its dark windows gleamed.

"Climb in, gentlemen, and we'll be on our way," Jeeves said as he held open the rear door with one hand. The other hand still held the silver automatic—not pointing at them but not away from them, either.

Frank and Joe looked into the spacious interior. They could see soft leather seats, a television set, and even a built-in bar.

"You do give your customers their money's worth," said Joe. "Battleships like this are for big wheels only."

"If you'll climb in," Jeeves repeated with a hint of impatience.

"Sure, sure," said Joe, and he tossed his duffel bag into the dark interior of the car. As soon as both boys were inside, the door behind them slammed, and they heard the click of its lock.

A second later a light came on, and they could see that the two side windows, the rear window, and the plastic shield that separated the driver from them were opaque.

"I thought windows like this were supposed to keep people from looking *in* while you could still look out," said Joe. "You know, part of the life-style of the rich and famous."

"These windows must have been custom-made for the rich and infamous," said Frank, pressing his nose against the glass as he tried to look out the side window. He could see nothing. "Somebody doesn't want us to see where we're going."

"Actually, the rich and famous aren't the only ones who use limos like this," Joe said.

"Who else does?" asked Frank.

"Funeral directors."

Frank grimaced, then finished Joe's thought. "Let's just hope this limo isn't being used for *our* funeral."

Chapter

2

THE DAY BEFORE, a ride to their own funeral had not been one of the Hardys' worries. Their main concern was that Christmas was just a week away, and they still hadn't bought any gifts.

In the morning, after breakfast, they were in Frank's room, planning their shopping.

"Agreed, then," said Joe. "What you get for Callie is your business." He was talking about Callie Shaw, Frank's steady girlfriend.

"Right," said Frank. "And what you get for half the girls in Bayport is *your* problem."

"It's the price of success," said Joe with a mock sigh.

"And of course we won't talk about what we're getting for each other," said Frank.

"Because it won't be worth mentioning," said Joe with a grin. "Personally, I've budgeted two dollars and ninety-eight cents, tax included, for your present."

"You shouldn't have told me—it makes me feel like a tightwad. Anyway, that leaves Dad and Mom and Aunt Gertrude. We'll buy gifts for them together."

"Maybe that computer of yours can come up with some gift ideas," suggested Joe. "We need some help. In fact, *I* need some help. Can you supply a little financial first aid? Maybe make me a small loan?"

"No way," said Frank. "The last upgrade I did on the computer put me near bankruptcy."

"Yeah, like that new engine in the van did to me," said Joe.

They sat in silence for a moment. Then Frank said, "Maybe you're right. Let's see if my computer can come up with some brilliant solution."

But before he could begin, the telephone in his room rang.

"Must be Callie," he said, going to answer it.

The person on the phone was a girl, but not Callie.

"Hi, Frank, it's Marcie Miller," she said. "Hope you don't mind my calling, but I needed to talk to you. Callie didn't want to give out your number at first, but I told her it was an emergency." She hesitated. "I told her it was a life-or-death situation."

Frank was instantly alert. Callie wouldn't have

urged someone to call for no reason. She was the most levelheaded person he knew.

"What's up?" he said.

"I'd rather tell you in person, at my house," Marcie said. "Please, could you come over right away? You and Joe. I need you both. I have to have some help, or—" She broke off. The desperation in her voice made it clear how urgently she needed them.

"We'll be right over," Frank promised.

"Thanks. Please hurry," she said and hung up.

"Come on. We have to get to Marcie Miller's place. Fast," Frank said. He headed for the closet to get his coat.

Joe didn't waste time asking questions. He could see from the gleam in Frank's eye that something interesting was cooking, and his appetite for action was as keen as his brother's. He raced to his room for his coat, beat Frank downstairs, and was already behind the wheel of the van warming up the motor in the icy morning air when Frank slid into the seat beside him.

On the drive to Marcie's, there was time to talk.

"Wonder what the problem is with Golden Girl?" said Joe, using his favorite nickname for Marcie.

"I always think of her as the rich little rich girl," said Frank. "But I guess that isn't fair. It isn't Marcie's fault that she has everything."

"Yeah," said Joe. "Looks, brains, personality,

9

plus all the things that her platinum card can buy.''

"Everything except a mother," said Frank, looking thoughtful. Marcie's mother had passed away when Marcie was born. "Maybe that's why everybody likes her. She definitely hasn't had *all* the breaks."

"She's lucky to have the kind of dad she has," said Joe, keeping his eyes on the road. Although the road had been plowed, there were still treacherous icy patches. Joe liked to drive fast, but he also drove well.

"Yeah, Mr. Miller is a real good guy—especially for a big-shot executive," said Frank. "He spends a lot of time with Marcie, talks with her, listens to her. He really tries to take the place of her mom."

"Marcie always says that she thinks he's tops," Joe agreed.

Joe parked the van beside the curb in front of Marcie's home, an imposing colonial mansion set back on a huge lawn blanketed with snow.

"We haven't been here since Marcie's Halloween party. Do you think the maid will remember us?" asked Frank.

Joe grinned as he rang the doorbell. "After the way you scared her with that fake skeleton, I don't think she'd *want* to remember you."

A young woman opened the door. It was Marcie—but this wasn't the Marcie that Frank and Joe knew. This girl was pale and unsmiling, and her movements were quick and nervous. She ushered the boys inside, then closed the door and leaned back against it. Her body sagged with relief. "Boy, am I glad to see you," she exclaimed.

"What's going on?" asked Frank.

"Come into the library and I'll show you," she said. Marcie led them down the hallway, continuing to talk as they followed her. "I never realized how big this house is until today. I can practically hear my footsteps echoing. Maybe it's because I'm almost never in it all alone. Dad's not here, today, though, and I sent the maid home."

On an antique oak table in the library was an expensive leather attaché case. Marcie snapped it open, and the Hardys' mouths dropped open.

Frank leaned closer. "Hundred-dollar bills. Are they all hundreds?"

"All of them," said Marcie. "I checked."

"That's a lot of cash," Joe finally managed to say. "What'd you do, rob a bank?"

Marcie caught her breath on a choking sob.

"Hey, sorry if I said anything wrong," Joe said hurriedly.

Marcie tried to pull herself together. "It's not your fault. You couldn't know. Nobody knows— not yet, anyway."

"Knows what?"

"About my dad," she said and buried her face in her hands, sobbing.

Frank and Joe waited. As active as they were, they knew that sometimes all they could do was wait.

Marcie calmed down after only a moment. She lifted her head from her hands, her eyes red and damp, but her face resolute. "I'm sorry. I know I can't help my dad if I go to pieces." She bit her lip, then continued in a steadier voice. "I'll tell you what happened. Then maybe you can help me make some sense out of it. And figure out what to do."

She sat down in one of the high-backed oak chairs by the table, and the Hardys sat down, too. In front of them the attaché case lay open like a question demanding an answer.

But Marcie didn't start with the money. She started with her dad.

"Let me say it fast, so I can get it out," she said. "My dad's in jail. Two plainclothes police officers came here and arrested him yesterday." She took a deep breath. "They've accused him of stealing—'embezzling' is the word they used— a fortune, millions and millions of dollars, from Maxtel. That's the company he's vice-president of. And—"

"Your dad?" said Frank, thinking of the distinguished-looking yet down-to-earth man who was Marcie's father.

"No way," said Joe, remembering when Marcie's dad had given not only money but also a lot of his own time and effort to help Marcie's high school class establish a shelter for the homeless.

"I know it, and you know it, but the law doesn't," said Marcie. "And this attaché case full of money makes it even worse."

"How so?" asked Frank, hoping the answer wasn't what he thought it might be.

"Dad called from jail early this morning and asked me to bring him some clothes and stuff, since they were holding him without bail," said Marcie. "Seems like a whole lot of big-time white-collar crooks—the same kind they say he is—have been doing vanishing acts lately, and they're not taking any chances."

"Yeah, I read about one the other day," said Joe. "Karl Ross, the takeover king. He took off."

"But what does that have to do with this money?" asked Frank.

"When I went to my dad's closet to get the clothes, I found this attaché case," said Marcie. "Normally I wouldn't have opened it, but I thought it might have something in it that he needed and forgot to tell me about. So I did. And it was a good thing. Because twenty minutes later, some cops showed up with a search warrant—and if I hadn't hidden the case in my room, they would have found it. You can imagine what it would have looked like to them."

"Yeah, I can imagine," said Frank, staring at the money.

"But you don't think—I mean, you *can't* think—" Marcie could go no further.

"Look, Marcie, he's your dad and all," Frank said gently. "But you have to see how it looks to somebody who isn't as involved."

"Don't worry, Marcie," Joe said, cutting in. "Frank always starts with the worst case. We both know your father well enough to know he's not a crook."

"Thanks, Joe," Marcie said, putting her hand on his arm. Then she turned to Frank. "Frank, I know you're not being unfair. It *does* look bad. Dad has a lawyer who can help him in court, but he needs somebody working on the outside to prove his innocence. That's why I called you two. Can you help? Will you?"

"We're not miracle workers, Marcie," Frank told her. "We'll try to find out what's going on, but we can't promise what the results will be. And if it turns out that you don't like what we find, we'll still have to tell the authorities."

"I'll take that chance," said Marcie with a glimmer of hope in her eyes for the first time.

Suddenly she frowned. "The trouble is, there's practically nothing to go on. Dad says the only person who can clear him of the charges against him is the company president, Adolf Tanner. He and Tanner were trying to buy some company in South America. First the money vanished, and then Tanner vanished. What's even worse, the police think my dad had something to do with

14

both things. They hinted to Dad that he could have wanted Tanner out of the way before Tanner discovered the money was gone.'' She paused. ''The charges against him are a lot worse than theft.''

''Then our first job is to find Tanner,'' said Frank.

Marcie shook her head. ''That's what everybody, including Dad, has been trying to do for the past week. No luck. It's as if Tanner disappeared into thin air.''

For a moment silence hung over the room. Abruptly the telephone rang, and Marcie sprang to answer it.

''Hello,'' she said, then listened for a second. ''Hold on, please.'' She covered the mouthpiece with the palm of her hand as she turned to the Hardys.

''It's for my dad. What should I do?''

Frank reacted instantly. ''Give me the phone.''

He spoke into the receiver, making his voice sound deeper and slower. ''Hello, Gregory Miller here.''

The woman's voice on the other end was the polite voice of a sales representative, the kind that sounded as if it had been programmed by a machine. ''Hello, Mr. Miller. This is Perfect Getaway Travel, Limited. I am returning your call about our special Perfect Getaway Travel plan.'' She paused. ''I am correct, am I not, Mr. Miller? You do want a Perfect Getaway, don't you?''

15

Chapter

3

"THAT'S RIGHT, I want to know about a Perfect Getaway," said Frank, keeping the rising excitement out of his voice. He motioned for Joe and Marcie to keep quiet as he switched on the speakerphone to let them listen in.

"Well, we here at Perfect Getaway realize that our clients are usually *very* pressed for time. I'm happy to say that we've arranged your reservation, and I'm calling to give you your itinerary," the voice said. "First of all, though, we must go over the matter of payment once again, to make sure it's completely understood."

"If we must, we must," said Frank.

"As I mentioned in our last conversation, the fee for our club will be seventy-five thousand dollars, to be paid in bills no larger than one-hundred," the woman continued smoothly.

"Needless to say, we cannot accept checks or credit cards."

"Of course," Frank agreed. "Now, if you'll tell me what I'm supposed to do, where I'm supposed to go."

"We will be sending you by messenger a map of southern Florida," said the woman. "On the map you will find a spot marked on a beach. That is where our representative will rendezvous with you tomorrow afternoon, if that is convenient for you."

"It's fine," said Frank. "The sooner the better."

"Most of our clients feel that way," the woman said. "Now, just one more detail. What will your name be?"

"Name?" said Frank.

"An essential part of our special Perfect Getaway plan is to leave your old self behind, including your name," said the woman. "From the moment you join us, we don't even want to *know* your old name or anything about you. In fact, we prefer to have merely a new *first* name for you. We and our clients have found that this is the best possible arrangement for all of us. In fact, after this call is completed, all record of your present name will be deleted from our files."

"I get it," said Frank. "What nobody knows can't hurt anybody."

"Exactly," the woman said. "Now, if you'll give us a name we can use for you . . ."

"What about—Frank? I think that has a nice ring to it."

"Fine, Frank," said the woman. "Well, if there's nothing else—"

"Uh, there's one other thing," said Frank.

"What's that?" asked the woman.

"I've got a partner," said Frank. "He's looking for a Perfect Getaway, too. In fact, he needs one very badly. May I bring him with me?"

"Please hold, sir, while I check with my supervisor," said the woman. A few moments later, she came back on the line. "Yes, we can accommodate your partner. That will be a total of one hundred fifty thousand dollars. And remember, nothing larger than hundred-dollar bills."

"No discount?" asked Frank indignantly. "A group rate, perhaps?"

"Wait a moment, I'll have to check," said the woman. Another pause followed. "Yes, we are able to offer you a special rate of one hundred twenty-five thousand dollars for two."

"That's more like it," said Frank.

"And what is your companion's name?"

"His name now or his new one?" asked Frank.

"His new one, of course," said the woman.

"Of course," said Frank. "What about, er, Joe? That should be easy for him to remember."

"Joe it is," said the voice. "Now, do you have any more questions?"

"Just one," said Frank. "What kind of clothes do we wear?"

"Dress as casually and inconspicuously as possible, for obvious reasons. And don't bother bringing much luggage. Perfect Getaway will provide you with a new wardrobe suitable for wherever your Perfect Getaway will take you."

"All included in your fee?" asked Frank, doing his best to sound like a suspicious customer.

"Of course, sir. One payment covers all."

"That sounds fine," Frank said.

"We'll do our best to take care of your every need," said the woman. "A satisfied customer is our best advertisement. As you said yourself when you contacted us, you got our name through a personal recommendation."

"Yes, that's right, I did," said Frank. "Well, so long. And thank you."

"Thank *you*," said the voice. "And we hope you have a Perfect Getaway."

There was a click, then a dial tone. Frank stared thoughtfully at the speaker in the middle of the desk before he hung up the receiver.

"So we're heading down to Florida," Joe said finally. "Great. We'll go home, pack our duffel bags, and get to the bottom of this Perfect Getaway stuff."

"Not so fast," said Frank. "I set up that meeting in Florida to keep our options open—but maybe we should tell the police about this."

Frank turned to Marcie, then hesitated. "Look, Marcie, I hate to say it, but this doesn't look good for your dad. I mean, apparently he

19

got in touch with this Perfect Getaway outfit right before he was arrested. Plus, he had that attaché case filled with the hundreds. We may be breaking the law if we don't inform the authorities. It could be important evidence in their case against him."

Much to his relief, Marcie didn't get mad. But she also didn't give up her position.

"Dad would never try to run away from anything," she said with absolute certainty. "There has to be another explanation. And I'm not saying that just because I'm his daughter."

"Frank, let's keep our options open, as you suggested," Joe said. "There has to be something we don't know. And I say we go down to Florida and find it before we present the cops with more evidence that makes Mr. Miller look guilty."

Frank still looked doubtful. "I appreciate the way both of you feel. But feelings aren't facts."

"Right," said Joe. "That's why we should go down to Florida—to get the facts."

"You have to," pleaded Marcie. "You two are the only ones who can help clear my dad."

Frank shrugged. "Okay. We'll go for two reasons. First, I can't picture your dad as a crook. And second, I wonder if Mr. Tanner called Perfect Getaway, too."

Joe grinned at Marcie. "I had a feeling he'd go. He doesn't like sitting around doing nothing any more than I do. And if it means taking a few chances—well, it's not the first time we've done it."

Frank couldn't dispute that. But he said soberly, "I want one thing understood. If we do find out that your dad was planning on vanishing, or if we find out anything else against him, we'll have to go to the cops with what we dig up. We can't be part of a cover-up."

Marcie nodded and said, "I understand, but I know there isn't a chance in the world you'll find out anything bad about him."

"Great, we're all set," said Joe. "We've got enough cash to convince Perfect Getaway that we're genuine and even to buy our airline tickets."

"I'll take care of the tickets," said Marcie. "I'll pay for them with a credit card. I'd go down with you, except that Dad might need me around, and I'm sure you two know what you're doing."

Frank was already leafing through a telephone book looking for the phone numbers of airlines with Florida routes. "Let's hope we can get a flight. Bookings over Christmas are tight."

"You can travel first class," Marcie said. "There are always seats available there."

"Money," said Joe, picking up the attaché case. "Wonderful what it can do."

The next day, though, as Joe sat with Frank in the locked backseat of the limo speeding toward an unknown destination, he wasn't so sure about the power of money.

He patted the attaché case on the seat between Frank and him and said, "This money got us into this dungeon on wheels. Let's hope it can get us out."

Frank signaled Joe to be quiet while he turned on the car's television set. Turning up the volume, he leaned over and whispered to his brother, "Be careful. The driver may be listening to make sure that we're the right guys."

Joe nodded his understanding.

Frank continued, "Things are happening faster than I expected. I thought we'd just make contact with Perfect Getaway, then wait while they made plans. Whatever we did, I thought we'd have time to call Marcie and fill her in. That way if something went wrong, we could count on some help showing up."

"Too late for that now," muttered Joe. "One item this limo lacks is a phone in the backseat." He shivered, and it wasn't because of the air-conditioning. "We've worked without a backup before, but when we climbed into this car, I felt as if we were entering another world. Like we were cutting all ties to the past, to everything we know. Creepy, huh?"

"You're not the only one who's spooked." Frank nodded in agreement.

"I wish we'd had time to let Dad know what

we were doing," said Joe, referring to their father, the famous private detective Fenton Hardy.

"I know what you mean," answered Frank. "But it's too late now—too late to tell anyone where we are."

Joe glanced at his watch. "We've been traveling for more than an hour. Wonder how much longer it'll be?"

"Not much—unless this limo can go underwater," said Frank. "We started out going south, and the car hasn't made any turns. That should put us at the tip of Florida—or beyond."

"What do you mean, 'beyond'?" asked Joe, glad to see that Frank's powers of observation and deduction hadn't been left behind.

"This highway continues as a causeway, linking all the tiny islands that form the Florida Keys, all the way to Key West," said Frank, looking at the map of the area that Perfect Getaway had sent.

Suddenly Joe stiffened. "The car's turning," he said.

"And slowing down," added Frank as he turned off the television. "We must have left the main highway."

The car continued at a slower speed. Then, after about ten minutes, it came to a stop. They heard the driver's door open.

The Hardys waited in tense silence for the car's back door to open or for the locks to click open.

23

"Why isn't Jeeves letting us out?" Joe asked nervously.

"Maybe he's gone to check with his boss. Or to get some help. Or both," Frank said speculatively.

Another three minutes of silence passed, while Joe watched the numbers on his digital watch change.

Then the lock clicked and the car door swung open.

Jeeves was there, and with him was a tall man with his hair shorn in a military crew cut. His clothes were military, too: sharply pressed green fatigues and polished army boots, and he carried a standard M-16 infantry rifle. But when Frank looked closer, he saw no insignia of rank or unit on the man's sleeves, and no name was stenciled on the strip of white material above the shirt pocket. Whatever army he belonged to was a private one.

Frank glanced sideways at Joe. Joe was checking the guy out, too, and doubtless had reached the same conclusion.

"If you will leave the car now, gentlemen, and accompany Bob here," Jeeves said, stepping aside to let them out.

Frank and Joe climbed out of the car and found themselves standing in front of a white-columned mansion that looked like it came straight off a movie set of the old South. But there was one thing different in this set. Through the breaks in the tropical mangrove trees edging the property, the Hardys could see a high wall topped by barbed wire.

Bob saw them trying to get their bearings, and motioned with his rifle. "Let's go. No sense in you looking around here. You ain't staying. This is just your jump-off spot."

Jeeves, gun in hand once more, couldn't resist adding, "Bob is quite right. You won't be staying—unless, of course, you are here under false pretenses." He smiled, clearly pleased with himself. "In that case, this place will be your final destination." His grin grew more ghoulish. "Or should I say, your *eternal* resting place."

Chapter

4

"FIRST WE TAKE care of business," Bob told the Hardys as he pressed the buzzer to the door of the mansion. Another man in fatigues and carrying an M-16 opened the door and waved them through.

The interior was a surprise. The outside of the mansion looked straight out of the South before the Civil War, but inside everything was strictly contemporary. The lighting was indirect, the walls were painted in soft pastels, the carpeting was thick and springy underfoot, the furniture was modern and sleek. It was like walking into an expensive international-style hotel.

Bob herded the Hardys into a room that had been turned into an office, where a pretty young woman was sitting behind a free-form desk. Its top was uncluttered except for a computer.

The young woman looked up at them, smiling automatically. When she saw two teenage boys approaching her instead of the middle-aged men she had expected, the smile wavered for an instant. She quickly replaced it. "Hi. I'm Sally," she said coolly. "If you'll tell me your names, we'll get you checked in."

Frank recognized her voice. She was the one he had talked to on the phone at Marcie's.

"Hi," he said. "I think I spoke to you before. I'm Frank. And this is Joe."

"Hi, Frank and Joe," Sally said suspiciously. She punched their names into the computer and looked at the monitor screen, which Frank and Joe couldn't see. Then she said, "Glad you arrived on time. Everything is so much simpler when our clients obey instructions. That will be one hundred twenty-five thousand dollars, please."

Frank put the attaché case on the table and opened it. "Shall I count it out, or do you want to?"

"I'd be happy to, sir," Sally said.

As she picked up the first bundle of bills, her whole manner changed abruptly. The unconvincing smile vanished from her face, her eyes focused like high-intensity lights on the bills, and her fingers moved as quickly as if they were machine parts, flipping through the bills amazingly quickly. After she had counted the bundle, she separated several bills from the rest and examined them with a penlight and a magnifying glass, which she took from a drawer.

"What's the matter, don't you trust us?" Frank asked quickly, suddenly wondering himself about all those hundreds. Were they funny money?

"Nothing personal, sir, just routine," said Sally automatically, not bothering to look up. She took another bundle of bills from the case and repeated the counting and checking.

Frank and Joe waited. The only sounds in the office were the rustling of the bills and Bob clearing his throat behind them. Neither Frank nor Joe turned around, but both could picture the M-16 in his hands. And they could be sure he was holding it ready.

Finally Sally looked up from the bundles of bills piled neatly on the desk in front of her. Her smile was switched back on. Whatever doubts she might have had about Frank and Joe seemed to have vanished.

"Everything seems to be in order," she said. "Now, what do you want to do with your remaining cash?" She pointed to the bundles of bills still in the attaché case. The case was still about three-quarters full. "Would you like to deposit the money in an account with us? Or do you prefer to keep it with you?"

"If it's all the same, we'll keep it with us," said Frank.

"I understand perfectly," Sally said. "In fact,

most of our clients prefer to keep their cash on hand. We cater to a very self-reliant kind of person. Survivors, that's how we like to think of them."

"Yes, well, it's a hard, cruel world out there. That's why we want to get away from it all," said Frank, fishing for information. "Just like all your other customers, right?"

But Sally only smiled politely and said, "Bob will show you to your suite now. I'm sure you'll want to freshen up. I hope you don't mind, but you two will have to share a suite, since you're being given a discount. Of course, if you wish to pay a bit more—"

"One suite will be fine," said Frank.

"Well, then, I hope you enjoy your stay." Sally snapped shut the attaché case and pushed it toward Frank.

Frank tried one last probe as he picked it up. "I hope this stay won't be too long. I mean, we've got to be moving."

"All in good time," she said. "There are a few formalities. But don't worry, I assure you that you won't be disturbed here. We are *very* secluded."

"Yes," said Joe. "I saw the fence out front. Can't say I liked it, though. Reminded me too much of a prison."

"It's for your own protection, sir." Sally smiled. "Bob, if you will escort our guests to their suite."

"Let's move it," said Bob. None of Sally's good manners had rubbed off on him. "You've got half an hour before your interview."

"Interview?" said Frank.

"What kind of interview?" asked Joe.

Bob cut off further conversation with a gesture of his gun.

He led them up a curving stairway and along a hall to a door on the second floor. "Make yourselves comfortable," he said. "I'll be back for you in half an hour."

Frank and Joe entered their room, and the door closed behind them. They weren't surprised to hear it being locked from the outside. They had already gotten the idea that they weren't totally trusted.

As soon as they were inside, Frank caught Joe's gaze, put his finger to his lips, then tapped that finger against his ear.

Joe got the message: just like the limo, the room might be bugged.

"You know, this place is gorgeous," Joe said in a loud voice as he began to check out one side of the room for listening devices, looking behind paintings, on the backs and bottoms of pieces of furniture, in vases, and under rugs.

"Perfect Getaway is really giving us our money's worth," said Frank, checking out the other side.

Working their way around the room, they met

on the far side, where they both shrugged and gestured to signify that they had found nothing.

Frank's eyes darted around the room, checking to see if they had missed anything. Then he glanced up and pointed at the old-fashioned chandelier hanging from the high ceiling. Joe nodded.

"I think I'll get some exercise," Frank said. "I need to work out some kinks from the trip."

"Good idea," said Joe. "Me, too."

He watched Frank get a chair and position it under the chandelier. Frank stood on the chair, then squatted down and made a stirrup with his hands. Joe nodded, recognizing a gymnastic stunt they had worked up the year before in a skit for a school show. Joe backed up a couple of steps, propelled himself forward, and leapt when he was about a yard from Frank, his right foot landing in Frank's linked hands. Frank heaved upward as Joe pushed off from his hands, and a second later Joe was standing on Frank's shoulders. Careful not to lose his balance on the chair or disturb Joe's balance on his shoulders, Frank straightened up slowly. It worked. Joe was up high enough to inspect the chandelier. He peered into it and saw a miniature black receiving device.

Joe leapt down, hit the carpet, and did a neat somersault, just to finish the routine off right. "Good workout," he said loudly. He pointed to the chandelier, put his finger to his lips, and nodded.

31

"Time for a nice, hot shower," said Frank. He went into the bathroom, and Joe followed him.

"Great shower, needle-point spray!" Frank shouted, as if Joe were still in the other room.

He then closed the door and turned the shower up full force. The din of the water hitting the aqua-colored plastic shower stall filled the bathroom.

Frank put his mouth close to Joe's ear. "Whisper. I don't think any bugs they might have in here could pick us up."

"This looks bad for Marcie's dad," Joe whispered back. "This operation sure seems to be set up to help crooks skip out."

"Right—and maybe it does even more than that," Frank answered. "It looks too elaborate for just an escape outfit. But we can worry about that later. Right now we have to worry about ourselves. We're in these people's hands, and unless we convince them we're their kind of guys, they're going to start squeezing really hard."

"Yeah, we've got to get our story together," whispered Joe. "I bet that's why they put us in here before the interview, so that if we tried to come up with some story, their bug would pick it up."

"You just figured that out?" whispered Frank.

"Okay, okay," Joe said with more than a trace of annoyance in his whisper. "If you're so smart, how do we explain how a couple of teens like us are loaded with cash and on the run from the law?"

"They were expecting Marcie's dad," whispered Frank. "So I think we should tell them that we were in on his embezzlement scheme."

"Sure, we really look like corporate types," Joe hissed sarcastically.

"Come on, Joe, the answer was sitting right there on Sally's desk."

Joe sat patiently, waiting for his brother to get to the punch line of what he was sure was a joke.

"I'm not kidding. We can claim that we were hackers for hire," Frank told him. "We can say we helped Mr. Miller rig his company's computers so he could get the money out of the country."

"And that when the cops grabbed him, we grabbed our share of the money—" Joe exclaimed.

"And ran," said Frank, finishing his brother's sentence.

Frank turned off the shower and opened the bathroom door. "Hey, that was great, Joe," he shouted into the other room. "You want to take one?"

Joe left the bathroom, then called back toward Frank, "Nah. You took too long. We're going to have our interview in a few minutes. Hope it doesn't drag on—I want to clear out of here fast. I can practically feel Uncle Sam breathing down my neck."

"What could they want to find out?" Frank asked as he came out of the bathroom. "The color of our money should have been enough."

"You can't blame them for checking us out," answered Joe. "In an operation like this, you have to be extra careful."

A minute later Bob opened their door without bothering to knock and beckoned to them to follow.

"Wait a sec," said Frank, and went to pick up the attaché case. "We'd better keep this with us."

Bob shrugged and said impatiently, "Let's go."

He led them down a hall to another room and opened the door. "Here are the two you wanted to see, sir," he said and gestured with his M-16 for the Hardys to go inside.

As they stepped into the room, they heard Bob leave and close the door behind them.

In front of them was a short, squat, balding man with a mustache. He, too, was wearing unmarked fatigues, but his whole presence indicated that he was an officer in whatever kind of force this was. He wasn't sitting behind his desk, but on top of it. One gleaming boot was tapping against the desk front as he looked the Hardys up and down.

"So you are Frank and Joe," he said. It was not a statement but a challenge.

"Right," said Frank.

"And who are you?" asked Joe.

The man smiled. "You can call me Alex."

"Glad to meet you, Alex," said Joe, extending his hand. "Now, how soon can you get us out of here?"

"Ah, you young people, always in such a hurry," Alex said with a sigh, ignoring Joe's outstretched hand. "In fact, you seem quite young to want to take one of our vacations, much less be able to afford it."

Frank had decided that the best way to weather this confrontation was to get this guy on the defensive, so he started talking fast and loud. "Look, I don't see why we have to go through this third-degree. The lady on the phone said there'd be no questions about our past."

Alex smiled. "It wouldn't be good for business to allow any undercover cops to travel along our underground railroad, would it?"

"If you lied on the phone," said Joe, "how can we trust you about anything?"

Alex sighed. "Come on, kid, you might be young, but you can't be that dumb. Who can you trust in this world? Nobody. But if it makes you feel any better, we'll keep our part of the bargain once we clear you. Not out of any sense of honor, but because it's good business. The only way we can keep getting customers is to have them pass the word that we give good value—a new start with a new name in a new place."

Frank pretended to think it over. Then he nodded. "Makes sense. Okay. Marcie Miller is a friend of ours. We met her father at a Halloween party, and he and I got to talking computers. When I told him about how some friends of mine had managed to get into the phone company's computers—"

Joe interrupted, continuing the story. "—he said that such a thing could never happen to his company's computers, that they were state-of-the-art. Later that night we tried it, and they were easy. They had a mainframe set up to take orders over the phone lines, and their security system was a joke. We could have wiped them out."

"But we didn't," interjected Frank. "We just got into the interoffice e-mail—that's electronic mail—system and left Miller a message. The computer wouldn't work for anyone in his company that day until—"

"—they said please," said Joe, laughing out loud.

"Sounds good," said Alex. "But that's nothing to make you start running."

"What came afterward wasn't just fun and games." Frank's face sobered. "Miller told us we were the answer to a businessman's prayer. Working together, with us slipping bogus orders into the computer at night and him moving the money during the day, we really took a bite out of the company. But it looks like he got too greedy and careless. We picked up our last payment just before the cops came to take him away.

When you called, it sounded like the answer to *our* prayers.''

Frank smiled at Alex, then at Joe. When he and his brother were on the same wavelength, it felt as if nothing and nobody could beat them.

''Well, Frank and Joe, you seem to have—'' Alex began.

Just then the phone rang. Alex picked it up and listened. Then his eyes narrowed and he said, ''Thanks. I'll take care of it.''

Without even a glance at the Hardys, he put down his phone, slid off the desk, and opened a drawer. Frank and Joe looked at each other uneasily. Alex's mood had clearly just changed— and it didn't look as if it had changed in their favor. When they looked back at Alex, they saw a .45 in his hand, pointed at them.

''There's one thing you didn't mention, Frank and Joe,'' he said, a smile spreading slowly across his face. ''Maybe you wanted to be modest. But let me tell you, it's a great big thrill to meet the famous Hardys.''

Chapter

5

"WHO'RE THEY?" SAID Joe with a puzzled look.

"Come on, you must have heard of them," said Alex. "They're Fenton Hardy's kids, and they like to play at being detectives like their old man."

"Oh, *those* Hardys," said Frank.

"What do *we* have to do with them?" asked Joe.

The door to the room opened. In walked Bob, his M-16 in one hand and a magazine in the other.

Alex glanced at its cover. "Hmm, *Advanced Computer Abstracts*. So, you're into computers, Frank?"

"What if I am?" said Frank defiantly, then stopped. He suddenly had a sick feeling in the pit of his stomach.

"You're not even going to ask me how I knew

this magazine was yours?" asked Alex with a gloating smile. "But I suppose you don't have to. You must realize that your name is on the address label pasted on it. A little careless, Frank. But I guess even the brightest boys make mistakes."

Frank didn't have an answer. He said feebly, "You went through our bags while we were down here."

"Too bad you didn't think of it sooner," said Alex.

"What are you going to do with us?" asked Frank, trying not to look at his brother. He could imagine the look that Joe was giving him.

"Do you have to ask?" inquired Alex, lowering his gun so it was pointed directly at Frank's heart.

Frank refused to give Alex the satisfaction of seeing him cringe. He kept his face expressionless and braced himself.

"Relax," Alex said. "You have a few more hours—until it gets dark. Then you can take a trip with a couple of our men to a neighboring key. It doesn't have a fine mansion like this one on it. In fact, it doesn't have anything on it but quicksand. We find it very handy. It's as though Mother Nature has given us the perfect disposal machine."

Then he turned to Bob. "Take them away."

"The cellar?" asked Bob.

"The cellar," said Alex. "You can leave that attaché case here. Money won't do you any good where you're going."

39

Bob herded Frank and Joe at gunpoint down the broad stairway to the first floor, then down a much narrower set of steps to an underground passage lined with wooden doors. It was dimly lit by a few light bulbs crudely installed on the ceiling.

"Surprise, huh?" said Bob. "Upstairs was where the owners lived the good life in the old days. Down here is where they used to stick slaves who got too uppity. To teach them a lesson, if you know what I mean."

They reached the end of the passage. Bob made them stand against the damp plaster wall next to the last door.

"Turn your pockets inside out," he instructed sharply. After they had dumped the contents of their pockets onto the floor, he said, "Open that door and get in."

They heard him slide the outside bolt shut.

"Hey, it's pitch black. What about some light?" Joe shouted.

"Get used to the dark. Pretend it's quicksand," Bob said, his voice muffled by the thick door.

Long minutes passed in the silent darkness.

Then Frank heard Joe whisper, "Think he's gone?"

"Probably," Frank whispered back. Then he said in a more normal tone, "I don't think we have to worry about bugs down here."

"I don't know if I should trust your judgment

40

after your brilliant move with that magazine," Joe said sourly.

"Look, I'm sorry," Frank said. "I was in the middle of an article, so I packed the magazine, intending to finish it and then chuck it. But things happened too fast, and it slipped my mind."

"Which leaves us slipping into quicksand— unless we can find a way out fast," said Joe. "Let's start looking."

A light flashed in his hand.

"Good, you've got your penlight," said Frank. "I knew you'd manage to palm something when that goon made us empty our pockets."

"Yeah," Joe agreed. "What'd you get?"

"This," said Frank, and showed Joe his Swiss army knife.

"We're in business," said Joe.

Frank knelt in front of the door. He examined it, his brow furrowed, concentrating. "Too bad it doesn't have a lock. There's nothing to pick. We have to get at that bolt."

He tested the wood with the tip of the longest blade on his knife.

"We're in luck," he said. "It's old and soft. I could pick it away with my fingernails if I had the time."

"But we don't," said Joe. "Get to work."

"Right," said Frank, and began gaining access to the outside bolt, while Joe provided light with his penlight. With the blade, Frank gouged out wood on the edge of the door; then he used the miniature saw on the Swiss army knife to remove larger chunks. Half an hour later, the metal of the outside bolt was exposed.

"Let's hope they've kept it well oiled," he said, and used the tip of his strongest blade to try to slide the bolt open.

It wouldn't budge.

"Back to work," said Frank, gritting his teeth and cutting at the wood again to widen the opening.

"Hurry it up," urged Joe. "They'll be coming for us any second."

"Thanks for the information," said Frank, wiping away the sweat that beaded his forehead.

Finally the hole looked large enough. "Let's see if I can reach it now," Frank said.

He managed to insert a couple of fingers into the hole and make contact with the metal of the bolt. The surface was rough and rusted. He tried to move it. It wouldn't budge. Finally he gave one last try—and felt it move just a fraction.

"I think I've got it going," he said. "But my fingers are starting to cramp."

"Let me take a crack at it," said Joe.

They exchanged places.

"It's moving, all right, but not much," Joe grunted. "It's really stiff." He withdrew his fingers and shook them to relieve the ache.

They traded places three more times, until Joe finally said, "That does it." He gave the door a push, and it swung open.

"Whew," said Joe. "That's cutting it close."

"I hope not too close," said Frank. "Let's see if we can make it out of here."

Swiftly they moved down the passageway and up the narrow stairs to the first floor. Joe went first, eager to be on the move. But he was cautious enough to stop midway up the stairs, and listen. At the top of the stairs, Joe slowly eased his head around the corner.

"Coast's clear," he whispered over his shoulder. "Let's go."

He raced for an open door. Frank was right on his heels.

They entered a recreation room that held a Ping-Pong table, a pool table, card tables, video games, a giant-screen TV, and soft-drink and snack machines. It, too, was deserted.

"Nice setup," remarked Joe. He went to a soft-drink machine and pressed a button. A plastic cup descended and was filled. "You don't even need change for it," he said, taking a long swallow. "They live pretty well here."

Frank shook his head impatiently. It was good to keep cool in tight spots, but sometimes Joe overdid it.

"We've been lucky so far," Frank said, "but let's get out of here before our luck runs out." Then he exclaimed, "Hey! What the—"

In one lightning motion, Joe had dropped his soda, grabbed a ball from the pool table, and let the ball fly—right at Frank.

43

There wasn't time for Frank to duck. He barely had a chance to blink as the ball whizzed by his ear. A *clunk* followed, and Frank wheeled around to see a young man in a white uniform toppling like a felled tree. Behind him, in the doorway of the room, another man in white stood with his mouth open in surprise.

The second man didn't get a chance to make a move. Frank connected with a karate chop. The man dropped to the floor, out like a light.

"Not a bad fastball, considering I haven't pitched since August," said Joe, crossing the room to join Frank near the two unconscious men.

"Glad your control was on," said Frank, rubbing the ear the pool ball had almost brushed.

"Trust me," Joe said. "They came through the door too suddenly for me to warn you. I had to move fast."

"And we have to get out of here just as fast," said Frank, but then he stopped himself in mid-movement. "On second thought, let's take time for a quick change."

He bent down to unbutton the clothes of the man at his feet.

"Got you," said Joe, nodding and following Frank's lead.

Minutes later Frank and Joe were clad in white suits that were a little too large and black patent shoes that pinched. Their own clothes had been torn into strips and used to tie and gag the two unconscious men.

"Now, let's find a way out of here," said Frank.

"Easy," said Joe as he raised a large window.

Although it was dark out, a full moon lit the cloudless sky, and the Hardys had to be careful to stay in the shadows of the shrubbery that bordered the side of the mansion.

"What now? The fence around this place is going to be tough to get over. Bet that wire on top is electrified," Joe said as they edged around the mansion toward the rear.

"Quick," Frank whispered suddenly. "Hit the ground!"

Joe had heard the same noise Frank had. They lay on their stomachs, holding their breath, as a group of about twenty men came out of the darkness on an asphalt path fifteen yards from them.

The men passed the spot where Frank and Joe were lying and entered the mansion through a rear door. Frank and Joe lay quietly for a couple more minutes before getting to their feet.

"That explains why the mansion was deserted," whispered Joe. "Most of the help was back there. Wonder what they were doing?"

"As long as they're not hunting us, I'm happy," said Frank. "Whatever they're doing, we have to get moving. In a little while, all those guys *will* be hunting us."

"Let's see how fast you can go," challenged

Joe. "Bet I can still beat you in the two hundred."

"You're on," said Frank, assuming a sprinter's crouch.

The two of them tore over the open lawn behind the mansion toward the asphalt path, and then raced along it.

At the point where the path entered a grove of mangrove trees, Joe came to a halt with a three-yard lead over Frank.

"As slow as ever," Joe panted as Frank stopped beside him.

"Make it five miles, and then see who's ahead," Frank answered automatically, looking behind them. There was still no sign of pursuit. And no fence ahead of them. He looked at the path. No telling where it led.

"Come on," Frank said, and they walked through the grove and emerged from the trees.

"Wow! Look at that," said Joe, stopping to stare at the view that opened out before them.

The path descended to a wharf that jutted out into the sea. Beyond the end of the wharf, the moonlight formed a ghostly ribbon on the smooth water. Ghostly in the moonlight, too, was a sleek white yacht, moored to the wharf.

"Maybe we won't have to swim for it after all," said Joe. "Not with a beauty like that to take us over the water."

"It's worth checking out," said Frank. "I

don't see any sign of life aboard. Maybe we can hijack it."

"Sounds good," said Joe, already moving toward the wharf.

"Careful, this wood is old—watch out for squeaks," whispered Frank when they reached the pier.

"Okay," Joe whispered back. "But there's no danger that I can see. Nobody is—"

A sudden beam of light froze him with his mouth open. Almost as quickly as the light had gone on, it went off.

It took just a second for the Hardys' vision to readjust to the moonlight.

And then they saw the figure of a man dressed in a uniform the same ghostly white as the yacht he was standing on.

But there was nothing ghostly about the man's voice. His shout shattered the stillness.

"Freeze, you two!"

The boys were trapped in the open, the moon hitting them like a spotlight, their moment of freedom over.

Chapter

6

" 'BOUT TIME YOU two showed up," said the man, speaking more softly. "Another five minutes, we would have left without you. They finished loading the ship a good ten minutes ago, and the tide's about to change."

"Uh, we can explain," said Frank quickly, hoping that he or Joe could come up with something fast.

"Save it for when we're below decks," the man said, then squinted at them. "Hey, where's your gear?"

"We sent it down with one of the guys on the loading detail," Frank said. "Didn't he bring it?"

The man gave a snort of disgust. "I can see they sent me a couple of goof-ups for this trip. Nobody brought your gear here—and it's too late to go back to find it. Doesn't matter, anyway.

There's plenty of uniforms on board, real pretty ones. So, you get aboard, too.''

"Okay, okay," said Joe, picking up on this new game. "But isn't this a lot of fuss over us showing up a couple of minutes late?"

"We stick to the rules in this outfit, and don't you forget it," snapped the man.

"Yes, sir. Right, sir," said Frank, and jumped from the wharf onto the deck of the yacht. Behind him came Joe, and then the man in the white uniform.

Joe stumbled over a rope on deck as they headed for a hatchway. "I could have broken my ankle," he complained. "Why don't you turn on some lights?"

"I can see it's going to be real fun teaching you morons the routine," the man said. "What can I expect, though, with last-minute replacements? If only my two regular stewards hadn't eaten those spoiled anchovies." He paused, then said, "Why do you think we don't have any lights? Security. Same reason everything on this trip is done the hard way, like not even using our radio. Nobody sees us, and nobody hears us. I wasn't even supposed to use my flashlight, but I had to check you out."

He opened the hatchway, and bright light shone out from the inside. All the windows and doors must have been blacked out. The man closed the door the moment they were in, then led them down the stairs going below decks.

"In here," said the man, and they entered a large wood-paneled cabin.

Joe uttered a low whistle of approval as he looked around at the luxurious surroundings.

"Yeah, this used to be some millionaire's yacht," said the man. "This cabin is mine, but yours is almost as nice. This ship is good duty. Do your jobs right, and maybe you'll get a permanent assignment."

"Hey, what do we call you?" said Frank.

"My organization name is Sam. What're yours?"

"Well, aboard this ship, I'm Frank," he said.

"And I'm Joe," said Joe.

"Frank. Joe. I'll remember that. And you do, too," said Sam.

"We'll do our best," promised Frank.

"First we have to get you outfitted," said Sam. As he led them out of the cabin and down the passageway, the yacht engine came to life. Under their feet, they felt the ship begin to move.

"We're in our own private world until landfall," said Sam. "This is my fifth trip, and I still haven't gotten used to it. Just like I can't get used to not knowing where we go. We just dock there and stay aboard." He shook his head. "Well, we don't want to know too much in this organization."

Sam took Frank and Joe to a supply room, where an attendant handed them uniforms consisting of black trousers, white shirts, black ties, white formal jackets, an extra pair of black shoes each, and enough socks, underwear, and toilet articles to replace the lost ones in their duffel bags.

Next, Sam took them to their cabin.

"Stow your gear and report to my cabin in ten minutes," he ordered and left them alone.

As they quickly changed into clothes that fit, Frank remarked, "Looks like we're going to be oceangoing waiters."

"I hope we wait on the captain's table," said Joe. "We could find out where we're headed."

"I'd sure like to find out *something*," said Frank. "The deeper we get into this Perfect Getaway outfit, the more questions I have. I mean, this all looks too big and elaborate just to help a handful of rich crooks skip the country—but maybe I'm underestimating the power of money."

Joe finished knotting his tie and looked at himself in the mirror. "How do I look?"

"You can serve me caviar anytime," said Frank. "Come on, let's get back to Sam and find out what we do next."

When they got to Sam's cabin, he looked them over, straightened Joe's tie, and said, "Okay, you two'll do. I know you're not experienced, but you can learn on the job. This trip'll be easy. We just have one passenger aboard. There were supposed to be three, but an hour before we sailed, the reception center called to say that the other two weren't coming.''

"They missed the boat, huh?" Joe asked innocently.

"Maybe they'll catch it on the next run you make," Frank suggested.

"Doubt it," said Sam. "When somebody's crossed off our passenger list, it doesn't mean his trip's canceled. It means *he's* canceled."

"So we've got only this one passenger to take care of," said Joe, to change the subject. "A VIP, huh?"

"All our passengers are VIPs," said Sam, smiling. "*They* think so, anyway—until they find out different."

"So, we give him special attention," said Frank.

"That's right. Extra special attention," said Sam, and his smile grew wider. He opened a drawer and took out a metal object the size of a pack of gum. He handed it to Frank. "I hope you know how to handle *this*."

Frank did. He looked at it and nodded. "Best miniature camera on the market. I've used this model lots of times." He didn't mention that he had learned to use it from the Network, a top-secret government agency that Joe and he occasionally helped.

"What do we do with the camera?" asked Frank.

"You wait until our passenger leaves his cabin,

and then you go through his stuff and photograph any papers you can find," said Sam.

"What kind of stuff are we looking for?" asked Joe.

Sam shrugged. "Beats me. The orders are to photograph any and all papers, period. I don't ask questions. I never find out *why* I'm doing anything."

"I couldn't care less," Frank said in a bored voice. "All I'm interested in is my pay."

"Right," said Joe. "What you don't know can't hurt you."

"That's a healthy attitude," Sam said. "Come on. I'll introduce you to the passenger. Igor is what we're supposed to call him. Some of these guys come up with really weird names for themselves."

Sam led the way to a door at the end of the passageway and knocked.

"Wait a minute," said a voice from inside. A key was turned in the lock, and the door swung open.

Facing them was a balding, moon-faced, middle-aged man in a rumpled white tropical suit. He looked like a marshmallow, but there was nothing soft about the icy blue eyes behind his rimless glasses. They were sharp and never rested as he looked over the three men at his door.

"No need to lock your door, sir," Sam said genially. "You're among friends here."

"That's for me to decide," the man called Igor

snapped back. His voice was cold and contemptuous, the voice of a man used to giving orders. "What do you want?"

"I want to introduce Frank and Joe here," said Sam, keeping the genial smile on his face with some effort. "They'll be here to serve your every need, twenty-four hours a day. Bring your drinks, launder your clothes, tidy your cabin when you take your meals at the captain's table or go on deck."

"I'm not eating at the captain's table, and I'm not going on deck," Igor said. "I'm staying in here, with my door locked. Although that really won't protect my privacy. I'm sure you've got keys to the lock."

"Of course not," Sam said indignantly. "You requested all the keys when you were brought aboard, and we gave them to you."

"I bet," Igor said, his voice still flat and hard. "Anyway, these two kids can serve me my meals in here—not that I'm expecting to have many. This trip can't take too long, can it?" For the first time, a faint note of uncertainty crept into Igor's voice—an uncertainty born of not being in complete control, possibly for the first time in his life.

"Not long at all," Sam assured him. "Just tonight, then the day after, and the following night. We reach our destination at dawn on the second day."

"I don't suppose I get to find out where that destination is?" said Igor.

"Not right now," said Sam. "You know the rules."

"Yeah, I found them out—too late," said Igor. "I had already gone too far to back out."

"I'm sure you'll find everything to your satisfaction," Sam assured him.

"I'm sure," Igor said sourly. "Okay, you can clear out now. I'll ring when I get hungry. Then you can bring me two chicken sandwiches on white toast with white meat only, and a bottle of diet soda. Got it?"

"Yes, sir," said Frank.

"Anything else?" asked Joe.

"Yeah, my privacy," said Igor. "Clear out until I ring."

As they walked back along the passageway, Frank murmured to Sam, "Well, there goes our chance to do the snooping."

"Are you kidding?" said Sam. "He thinks he's smart. I have something to cut him down to size. Come to my cabin."

In his cabin, Sam pulled out a brown glass vial of pills. He took one out, handed it to Frank, and replaced the jar in his desk drawer.

"When Igor rings for his diet soda, crush this pill and put it in the drink," Sam said. "In about thirty minutes it'll take effect. After that, he'll be out like a light for at least five hours. You'd be able to break his door in and he wouldn't notice."

Then Sam snapped his fingers and said, "Oh,

yeah, I almost forgot.'' He opened another drawer. "Here's the key to his cabin."

"So he was right—you did hold out on him," said Frank.

"He knows how the game is played," said Sam with a shrug. "The thing is, he doesn't know he's a sure loser, because we have all the cards."

"I'd almost pity him—if I hadn't met him," said Frank.

An hour later Igor rang for his food, and Joe brought the sandwiches and drugged soda.

"Bread's stale," Igor complained, testing it with his finger. "Not much fizz in the soda. And your jacket isn't buttoned up all the way, boy."

"Sorry, sir," said Joe.

"If you think I'm giving you or your sidekick a tip, you're crazy," said Igor, and waved him away.

As soon as Joe was back in the passageway, he heard Igor lock the door to his cabin again.

Joe went back to his cabin.

"I wonder what Igor did in the real world, other than bully anyone who crossed his path," Joe said to Frank as he climbed up to the upper bunk to rest before they went into action.

Frank looked at his watch. "We'll give him an hour. By that time he'll be out of the picture, and we can start finding out about him."

"Real nice of Sam to give us the go-ahead to do some investigating," said Joe. "Makes it easier."

"It sure does, and we need all the breaks we can get," said Frank. "While you were gone, I went down to the wardroom. Nobody on this crew seems to know anything about anything—or if they do, they're not talking."

"That never stopped you from learning anything before," replied Joe.

Frank thought for a moment. "My guess is that they really don't know anything," he went on. "Whoever set up this operation has fragmented it so that nobody knows the whole picture. From what Sam said, there's no communication between Florida and this ship, and there's no communication between this ship and wherever it docks. Anyone following the trail would hit one dead end after another."

"Look, do me a favor and don't use the expression 'dead end,' " Joe said wryly.

"Okay," said Frank, grinning. "At least we've got one door we can open." He tapped the key to Igor's cabin in the palm of his hand.

Half an hour later they stood in front of that door.

"First we check to make sure the pill has taken effect," whispered Frank.

He knocked loudly on the door.

They waited. No answer.

"Sam was right," said Joe. "Igor must be dead to the world." He grinned. "Oops—there's that dirty word again."

"Anyway, this looks like it'll be safe enough,"

said Frank. He inserted the key, turned it, heard the lock click, and pushed open the door.

Joe went in first.

"It won't hurt to turn on the light," he said, flicking the switch.

The light came on. Igor lay motionless, a huddled lump beneath the blankets.

"Sleeping like a baby." Joe grinned as he moved forward and let Frank enter.

Frank stepped in—and stopped abruptly.

Not because he wanted to. He had no choice.

An arm had snaked out from behind the door and wrapped around his neck, right under his chin, jerking his head back.

At the same moment, something cold and sharp pressed lightly but firmly against his exposed throat, directly over his jugular vein.

Igor's voice hissed in his ear.

"This knife is razor-sharp. The slightest move—and you're dead."

Chapter

7

THE DAY FRANK earned his brown belt, his teacher had given him a piece of advice: "You have attained a certain level of skill, but do not let pride blind you to its limits. There are times when you can do nothing but wait for the moment to strike."

The cold steel of the knife against his throat was all Frank needed to confirm that the slightest move on his part, no matter how fast or smooth, would leave his throat slit wide open.

"Joe, don't move or I'm dead," he said, trying not to disturb the razor-edged blade.

Joe turned slowly, his hands away from his body so Igor could see that he had no weapon.

"Mister, I'm not going to try anything," said Joe.

"I'm glad to know that you two are not entirely

stupid," said Igor. "I couldn't be sure. After all, you were idiotic enough to think I'd allow you to drug me so you could search my things."

"How'd you catch on to it?" asked Frank. He wanted to keep Igor occupied talking. The more he talked, the better Frank's chances for figuring an escape. He knew that the least increase in pressure on the blade would set off a geyser of blood.

"How do you think?" Igor said contemptuously. "I haven't survived in this world by trusting people. I've done it by staying one trick ahead of them. Like the way I kept this knife concealed in my umbrella handle when you searched me for weapons. You're like a bunch of children playing a game of double-cross with me. I've played and beaten masters at it."

Igor chuckled, and the knife jiggled.

"Hey, watch it," Frank gasped.

"You mean you don't want to die?" Igor asked, chuckling louder as Frank winced and Joe watched in helpless horror. "I knew you people would try to squeeze every cent out of me—the money I'm carrying as well as everything that I've hidden around the world."

"Look, mister," said Frank desperately, "we're just hired hands. We get orders and we follow them."

"I know that," said Igor in a bored voice. "And that's the only reason I'm going to let you live. In fact, I'm going to offer you the chance to live very well indeed. What would you two say to a twenty-thousand-dollar bonus? That's twenty thousand dollars apiece."

"For what?" asked Joe.

Frank cut in quickly. "What does it matter? For twenty grand, I'll do anything you can dream up."

"That's what I thought you'd say," said Igor with satisfaction. "One good thing about dealing with hired help—you can always hire them yourself if you pay the right price."

He let Frank go. Frank let out a long breath of relief, touching his throat gingerly, then glanced at his fingertips. No blood.

"Let me show you something, so you'll know you can trust me, and so then I can trust you," Igor said. He went to his bunk and pulled away the blanket. Under the blanket was a pile of clothes bundled up to give the illusion of someone sleeping there. He reached under the clothes and pulled out an attaché case.

The attaché case looked familiar.

So did its contents.

Hundred-dollar bills.

The only difference between this case and the one that Frank and Joe had left back in Florida was that this one had many more bills left in it. It was still packed full.

"In case you have any idea of trying to take the whole bundle, forget it," said Igor. "If you do, I'll report you to your superiors. And also forget any idea of shutting my mouth before I can do that. I'm sure your bosses would deal very harshly with anybody who killed their golden goose.''

"Boy, you don't trust anybody, do you?" asked Joe, shaking his head.

"Should I?" Igor replied. "The only thing I trust is the power of money. It's gotten me this far, and it will get me my freedom.''

"But aren't you worried?" Frank asked. "I mean, if they take that, it's all over for you.''

Igor snickered. "You think *this* is money? But I suppose you do. It must look like a lot to guys like you. It's small change. Pocket money.''

"Big pockets," commented Joe.

"I'm a big man," said Igor proudly. "I hope you realize that by now.''

"We do," said Joe.

"And with the cash you're laying out, we're your boys," said Frank. "What do you want us to do?"

"Tell me where your bosses are taking me, what they plan to do with me," said Igor. Despite his show of bravado, he was unable to hide his uncertainty.

"We'd be glad to, only there's a hitch," said Frank.

"They don't tell the hired help anything," finished Joe.

Igor didn't seem surprised. He nodded. "Makes sense. Whoever runs this outfit is smart.

I'll give him credit for that. He doesn't trust anybody, either. Okay, here's the deal. Sniff around, find out what I want to know, and warn me about any other dirty tricks your bosses plan to pull on me. Do that, and I'll give you each the twenty thousand I promised, plus a bonus." Igor took a handful of bills out of the attaché case. "Here's a thousand apiece to whet your appetites for what's to come if you deliver."

"You've got yourself a deal, mister," said Joe, pocketing the bills.

"Yes, sir, we'll start investigating right away," said Frank. "We'll get back to you as soon as we learn anything."

"Okay, buzz off," said Igor, waving his hand dismissively. "And when they ask you what you found in here, tell them about the attaché case and say there was nothing else you could find. That should satisfy them."

"Thanks, sir," Frank said, still working on buttering him up. "You think of everything."

"That's why I *have* everything," said Igor. He pulled out a cigar and was lighting it with a gold lighter as the Hardys left.

Out in the passageway, Frank turned to Joe. "I don't feel like I'm on a boat. I feel like I'm swimming in the middle of a sea—a sea full of sharks."

"Yeah, and they're all ravenous," said Joe.

"Well, let's go feed Sam the line that Igor

63

cooked up," said Frank. "Hopefully, it'll keep him from snapping at us."

To their relief, Sam swallowed the story. He shrugged and said, "Well, at least we did our job. They can't blame us if we didn't come up with anything. It won't be the first time."

"What will they do, without the extra information on the passenger?" asked Frank.

"Beats me," said Sam. "They'll pick him up with the rest of our cargo, and that's the last we'll see of him."

"And where will they take him?" Frank persisted.

Sam grimaced wearily. "I already told you, our job is to deliver stuff. After that, we don't have anything to do with it." He looked sharply at Frank. "Hey, what makes you so curious, anyway?"

Joe interrupted hastily. "Frank is naturally nosy. Gets him in trouble, I always say. All *I* want to know is what we're supposed to do now. Do we get some time off?"

"You alternate shifts waiting in the galley," said Sam. "One of you has to be on call in case Igor rings. The other can sack out in the cabin, or play cards or whatever in the rec room. But watch out for the off-limits sign. It's not for decoration. On this ship, if you break a rule, you don't just say goodbye to your job. You say goodbye, period."

"Got you," said Frank.

"No problem," said Joe.

"Me, I'm going to get some shut-eye," said Sam, stretching and yawning. "Don't wake me unless there's an emergency. There won't be much time to sleep. We'll be unloading in less than twenty-four hours, and then clearing out in a hurry."

Frank glanced at his watch in surprise. "I didn't realize it was day already. With everything blacked out, I can't tell night from day."

"Yeah, it is weird, huh," Sam agreed as he went to lie down in his bunk. "The bosses love to keep us all in the dark."

By the time Frank and Joe reached the door, Sam was already snoring. Frank closed the door softly, then said, "I'll take first shift in the galley. I'll try to find out if the cook knows anything. The way this operation is set up, I don't have much hope, though."

"I'll do some nosing around myself," said Joe.

"Hey, be careful," said Frank.

"Sure, you know me," said Joe.

"That's the trouble," Frank said with a grimace.

Joe slapped Frank on the shoulder and watched him head for the galley. Then Joe made a beeline for the one thing he always found irresistible—an off-limits sign.

Sam had made sure to point it out to the Hardys on their fast tour of the ship. But even if he hadn't, there was no way to miss it. Posted right next to a stairway, it was three feet by three feet with bright red letters: CAUTION. OFF-LIMITS. NO UNAUTHORIZED PERSONNEL PAST THIS POINT. ALL VIOLATORS PUNISHED SEVERELY! The word "severely" was underlined in black.

Joe glanced quickly up and down the passageway to make sure nobody was coming, then darted down the stairway.

He descended into a dimly lit cargo hold. Several dozen unmarked wooden crates filled it. He shone his penlight on a few. As Joe walked around the cases, the smell of Cosmoline, the sweet, sticky grease that arms manufacturers use to pack their wares, filled his nostrils. The hold smelled like the National Guard Armory back in Bayport.

I have an idea what these things hold, he thought as he took out the Swiss army knife that had come with his steward's uniform. He pried open a crate and reached inside.

Yuck, he thought, and pulled back his hand. His fingers were covered with the dark grease that he had been smelling.

Well, my hands can't get any greasier, he decided, and pulled the partially opened lid wider so that he could shove in both hands. He took a firm grip on the grease-covered metal he felt and pulled it out. He was holding a submachine gun. He quickly replaced the weapon and put the lid back on the crate, then wiped his hands on a rag. He looked around the hold at the other crates.

"There must be a whole arsenal down here," he muttered. As he looked around one last time, he noticed a group of fiberglass and steel boxes sitting in one corner of the hold.

What else do they need? he wondered as he moved to open the top box. There, nestled in a foam cradle, was a machine that so surprised Joe that it took him one long moment to recognize what it was—a lie detector.

"Guns and gadgets! What *is* going on here?" he whispered. "I've got to tell F—"

Just then he heard a sound. He squeezed himself into a perfect hiding place made by a gap between two crates.

He could just make out the high-pitched voices of two men who seemed to be stationary. They were clearly arguing about something.

Joe carefully edged his way between the crates toward the voices. He rounded the last crate in the row and found himself facing a steel door. The door was open a crack, and the voices were coming from inside.

"I'm starving," said one voice. "I'm going upstairs to get some chow."

"You know the orders," said a second voice. "No mingling with the crew. We're supposed to keep out of sight until we get off-loaded tomorrow."

"Just my luck to be stuck with a by-the-book partner," said the first man.

"I'm making the same money you are," said the second. "And I'm not going to risk losing it."

"Well, there's no way *I'm* going to wait one minute more to get fed," retorted the first man. He pulled open the door and stepped out.

It happened too suddenly for Joe to hide. The man and Joe stared each other in the eye.

Joe opened his mouth, searching for some kind of explanation. But the man wasn't waiting for an explanation. Before Joe could blink, the guy launched a savage left hook.

Before the fist connected with his jaw, all Joe had time to do was form a single word in his mind. Caught! he thought, and then the punch sent him spinning into a pitch-black night streaked with multicolored shooting stars of pain.

Chapter

8

JOE WAS DOWN but not out. Even with his mind
teetering on the brink of consciousness, his body
reacted instinctively. The moment he hit the
floor, he started rolling, away from the fist that
had sent him heading toward dreamland. At the
same time, Joe shook his head, trying to clear
away the cobwebs.

The next couple of seconds seemed like hours
as he stopped rolling, tensed his legs to get to his
feet, and forced his eyes to open, although that
was the last thing he wanted to do.

Through a blur, he saw that the man had followed him. What Joe could see all too clearly,
but couldn't do anything about, was the tip of the
man's boot heading straight toward his chin.

It never made it.

There was a clang so loud that for an instant

Joe thought someone was pounding a gong inside his head. Then there was a series of crashing noises, like the sound of dishes breaking.

On his hands and knees, still dazed, Joe watched helplessly as Frank lifted the steel tray and brought it down on the back of the man's head again. Then he whirled around to face the other man, who was coming out of the room.

He swung the tray in a level arc so that the edge caught the second man in the stomach. Then, as the man doubled over, Frank lifted the tray up and—crack—it hit the bottom of the man's chin, snapping his head back. He toppled backward, hit a wall, and crumpled to the floor.

Frank gave both fallen men a glance to make sure they were unconscious. Then he went to Joe, who was still trying to struggle to his feet.

"You okay?" he asked, helping Joe up.

Joe touched his chin gingerly and winced slightly. "Bruised but nothing broken," he said. "Thanks for showing up in time. The tip of that guy's boot could have done a lot more damage than his fist. How did you get here, anyway?"

"Bit of luck," said Frank. "While I was sitting around in the galley, the cook told me to rouse Sam. Seems it was Sam's job to deliver chow to these guys down here. Nobody else was supposed to talk to them. But when I told the cook that Sam was sacked out and would get real mad if I woke him up, the cook decided it wouldn't hurt for me to bring the food down, if I did it real fast and kept my mouth shut. Needless to say, I was glad to oblige. It seemed like a terrific chance to find out more about what's happening. I didn't realize it'd also be a chance to get you out of a jam.''

Joe couldn't argue. "No risks, no rewards," he said weakly. "And for this risk, I discovered that this hold is filled with crates of weapons and some really weird stuff. I thought we were dealing with arms smugglers until I found a lie detector and a bunch of other electronic equipment over in the corner. Now I don't know what's going on here.''

"Neither do I," said Frank. "We keep uncovering more questions than answers.''

"I did learn one thing," Joe replied. "I overheard these two guys talking. Seems they've taken jobs with whoever is running this show. From what they said, they're supposed to be picked up with the cargo.''

"Hey, that *is* good," said Frank, looking at the two unconscious men with new interest. "Come on, let's tie them up fast, before they come to. Then we can find out what they know.''

They took some rope off one of the crates and used it to tie up the men. But by the time they had tied the last knots and were waiting for the men to regain consciousness, Frank was having second thoughts about their chances of getting information.

"I'll bet they don't know any more than anybody else," he said. "Every part of this operation is kept separate from every other part. These guys wouldn't be told anything until they moved on to the next part of the operation.''

"Right," said Joe. "If we want to find out what's going on and where, we'll have to do it by ourselves.''

"Too bad we're not in these guys' shoes,'' said Frank. Then he paused, looking at the pair with new interest.

Joe was quiet, too, as he looked at them. Then he asked, "Are you thinking what I am?''

"Probably," said Frank. "The idea is crazy enough.''

"Crazy enough to work," Joe said. "These guys are about our sizes.''

"And their hair coloring is close to ours, too," said Frank, warming to the idea. "One's got brown hair like mine; the other is blond like you. We could pass for them if we managed to dodge the crew members who've seen us already.''

"Should have known you'd be ready to go for it," Joe said, grinning. This was more like it, he thought. He and Frank were swinging into action. It was time to stop running from danger, time to launch an attack.

Meanwhile, Frank was thinking out loud.

"Getaway's policy of keeping its employees in the dark is its strength, but also its weakness," he said. "It's impossible to trace them from Florida to wherever headquarters is. But on the other hand, each time we get past one of the roadblocks they've set up, nobody can chase us or call ahead to warn anybody about us. Because nobody knows where we're going after we leave their particular operation."

"So the same shield that protects the higher-ups protects us, too," said Joe, grinning.

"Not exactly," said Frank. "Sooner or later, we're going to run into somebody who knows enough of what's going on to know that we don't belong here. And we are a long way from any sort of backup. When we run out of places to go, we have a problem. A *real* problem."

"So, we make sure that we always have an escape route open," said Joe, shrugging. "As long as we keep moving, I think we're in good shape."

"I hope so," said Frank, then turned back to the problem at hand. "First thing we have to do is see Igor."

"Why?" asked Joe. "You don't trust him, do you?"

"No," said Frank. "But we have to make sure he doesn't give us away when he sees us. He's going to be picked up at the same time as the cargo and us."

Frank and Joe hauled the two limp men into the back room and made sure the ropes that bound them were secure. Then they put gags in the men's mouths. They planned to come back when the ship neared the shore, and put on the men's khakis.

Then they went to Igor's cabin.

He was glad to see them.

"What did you find out?" he asked. "Remember, no info, no more money."

"Sorry, pal," said Joe, shrugging. "Nobody knows anything."

"I should have known," said Igor with disgust. "I was dumb to give you two a penny. In fact, I want my money back."

"What are you going to do if we don't hand it over?" Joe sneered, acting the part of a young thug. "You figure on taking it from us?"

"I won't have to," said Igor smugly. "I'll simply report that someone stole two thousand dollars from me, and your superiors will take it from you for me."

"You're a real nice guy, aren't you," said Joe, waving a clenched fist in front of Igor's eyes. "I've got half a mind to—"

Frank cut in on his tirade. "Cool it, Joe. Use that half a mind of yours. Igor's got a lot more than two thousand dollars for us if we treat him right."

Frank turned to the balding businessman and apologized. "Don't let my buddy bother you. We know that we didn't come up with much, but we think we can give you your money's worth. Actually, we can do something that's worth a lot more than the twenty thousand that you offered us."

"So far we agree on one thing—neither of you

74

has earned the thousand I gave you," Igor said angrily. "What do you propose to do to earn any more of my money?"

"We made a deal with two guys we ran into," said Frank. "They're new recruits who are going to the same place you are. We gave them a thousand apiece to let us go in their places. That way, we'll be able to look out for you, keep you posted, and keep you protected."

"For a price," said Joe in a harsh voice. "A bigger one than you offered. We had to pay off those two guys, and we're taking more risks. We want our payoff doubled."

"Highway robbery," snapped Igor.

"Take it or leave it," said Frank.

Igor looked at their faces. Both of them kept their expressions flat and cold. Igor shrugged. "Okay. I'll pay. You can't blame me for wanting to negotiate a bit, though. Lifetime habits are hard to break."

He gave them a big, friendly smile that was about as convincing as the sun rising in the west.

"Sure," said Frank, giving him the same kind of smile in return. "No hard feelings."

"So long as we get the cash," said Joe, concluding the negotiations.

After they left Igor's cabin, Frank said, "That worked fine. The one way to convince him we're on the up-and-up was to convince him we'd do anything for money. That's the only thing he believes in."

Then he added, "I'm heading back to the galley before they come looking for me. We don't want anybody wandering down in the hold and spotting those two guys we tied up. We'll make the clothing switch as close to landfall as we can. Cut down our chances of being caught."

"Right," said Joe. "I'll get some sleep and then relieve you. Wake me when you get tired."

They parted in the passageway, and Joe went to their cabin.

He hadn't realized how tired he was until he saw his bunk. He didn't bother taking off all his clothes, just his white steward's jacket and his black shoes. He lay down in the bunk and was sound asleep as soon as his head hit the pillow.

His sleep was deep—so deep that even when he started dreaming he knew it was all a dream, as if he were standing a safe distance outside of himself, so that nothing could really hurt him.

He saw Jeeves, the chauffeur, pointing a gun at him and saying in his British accent, "Better start running now, sir, better start running fast, faster than my bullets."

He saw himself running, stumbling over sand that kept slipping beneath his feet, so that he didn't go forward but just kept digging himself deeper and deeper into a hole.

Finally he was at the bottom of the hole, looking up at the light of the sky above. And then the light was blotted out by a face that belonged to

Alex, the man who had grilled him and Frank at the Florida mansion.

Alex was smiling a sneering, triumphant smile and saying, "I didn't have to put you in quicksand, after all. You've dug your own grave."

Then Alex began kicking sand down onto Joe's upturned face, and Joe heard himself shouting desperately, "Frank, come on, time to get going! Move it!"

Then Alex's face was gone, and there was Frank's, close to him, right above him.

"Frank, I knew you'd show up. You know I'd do the same for you," Joe said in relief. Then he saw that Frank's face wasn't smiling, but tight-lipped and grim.

And he suddenly realized that Frank's hand was on his shoulder, shaking him.

Shaking him awake.

He sat up in bed and looked groggily past Frank, and saw Sam standing in the doorway with a gun in his hand and a look of vicious anger on his face.

And Joe knew that this was no dream.

It was a nightmare made real.

Chapter
9

"GET ON YOUR feet—*fast*," said Sam in a snarl that shredded the last doubts Joe had that he was awake and that this was all real.

Joe sat up, swung himself down out of his bunk, and stood beside Frank. He needed no prompting to follow Frank's lead when his brother put both hands in the air.

"What happened?" he asked.

"I was in the galley about half an hour ago when Sam rang and told me to bring him some coffee. When I did, he shoved this gun in my face and told me to lead him to you. I didn't have any choice."

"And now you don't have any chance," said Sam. "You two kids got your nerve, trying to play me for a sucker."

"How'd you find out?" asked Joe.

"How do you think?" said Sam. "When I woke up from my little nap, I remembered I was supposed to bring those guys down in the hold their chow. I went to the galley and found out that Frank had already gone. After I chewed out the cook for breaking the off-limits rule, I went down to make sure Frank kept his mouth shut about what was down there. I guess you know what I found."

"I guess I do," said Joe, his stomach sinking.

"And I guess you know what's going to happen to you now," said Sam.

"I really don't want to find out," said Joe, searching desperately for a way out of this jam. He hoped Frank was doing the same.

Frank shrugged, apparently unconcerned, and said, "I suppose our luck had to run out sometime. You have to admit, though, we got pretty far."

"And you're going to keep going far—all the way to the bottom of the sea," said Sam.

"What're you going to do?" asked Frank. "Make us walk the plank?"

"No, that would be too public," said Sam. "You won't leave this room alive. After I shoot you two, the only ones who will notice are the fish when you sink past them in the water."

"Gee," said Frank, "I hate to make you miss any sleep while you're waiting for a chance to toss us over the side undetected. You've had so little rest since we left port."

THE HARDY BOYS CASEFILES

"Yeah, well, I can sleep all the way back to Florida on the return trip. Not that I wouldn't mind a little sack-time right now, but—" Sam paused to give a big yawn. "Yeah, wouldn't mind a"—he gave another yawn—"nap. Funny, I feel kind of—" He shook his head, as if trying to clear it.

"Maybe you should sit down," Frank suggested. "You look tired. *Really* tired."

"Maybe I will," said Sam, sitting down. "But don't you two get any—" Another yawn. "Remember, I still got this—" And as his eyes closed and his head slumped forward, the gun dropped from his fingers and clattered to the floor.

"Whew," said Frank with relief. "Thought that stuff would never get to work."

"Stuff?" said Joe. "What stuff? What happened?"

"On my way back to the galley, I figured I'd look in on Sam to make sure he was still napping," said Frank. "He was gone, so I decided to use the opportunity to lift some sleeping pills from that bottle he put back in his drawer. I figured we could use them to knock him out before we jumped ship, since he was the only one who might stop us. Then, when I got back to the galley and he rang for coffee, I saw my chance to knock him out of action. I put in a triple dose. Luckily, he gulped down the coffee while he was questioning me back in his cabin. From then on,

I had to hold my breath and pray he'd drop off before he knocked us off."

"Think he'll sleep until we're off the ship and beyond his reach?" said Joe, looking down at Sam, who had slipped off the chair and lay snoring on the floor with a peaceful smile on his face.

"From what he said about those pills, we stand a good chance," said Frank. He stooped down to pick up Sam's gun and concealed it in his shirt. "Come on, help me lug Sam back to his cabin. From what the cook said, he's known for liking lots of shut-eye. We have to hope that nobody thinks it too strange if he stays sacked out."

As they hauled Sam down the passageway, they passed a crewman, who glanced at them curiously.

"Sam here had a few too many," Joe told him. "I warned him, but he wouldn't listen."

"Yeah," said Frank. "He's out like a light, and he weighs a ton. Wouldn't be surprised if he sleeps right through the unloading. Leave us to do his work for him."

"It wouldn't be the first time Sam pulled a stunt like that," said the crewman. "The guy drinks like a fish and sleeps like a log." The man looked at Sam, who by now was snoring loudly. He shook his head with disgust and continued on his way.

"This may actually work," said Joe as they deposited Sam onto his bunk.

"Don't my plans always work?" Frank replied with a grin.

"I won't answer that," said Joe. "I want to stay optimistic."

"You've got to keep the faith," chided Frank. "Now, let's go after those two guys in the hold. They should still be where we found them, since they're not supposed to show themselves to the crew."

Again Frank was on target. When he knocked on the door of the cabin in the cargo hold, a voice answered from within, "Who's there?"

"Sam," Frank answered.

The door swung open, and a minute later the two men were backed up against a wall, their hands over their heads, their eyes fixed on the gun in Frank's hand.

Upon questioning, they gave their names as Dave and Mike.

Frank could have gotten their last names, too— the fear in their eyes told him that. But their last names weren't what he was interested in. He wanted to find out just one thing.

"Does either of you know where you're supposed to be going?" he demanded in a harsh voice. "Don't play games. Tell me the truth. I get very upset when people lie to me."

"Hey, guys, cool it," Dave said hurriedly. "No sweat. I'll tell you anything I can."

"Me, too," Mike seconded. "I'm just in this

for the money. And there's no amount of money worth dying for.''

"Good to see that both of you are using your heads," said Frank. "Now, talk."

"Trouble is," said Dave, "there's not much I can tell you. All I know is I answered an ad for adventurers only, and I was promised really good pay for two years' work if I followed orders and didn't ask any questions."

"Same with me," said Mike. "The guy who hired me wouldn't tell me where I was going. I was just supposed to be picked up on a beach near Miami, which I was, by limo, along with Dave here. We couldn't even see out the limo windows. Next thing we knew, we were being grilled by some guy in a big old house, and then we were stuck down here and told to stay here until we were off-loaded. Honest, we're in the dark about this whole deal."

"You've got to believe us," pleaded Dave, staring at the revolver in Frank's hand, sweat beading his forehead.

"I don't know why I should, but I do," Frank said in a grudging voice.

"You guys are lucky we're such trusting souls," said Joe, silently agreeing with his brother that the guys' stories made sense. "But don't push your luck. One wrong move, and we'll turn out your lights for good."

"Yes, sir," said Mike.

"Anything you say," said Dave.

They were as good as their word. Frank and Joe quickly traded clothes with them, then tied them up and gagged them once again.

"Luckily, they don't know where we're going, so they can't help anyone find us," said Joe.

Frank nodded, then stifled a yawn. "Maybe we ought to join Sam in dreamland for a couple of hours. There's nothing to do now but wait for landfall at dawn."

Joe found himself yawning, too. "Guess you're right."

"I'll set the alarm on Mike's watch to wake us at five," said Frank.

"Hope there are no rude awakenings before that," said Joe soberly, climbing up into the upper bunk in Dave and Mike's quarters. Frank lay down in the lower one.

It seemed like only minutes before the beeping of the watch woke them. They had barely washed up in the lavatory connected with the cabin when they heard the sound of men and machinery outside in the hold.

"Let's get out of here before somebody comes and sees these two tied up," said Frank. He started to hide the gun in his shirt again, then stopped and shook his head. He thrust it under the mattress of the bottom bunk. "We're better off without this. Dad always says that carrying a gun usually gets you into more trouble than it gets you out of. What we need is brainpower, not firepower."

"Right," agreed Joe. "Anyway, we promised Dad we'd leave guns alone unless it was life or death." Then he added, smacking his fist in his palm, "Though muscle power can come in handy, and Dad can't complain about that."

"Spoken like a true muscle-head," Frank said, then ducked a mock punch that Joe threw at him. Then sounds outside the cabin jerked them back to reality. This was no time for joking. It was time to save their skins.

Frank opened the door and looked out cautiously. Crewmen were loading the crates in the hold onto wooden pallets, attaching the pallets to cables descending from the open cargo hatch above, and standing aside to watch them being lifted up and away.

"Wonder where the stuff is going?" Frank muttered, leaving the cabin and signaling to Joe that it was safe to follow. Everyone was too busy to notice them.

"We'll find out quickly enough," said Joe. "Let's get up on deck fast, before the activity slows down."

Minutes later they stood on deck in the faint early-morning light. The yacht was anchored close to shore in a natural deep-water cove. On the shore, a tall crane was lifting the loaded pallets out of the hold and depositing them on the ground. There, men driving forklifts were picking up the pallets and carrying them into an opening in a thick tropical forest.

"I can see why they picked this time of day to unload," said Frank. "There's enough light to see, but it's still dim enough for them to avoid easy detection. Their security never lets up."

Just then a voice from behind made them wheel around. "Mike? Dave? About time you two showed up."

A man in crisply pressed khakis with a gleaming leather belt around his waist stood facing them. He was slapping his hand impatiently against his thigh below a holster that hung from his belt. The expression on his face told Frank and Joe that his eyes, invisible behind dark aviator sunglasses, were glaring at them. Although he wore no sign of rank, it was clear who was in command.

Both Hardys snapped to attention.

"Sorry, sir," Frank said.

"The guy on the ship was late waking us," said Joe.

"I haven't got time to listen to your excuses," the man said. "Which of you is which?"

"Mike here," said Frank.

"Dave here," said Joe.

"Okay," the man said. "Continue using first names only, but now you're Mike Seven, and you're Dave Eleven, to avoid confusion among personnel. Got it?"

"Yes, sir," Frank and Joe responded in unison.

"Now, lift your arms above your heads, both of you," the officer ordered.

86

Frank and Joe instantly obeyed, and the officer quickly frisked them.

"Good," he said, stepping back and indicating that they could lower their hands. "Some recruits disregard instructions and arrive armed, which is bad news for everybody. Some guys are too dumb to live."

"Not us, sir," said Frank fervently.

"We know how to obey orders," Joe seconded.

"That's a very healthy attitude—healthy for you," said the commander. "Now, let's move it."

He led the way off the yacht onto the gangway that stretched between the ship and shore. As soon as they were on land, the commander nodded to a crew of men in nearly identical khakis, who started unhooking the gangway, getting ready to wheel it away.

The commander marched Frank and Joe toward the opening in the forest where the cargo was being taken. The light was still too dim for them to see what was in the jungle shadows.

Only when they reached the edge of the forest could they see what was waiting for them.

Waiting among the trees was a train—a small diesel locomotive with a passenger car and a string of five boxcars.

"Put your eyes back in your heads—it's real," snapped the man. "All aboard."

Frank and Joe climbed into the passenger car. It was the kind seen in old black-and-white

European movies, with a passageway running beside several separate compartments. Each compartment contained seating for six, three seats facing three more.

As they passed the first compartment, they saw Igor sitting inside, flanked by stone-faced men in khaki. He was trying to look at ease, but sweat was pouring down his face.

"You two are in luck," the commander said. "You get a compartment all to yourselves. There aren't many passengers this trip. Make yourselves comfortable. See you in a couple of hours when we reach the ranch. Your orientation starts there."

Frank and Joe sat facing each other on the faded blue plush seats of the compartment. Both peered out the window. All they could see was a thick rain forest of very tall trees.

Frank slid open the window, stuck his head out, and looked upward. After several moments, he pulled his head in again. "Pretty clever. They've extended nets between the tops of the trees on both sides of the tracks and covered the nets with foliage. Looks like they've laced the top branches together, too. They've made sure that nobody can spot the tracks from above. It's as if we're in a tunnel."

There was a gentle lurch, and the train started moving.

"Remember how Alex mentioned their underground railway, Joe? I read about the original one—the operation that helped runaway slaves escape from the South before the Civil War," Frank said. "Guess you could call this the *underworld* railway."

"Yeah, the Crime Rail Express," said Joe. "Just wish I knew where it was heading."

Frank nodded in agreement as he squinted out the window, but he could see less and less as the light at the opening of the tunnel faded behind them. The train sped on, deeper and deeper into the darkness of the unknown.

Chapter

10

"BET YOU ALL are a mite curious about this railway," said the tall man in a cowboy hat and the now-familiar khakis. He had met them as they got off the train at a distant corner of the ranch.

But even if the Hardys had not been told, they would have been able to guess that this man, introduced only as "Chief," was in absolute control of this huge highland ranch at the edge of the jungle.

"Yes, Chief," Frank and Joe answered as they had been instructed to do.

"Real interesting story, that railway," said the man. He was smiling with his mouth, but his eyes stayed hard. He kept Frank and Joe standing at stiff attention while he paced in front of them, the jungle a backdrop. He was making sure they knew who was in charge there. "It was built by an

American about ninety years ago. He saw those little countries here in Central America all split by civil wars and fighting with each other, and he figured that a good, enterprising American could come down here and take charge. Carve out his territory, just like a man used to be able to do in the West before all the land got settled. Well, this fellow came down here and did just that. Built this ranch, declared it an independent country with himself as president for life, ran a railroad to the sea, and had himself sitting pretty. Trouble was, the folks down here got their act together and put this fellow in front of a firing squad, and that was that. The ranch, his little kingdom, went to seed, and the railway tracks were overgrown by jungle—until I came along. You might say I'm following in that fellow's footsteps, except I'm not making his mistakes. You see, I know how to protect myself. I know what to protect myself with. And you boys know what that is?''

He looked at Frank and Joe, demanding an answer.

"Guns?" said Joe.

"Sure, I got them," said the chief. "But I'm talking about something more powerful. The most powerful thing in the world.''

"You don't mean atomic weapons?'' said Frank, trying not to shudder.

"Nah, don't need them with what I've got, though I expect I could get some if I wanted to,'' the chief said, his grin widening. "What I'm talking about is money. Money and information. That's all I need."

Frank and Joe exchanged a quick glance. Once again, just when they thought they'd found the answer to some of their questions, they'd discovered that all they had was a new set of questions.

"Yes, sir, money nearly does it all," the chief went on. "But I don't have to tell you two that. Money is what got you down here, right?"

"Yes, Chief," Frank and Joe answered.

"But I've got news for you," the chief went on. "All the money in the world can't get you out of here, and you remember that. Nobody leaves here before I say they can. Nobody leaves here alive, that is. You got that?"

"Yes, Chief," the Hardys responded again.

"Glad you got the message," said the chief. "Now, you boys follow orders, keep your noses clean, and maybe when your two years are up I'll figure I can trust you and let you go home. But remember—one little foul-up and you two ain't going nowhere, except six feet under the ground."

"Yes, Chief," said the Hardys, beginning to feel like broken records.

"Okay, you can go now," the chief said. "Dimitri!" he called. "Assign these boys their duties." He turned and strode away.

Dimitri, the man who had ridden on the train with them, walked over and joined them.

"Did the chief give you his orientation speech?" Dimitri asked.

"Yeah, if that's what you call it," said Joe.

"That's what I call it," Dimitri said in a voice that made it clear that he didn't like wisecracking. Then he commanded, "Come with me. Time to get that cargo off the train."

He drove Frank and Joe in a jeep to the boxcars, where men were loading the weapon crates onto a large flatbed track.

"Start sweating," he told the Hardys, and they joined the others working in the broiling heat. Even there in the highlands, on a plateau above the rain forest, it was clear that this was Central America. They could feel the sun directly overhead, beating straight down on their backs as they worked.

When all the crates had been loaded, Frank and Joe climbed into the back of the truck with the other men, and the truck started rolling. It bounced along a dirt road that cut through lush grassland dotted with herds of cattle until it reached the bank of a wide, slow-moving river.

Dimitri climbed out of the front of the truck and told the men to climb down from the back. He pulled a walkie-talkie and snapped it on. Frank and Joe, standing close to him, could hear him speaking in Spanish.

After he had finished, he said, "Okay, men, we wait here. Shouldn't take long for them to cross over."

Joe peered toward the other side of the river. Jungle grew down to the opposite bank.

"Who are we expecting?" he asked.

"Bandits. Guerrillas. Freedom fighters. Call them whatever you want," said Dimitri with a shrug. "They're our first line of defense and the main reason that no prisoner ever gets very far. We keep them supplied with arms and ammunition, and they guard our perimeter. What they do with the guns the rest of the time is their own business."

Two large, flat-bottomed boats were crossing the river, propelled by loudly chugging engines. Aboard them were bearded men in jungle camouflage uniforms.

When they had reached the near bank, Dimitri turned to his men. "Load the stuff aboard."

Frank and Joe teamed up to haul crates aboard the boats. They were able to talk in whispers as they worked.

"They've sure got this place sewn up tight," muttered Frank, grunting as he bent to lift one end of a heavy crate. "Thick jungle all around, bandits hiding behind trees."

"Kind of a funny setup for the Perfect Getaway," Joe agreed as he lifted the crate's other end. "I mean, what do they need a ranch for? A couple of plastic surgeons and an acting coach ought to be enough." The two boys carefully boarded the first boat, lugging the crate between them, and set it down at the feet of a surly-looking bandit. Keeping silent until they were once again on land, they continued their conversation as they loaded several more crates.

"Something smells rotten here," Joe murmured. "And I don't think it's the river water, either."

"What has me worried is how *we'll* manage to get out of here," Frank answered. "The only way I can think of is to somehow get word to Dad or the Gray Man."

Joe frowned. The Gray Man was the Hardys' contact in a top-secret American intelligence operation and a hard man to get hold of. They'd helped the operation out more than once. But the only way they knew of to contact him was via modem from Frank's home computer. They were a long way from that computer now.

"Well, it's only a two-year enlistment," Joe joked lamely as they loaded the last crate onto the boat. "It'll fly before we know it."

"Yeah, sure," Frank muttered.

After the loading was finished and the boats were heading back across the river, Dimitri told Frank and Joe to climb into his jeep while he sent the other men back to the truck.

Dimitri sat in back with the Hardys and told his driver, "We're making a tour of the ranch so our new men here understand the layout. You know, the standard orientation tour."

The man said, "Yes, sir," and started the jeep back over the dirt road.

Again they passed the grazing cattle, and Dimitri explained, "That's where we get our beef.
Not to mention that the chief likes to play cowboy. He rides a horse and lassos steer, brands
them, that kind of stuff." Dimitri smiled, as if at
a private joke. "It's one of his favorite hobbies."

The jeep turned onto another dirt road, and
they drove to where the grassland turned into
fields of corn and grain and vegetables.

"This is where we get the rest of our food,"
Dimitri explained. "The chief has made this
ranch practically self-supporting."

"How many people live here?" Frank asked.

"Oh, plenty." Dimitri gazed off into the distance. "And they stay a long time."

"Is it expensive?" Joe exchanged glances with
Frank. They needed information, but weren't
sure how far they could push Dimitri without his
getting suspicious. At the moment, he seemed
not to notice how curious these two young recruits were.

"You never saw anything so expensive in your
life," he bragged. "See that?" He pointed toward
a large complex that had just become visible in
the distance, at the edge of the surrounding jungle. "That's the ranch house. Only the truly elite
can afford to stay there. A suite in the big house
costs fifty thousand a month, and that's just for a
room and continental breakfast, no more. You
pay for extras. A good meal costs a thousand

bucks. Clean sheets, five hundred. Laundry and dry cleaning, a grand a week.''

"Why would anyone pay that much?" Frank asked incredulously. "How ritzy can the place be?"

"Oh, it's ritzy, all right. But that's not why people stay. See, the catch is, it costs five million dollars in cash to check *out*."

"Five m—" Frank started to say, but Joe stopped him with a nudge in the ribs and a gesture toward the cornfield to one side of them. There, a group of men and women chopped wearily at some weeds. A man in khakis with a rifle in the crook of his arm was overseeing them. As the jeep drew closer, Frank and Joe could see that, while most of the workers were probably locals, a few among them were middle-aged, paunchy, sunburned, and obviously not accustomed to fieldwork. All wore ragged clothing and frayed straw hats that did little to keep out the burning sun as they hacked methodically at the soil. They were clearly bone-weary.

Suddenly there was a small commotion. One of the workers had fallen to the ground and lay still, face down. The other workers gathered around him.

Dimitri told his driver to head over to the scene of the trouble so that he could check it out. When the jeep arrived, Dimitri climbed out, followed by Frank and Joe.

By now the man who had collapsed was being

helped to his feet by fellow workers, while the guard looked on in a bored way.

Frank and Joe could see that the man was in late middle-age, with a stubble of beard on his hollowed-out cheeks and dark circles of fatigue under his watery blue eyes.

Something stirred in Frank's memory. He was sure he had seen that face before. But he couldn't remember where.

Dimitri, though, knew who the man was. "Hans? Causing trouble again? Won't you ever learn?"

Something inside the man seemed to snap. He straightened up, his nostrils flared with anger, his eyes ablaze. For a moment he was no longer a cowering field-worker. His voice was the voice of someone who was used to being in command. "Stop with this 'Hans' nonsense! I am sick of these silly games you play here. Call me by my right name, at least. Karl, Karl Ross. A man who could buy and sell you a million times over!"

A shiver ran through Frank. Karl Ross. Now he remembered where he had seen that face: on the front page of the newspaper when the financier had mysteriously disappeared, just before he was to be indicted for stealing millions in the stock market.

Dimitri's voice was laced with sarcasm as he said, "Hans, maybe that was true once, but you're broke now. And the ranch is your home. Don't you like it here? Maybe you should try to escape again. Next time you get lost in the jungle, the guard might not find you and bring you back. You might get away and keep going until the jaguars or snakes or alligators finish you off. Or you could cross the river and have our friends over there nab you."

Dimitri turned to Frank and Joe. "I heard that Hans here was a real smart operator on the outside. But he's acted real dumb around here. After he went broke, he had a real nice job in the ranch kitchen washing dishes. But he gave it all up when he tried to get away. Guess he thought escaping from here would be as easy as escaping from the States."

"What do you want me to do with him, sir?" the guard asked Dimitri.

"Get him back to work," said Dimitri. "If he drops, let him lie in the dirt. He's not going anywhere—are you, Hans? And remember, if you cause any more trouble, we cut your rations in half."

The fire had faded from Karl Ross's eyes. His voice was a whimper. "But it's such a very little bit already. Maybe if I ate a little more, I could work better. Nothing much. Some extra margarine, maybe. It makes the bread taste so much better."

"Well, if you're very good, we'll see about that," said Dimitri, smiling. "We might even give you some meat on Sundays. How does that sound, Hans? You don't mind my calling you 'Hans,' do you, Hans?"

"No, no, not at all," Karl Ross said. "Please, forget my little outburst. It was the sun. Yes, a touch of sun. A little meat, you said? Maybe this Sunday? It has been so long."

Karl Ross picked up his hoe and began hacking at the weeds with as much vigor as his bent body could muster. Dimitri watched with a smirk on his face, then climbed back into the jeep. Frank and Joe, both feeling queasy, followed him, and the jeep drove off.

"Guess you've seen enough," Dimitri said. "You get the idea how we operate here."

"Yeah, we've got the idea," said Frank, masking his disgust.

"Sure do," agreed Joe.

"Anyway, you won't be working out here," said Dimitri. "You've been assigned to the ranch house staff. Easy duty. You even have your living quarters there, so you don't have to live in the barracks. I'll take you there now to be briefed."

When they reached the ranch house—a rambling, two-story, colonial-style structure built around a central courtyard—Dimitri offered a few words of caution. "Like I said, it's easy duty, but there is one hitch. You're going to be working right under the chief, and sometimes he's—well, a little extreme. The guys before you made the mistake of acting surprised at some of the stuff he did—and they're out guarding the jungle now, fighting mosquitoes. So, if you know what's good for you, you'll keep your noses clean and do exactly what you're told.''

Dimitri left Frank and Joe with the front door guard, who said to them, ''You can pick up your gear and bedding and get settled later. The chief wants you right now. On the double.''

''Where do we go?'' asked Frank.

''Down that hall there and through the door at the end,'' said the guard. ''It leads to the courtyard.''

''What do you think?'' asked Joe as he and Frank started down the wide, high-ceilinged hall. ''Is it worth fifty thousand a month?''

''It's not bad,'' Frank said as the two brothers looked around at the sweeping Spanish-tiled stairways, huge oil paintings, and antique carpets. ''But even that much money isn't enough to keep an organization like this going. Think about it. The house in Florida, the yacht, the private railroad, the ranch—it's got to cost more than a small country.''

''The world's greatest scam for the world's biggest crooks.'' Joe shook his head in disbelief. ''Can you imagine how Karl Ross reacted when he got here and found out what he'd laid out his money for? A prison a lot worse than the one he was escaping. Not such a Perfect Getaway.''

''At least they haven't killed him,'' said Frank.

''Yeah—but that's the question. Why haven't they? They've gotten all they can from him.'' Joe paused to straighten what looked like a small but genuine Rembrandt painting.

"Lucky we got assigned to headquarters," Frank said. "This'll make it a lot easier to fill in all the blanks about what's going on here."

"There's one blank I want filled in right away," said Joe.

"What's that?" asked Frank.

"What Dimitri said, that bit about the chief acting extreme," said Joe. "What could be more extreme than what we've already seen and heard around here?"

Suddenly, through the half-open door leading to the courtyard, there came a hideous human scream.

"You know, Joe," said Frank, "I've got a hunch we're about to find out."

Chapter

11

THE ONLY INHABITANTS of the large central
courtyard were half a dozen bright green parrots
cackling at one another in the branches of a
twenty-foot palm tree. The entire courtyard was
filled with lush, tropical trees, flowers, and plants
in an apparent effort to bring some of the jungle
into the heart of the ranch complex. In the center
of this miniature jungle, an elaborate fountain
paved with hand-painted tiles sent streams of
water up into the humid air.

Frank and Joe were in no mood to enjoy the
scenery, though. Another horrible scream
pierced the air, and this time it was clear that the
sound was coming from behind a closed door at
the opposite end of the courtyard.

"Come on," said Frank, and he led the way

THE HARDY BOYS CASEFILES

through the trees, causing the parrots to squawk indignantly overhead.

"Frank, maybe we should—" Joe said as they reached the far door.

"Ssh," Frank warned him and cracked the door open to peer inside. Just then another nerve-shattering scream washed over them.

"I told you, I don't have any!" a voice cried out. Frank hestiated. The voice was familiar. He motioned to Joe, and the two boys slipped through the door.

This section of the ranch was radically different from the main entryway, and something about it made the Hardys' skin crawl. The narrow, low-ceilinged hall was painted antiseptic white. The lighting was fluorescent. The floor was green linoleum.

"Looks like the infirmary at school," Joe whispered.

Voices came from a room at the end of the hall, where a door had been left ajar. The two voices were too low now to decipher, but they sounded familiar. Frank and Joe moved toward them and cautiously looked into the room.

Igor, his clothes torn and muddy and his face cut, was sitting in a dentist's chair. An IV plugged into his wrist fed what looked like a glucose solution into his bloodstream.

The other man was the chief. He wore his khakis and cowboy hat and was standing on the other side of the chair. Near him was a table loaded down with a lie detector, a voice-stress analyzer, and other complicated electronic equipment that even Frank had never seen before. The chief held a syringe in one hand and was adjusting his equipment with the other, while talking to Igor in a low monotone. When he saw Frank and Joe, he stopped talking.

Remembering Dimitri's warning, Frank and Joe were careful to show no surprise at the scene. Keeping their faces expressionless, they entered the room, saluted, and said in unison, "Reporting for duty as ordered, sir."

"Glad you're on board, boys," the chief said, his western accent more pronounced than ever. "I was just warming up Igor here a little bit. Seems he's a bit shy about telling me where he's stashed his cache."

"I told you, I have no cache," Igor protested, unable to take his eyes off the syringe, whose tip bubbled with an odd-looking blue liquid. "Please, you have to believe me."

"Sure I believe you, partner," said the chief, smiling. "Just like I believe all the folks who come visiting us here. All those poor, poor fellows. None of them with a red cent stashed away, except for what they brought with them. And you, you don't even have that anymore, do you?"

The chief checked the level of the IV solution. Then he held up the syringe and squeezed it until a tiny blue bubble dripped down the side. "Yep, poor old Igor here had the unfortunate idea of trying to cut out once he saw it wasn't quite the palace he'd envisioned," the chief said, reaching for Igor's free arm. "Seems he jumped the train as it was slowing down outside the ranch. The guards caught him, naturally. And if they hadn't, the snakes sure would have. The penalty for an escape attempt at Rancho Getaway is the forfeiting of all a man's available money. Sad to say, Mr. Igor here doesn't seem to have the extra savings for even one more night alive."

"I liquidated all my assets before I left the States," Igor babbled frantically, watching in horror as the chief prepared to inject him with the poisonous-looking blue chemical. "Gave it all away. I didn't think I'd need it anymore—"

"That plus a dollar will get you a cup of coffee," the chief said impatiently. "Now, this won't hurt much. You'll just feel a cold shiver up your spine. Kind of like a rattlesnake bite. Hold him down, boys, will you? He's squirming around too much."

Frank and Joe stepped forward hesitantly and placed their hands on Igor's shoulders, ignoring the desperate, mute appeal for help in his eyes. The chief brought the syringe closer to the surface of Igor's skin and lined up the needle with a vein. Joe's eyes sought out Frank's in alarm. Each knew what the other was thinking. How long could they let this go on? Igor might be a crook, but nobody deserved this.

The chief pulled back his finger to plunge the

needle in. Joe tensed his legs, ready to tackle him in an instant.

"Okay, okay, you win!" Igor's voice was hoarse with fear. "I've got savings. Swiss bank accounts. You can have it all. Just get that thing away from me!"

The chief smiled and stepped back. Relieved, Frank and Joe released their hold on Igor. "I knew you'd come to your senses," the chief said, setting the syringe on the table and reaching for a pad and pencil. "If you'll just give me the account numbers, I think we might have ourselves a deal."

As Igor, half-mad with relief and fear, rattled off a string of account numbers from memory, Joe and Frank exchanged glances. "Extreme" wasn't the word for the chief. "Crazy" was closer.

Except that if the chief was crazy, it was like a fox.

A rabidly cruel fox.

"That's all?" the chief mumbled as he copied down the last of the account numbers. There were almost a dozen, all in Swiss and offshore banks, the kind that operate by number only instead of by name, appearance, or proper ID. "You wouldn't be holding out on me again, I hope, Igor."

"Are you kidding? Money's not everything, you know."

The chief chuckled. "Untie him," he commanded the Hardys as he started out of the room. "We'll go inside and get these funds transferred so Igor here can relax and take a shower in his room. You two come along, to keep guard."

The chief's office was ultramodern, except for pictures of the Old West and the mounted head of a longhorn steer that jutted out of the wall behind his chrome-and-marble desk.

The chief motioned for Igor to sit down facing the desk and ordered Frank and Joe to stand guard near the door. "Make yourself comfortable," he said to Igor. "I'm going to check these little old numbers out. We've got a communications setup here that can do that in no time flat." He started to leave, then paused. "I forgot," he said to the Hardys. "You two haven't been issued weapons yet. Until that happens, you can use this."

The chief took a pearl-handled six-gun out of a cabinet near the desk and tossed it to Joe. Then he left the room.

As soon as he was gone, shutting the door behind him, Igor turned eagerly to the Hardys.

"You two have to help me escape," he said. "That money I promised you before—well, I'll triple it. Quadruple it. Anything."

"What are you going to pay us with?" said Frank, keeping up a show of suspicion. No sense in blowing his and Joe's cover.

"Yeah," Joe seconded him. "Looks like the chief has all your cash."

Despite his sorry state, Igor looked at him with contempt. "You think I gave him all my bank account numbers? Don't be a fool. With crooks like him, you've always got to keep your highest cards back, just in case he threatens you again. Those accounts I gave him were chicken feed. I've got something worth more than all of them put together. Millions, I tell you, millions."

"Millions?" Frank said, pretending to think it over. "What could be worth that much?"

"Information, my friend." Igor leaned toward him, and the Hardys again saw the look of raw desperation they'd witnessed when the chief had threatened to put him out. He was a cornered animal, they realized, and he'd fight tooth and claw before allowing himself to become someone else's prey. "Stock tips. Insider scams. Who's going to make the next takeover bid and when. I put half the people in the top five hundred where they are today. I can even do a little blackmail if I have to. Why do you think I'm on the run? Because I've got a direct line to the really big money, boys, and I know how to redirect it."

While Igor was trying to persuade the boys to help him, Frank was thinking fast. He and Joe had to get out of this place, anyway, had to report this ranch to the authorities. There were valid reasons for taking Igor along. They could hand him over to the law, which would make him pay for his crimes. Whatever those crimes were, they couldn't be bad enough to justify leaving him to the chief.

"Sounds good," he said cautiously to Igor. "But I have to see what my buddy here thinks."

"It's a deal," said Joe. "But remember, we don't let you out of our sight until we have the money in our hands. And I'll have *this* in my hand all the time." He indicated the six-gun he was holding.

"Afraid that gun's not much good to you," said the chief's voice. They whirled around to see him standing in the doorway. In his hand was another six-gun, the twin of the one he'd given Joe. "That gun I tossed you isn't loaded. But the one I have is."

Frank realized instantly what had happened. "You've got your office bugged!"

"Smart boy," said the chief, and made a brief gesture with his gun toward the mounted steer head on the wall. "That steer has ears. But you should have been smarter sooner. You two boys made the same mistake as the two boys you're replacing. They stood here in this very room with that big-deal financier from New York, Karl Ross was his name, and they listened to him when he talked about the money he was holding out on me. You won't be seeing them around anymore. And as for Ross, he's not going to be bribing anybody else, because he's got no money and no special contacts left to bribe them with."

"A setup," Igor murmured, unable to believe

he'd been had. "You were planning this all along."

"Sure I was, partner." The chief swung his icy gaze to the exhausted man. "Even your liquid assets aren't enough to make a profit on a place like this. What I need is power. Knowledge. Leverage. I need to own people. That's what gives the ranch the sweet smell of success."

Slumped in his chair, Igor looked like a deflated balloon. The presence of lie detectors and similar equipment in the back room clearly made more sense to him now. With a gesture of defeat, he picked up a pen and starting writing down names on a piece of paper.

"That's right," the chief said, peering over his shoulder. "Whatever you can give me. Just make sure I can make it stick. You already told me what I can get out of this—'millions, I tell you, millions.' "

Igor didn't answer. He continued writing, lost in silent despair.

"Now that our business is over with, I get to deal with you two boys," said the chief, smiling. "That's the fun part. I figure we can have a little lassoing contest in the corral out back. I used to be a pretty fair cowhand years ago. I grew up on a ranch like this, but smaller. I'll tell you what. If you can make it to the corral gate, you'll get to work in the fields. If you don't make it, you're going to fertilize them. I'm afraid the two boys before you were a mite slow—disappointing, really. I'd hoped for more of a challenge. But you two look very fit. Maybe you'll give me a run for your money. Or I guess I should say, a run for your lives."

The chief looked Frank and Joe up and down as though he were inspecting livestock. "I'll take you one by one. Who wants to be first?"

"Me," Frank and Joe said at the same time.

"Believe me, my buddy is as slow as molasses," Joe added quickly, before Frank could say anything. "He's strictly long distance, not a sprinter like me."

The chief said nothing, just continued to size them up. Then he nodded. "Okay, I believe you. You first, boy. And remember, I want to see some speed."

"You'll get it," said Joe with a show of bravado. "No way you're going to get that rope around me, old man."

The chief grinned, looking delighted. "That's what I like to see, a little spunk. Roping you in is going to be the most fun I've had in a month of Sundays." He turned to the others. "You two can wait here while I play my little game with your friend."

Holding his gun on Joe, he motioned him out of the office, then locked the door as he left. He and Joe walked back to the large corral behind the ranch house, an elaborate construction with high walls of corrugated metal, an attached stable, and all the paraphernalia necessary for a real big-time rodeo.

"Go on, get in there," the chief said, pushing Joe into the corral and locking the gate after him. "I don't figure you're going to make it to the gate," he explained. "But even if you do, if my horse stumbles or something, you're still not going to get away. The only thing you're going to escape is the cemetery."

"Fair enough," said Joe, doing some stretch exercises to loosen up his muscles. "Just watch my dust."

The chief shook his head. "It will be fun cutting you down to size. Maybe I'll even put my brand on you." There was a nasty edge to his voice. "I wonder where I should put it. The center of your forehead might look good. Move on out to the middle, now. I'll be there in a minute."

Joe watched the chief head for the stable, then turned and surveyed the large corral. Halfway across it was a long distance for a sprint. Joe started across, slowly. From the stable, he heard the whinny of a horse. Then suddenly, behind him, he heard the crack of a gun.

The chief sat astride a palomino in a cubicle near the gate. The six-gun in his right hand was pointed in the air, and his left hand rested on the lasso that was wrapped around the saddle horn. "Coming out of chute number three!" the chief shouted in a rodeo announcer's voice, and shoved the gun into the holster at his hip. The door of the cubicle shot up, and the horse raced right for Joe as the chief gave a wild, ear-shattering whoop.

At the first sound, Joe started moving, as fast a start as he had ever made. His feet were pumping beneath him, his heart was pounding in his chest, and his lungs felt as if they would burst. He rounded the corral, approaching the gate from the opposite side, steadily getting closer.

Then he felt the rope drop down over his shoulders and tighten.

And he heard the chief's cry of triumph. "You lost, boy. You're dead!"

Chapter
12

THAT WAS WHAT Joe had been waiting for.

As soon as he felt the rope tighten around him, he came to an abrupt halt. At the same moment he grabbed the rope in both hands and yanked with every ounce of his strength, praying that he had made his move fast enough to stop the chief from bracing himself in the saddle.

It worked, just as Joe had gambled it would. Caught by surprise, the chief didn't have time either to brace himself or to let go of the rope. Instead, his hands instinctively tightened on the rope, and he flew out of the saddle, hitting the ground flat on his face.

Before the chief could roll over and draw his gun, Joe straddled him and grabbed the gun from his holster.

Joe stood up, shrugging off the rope that still

hung loosely around him. "Okay, Chief, on your feet. The game's over, and guess who won? In case you don't know, keep your hands in the air—or as you'd say, reach for the sky, partner."

The chief looked at the gun, and followed orders. But his eyes were blazing. "You're not going to get away with this, boy," he snarled. "You're going to pay."

"Unless you follow orders, *you're* going to get paid off—with this," said Joe and raised the gun so that it was pointing right between the chief's eyes. He wanted to make sure the chief believed he would use it—because Joe had a feeling that he wouldn't be able to, even in a pinch.

"Okay, okay, boy," the chief said hurriedly. "Just be careful of that piece. The trigger's kind of sensitive. The least little thing will set it off."

"Fine," said Joe. "Make sure you don't supply that least little thing."

The chief didn't have to be told where they were going. He unlocked the gate and headed out of the dusty corral and back to his office, where he unlocked the door without being told.

Igor's mouth dropped open when he saw the chief enter, with Joe following, gun in hand. "How did you—" he started to ask.

But before he could finish, Frank grinned and said, "I figured you'd pull it off."

"You should have seen it," Joe said.

"Both you boys better fasten onto one idea now," said the chief, careful not to make any sudden moves but not hiding the menace in his voice. "No way you're getting away with this. You can't escape. There's jungle all around. And the longer you hold me, the rougher I'm going to be on you when you realize you can't escape and have to give up."

"Maybe he's right," Igor said. "Perhaps we can make a deal."

"You never learn, do you?" said Joe with disgust. "You can't make a deal with someone like him."

"Besides, we won't have to make a deal—not when we can make tracks," said Frank, his eyes lighting up.

Joe recognized that light. Frank had an idea.

"What kind of tracks?" asked Igor.

"Railroad tracks," said Frank. "We arrived by train, and we can leave the same way."

By now Joe had the idea. He pointed at the chief with his gun. "Yeah, we've got our ticket right here."

"What makes you boys think—" the chief began.

"We don't think, we *know,*" said Frank. "We *know* that you're going to pick up that phone and order the train to get ready. We *know* that you're going to order that all your 'guests' be rounded up and put in a ventilated boxcar. We *know* that the train's going to pull out of here in a couple of hours, with us and you aboard. And, oh yes, we *know* that there'll be enough provisions on it to

117

feed everybody until that yacht arrives on its regular run to the coast and you can give orders for it to take us back to the States.''

"You want to know *how* we know all that?" Joe chimed in. "*We* know that *you* know what'll happen to you if you don't do just what we say."

The chief looked at the gun staring him in the face, and picked up the phone.

He made three calls, never taking his eyes from the gun. With the first call he ordered that the train be readied; with the second, that the boxcars be loaded with all the guests from the ranch; and with the third, that four days' worth of food and drink be loaded in another boxcar.

When he was asked if any men would be required to go along as guards, the chief gave a glance at the gun and said, no, the two men he had with him would be enough.

That was the only question he was asked. Frank, listening closely for any signs of trickery, wasn't surprised. The chief was the kind of boss who gave orders and demanded unquestioning obedience.

Meanwhile, Igor was rejoicing. "Great work," he said. "When we get out of this, I'll give you that bonus I promised. Or, if you prefer, you can give me that money to invest, and I'll make you really rich."

"Thanks, we might consider that," said Frank, barely able to suppress a grin. Igor simply couldn't pass up an opportunity to try a scam, even under these circumstances.

"Yeah," said Joe, keeping a straight face, too. "We could use the help of a financial whiz like you."

Igor gave them a genial smile. Then his expression clouded. "There's one thing I don't understand. Why are we taking along those others? They all must be broke by now. What good are they?"

Frank tried to think of an explanation that would satisfy Igor. "They might have money still hidden away. You never know."

"I doubt it—but I'll leave that to you," said Igor. "I believe in the free enterprise system." He rubbed his hands together in anticipation.

Frank and Joe knew that this wasn't the time to let Igor know that he and the others were heading back to the States to be put into the hands of the law. Frank did figure, though, that it was time to find out more about Igor.

"Say, Igor," he said, "since we're going to be partners, we should know your real name."

"I understand. It never hurts to be prudent," said Igor, still smiling his oily smile. "Perhaps you've read about me. My name is Tanner. Adolf Tanner."

Frank and Joe glanced at each other. Adolf Tanner, Gregory Miller's boss. The guy who had disappeared, leaving Marcie's father holding the bag.

THE HARDY BOYS CASEFILES

"Adolf Tanner," said Frank, wrinkling his brow, pretending to try to remember the name. "Seems to me I did read something about you. You vanished, but somebody working with you got caught."

"Some guy called Muller or Milner or something like that," added Joe.

"Miller," Tanner said. "Gregory Miller. He worked under me, not with me. Your typical Boy Scout. Before I left, I doctored my books to make it look like he was the one milking my company. For insurance, I had one of my men stick a briefcase full of cash in his closet to make it look like he was planning to escape. If I'm lucky, the police will also suspect him of doing away with me to cover his thefts. He'll wind up in jail, and I'll be in the clear. Beautiful, you have to admit."

"I have to hand it to you, you are one shrewd operator," said Frank.

Now, especially, both Hardys couldn't wait to get back to the States. They had solved the mystery they had set out to solve. They had found out the truth about Marcie's father. They had caught the real crook, and it should be simple enough to prove that Mr. Miller had only called Perfect Getaway in an effort to track down Tanner. How he had heard about it, they'd have to ask him later. Now all they had to do was deliver their catch.

They didn't have long to wait for the delivery mechanism to start operating.

120

In half an hour the chief's phone began ringing.

Each time it rang, the chief picked up the receiver and merely listened to the caller. Then he said, "Very good," hung up, and relayed the information.

The train was made ready and turned around to head back toward the sea.

The supplies were loaded into a boxcar.

Finally, the prisoners were loaded aboard.

"Time to move out," said Joe. "I'm putting this gun in my pocket, but my hand's going to be resting on it. One wrong move from you, Chief, and you'll find out how fast I can pull the trigger. Hope I'm coming through loud and clear."

The chief nodded. With Joe right behind him, he led the way out of the room. He looked neither to his right nor his left as the group passed the guards at the entrance of the ranch house and climbed into a waiting jeep, Joe sitting close beside the chief. The sun had set, and a full moon was just rising, bathing the land in a silvery glow.

The jeep drove them to the ghostly train, shimmering in the moonlight. Only a dim light from the train's interior added to that illumination. Security, as always, was tight.

Dimitri was waiting with a squad of men. He opened the jeep door and stood at attention as the chief climbed out, followed by the others, with Joe in the lead.

"Hey, where do you think you're going, Igor?"

Dimitri barked. "You go back in the boxcar with the other prisoners."

Tanner opened his mouth to protest, then caught himself. It was clearly all he could do to keep from winking at Joe and Frank as he responded meekly, "Yes, sir. Sorry, sir."

After he was led off, the chief and the Hardys entered the passenger car, followed by Dimitri.

"Will there be anything else, Chief?" Dimitri asked.

The chief's eyes flicked around to meet Joe's hard gaze. Then he looked at Dimitri and said, "No. You're dismissed. Tell the engineer to get the train moving."

After Dimitri left, the chief and the Hardys sat silently in their compartment until the train started rolling.

"Glad to see you're being sensible," Joe said. "That means you're going to stay alive. Don't look so mad, though. Life in jail won't be so bad. I'm sure you'll be out in twenty or thirty years."

"You—" began the chief. But when Joe pulled out his gun, the chief swallowed the rest of his sentence.

"Time to make some changes," said Frank, checking out the window to make sure that the ranch was out of sight. "Let's pay a visit to the engineer."

Herding the chief ahead of them, they moved forward through the passenger car and then through a door that connected it with the engineer's compartment.

The engineer had the train controls set on automatic. He was sitting back in his seat with his eyes closed.

Frank tapped him on the shoulder. He looked up, saw the chief, and leapt to his feet.

"Sorry, sir," he babbled. "Just taking a little break. Won't happen again, I—"

Then he saw the gun in Joe's hand.

"We want you to do us a favor," Joe said. "Show us how to run this thing. We want to expand our occupational skills."

A half hour later the chief and the engineer were tied up in the passenger car, and Joe and Frank were at the controls.

"Tanner seemed a little disappointed that he had to go second-class."

"I'm afraid Tanner has a lot of disappointments coming up," said Joe as he moved a lever to speed up the train. "This is fun. When I was a kid, I always wanted to drive a train."

"Okay, Casey Jones, just keep your eyes on the tracks and don't lose your head," said Frank.

"You know me," said Joe, increasing the speed still more.

"That's the trouble," said Frank. "I don't want to have survived all of this only to wind up in an old-fashioned train wreck."

"No problem," said Joe. "Clear track ahead."

Frank couldn't argue. The front lights of

the train had come on when the train entered the tunnel formed by the foliage overhead. The gleaming rails stretched unbroken into the darkness.

After a while Joe rubbed his eyes. "I have to admit, this job is tougher than it looks. Those rails are almost hypnotic, and we haven't had a decent night of sleep since we left Bayport."

"You're right about that," said Frank. "Good thing we're practically at the end of the tunnel." He couldn't stop his mouth from opening in a wide yawn.

Then his eyes widened, and his yawn froze. For a second all he could do was make a gasping sound.

Then he choked out, "Put on the brakes—or we'll crash!"

He didn't really have to say anything. Joe, too, had spotted the felled trees lying across the track. He yanked on the brakes and started breathing again only when he felt the train come to a stop with a loud hiss and an ear-piercing screech.

"Let's get out and see—" Frank began.

But he and Joe only had to glance out the window behind them to see what had happened.

Dimitri was standing there, gun in hand.

And from the darkness behind Dimitri came a voice that they recognized all too well.

"Hello, Hardys. Long time, no see."

Chapter

13

FRANK AND JOE instantly recognized the squat man with a mustache who held them at gunpoint.

"Alex!" Frank managed to say.

"How did you get here?" said Joe in a stunned voice, remembering their last sight of Alex in the mansion on the Florida key.

Alex smiled. "Me, explain anything to brilliant detectives like the Hardys?" he said sarcastically. "I wouldn't be so presumptuous. I'll let you try to figure it out, until we get you back to the ranch. If you still don't know, the chief can explain—before he tells you what he's decided to do with you." Alex's smile widened. "I want to be around for *that*. Should be fun."

A half hour later Frank and Joe were back at the ranch, along with the chief, Alex, and a squad of armed guards. They had all been flown there in the same helicopter that Alex and the guards had used to beat the train to the end of the tracks. A few men had been left behind to turn the train around and return its human cargo to captivity.

When they were all in the chief's office, Alex asked the two boys, "Well, have you figured out how I got here yet?"

Frank had been thinking about it the whole trip back. "You must have had some kind of emergency plan, in case somebody got through your security shield," he said. "I should have thought of that. The chief would want to cover his bases in case somebody goofed up."

"Now you're talking horse sense, boy," said the chief. "Too bad you thought about it too late. As soon as that fool you put to sleep on the ship woke up, he found those two recruits tied up and reported what had happened to the captain. The captain then went to his safe and got out a sealed envelope he'd been told was to be used only if somebody slipped past what you call our 'security shield.' There was a phone number in there. As soon as the ship got to the nearest island, he made the call and talked to Alex, who took it from there. The captain never even had to break radio silence."

"All according to the chief's faultless plan," said Alex, shamelessly flattering the old man. "The chief thought of everything. All I had to do was open my own sealed envelope, which gave me a flight plan to the ranch. I flew down in a company plane, and when I arrived here and heard that a couple of new recruits named Mike and Dave were with the chief and the prisoners on a train trip to the coast, it was easy to see what was happening. All I had to do was load up the ranch helicopter with men and cut you off." He slapped his thigh with boisterous amusement. "Sure did get a kick out of seeing the look on your faces. You looked like you'd seen a ghost."

"And now we'll see what's going to happen to you," said the chief, enjoying the look that now appeared on the Hardys' faces. "We could just kill you. A couple of bullets in the back of the neck and that would be that. But after what you've done to me, that's not enough. I think you need to sweat a little."

The old man pulled off his cowboy hat as he walked close to the two boys. His voice hardened as he wiped the sweat from his face and said, "Fact is, boys, I want to see the two of you sweat blood. And I know how to make you do it."

As he watched the brothers' faces tighten in apprehension, his booming laugh filled the room. "I don't think I'll tell you how. I'll let you start sweating now, and you can sweat the whole night through. Then tomorrow I'll let you in on my little surprise. We'll see if you boys can really take it."

He turned to his guards. "Put them in the lockup. And turn up the heat."

* * *

The lockup was a windowless white room. There was no furniture—not even a crude cot or bolted-down chair such as one would expect to find in the lowliest jail cell. Hanging down above the door was a 500-watt light that could have driven away the shadows on a city block. In that small room, the glare reflected off the stone floor and the steel door and turned the tiny chamber into an oven.

Joe used the palm of his hand to wipe away the sweat pouring down his face. "Whew! Must be a hundred degrees in here."

Frank was sweating just as hard. "Right, and they didn't leave us a drop of water."

"Then that means we've got to get out of here—fast. But how?" asked Joe.

Frank started to say something but then, grinning ruefully, put a finger to his lips to indicate that they'd have to work in silence. They couldn't afford to let the chief overhear their plans. Then he realized that he had no plan. Shrugging his shoulders, he sat down on the floor to think. And sweat.

Joe wouldn't join him. He couldn't. His restless nature demanded that he do *something*. He paced around and around the cell. Finally he dropped to the floor beside Frank and said in a whisper, "I hope you've figured a way out of this box. I've looked over the doors, the walls, the floor—every inch of it—and I think they've really got us this time."

Frank replied in a voice no louder than his brother's, "Sometimes all we can do is wait and save our energy for when there's an opening."

"Listen, Frank," snapped Joe, "waiting I can put up with, but baking's too much. I'm going to knock out this light, at least. Much more of this heat, and come morning all they're going to find are a couple of crispy critters."

Joe backed up against the far wall and charged full speed at the door. The instant before he would have crashed into the weighty steel sheet, he leapt skyward like a basketball player going up for a slam dunk. At the top of his jump he caught hold of the heavy steel pipe from which the light was suspended. Slowly, feeling the heat of the scalding globe only inches away, he pulled himself up until he could brace one arm over the bar.

As he reached out to smash the bulb Frank suddenly jumped to his feet. "Wait," he said sharply.

Joe stared disbelievingly at his brother.

"Frank, if you have an idea, it better be a fast one. I don't know which I'm going to do first— fry or fall down."

"Then be quiet and listen," Frank said softly. "Don't unscrew the bulb, unscrew the *fixture*. There should be some slack in the wire. If we can pull it down as far as the door, then maybe we can give the guards a hot welcome."

"All right," whispered Joe enthusiastically.

"Then we can arrange for one of those openings you were talking about."

With no tools and only their thin khaki shirts to protect them from the searing heat of the light, it took Frank and Joe hours to set their trap. By the time they were finished, they figured it was only a couple of hours before dawn.

"Now, how do we issue invitations to this party?" asked Joe.

"Easy," Frank answered. He wrapped his hands in the scorched remains of his khaki shirt and, grasping the now-dangling wire close to the bulb, he smashed the globe against the door and began screaming.

After the hours of silence, Frank's cries tore open the night. The two boys could hear the sound of running footsteps.

"What's going on in there?" a gruff voice demanded.

"The light exploded and I think my brother's all cut up!" Joe said urgently.

"He's going to be worse than that if he doesn't shut up," the man growled. Frank's screams continued.

"Your boss won't like it if Frank's hurt when he comes for him," Joe said pleadingly.

"Okay, but both of you stand back while I open up the door," the guard grumbled.

The boys listened to the sound of a key turning in the lock. The minute it clicked open, Frank, still holding the wire, jabbed the metal base of the shattered bulb against the steel door. The darkness was illuminated by a blue flash! And the boys heard a single, choked cry as the surge of electricity flowed through the steel door and into the man behind it.

Frank jerked the bulb back, and Joe reached for the door handle. When the door swung open, the cool night air tasted like springwater to the two parched prisoners.

After carrying the unconscious guard into the cell, they bound and gagged him with the remains of their shirts. Locking the door behind them, they took his keys and set out to explore the house.

"The first thing we have to do is find some weapons," Joe whispered. "I won't go back in that room. And I don't want to know what else the chief has planned for us."

"Me, neither, but if we want to get out of here alive, we have to get some help," Frank replied as he opened the outer door and inched carefully into the courtyard. The sky was the hazy gray of the last hours before dawn.

Across the courtyard, the boys could see the ranch-house guard, tipped back in one of the easy chairs sleeping.

"I'd hate to be in his shoes when the chief finds us gone," murmured Joe.

"Be quiet or we won't be." Frank eased open the door to the main hall of the house.

Once they were inside, Joe indicated that they

should go upstairs, but Frank shook his head. He pointed up and mouthed the word "guests." Then he pointed at the heavy oak door at the end of the hall and pantomimed the words "the chief." An angry look appeared on Joe's face and he began striding toward the door.

Frank grabbed him by the arm and whispered fiercely, "We don't want him now, Joe. What we want is a way out of here. He has to have some way of communicating with the outside world. If we can get a message out, we can hide in the jungle and wait until the cavalry arrives."

Joe kept going, almost dragging Frank down the hall. Just before they reached the chief's door, they came to a much less impressive oak door bearing a sign that read: RESTRICTED— STAFF ONLY. It was locked, but the keys they had taken from the unconscious guard let them in.

There, in a tiny alcove, they found themselves facing three doors, each bearing a lettered sign. When they read them—LOUNGE, ARMORY, COM- MUNICATIONS—Frank punched the air and whis- pered a heartfelt, "All ri-i-ight!"

Joe turned to him and said in a barely audible voice, "I think Santa has just delivered, even if he did forget the swimsuit."

A moment's celebration was all they could afford. As soon as Joe had the armory door open, he tossed the keys to Frank, who entered the communications room.

The armory was a policeman's nightmare—a

terrorist's dream come true. Joe was surrounded by racks of M-16s. Crates of .223 caliber, full-metal-jacketed ammunition lined the wall. And in a cabinet at the back of the storeroom were enough C-4 plastic explosives to move the ranch house and all its occupants into another country. Joe realized that for the first time in many hours he was smiling. He cleared a space on the table in the center of the room and went to work.

When Frank walked into the communications room, it was like coming home. Low counters lined the walls, and sitting on them were two computers and an extremely sophisticated radio setup.

When Frank booted up the two computers, he immediately discovered two things. First, one of the computers was used to do nothing except direct a rooftop microwave antenna that linked the ranch to the nearest phone system. Second, the other computer—the one used to assemble a message to go out over the antenna—required a password. A password he didn't have. He settled in before the computer, determined to use every hacker trick he knew.

When Joe walked in about forty minutes later, he stared over his brother's shoulder at the CRT. He watched as the words PLEASE ENTER PASS-WORD appeared on the screen, followed by the key clicks of Frank trying one stunt after another.

"Why do you always try the hard way, Frank?" Joe asked. "Let me go get the chief.

He'll tell us his password if I ask him just right."
Frank knew how his brother would ask—with his
fists.

"Give me a few more minutes. So far I've
figured out that the password is six characters
long and that the only person who uses this
computer is the chief himself." Frank didn't look
up from the keyboard as he spoke.

"Well, don't let me rush you," Joe said calmly,
"but I've planted a few surprises around the
house that are due to go off in about—let's see—
eight minutes."

Frank's fingers froze as he turned to gaze at his
grinning brother.

The look on Joe's face told Frank all he needed
to know. As he turned back toward the computer,
he said, "And I guess we don't want to be anywhere nearby when your 'surprises' go off, do
we?"

"Nope."

Frank mentally reviewed the list of words he'd
tried, the ways he'd attempted to bypass the
computer's security system. For once, he was
sure that the chief had been too confident. He felt
as if the answer to this puzzle was right on the tip
of his tongue. Yes!—he had it.

"Hey, Joe, if you wanted one word to describe
the chief, what would it be?" he asked. He answered the question himself as he typed in the six
letters needed to control the computer, C-O-W-
B-O-Y. The screen went blank for a moment, and

then a menu of all the computer's functions and files appeared.

Frank was totally in his element now. As Joe counted off the seconds, he scanned a file here, set up a short program there, and set up a message that would end up on his hacker friend Phil Cohen's computer back in Bayport.

"Frank, if we don't go *right* now, we are going to get caught when the fireworks go off," Joe said, his voice tight with tension.

"Just one more thing," Frank replied. "I want to see this file called 'auction.' I think that it has the answer to a lot of our qu—"

"Look, answers won't matter in just about one minute." Joe grabbed his brother's arm and literally dragged him out of the room and into the hallway. Speed, not silence, was what was important now. The sound of their footsteps must have awakened the guard, because as they tore through the courtyard they could hear him shouting behind them.

Joe led Frank through the gate at the back of the courtyard and toward the corral. Standing there was the chief's palomino, saddled and waiting. "Sorry about this, but I could only find one horse," Joe panted.

Two shots whistled past as Joe leapt into the saddle and Frank mounted behind him, taking a firm grip on Joe's shoulders.

"Let's go," Joe shouted, and kicked the palomino's sides. The horse got the message. It was off like a shot, racing across the grassland toward the jungle. "We'll follow the tracks," Joe shouted.

There was more gunfire coming from behind them. Just then, Frank heard a tremendous explosion. Looking back, he saw the trucks burst into flames and watched the locomotive rise up off the tracks and fall over in almost slow motion. The chief's men were all scrambling for cover.

"It'll take them a while to come after us," Joe shouted.

"It'll take them a while to figure out they're all in one piece," Frank answered. The two brothers began laughing, relieved to be, at least for the moment, safe and free.

About half a mile down the track the horse began to slow down. Joe pulled on the reins and brought it to a halt. He knew that a good horse could burst its heart running, and that was the last thing he wanted to happen to this animal. The two boys climbed off it. Joe looked at the horse's heaving flanks and the froth coming from its mouth. "Sorry to have worked you so hard, pal," Joe said. "But it was for a good cause. You can take off now." He gave it an affectionate pat on the flanks and grinned as the horse trotted easily away down the track, relieved of its double burden.

"Time to get off these tracks," said Frank. He looked at the mass of jungle on both sides of them.

"Hey, you didn't really believe that stuff they told us about this jungle being filled with alligators and snakes and jaguars, did you?" Joe said.

"Not a bit," said Frank. "Scare talk."

They pushed their way into the foliage, but it was hard going. The ground was soft, the trees thick, and vines lay like trip wire all around. A hundred different kinds of insects buzzed around their heads, all of them having a feast on every inch of exposed flesh.

"We're not leaving much of a trail," said Joe, looking behind them. "It's as if the jungle grows right back as soon as we've passed through it."

"As if it were swallowing us," said Frank. "As soon as we reach civilization, we can get hold of the police or the army or whatever they have down here, and tell them what's going on at the ranch," said Frank. "We can also contact the U.S. embassy. That'll cook the chief's goose, if it wasn't cooked already."

"Nah. I set the charges in the house small enough to just make noise. The others blew up the trucks and train," said Joe, pausing to wipe sweat off his face and brush away a cloud of gnats. "I can hardly wait until—" He suddenly gave Frank a violent shove, sending his brother sprawling.

"Hey, what the—" Frank demanded, then followed where Joe's finger was pointing.

The black snake lay where Frank had been about to step. It raised its head and looked at them with glittering, unblinking eyes. Then it hissed softly and slithered away.

"Thanks," said Frank. "I owe you one."

"Anytime," said Joe. "Here, let me help you up."

He bent over to help Frank out of the tangle of foliage in which he lay.

Before Joe could straighten up, Frank grabbed his arm and pulled him down to land face forward in the same foliage.

Joe rolled over on his back, lifted his head, and saw what had caused his brother to react with lightning speed.

The body of a jaguar, leaping from a tree branch.

The jaguar now stood motionless a few feet away, its balance restored instantly after its miss. Its eyes flicked from Joe to Frank and back again, picking its prey.

Then it let out a vicious snarl. Frank and Joe saw its haunches tensing, ready to spring. It bared its fangs and extended its claws for the kill.

Chapter
14

DESPERATELY FRANK AND Joe tried to scramble to their feet, even though they knew they didn't stand a chance of escaping so fast an animal.

The jaguar snarled again—but this time its snarl was obliterated by the crack of a rifle and the whine of a bullet.

The bullet missed, thudding into a tree behind the big cat. But it was enough to send the animal disappearing into the jungle in two giant bounds.

By this time the Hardys were on their feet. They looked around and saw the man who had saved them. Half concealed by a tree was a dark-skinned man wearing the loose cotton pants and shirt and wide-brimmed straw hat of a local farmer. But the gleaming semiautomatic rifle in his hands wasn't designed for raising crops.

Joe grinned and waved his hand. "Hey, thanks, pal!"

The man merely stood and stared at them, his face and dark eyes expressionless.

Frank looked at his brother. "You expect him to understand you? Let me try my Spanish on him."

"*What* Spanish?" asked Joe.

"Listen and find out," said Frank. He turned toward the man. "*Muchas gracias, amigo,*" he said, almost using up his entire command of the language.

The man continued to stand and stare at them. Suspicion shone in his eyes.

"Maybe he thinks we're bandits or something," Frank said to Joe. "I'll straighten him out." He turned to the man, pointed at Joe and then at himself, and said, "*Americanos.*"

Instantly the man's gun was up, pointed straight at Frank's chest.

"Uh, Frank, I think you said the wrong thing," Joe muttered.

The man indicated that they should raise their hands in the air, which they did.

Then he took a length of cord from his pocket, and gestured to indicate that Frank and Joe should lie face down on the ground, with their hands behind them, to be tied up.

Again Frank and Joe instantly obeyed.

It was Frank whose hands the man started to tie first. Which meant that it was Frank who had the chance to kick back with his feet, knocking the man off balance, and sending his rifle flying.

Instantly Joe was on his feet, finishing the job with a right to the man's jaw.

Frank stood up and looked down at the unconscious man. "That was almost too easy," he said.

"Guess the guy wasn't used to people fighting back when he had them under the gun," said Joe, kneeling down to tie the man up with his own cord.

"Well, not too many people have had the practice we've had," said Frank. He stooped down and drew the man's machete from his belt. "We can use this to hack through the jungle."

Joe retrieved the rifle. "I don't think even Dad would object to us taking this, too. This is one spot where a gun will come in handy."

"Right," said Frank. "Jaguars aren't an endangered species around here. We are."

They tied the man up and propped him against a tree. Then they revived him.

"He should be able to work himself free in an hour or two," said Frank as he started to slash a trail through the undergrowth with the machete. Then he said, "Hey, what do we have here?"

"Some kind of path," said Joe. "This trip gets easier and easier. Now we can really make time."

"What say we try jogging?" said Frank. "See how a sprinter like you can do over the long run."

"Okay, marathon man," said Joe, breaking into a jog. "First one to run out of steam is a—"

A burst of semiautomatic weapon fire plowed a line of bullets right in front of Joe's feet, bringing the two of them to an abrupt halt.

Out of the undergrowth stepped four soldiers in camouflage uniforms and helmets. All carried semiautomatic rifles.

Frank and Joe didn't have to be told to drop the machete and rifle and raise their hands high.

"They probably think we're guerrillas," Frank muttered to Joe.

"Yeah, that rifle I was carrying didn't help," said Joe. "Guess Dad was right, after all. Guns do get you in hot water."

The soldiers advanced toward them, weapons at the ready. The expressions on their faces made it clear that they were not only ready but eager to shoot first and ask questions later.

"I'll give the magic word one more try," Frank said to Joe. Then he called out to the soldiers, *"Americanos."*

This time it worked. Their faces broke into smiles.

"Speak English?" Frank asked them hopefully. *"Inglés?"*

Still smiling, a soldier with three stripes on his uniform shook his head, but waved for them to follow him, while another soldier scooped up the rifle and machete.

Half an hour down the trail and then twenty minutes along another trail, they came to a jungle army outpost surrounded by barbed wire and machine-gun emplacements.

The soldiers led Frank and Joe through the front gate and into a tent where an officer with silver bars on his shoulders was sitting.

The sergeant spoke to him in Spanish, and then the officer said to the Hardys in perfect, unaccented English, "So you're Americans? What happened? How did you get here?"

Frank and Joe were happy to tell him, beginning with the man they had knocked out in the jungle.

The officer nodded. "A local bandit, though they call themselves guerrillas. We're stationed here to try to control them. I'll send a couple of men to pick him up. But you still didn't tell me what you were doing in this jungle originally. And I'm afraid you're going to have to. This isn't a place for tourists, you know."

"You may have a hard time believing our story," warned Frank. "But you will when you check it out."

By the time Frank and Joe finished telling him about the ranch and what was going on there, the officer's face was serious.

"You do believe us, don't you?" Frank said.

"Honest, we're telling the truth," added Joe.

The officer nodded. "I believe you. It's too incredible a story for you to have made up. And to think we believed that the ranch was an agricultural experiment."

Then he stood up. "Please wait here. I have to radio headquarters to find out how to move against this vipers' nest. It's too important for me to decide alone."

After he left, Joe said, "Hope the captain lets us come along when they go after the ranch. I'd really love to see the chief's face when they close him down."

"I just want to get my hands on Tanner and take him back to the States," said Frank. "I hate to think of Marcie's dad sweating it out in jail."

There was a smile on the captain's face when he returned. "Good news. They're sending a helicopter right away to take you to headquarters. Then, after you give them the details of how the ranch is set up, they'll move in on it immediately."

"Great," said Joe. "Think we can go along?"

"I'm sure it can be arranged," the captain said, "considering all the help you've been. Now, perhaps you'd like a bite to eat while you wait."

"Wouldn't mind," said Joe. "I could eat a horse."

"Or even a jaguar," seconded Frank with a grin.

"I'm afraid you'll have to settle for steaks," the captain said. "But I don't think you'll find them bad."

The captain's promise was an understatement. When Frank and Joe sat down in the mess tent, the steaks that were set before them were filet mignons, three inches thick, tender and juicy. With them came baked potatoes and salad. And, afterward, chocolate ice cream.

"Great," said Joe, spooning up the last of his dessert in a hurry, since he had just heard the sound of a helicopter descending outside.

"Sensational," said Frank. "Thanks a million, Captain."

"It's the least we could do," said a voice from behind them. "Condemned men are entitled to a hearty last meal."

They didn't have to turn their heads to recognize who had spoken.

Alex.

They turned to see Dimitri standing beside him. Both men were holding .45s.

Frank was the first to say what he and Joe realized at the same moment.

"You're in on this," he accused the captain.

The captain shrugged and leaned back in his chair, a lazy smile playing across his face. "I like to think of it as hardship pay. Jungle duty is no picnic. Earning a little extra from the chief eases the discomfort, and catching idiots like you relieves the boredom. Besides which, the ranch furnishes us with those excellent steaks that you so enjoyed."

"You'll earn an extra bonus for these two," Alex promised him. Then he said gloatingly to the Hardys, "I told you there was no place to go. We warn everyone about all the dangers of fleeing the ranch without mentioning the captain here. That way we can weed out the ones like you who refuse to abandon hope of escape.''

Dimitri gestured with his gun for Frank and Joe to get to their feet. ''Come on. The chopper is waiting—and so is the chief,'' he added with a nasty grin.

Prodding them with his gun barrel, Alex steered Frank and Joe into the helicopter. The Hardys took seats, trying not to think about what was in store.

The trip back to the ranch passed in silence except for the roar of the motor and the thump of the blades. Frank and Joe sat between Alex and Dimitri. Each of the Hardys had a gun barrel pressed against his side the whole way.

Waiting for them at the helicopter pad were ten guards with their guns drawn. The chief was taking no chances that Joe and Frank might spoil his fun again.

''You don't know how glad I am to see you boys,'' the chief said. His jaw was tight, his face pale with anger. He looked like a spoiled child who'd had his toys taken away.

Frank and Joe looked around at Joe's destructive handiwork. A pall of smoke still hung over the ranch from the burning trucks. The locomotive lay alongside the tracks like a toppled giant. When they looked back at the chief, he appeared even angrier than before. The chief waved the guards away and drew his pearl-handled revolver to cover Joe and Frank.

"Boys, we're going to have us a party. And you're going to be the entertainment," the old man said bitterly. He gestured back at the house. "Everybody'll be here. Because every last one of them has got to learn that nobody crosses me and lives."

As the boys watched, the guards began driving the men—all the men—from the house, from the barracks, in from the fields to the clearing beside the helipad. The prisoners formed a semicircle around the trio. Behind the prisoners stood the guards, guns up, ready for anything.

"We don't need trouble here," the chief shouted. "And these boys are trouble. Every once in a while, I think that you people need to be shown just exactly what can happen if we think that you're trouble!"

He stepped close to the two brothers, an evil glint in his eyes, and spoke softly, so softly that only they could hear him. "You two have any last words before I put a bullet through your brains?"

Frank looked at his brother and said, "Joe, it's been—" But he never got to finish that sentence. Joe finished it for him, shouting, "Fun!" And then the world seemed to explode around them.

Chapter

15

FRANK WAS ALIVE, but he didn't know why. He kept trying to walk until he realized that he was lying flat on his back, deaf and dizzy. All he could see was dust and smoke—and Joe sticking the muzzle of a pearl-handled revolver in the chief's ear.

What he could see of Joe's face was grim. As Frank got to his knees, he saw that the prisoners and their guards were as confused as he. But when he looked back at the ranch house—no, where the ranch house had *been*—he began to understand. And when Frank looked at Joe and the chief, Joe nodded happily. The chief simply stared, stunned by the blast and the loss of his little kingdom.

Joe was shouting something at Frank, but all Frank could do was shake his head from side to side and point at his ears. Finally, Joe dragged the chief closer to his brother and screamed at him from inches away. "Look behind you! There's the cavalry!"

When Frank turned around, he saw three large troop-carrying choppers coming in low over the tree line. They were close enough now that the men on the ground who couldn't hear them could feel them. There was no fight left in any of them. A couple of the men started a dash for the jungle, but when one of the choppers circled around to head them off, they slowed to a walk, then stopped to await their captors.

As soon as Frank and Joe saw the troops pouring out of the helicopters, they shouted as loudly as they could, *"Amigos, amigos!"*

Frank nudged his brother and muttered, "Get rid of that gun before one of these trigger-happy commandos decides to shoot you."

Joe dropped the gun like a hot potato, but kept the chief well away from it.

When the two boys saw who was walking alongside the strike force's commander, their jaws dropped. "Dad!" they shouted together.

"Hello, sons," a grinning Fenton Hardy said. "I thought I was going to get to rescue you this time, but it looks like I'm a little late. Your friend Phil got me up in the middle of the night with a wild story about you sending him somebody's secret files, and I've been flying ever since."

"Dad," said Frank, "I don't even know what

happened here, but I think that maybe Joe has some explaining to do."

Joe laughed at his brother's amazement, as well as at the sight of the chief being herded into the corral with the rest of his men. He groped inside his pants pocket and pulled out what looked like a miniature walkie-talkie. "Well, when I spotted this in the chief's armory, I figured that if we ran into any real trouble during our escape, we could bluff our way out with this radio detonator."

Joe stopped for a moment to look at his father and the brother who had been through so much with him. A wide grin spread across his face as he continued, "And I figured it would work even better if it wasn't a bluff, so I rigged a whole case of plastic explosives to go off if I pressed the button. I think that everything in the place went off instead."

Frank peered at his brother, not yet certain whether he was serious. "Why didn't you tell me about that thing? We could have been blown to bits!"

"Frank," Joe said a little heatedly, "we were *about* to be blown to—"

"Calm down, guys. You can argue later. Right now, there's a gentleman over here who'd like to meet you and thank you." Fenton Hardy took one son under each arm and walked the two of them over to the lead helicopter. Sitting inside was a dignified gentleman in his late fifties. He introduced himself to them as General Juan Rodriguez of the Special Forces.

"Gentlemen," he began in his softly accented English, "I bring you personal greetings from my president. We have known about this place for some time, but were unable to move against it. You have cured a cancer on our land."

He stepped out of the chopper to survey the ranch. As he turned, staring intently at the charred rubble that had been the beautiful ranch house, at the toppled locomotive and the smoking ruin of the ranch's rolling stock, he muttered, "But we did expect to get to help in the treatment."

"General," Frank said inquiringly, "how did the chief get away with this for so long?"

"Frank," the general said with a sigh, "men are weak when it comes to money. I am certain that we will discover that a number of our young officers currently in the field have been corrupted."

"Sir," Joe said, thinking of the captain in the jungle with his juicy steaks, "there may not be all that many bad apples in your barrel. But we can show you one very bad one." He smiled at the thought of that man's arrest.

"But if you couldn't shut down the chief before," asked Frank, "why now?"

"Did you read any of the computer files you sent out to Phil?" Fenton asked his son. "They were dynamite—economic, social, and political dynamite for this country and a number of others. The chief had been using them for blackmail or simply selling the information he got out of these men to the highest bidder. The underworld railway was an equal-opportunity corrupter."

"Let me finish this part of the story," interjected the general. "One of the files that your father shared with me detailed not only the fact that the ranch was the major source of arms for the rebels who have been plaguing our country for years, but also that many of their raids had been planned at this very ranch. One of those raids cost the life of my wife." The general stopped for a moment to collect himself. "So I thank you as much as my country thanks you."

"It looks like all you have to worry about now," said Joe, trying to lighten the mood, "is whether you have enough jail cells for all these guys."

The general smiled. He took one more look around and then silently, seriously shook hands with each of the boys. "Now, my young friends, the least that my country and I can do to repay you is to put you on a helicopter and then onto a plane and fly you home for Christmas."

As soon as he said the word "Christmas," Frank clapped his hand to his forehead. "Ouch!" he said. "I just thought of something."

"What's that?" the general asked, concerned. It was apparent that he was worried that some essential part of the case that they were building was missing. Perhaps one of the important crooks had gotten away.

"Christmas!" said Frank. "Joe and I still haven't done any of our Christmas shopping!"

Joe was the first to grin in relief, followed by the other two.

"Son," said Fenton Hardy, "don't worry. There are still four more shopping days. And besides, this Christmas I think that we'll all be happy with the gift you've already given us—the two of you back home and alive."

The Borgia Dagger

Chapter

1

FRANK HARDY'S EYES widened. "Watch out!" he shouted. He ran to stop Callie Shaw before she took another step. With catlike reflexes, he sprang after her. Whipping his arm around her, he pulled her back just in time.

"Wh-what are you doing?" Callie sputtered as she stumbled backward over the dirt path and clutched Frank. She looked around for the unknown menace. But all she noticed was the swaying of the rushes in the wind, and the silver blue surface of the river as it raced by.

Frank loosened his grip. With a sigh of relief, he cast his glance down to a spot on the ground. "It's poison ivy," he said. "You just missed stepping in it."

Callie looked at him in disbelief. *"Poison ivy?"* she cried. "You scared me like that because of a little poison ivy? I thought we were in danger of losing our lives or something!"

1

"Well, poison ivy isn't a whole lot of fun, you know." Frank said, slightly embarrassed.

Callie straightened herself out and picked up the picnic basket she had dropped. "Frank, relax—you're not working today, okay? This is exactly why I wanted to have this picnic. I mean, here we are in this beautiful little forest with a river beside us—it's June, the sun is out, you're not working on a case right now, and"—she smiled up at him—"we're finally all alone."

"You're right," Frank said, gently wrapping his arms around his girlfriend. "I overreacted—a little. I guess I'm still jumpy from tracking down guerrillas in the jungles of Central America."

A breeze wafted past them, carrying the strong, sweet smell of honeysuckle. "I'm glad you're deciding to wind down, Frank," Callie said. "Sometimes I think you'll never learn how to relax."

Frank chuckled. "You don't need to worry about *that*, Callie."

"I wouldn't dream of doing anything right now," she answered, looking directly into his eyes.

"Next time," Frank whispered, returning her tender gaze, "I'll let you step right into the stuff."

Callie pushed herself away from him. "You really know how to sweet-talk a girl, don't you, Frank Hardy?"

Frank tried to choke back a laugh. "Oh, Callie, come on, I was kidding—"

"Very funny, Frank. I went through all the trouble to make sandwiches, then I found this remote spot fifteen miles from Bayport—"

Just then a loud voice rang out through the woods. "TOOOOO BEEEEEE, . . ."

"What's that?" Frank said.

"And all you can do is make fun of—" Callie suddenly stopped and listened.

"OR NOT TOOOO BEEEE; . . ."

"I don't know," she said. "Sounds like someone reciting poetry."

"THAAAT IS THE QUESTION: . . ."

"No—not poetry," Frank said, frowning as he thought. "It's from *Hamlet*—Act Three, Scene One, where Hamlet considers suicide."

"It's probably some frustrated actor sounding off. Let's see if we can find a quieter spot."

"Actually, that guy's voice sounds kind of strange. What do you think, Callie?"

They listened again to the booming voice.

"TO DIE, TO SLEEEEP—NO MORE! . . ."

"He does sound odd," Callie admitted. "But—"

"Come on, let's check it out," Frank interrupted, eagerly making his way down the hill toward the river. Reluctantly, Callie followed.

"FOR IN THAT SLEEP OF DEATH WHAT DREAMS MAY COME, . . ."

"Now he sounds *really* weird," Callie remarked as they followed a bend in the river.

Just ahead of them, an old wooden bridge drooped over the river. Its supports were cracked, and its rotting floorboards dangled in the air. On either end hung tattered strips of orange tape that had once stretched across the bridge to stop people from crossing.

It seemed that common sense alone would have prevented anyone from stepping onto the bridge—especially with the strong currents of the river below.

Just then Callie and Frank made out a dark figure in the sun's glare. A silver-haired man in black clothing stood in the middle of the bridge, facing away from them.

"FOR WHOOO WOULD BEAR THE WHIPS AND SCORNNNS OF TIIIME, . . ."

"He's a lunatic, Frank!" Callie whispered. "Listen to him!"

Frank picked up his pace as the man raised his arms upward. "I *am* listening. This is the part where Hamlet thinks of ending his life with—"

"WHEN HE HIMSELF MIGHT HIS QUIETUS MAKE WITH—"

"What's he got in his hand?" Callie asked.

"I can't tell—"

"A BARE BODKIN!"

"What's a bare bodkin?"

Frank burst into a sprint toward the bridge. "It's a dagger! This guy's serious!"

4

Callie immediately shouted, "Don't do it, sir! Everything will be all right!"

Startled, the man spun around to see the two of them running along the riverbank. His face was lined with wrinkles, and despite his look of utter weariness and despair, not a hair was out of place.

"Stay your futile efforts, foolish youths!" the man shouted. "All is lost; my time is at hand!"

With a sweeping gesture, he raised the dagger high and pointed it toward his own chest.

Frank could see there was no time to climb up to the man. He slid into the mud just under the end of the bridge.

"Into the great everlasting I commend my spirit!" the man bellowed, ready to plunge his knife downward.

"Noooooo!" Callie screamed.

At that moment Frank grabbed onto one of the bridge's broken supports and shook it with all his strength. The old bridge creaked and wobbled. Losing his balance, the man reached out with one hand to grab the railing. Splintering planks flew in all directions.

Then, with a *crack* that echoed all along the river, the wooden support gave way. One side of the bridge jerked down, and the man slid feet first on his stomach into the roaring current, his right hand still clutching the dagger.

A bloodcurdling scream sliced the air just before his silvery mane disappeared below the surface. Callie stared in horror as the current carried the man toward her.

"He's heading for the rocks!" she cried.

Gasping and flailing, the man lifted his head out of the water. "Help me! I can't swim!" he managed to sputter.

Instantly, both Frank and Callie dove in after him. The man bobbed up just above and then below the surface. He looked panic-stricken. Fighting the current, they caught up to him. Callie reached for his shoulders—only to be met by the gleaming blade of the dagger as it *whooshed* through the air, inches from her face.

"I can't get near him!" Callie shouted.

"You've got to calm down, sir!" Frank called out. "Just keep your arms still! You'll float long enough for me to bring you in!"

"I—can't—swim—" the man repeated, choking on silt-laden water. Frank realized the man was unable to help; he was blind with fear.

With a powerful lunge, Frank grabbed him around the chest. The man kicked and thrashed even harder, waving the knife in his hand.

"Watch it!" yelled Callie.

Keeping his right arm around the man, Frank reached across and grasped the man's right forearm with his free hand. He jammed his thumb into a pressure point on the wrist and swung the man's arm upward. The dagger flew into the air and plopped into the river ten feet upstream.

By then the man was beginning to lose strength.

As Frank struggled to swim with him, Callie glanced up and was startled to see a line of jagged rocks only fifty feet away.

"You have to let him go, Frank," Callie said. "We'll never get away in time!"

"He's unconscious! Help me out!"

Straining with the effort, Callie swam to Frank and grabbed one of the man's arms. Together, they slowly towed him to the riverbank, narrowly missing the rocks.

They laid the man's limp body on the wet ground. After a minute of Frank's mouth-to-mouth resuscitation, the man suddenly coughed and came to.

"Wha—where—" he sputtered, trying to focus his eyes. "I'm alive, aren't I?"

"You survived without a scratch," Frank said. "Looked like you were having a rough time up there, huh?"

" 'A rough time,' he says," the man muttered. His voice was weak but full of anger. "Oh, callow, fallow youth—you do still believe in the unquestioned perseverance of life at any cost, don't you?"

"Wait a minute," Frank said firmly. "Let's have it slowly, and in English. Who are you, and what were you doing up there?"

"*I* am a troubled man, sir," the stranger answered, throwing back his head in a grand gesture as Callie helped him to sit up. "Tyrone Grant is the name." He dropped his gaze downward and nodded sadly. "Yes, *the* Tyrone Grant of the stage and screen. Don't be shocked."

Hearing nothing but silence from Frank and Callie, he looked up to see their blank stares. "I can see you don't frequent the art movie houses, do you?"

Frank and Callie shook their heads.

"Just as well. I'd shatter your image of me. Now I'd like to ask *you* a question. Just what right do you have in trying to keep me from my task?"

"I don't care what you say, Mr. Grant," Callie said softly, "suicide is never the answer. Think of your family—"

Grant's steel gray eyes bored into Callie. "My family? You must mean that woman I was once married to, who left me for a Hollywood film editor!"

"I-I'm sorry to hear that," Callie said.

"Oh, I haven't even begun yet. There's not much work these days in 'quality' films, you know. I was barely paying the bills with my nonacting job—and now I've lost that, too! What does a man of my age and circumstances have to live for? What? What?" He looked around at the ground. "Where's my dagger?"

"I'm afraid it's in the river, Mr. Grant," Frank said. "Listen, why don't you let us give you a ride home? Maybe you should get some rest, think things over."

"That knife was a Grant family heirloom! I'll

sue! Not only do you rob me of the dignity of killing myself, but you save my life *and* throw away the most treasured possession. . . .''

Callie and Frank looked at each other and rolled their eyes. As they turned to climb the hill, they beckoned Grant to come with them.

Grant complained all the way, but he did follow them up the hill and through the woods to Callie's car. Callie pulled an old wool blanket out of the trunk and gave it to Grant to wrap around himself.

By the time Callie started the car, Grant was sobbing in the back seat.

"Please, Mr. Grant," Callie said. "I'm sure everything will work out. Why don't you tell me your address?"

"Ninety-four Lakeview Avenue!" he answered, brushing away tears with the back of his hand. "And if you insist on preserving my life, you could at least have the courtesy to give me a tissue!"

As Frank handed back a tissue, Callie entered a section of Bayport that was unfamiliar to her. Grant continued to complain as she drove through the outskirts of the city. Just past a bait-and-tackle store was a sharp bend in the road. Callie approached at thirty miles an hour.

"Slow down," Frank whispered. "You're driving too fast!"

Callie braked, gritting her teeth. She didn't usually drive fast, but this time she'd had enough.

Frank and she had risked their lives to save Grant's, and the actor wasn't the least bit grateful.

"And furthermore," Grant said, in a booming voice, "I would appreciate your *not* leaking this to the press!"

Abruptly Callie stopped the car and whirled around to face Grant.

"Mr. Grant!" she said sharply. "I've listened for long enough. Like it or not, we just saved your life. Now will you please . . ." she said, not finishing the thought as she pulled onto the street again.

Grant's face lost all its color as he stared silently past Callie and out the windshield. A minute later Frank grabbed the steering wheel of the car, which was entering a blind turn too quickly. "Callie, pay attention!" Frank shouted.

A blue flatbed truck whizzed around the corner, blowing its horn and just missing them.

"You see what you're making me do, Mr. Grant?" Callie said. They all breathed a sigh of relief, even Tyrone Grant, as Callie slowed the car for the turn.

And suddenly there, in the wrong lane, was a fiery red sports car convertible, hurtling straight toward them!

Chapter

2

"HANG ON!" CALLIE screamed as she yanked the steering wheel far to the right. The car swerved into a guardrail and bounced off, just as the sports car spun away from them, its tires squealing.

Crrrunch! A sickening noise filled the air as Callie pulled her car to a stop on the side of the road. Callie and Frank turned and saw the red car nudged up against a telephone pole.

"Are you all right?" Frank asked.

"Fine," Callie said. "I think we got the better end of the deal."

They both hopped out and ran to the other car. It was only dented in a bit in the front.

"I'm fine, too, you know!" Grant shouted after them. "What's become of your great concern for *my* life?"

As Frank and Callie approached the left door, it flew open. A shrill voice pierced the air:

11

THE HARDY BOYS CASEFILES

"Why don't you watch where you're driving?"
Brushing herself off, a tall redheaded girl of about
eighteen climbed out of the car. She adjusted her
three gold necklaces and smoothed down the
wrinkles on her tight jumpsuit. She shot a poison-
ous glare at Frank and Callie before putting on
her sunglasses. Then she walked over to Frank
and Callie. There was something very familiar
about her, Frank thought.

"Look what you've done to my Lamborghini!"
she cried out. "It's ruined!"

"Well, hardly that. I am awfully sorry about it,
though," Callie said. "But I think *you* were the
one—"

"Don't try to lay the blame on me! I—"

"Look," Frank interrupted, "the insurance
companies will settle it. You have to exchange
insurance information. The only important thing
now is, how are you?"

The redheaded girl sneered. "I *was* fine until
you came along. Now I have to call a cab and call
my garage—and I'm late enough as it is!"

She marched back to the driver's seat and
pulled a mobile phone out of the car. Frank tried
to remember where he'd seen her face before.

"Hello, Harley?" she said into the phone.
"Hello? I can't hear you. . . . Yes, it's me. . . .
Tessa! . . . Tessa! . . . What? . . ." With a
frustrated cry, she threw the phone back in the
car.

"It's broken!" she said. "What am I supposed to do now? Walk?"

Fighting an urge to tell her off, Callie said, "Well, my car is okay. Can I give you a ride?"

"Were *you* driving?" the girl asked bitterly.

"Yes."

"I'll go, but only if *he* drives," she said, waving a finger at Frank.

Callie shrugged her shoulders and headed back to her car, giving Frank a look of exasperation as she passed him.

Frank tried to take the girl's arm but she drew away. Throwing back her silky red hair, she walked toward Callie's car.

"By the way," Frank called after her, "aren't you Tessa Carpenter, the one I read about—"

"—in *Personality* magazine," Tessa said sarcastically, finishing Frank's sentence. "Yes, that's me. Ridiculous article, wasn't it? 'Bayport's poor little rich debutante—heiress to the famed Cliffside Mansion and the area's largest art collection . . . but how has she survived the tragic loss of her parents?' " She rolled her eyes. "*Now* I suppose you want to be my best friend, like everyone else."

I wouldn't dream of it, Frank thought to himself as they both climbed into the car. But to Tessa, he just chuckled and said, "No, no, I was just interested in your story. Seems like a huge place for one person to live."

After making her phone calls from a nearby

phone booth, Tessa climbed into the backseat cautiously, as if she were entering a garbage truck. "The Bayport Museum—and fast," she said to Frank.

By this time, Tyrone Grant had curled himself into a ball in his half of the backseat, wrapped from head to toe in the blanket Callie had given him. Tessa peered at him over her sunglasses. "You didn't put me back here with a sick person, did you?"

Grant's only reaction was to shift slightly under the blanket.

"Well, not exactly," Frank said. "He's okay, probably just exhausted. What's happening at the museum? Checking on the Carpenter collection?"

Tessa smirked. "Not checking on it. Taking it back."

"Really?" Frank said. "*Personality* says the collection makes up about half the museum!"

"They're wrong," Tessa answered dryly. "It's about sixty percent. But it all belongs to me now, and I've decided the paintings would spruce up the house."

I wonder what the curator says about this, Frank thought.

He soon found out. As they approached the museum, they noticed a group of five men gathered around a truck at the side of the building. Four of them wore plain gray uniforms and were trying to load large crates onto the truck. The fifth was a stocky man in a dark blue suit and wire-rimmed glasses. As the workmen brought the crates to the truck, the fifth man was shouting and gesturing angrily, his thinning blond hair flopping in front of his reddened face. It appeared that he was trying to keep the men from working.

"This is the last straw," Tessa muttered under her breath. "I have to talk to the fat guy," she said to Frank.

Frank drove up a circular driveway to the side of the museum and Tessa hopped out. "Albert, Albert," she said, shaking her head. "What *are* you doing to these poor men?"

The man wiped his brow with a handkerchief and pushed up his glasses. "Miss Carpenter, may I remind you that this artwork is on *permanent* loan to the museum—as per our agreement with your family, signed thirty years ago by your grandfather! As curator, I cannot let these out of my sight!"

Tessa nodded patiently. "Albert, you yourself said you couldn't find this so-called agreement, remember?"

"You've got to give me some time! After the fire last year, we moved all our old files to the warehouse upstate, and many things got mixed up—"

"Look," Tessa said, continuing, "you've seen a copy of my parents' will. The collection belongs to me now, and I want it back. Besides, don't

15

you think you've had these things long enough? Maybe it's time to redecorate."

"*Redecorate?* Young lady, we are talking about a museum, not a bedroom! These are priceless paintings and sculptures—the museum is nothing without them!"

Tessa let out a lighthearted laugh. "Oh, please don't take it so seriously! You should just be glad you had them for so long!"

"Glad we had them! Why, your actions are illegal. Your parents would never have allowed this."

As the man stammered in shock, one of the workmen tried to push past him. "Come on, Mr. Ruppenthal, this stuff is heavy. Listen to the girl."

"Over my dead body," Ruppenthal said, shoving the workman back.

Thrown off balance, the workman fell onto the ground. "Okay, buster," he said as he picked himself up, "if you say so."

With that, he let loose with an uppercut that caught Ruppenthal squarely in the jaw. After Ruppenthal fell, three museum officials rushed out of the building to come to his aid. One of them sank a fist into the workman's stomach, sending him flying into a crate.

Rubbing his jaw, Ruppenthal yelled, "Watch it, Felipe! That's the Rodin statue!"

Instantly a melee broke out—workmen against

museum staff. Ruppenthal darted around, trying to move the artwork out of the way.

Frank watched the scene in amazement. "I'm going to try to stop this! You call Joe from the corner pay phone!" he said to Callie, and he ran toward the fight.

. He pulled Felipe off one of the workmen. Then he spun around just in time to see another workman running toward him with his fists balled.

"I don't believe we've met," Frank said, extending his right hand. The workman uncorked a haymaker, which Frank easily ducked, sending the man tumbling.

"Ease up, fellas, let's talk this over!" Frank shouted to no avail. A museum worker jumped on him from behind, trying to wrestle him to the ground. But Frank remained upright, lifting the man off his feet and hurling him in the direction of Tessa, who was watching wide-eyed while backing away toward Callie's car.

Within moments came a welcome sound—the high-pitched wail of a police siren. Frank looked up the driveway to see two familiar sights—the patrol car of Officer Con Riley and the Hardy brothers' black van.

"All right, boys, playtime is over!" Officer Riley's voice barked over the patrol car's megaphone. The men all let go of one another and tried to look as nonchalant as possible.

Officer Riley, his partner, and Callie walked up

to the scene. They were followed by Frank's brother Joe, who had hopped out of the van.

"All right, Ruppenthal," Officer Riley said. "What happened here? Does this have to do with the Carpenter items?"

"That's right, Officer," Ruppenthal answered. "These men are forcibly trying to remove this artwork!"

"Or are you 'forcibly' trying to prevent them?" said Officer Riley with a knowing look. "Miss Carpenter already called me about this. I'm afraid that unless you can produce an agreement that says the artwork belongs to you, you'll have to let these men do their job."

"But—but—"

"You can protest all you want in court, my friend. Not here."

As Ruppenthal and Officer Riley argued, Joe joined his brother. He glanced around at the group of burly men, all of whom were now disheveled.

Joe whistled in awe and ran his fingers through his blond hair. "Whew, looks like I missed a big one," he said. "How was it?"

"Fine," said Frank with a smile, massaging a bruised arm. "But we missed you."

With a mischievous grin and a gleam in his blue eyes, Joe moved closer to his brother and said softly, "By the way, who's the redhead in the jumpsuit?"

Frank chuckled. "Believe me, you wouldn't be—"

Suddenly a loud scream ripped through the conversation. All heads turned to the end of the driveway.

There, up against Callie's car, Tessa Carpenter was frozen in fear. Around her neck was a pair of hands. Her body shook as the strangler repeatedly slammed her against the car.

Frank and Joe raced up the driveway, with Callie right behind. "It's Grant!" she cried out in disbelief. "He's trying to kill Tessa!"

Chapter

3

WHILE FRANK WENT to help Tessa, Joe grabbed Grant by his still-soggy collar and pulled him backward. "Tessa, are you okay?" Frank asked.

"I'm—fine," Tessa said with both hands on her throat. "Just a little dizzy."

"I've had enough, Tessa Carpenter!" Grant shouted, gesturing wildly at Tessa. "I had hoped to escape your mocking glance for good! But no—still you torment me!"

Frank slid in front of Tessa, who cowered in fright. Grant tried to lunge for her again, pulling against Joe's tight grip. Within seconds, Officer Riley and his partner arrived. They yanked Grant away and slapped handcuffs on him. Callie and Joe stood by Frank.

"Forgive me, Officer," Grant said, his voice cracking with emotion. "She has forced me to do things I'd never dreamed of!"

When Officer Riley had a good look at Grant,

his face lit up. "Say, aren't you the fella in the new flick? What's it called—*Horror High School III?*"

Grant turned red and looked at the ground. "A cameo role," he said, grimacing.

Frank turned to Tessa. "Sure you're okay?"

Tessa leaned against Frank's broad chest to steady herself. "Yes, I think so," she said faintly. She glanced up at him, her eyes filled with relief and admiration. "Thanks to you."

Joe rubbed his hand. The outline of human teeth—Grant's teeth—was beginning to rise up in a welt. Great, he thought, I get rabies, and Frank walks off with the glory. "It was nothing!" he called out. "We're happy to help you—"

Tessa just looked at him blankly and turned back to Frank. "How can I possibly repay you for saving me from that horrible man—"

"I heard that, Tessa!" Grant called out. "Funny how your opinion of me has changed over the years!"

"Calm down, Mr. Grant," Frank said. He looked back at Tessa. "You *know* this man?"

Tessa gave Grant an icy stare. "You bet I do. And his name isn't Grant either. It's Edwin Squinder. He used to work for my parents—"

"Bless their souls! I don't know how those two marvelous people could have created a monster like her," Squinder said. "For twenty years I was their chauffeur—on call, day and night. But was I unhappy? No! The Carpenters treated me like

21

family! I lived on the grounds of the mansion—
even took care of Tessa when she was little. For
them, I gladly gave up a promising career in the
theater!" He looked squarely into Tessa's eyes.
"And in return, they left her money to retain me
for life!"

"Your act isn't working, Edwin," Tessa said.
She shook her head with scorn and turned to the
others. "How could I retain someone who
couldn't do his job? Who spent day and night in
front of the TV set, imitating actors in old movies?"

"Who refused to drive you to parties on his
one night off a week! That's all it was!" Squinder
shouted. "A year ago she fired me—and all her
other servants—because she's spent almost all
her inheritance on clothes, cars, wild parties—"

"Okay, okay, enough of this," Officer Riley
said. "Miss, do you want to press charges?"

Squinder suddenly looked frightened. "Please,
Tessa. If you have a heart, don't do it. You know
I'm not a violent man. I just—flew off the handle.
Times have been rough."

Tessa sighed. "No, Officer, I can't be bothered. I think Mr. Squinder will know better than
to mess with me again."

Officer Riley looked surprised, but let go of
Squinder and unlocked the handcuffs on his
wrists. "If you say so."

"Thank you," Squinder said softly. He

brushed himself off, lifted his chin high, and walked away.

"I'm not sure we should let him go," Frank said. "A few hours ago he was about to commit suicide."

Tessa nodded. "I'm not surprised. He does this every few months—but only when he knows people are around to stop him. It's his eccentric way of dealing with his failure as an actor. He's crazy, but harmless."

When Squinder was out of sight, Officer Riley said, "I don't like the looks of him. Be sure to call us right away if there's any more trouble. Frank, I think you or your brother ought to give Miss Carpenter a ride home." With a smile and a wink, he tipped his cap and walked back to the squad car with his partner.

Callie thought she sensed a special meaning behind Officer Riley's wink, and she wasn't so sure she liked it. Especially when she caught a glimpse of the way Tessa was looking at Frank.

"You know, Frank," Tessa said, flashing a warm smile, "you handled Squinder beautifully. And I just couldn't believe how you singlehandedly took on all those men by the truck!"

"It was nothing," Frank mumbled, feeling uncomfortable under Callie's burning gaze.

"Listen," Tessa went on, touching Frank's hand, "I'm having a big party tonight in my house—sort of a celebration for the arrival of the artwork. I'd *love* for you to come!"

Frank cleared his throat and cast a nervous glance at Joe and Callie. "Oh!" Tessa said, following Frank's glance. "You can bring your friends too."

At that, Joe stepped forward with a broad smile and an outstretched hand. "I'm Joe Hardy, Tessa—Frank's brother."

"Nice to meet you," Tessa replied. "And is this your sister?"

Callie looked as though a chill had shot through her. "No," she said dryly, "I'm just the driver."

"This is Callie Shaw," Frank added quickly. "She's—"

Joe could barely contain himself. "We'd be happy to come to your party, Tessa! Listen, I'm free right now. Can I give you a ride home?"

Tessa's smile fell slightly, and she looked over at Frank, as if expecting him to offer her a ride too.

Feeling relieved, Frank said, "Thanks, Joe. I'll go with Callie. See you later." He headed after Callie, who was already walking to her car, while Joe flirted with Tessa on the way to the van.

" 'And is this your sister?' " Callie said, mocking Tessa's voice. "Sorry, Frank, I can't help it, she makes me furious! Did you catch the way she was looking at you?"

Frank put his arm around Callie. "I know," he said. "She's obviously spoiled rotten. But don't worry about me. It's Joe who seems to be falling for her."

Callie took out her keys as Frank went around to the passenger side of her car. "Yeah, but she definitely has her eye on you. Did you see how disappointed she looked when she knew Joe was taking her home?"

"But, Callie, don't you see? It doesn't matter!" They sank into the car's bucket seats, and Frank leaned over to Callie with a glowing smile. "This man has eyes for only one ravishing beauty—you!"

Callie started to put the key in the steering column, but stopped when Frank brought his face closer and gave her a kiss. At that moment, Tessa Carpenter faded from memory.

"I'm sorry, Frank," Callie said. "I guess I'm just upset that our day together had to be spoiled like this."

"I'll make it up to you, Callie, I promise. Next Saturday we'll—"

"I was thinking of something sooner than next Saturday," Callie said eagerly. "Why don't we go see a movie tonight?"

Frank looked at her blankly. "Tonight? Well— we can't."

"Why not?"

"Did you forget? We've been invited to a party."

"Party?" Callie had no idea what he meant. Then it dawned on her. "You mean at Tessa's?"

"Well, yeah!" Frank said with a shrug. "I mean, we agreed. It might be fun—"

Callie's face clouded over. She started the car and pushed her foot down on the accelerator. Frank fell back in his seat.

"Fine," she said, glaring straight ahead. "You go ahead. *I* have other plans."

"Why so glum, chum? This party's going to be the hottest ticket in town!" Joe called out from the bathroom as he stood in front of the mirror, combing his hair.

Frank yanked on good black socks and stared at the bedroom carpet. "I don't know, Joe, I just can't get excited about it." He plopped himself down on the bed and flipped through a copy of *Personality* magazine that Joe had left lying open.

"Well, you won't believe her house." Joe leaned into the room and gestured with his comb. "When I drove her home she told me to go up this narrow road through the woods—only it turned out not to be a road, but her *driveway*! At the end there was this enormous brick mansion— a lawn the size of a football field, servants' cottage, in-ground pool—"

"Hmm. There's a picture of it here in the magazine."

"Right. And that's not even the best part— read the section about the Borgia Dagger," Joe said, walking into the bedroom.

"The what?" Frank flipped through the pages and saw the headline: HEIRESS INHERITS CARPEN-

TER COLLECTION—INCLUDING DEADLY BORGIA DAGGER!

"Part of that museum collection," explained Joe, "is a jeweled knife that once belonged to this sinister Italian family about four hundred years ago. They were all religious and military leaders, but they were also cold-blooded murderers! Legend has it that the dagger Tessa has is cursed."

"What kind of curse?"

Joe continued in a low, creepy voice. "The owner of the dagger will die within a few months of having touched it." He opened his eyes wide and let out a deep, diabolical laugh. "Yaaaa-haaa-haaa-haa—"

Abruptly Joe ducked and just missed being hit by the rolled-up copy of *Personality* that Frank had hurled at him.

Approaching the mansion in the dark, even Frank was impressed. Four pointed spires rose from the roof like the towers of a castle. A porch, shrubbery and flower beds surrounded it, and a rolling lawn stretched far into woods in all directions. There were no other houses visible. Loud music echoed through the night air and lights glared from four bay windows on the first floor.

They parked the van and walked inside. Immediately Joe felt that his blue suit wasn't right. There seemed to be two types of guests: One type wore expensive tuxedos and evening gowns. The other type wore more casual clothing, but Joe

27

could immediately tell it was just as expensive. Standing among them, a wiry man scribbled notes on a small yellow pad.

"Probably a society columnist," Joe whispered to Frank.

"It's Frank and Joe! Come on in!" Tessa's voice floated toward them over the noise of the crowd. From behind a group of laughing people, she emerged.

Frank thought Joe's jaw would drop off. Tessa wore a slinky, full-length gown with silver sequins and high-heeled silver shoes. She grabbed both of their hands and pulled them toward a tall, dimpled guy with dark brown hair. He was about six-foot-one and eighteen years old, same age and height as Frank—only he looked as though he had just stepped out of a movie.

"Frank and Joe Hardy, meet Harley Welles." Harley's teeth were blindingly white as he grinned and said hello.

Next to Harley was a tiny, white-haired woman who looked about fifty years older than anyone else in the room. Her gray-green eyes twinkled behind thick glasses as Tessa introduced her. "And this," Tessa said, "is my very dearest friend, Dr. Harriet Lansdale. I've known her longer than anyone in the world."

Dr. Lansdale's shoulder shook as she chuckled. "That's because I delivered her!" she said. "Welcome to Cliffside Heights. I hope the two of you will come back in the daytime to see the grounds someday. Tessa has lovely gardens.''

''Aunt Harriet is semiretired,'' Tessa said. ''She works only part-time now, at the Cliffside Country Club—the rest of the time she spends gardening. Here and at her own home.''

Frank nodded and looked around. They were in a huge parlor, its walls crammed with gold-framed paintings. A towering marble statue of a Greek warrior stretched to the ceiling in a corner between a bookcase and a sideboard.

Just then the doorbell rang. ''Harley, be a dear and go into the kitchen for some more cups! Excuse me,'' Tessa said, and she went to open the door.

''Come and look at the collection,'' Dr. Lansdale said, leading the way for Frank and Joe to follow. ''Personally, I'm trying to convince her to return everything, but we might as well appreciate it while it's here.''

Joe looked longingly at the buffet table that stretched across the middle of the room and ended near the Greek statue. They were moving toward the old sideboard.

Three teenagers dressed in fringed leather jackets were standing around a glass case resting on top of the dark carved-wood piece.

''Excuse me, Muffy,'' Dr. Lansdale said to one of the girls in the group. They parted as the doctor edged up, pointing to the glass case. Inside

29

it, on a purple satin cushion, was a long knife that reflected the light off its gold-and-jeweled handle.

"Here's the centerpiece of the collection," Dr. Lansdale continued, "the Borgia Dagger that you've probably read about."

"Oh, wow, it is incredible!" Muffy said, lifting up the lid of the case and taking out the dagger.

Suddenly a voice bellowed, "See what I mean? Look at that—they think it's a toy!"

Frank and Joe turned to see Albert Ruppenthal rushing across the room, followed by Tessa. Ruppenthal grabbed the dagger from Muffy and put it back on the satin cushion.

"I really didn't mean to interrupt, Miss Carpenter," Ruppenthal said. "I thought I'd come over, apologize, and quietly try to persuade you to give back the collection—but this is outrageous!" He glanced at the dagger, which was now being examined by several other guests. "Do you realize how much that dagger is worth?"

Tessa smiled sweetly. "Of course I do, Albert!" She picked it up, and a hush fell over the room as, carrying it, she sauntered over to the buffet table.

Timidly, one of the teenagers said, "Tessa, remember the curse on that thing! If the owner touches it, it's curtains!"

Tessa threw back her head in defiant laughter. She turned to Ruppenthal, pointing at him with the dagger. "Albert, you look hungry. Would you like an appetizer?"

The Borgia Dagger

Ruppenthal's face went white with shock as Tessa sliced into a wedge of cheese with the Borgia Dagger. She stabbed the tip of the blade into the slice she had cut, then walked back to the sideboard and offered the cheese to the curator with a mocking smile.

A split second later the lights went out, and the music cut off in midsong. All the partygoers held their breath in a silence that seemed to last forever.

Then came a crash and a scream—Tessa's scream.

Chapter
4

THE LIGHTS CAME back on, and Frank and Joe stared at the marble statue—or rather, at its pieces on the floor. Part of the sideboard was splintered, and shards from shattered glassware lay all around.

And crouched under the sideboard, the Borgia dagger still in her hand, was Tessa, her face white with shock.

Frank, Joe, and Dr. Lansdale knelt down beside her. "Did the statue hit you?" Joe asked, his voice edged with concern.

Ruppenthal stood gaping over the statue. "Twenty-three hundred years old . . ." he murmured as tears formed in the corners of his eyes.

Tessa was shaking with fright. She looked past Joe and saw Frank. With a choked sob, she let go of the dagger and stood up and threw her arms around him. "Oh, Frank, I was almost killed!"

The crowd started to murmur. Smothered by

Tessa's embrace, Frank said, "Well, you seem to be okay. Why don't you just—uh, sit back and relax a little." As Tessa let go, Frank looked around uncomfortably.

"Mind if someone tells me what's going on here?" a voice said from above.

Frank looked up to see Harley towering over him. This time the glittery smile was gone, replaced by tightly pursed lips.

"Looks to me like an accident," Frank replied.

"I—I can't figure it out, Harley," Tessa said. "There was a blackout, and someone must have knocked over the Roman statue—"

"Greek!" Ruppenthal cried, now sitting on the floor with his head in his hands.

Harley knelt down and helped Tessa over to a sofa, while Joe quietly picked up the dagger and put it back in the glass case, which was mercifully spared.

Dr. Lansdale, who had disappeared, returned with a dampened towel. She sat next to Tessa and put it on her forehead. All around them, guests from the party gathered.

Holding Tessa's hand, Dr. Lansdale smiled and said, "You know, if I were a superstitious person, I'd think this incident was connected to that silly Borgia curse." She looked at the concerned faces around her and chuckled. "And I see I'm not the only one who's thought of it."

Tessa swallowed nervously. Beads of sweat

collected on her brow. "What do you know about the curse, Aunt Harriet?"

"Dear child, I really don't think you ought to worry about it."

"Oh, please," Tessa said. "Maybe if I hear how silly it is, I *won't* worry."

Dr. Lansdale sighed. "Well, if you insist." She sat back and fell silent, as if trying to remember the details. The guests all gathered closer around her.

"I must say it's a rather gruesome tale. The Borgias were one of the wealthiest and most influential families in Italy around the turn of the sixteenth century—and there were bound to be a few black sheep among them." She nodded slowly. "Well, the history books don't record it, but legend says that the worst one, the one whose name caused people to shake with fear, was Armando Borgia. He was a nephew of the duke, and he had an interesting collection in his basement— a collection of bodies."

Joe noticed a shudder run through Tessa. Dr. Lansdale placed her hand on Tessa's and said, "Oh, honey, you look petrified. I didn't mean for this silly old wives' tale to scare you. I'll stop."

"No, go on!" Tessa pleaded. "Maybe if I hear about it, it won't seem so scary."

Joe could see the tension on Tessa's face. He knew it would only be worse if Dr. Lansdale continued. "Maybe you'd better not," he said into her ear.

"It's all right, Joe," Dr. Lansdale answered. "I understand your concern, but sometimes this is the best treatment for fear." She turned back to Tessa. "Now then, this Armando Borgia was supposedly the cruelest landowner in Italy. He purposely charged rents that were outrageous in order to keep the peasants weak and overworked. They wouldn't be able to rebel then. He married several women, only to cast each wife into the street when he tired of her—including Marisol Allegra—a breathtaking Spanish-Italian beauty by all accounts, of noble blood, young, trusting—"

"Tell me about the dagger, Aunt Harriet," Tessa said, shaking.

"Yes, of course. You see, Armando rarely left his palace and gardens—but when he did one day, he was shocked to see the streets full of dirty, homeless beggars. Of course, he was the one who had forced them to live like that because they couldn't afford his rents. But to Armando, they were nothing more than human garbage— garbage to be gotten rid of."

"So he killed them?" Tessa asked.

"One by one," Dr. Lansdale said, "he invited the beggars into the palace. He allowed them to wash up and eat until they could hold no more. Most were tearful with gratitude—and then they were invited to see the wine cellar.

"They never came back up.

"It is said that Armando disposed of each of

them with one quick plunge of his jeweled dagger to the victim's heart. The bodies were stacked neatly in the cellar and left there until the end of the week, when they were buried in a single pauper's grave.''

Out of the corner of his eye, Frank noticed the society columnist furiously taking notes.

"No one caught on," Dr. Lansdale said. "All people noticed was that the streets were becoming free of beggars."

Suddenly Dr. Lansdale's voice became softer. All of the guests leaned closer to hear.

"One night, as Armando was half-asleep, his door was pushed open. Thinking it was a servant, he just grumbled and turned over.

"But it wasn't a servant. One of his victims had been lying in the cellar—the knife had just missed her heart—alive. With her last ounce of strength, she had dragged herself up to Armando's bedroom, and found the blood-stained dagger.''

"Well, that's ridiculous," Tessa said. "How could she have known where to go? . . ." Tessa cut herself off as she realized the answer.

"That's right, Tessa," Dr. Lansdale said. "The beggar woman was Marisol, one of Armando's wives. Not even Armando had recognized her, so changed was she after having been forced into the street. Poverty and wretchedness had driven her to insanity.

"With the life flowing out of her, Marisol flung

36

open the bedroom shutters, letting in the light of the full moon. And as she raised the dagger over Armando's bed, she screamed his name so loud they say it shattered the windows in the room."

By now the parlor had become so quiet, Frank could hear the beating of his own heart.

"When a servant found them both slumped on the bed, Armando's eyes were wide with the horror of recognition—and the letter *B* had been drawn on his forehead in blood.

"From that day on, the legend goes, whoever takes possession of the dagger dies mysteriously within four months of having touched it."

Dr. Landsdale shrugged her shoulders and gave a small laugh. "Well, aren't you all grim! Don't you see how absurd the story is? I mean, after all, the museum has had this dagger for decades, and no one has died mysteriously—isn't that so, Mr. Ruppenthal?"

Ruppenthal loosened his collar and looked at the floor. "Well—uh, to tell you the truth, no one ever dared touch it while it was at the museum."

Tessa moved to get off the couch, but swayed dangerously. "Aunt Harriet, would you please show the guests out? I think I'd better stay here," she said.

"Of course, sweetheart. But please don't take this thing so seriously. I hope I haven't made matters worse."

"We'll stay awhile, help with things," Joe said eagerly.

Frank narrowed his eyes at his brother. "Thanks a lot, pal," he murmured.

The first guest to go was Ruppenthal, who stormed off in anger. Dr. Lansdale went to the front door and said goodbye to everyone quietly as they left the mansion.

Frank and Joe helped the hired help carry dishes to the kitchen for a half hour, and when they were done, Tessa was still on the couch, fast asleep. They tiptoed out the front door and onto the porch. "Were you hoping to be hired as a butler or something?" Frank asked.

But Joe was deep in thought. "That was the weirdest story I ever heard," he said.

"Well, something about it smells a little funny to me."

"Like the fact that everything was normal before Ruppenthal got there?"

"Yes. And also how Dr. Lansdale wouldn't stop telling that crazy story, even when she knew Tessa was scared out of her wits."

"Well, I tried to get her to stop—" Joe cut himself short, his eyes focused beyond the side of the house.

"What is it, Joe?"

"Shh. The servants' cottage!"

Frank wheeled around to see a dark figure climbing out of the cottage window. "He's heading toward the front of the house," Frank whispered. "Let's give him a surprise." The brothers quietly sneaked down the front stairs and ducked behind the surrounding bushes.

"Do you think he saw us?" Joe whispered.

"We'll find out soon enough," Frank answered.

He was right. As they carefully peered around the side of the house, they froze.

Inches from their faces was the muzzle of a silver-plated revolver.

"Gentlemen, to what do I owe the pleasure of our meeting?" Stepping out of the shadows, his finger poised over the trigger of the gun, was Edwin Squinder.

Chapter

5

"I WOULDN'T RECOMMEND pulling that trigger," Joe said calmly, his hands in the air.

"Spoken bravely," Squinder said. "Now let me give you *my* recommendation. You had better not say a word to Tess—"

"Who's there?" Tessa's voice called out from above the stairs.

Frank and Joe looked up to the tops of their raised hands. They heard a door open, then Tessa's face appeared over them, peering down from the porch. "What in heaven's—Edwin, put down the gun!"

"Never!" Squinder said. "Never again shall I be a slave to your every whim!"

Harley appeared beside Tessa at the top of the stairs. He rolled his eyes when he saw Squinder. "Ease up, Edwin," he said.

"And as for your snide boyfriend—" Squinder continued.

"We all know how you feel, Edwin," Tessa said patiently. She walked down the stone steps with her hand out. "Now will you give me that before I have you arrested for trespassing and stealing?"

"Stealing?" Squinder answered. "Your father *gave* me this gun, and I was foolish enough to leave it here when I was forced off the premises. I only came back here to reclaim what is rightfully mine!" He pointed the revolver at his head. "The only person this gun was meant to hurt is myself. And this time I will not be foiled in my attempt—"

"Well, it may help if you buy some bullets," Tessa said. "First of all, my father *lent* you that gun, to scare away robbers—it was never loaded. Second, what was once my father's is now mine. Third, you're already on thin ice with the police after this afternoon. So,"—she reached out, with her palm up—"if you please?"

Squinder's eyes darted from side to side.

"Give it to her and go home, Edwin," Harley said, joining them at the foot of the stairs. "You need some rest."

Finally Squinder lowered the revolver. "Very well," he said, his voice trembling, "I shall return to the miserable little flat I have been calling a home—and lie awake thinking of other ways to escape the bitter life to which I have been doomed!"

With a grand gesture, he placed the revolver in Tessa's hand and strode away.

As Squinder disappeared down the driveway, Joe said to Tessa, "Will you be all right here alone? We could—"

"She won't be alone," Harley snapped. "Dr. Lansdale and I will stay here tonight. Tomorrow we'll make sure she spends the day relaxing at the club. Tessa will be well taken care of, thank you."

"Okay, fine," Frank said, pulling his brother away from the house. "Good night, Tessa. Thanks for inviting us."

"My pleasure," Tessa called back. "Be sure to come by again, anytime!"

Frank and Joe climbed into the van. "Do you think she really meant that, about coming by anytime?" Joe asked as he started the engine.

"Haven't you had enough of her and her snooty friends, Joe? She's definitely not your type."

"That's not what I mean! I think we have a case here. It's obvious someone has it in for Tessa."

Frank nodded thoughtfully as the van rolled down the driveway. "You're right. And I put Squinder high on the list of suspects. I don't think he's as flaky as he lets on."

"Right. I mean, he's probably the only person who knows where to find the fuse box in order to kill the lights—and I thought his alibi about re-claiming the gun was pretty lame."

"There's only one problem," Frank said. "There must have been two people—one to turn off the lights and the other to push the statue. And I have an idea who the other one is—"

They looked at each other and said at the same time, "Ruppenthal!"

As they drove back to their parents' house, Frank and Joe tossed around a couple of questions: Would Ruppenthal *really* have destroyed a valuable work of art just to scare Tessa? And if Squinder were to blame, why didn't he flee immediately after the incident?

There were far more questions than answers. And although they wouldn't admit it to each other, one thought was nagging at both of them: Maybe it was useless even to wonder. Maybe the curse of the Borgia dagger wasn't an old wives' tale after all.

"I suppose I'll forgive you, Frank," Callie said with a smile. "But for a bright guy, you can be pretty thoughtless sometimes!"

"Guilty as charged," Frank replied. "But I'm changing!" He jumped out of his chair and ran over to his parents' refrigerator. "Can I get you some fruit juice, some leftover ham?"

Callie laughed. "There's enough ham in this room already!"

Frank sat back down at the kitchen table. He

shrugged his shoulders and said, "I may have done a thoughtless thing last night, but you have to admit we stumbled into an interesting case."

"Okay, I admit it! From what you've said, both Squinder and Ruppenthal seem pretty suspicious to me. And I'm not so sure that old woman doctor is as innocent as she sounds."

"With someone like Tessa, you never know how many people might have a grudge against her."

"Well, to be honest, Frank, I really think you should keep your distance. I mean, no one has asked you to do anything, after all. And I have a feeling that hanging around Tessa Carpenter will bring you nothing but trouble."

"Maybe . . ." Frank said absentmindedly.

Just then Joe came into the kitchen. "Oh, hi, Callie! You ready to hit the road, Frank?"

"I think so. Callie just stopped by; we were having a talk."

"Where are you guys going?" Callie asked.

Frank and Joe exchanged glances. "Um, well . . ." Frank said, adjusting his collar. "We thought we'd go to the museum—"

Callie's eyes narrowed. She folded her arms. "I see," she said. "Anything there in particular you wanted to see? Or should I say, any*one?*"

Both Frank and Joe started to speak at once, but Callie cut them off.

"I know, you don't want to mention any names, but the initials are Albert Ruppenthal's,

44

right? You'd rather spend time with this Tessa Carpenter case than with me!''

"That's not it, Callie, really—" Frank said.

Callie smiled. "I know. I'm just giving you grief. I know you won't be satisfied unless you follow up this hunch."

Frank grinned. "I'll make it up to you—why don't we see a movie this evening? Something *you* want to see!"

"Great." As Joe scooted out the door, Callie grabbed Frank's hand and gave it a squeeze. "I *do* feel better after our talk," she whispered. "Thanks."

They all went out the front door, Callie to her car and the brothers to the waiting van.

The Hardys smiled and waved to Callie as she drove away.

"I'm surprised she didn't want to help out," Joe said as soon as Callie was out of sight.

Frank grinned and shook his head. "Not this case. I have a feeling Callie's not *too* concerned about whatever happens to Tessa."

"I guess you're right," Joe said. He put the van in gear. "Next stop, Bayport Museum."

As they approached the museum, the first thing they noticed was that the parking lot was almost totally empty.

"It's open on Sundays, isn't it?" Joe asked.

"Sure is," answered Frank as Joe pulled into a

45

spot. He looked at his watch. "Eleven-thirty—should be peak business time."

They got out of the van and walked inside. After paying their donations, they went into the main exhibit room.

Immediately, they realized why Ruppenthal had become so upset. Where large paintings had once crowded the walls, there were now rectangles that were still painted the original color—beige. All around these spots the walls had faded to a lighter shade. Glass exhibit cases were half-empty, and a museum guard slept in a chair in the corner.

"It's like a tomb in here," Joe whispered.

"I guess word travels fast," Frank mused. "Looks like the Carpenter Collection really was the backbone of this place."

They both turned when they heard the echo of footsteps in the hallway behind them.

"You can go home, Mr. Harris!" a familiar voice called out. The guard in the corner woke up with a start. "It doesn't look too hopeful. I think I'll close up till—"

Albert Ruppenthal cut himself short as he entered the room. "Well, well, a couple of paying visitors," he said. "Enough income to pay for today's electric bill, perhaps. Or have you been sent by your girlfriend to bring me news of more destroyed artwork?"

"We felt very bad about the statue, Mr. Ruppenthal," Frank said, shaking his head. "Actually, we wondered if we could ask you a few questions about it."

Ruppenthal fell silent for a few moments. His eyes moved from Frank to Joe and back again, as if sizing them up, trying to decide something. Finally he said, "All right, let's talk. I have a few questions for you, too."

Together they walked down the hall and through a door that said Authorized Persons Only. Inside the door was a large office with about six desks. Ruppenthal led Frank and Joe to the other end of the office, where a glass door led to several private offices.

Ushering the brothers into his private office, Ruppenthal immediately closed the door and drew the blinds over the windows.

"Have a seat. Now, I feel funny about doing this, but it seems to me you two are very close to Tessa Carpenter."

"Well, I don't know if *close* is—" Joe began to say.

"Yes, we are," Frank butted in. "I'm Frank Hardy and this is my brother Joe. We were schoolmates with Tessa at school."

Joe gave his brother a puzzled look. "Fine, fine," Ruppenthal said, sounding a bit distracted. "I noticed, too, that she seems to depend on *you* an awful lot, Frank. Softens up a bit when you're around—"

Frank shrugged his shoulders and smiled modestly.

Ruppenthal leaned over his desk, glaring at Frank and Joe. "I'll give it to you straight. This museum is in danger of folding. If we don't have the artwork, people won't come. If we don't have the people, companies and agencies will refuse to fund us. But the main thing is, what Tessa is doing is illegal."

"So you want us to find the agreeement," Joe said.

"No," Ruppenthal said, sitting back in his chair. "I have people looking for it, but I'm afraid it's lost or destroyed. What I have in mind is something much more exciting."

Frank and Joe watched as Ruppenthal reached into his top desk drawer.

"The museum has a small reserve fund," he continued. "It has been building over the years for use in extreme emergency. Until now it hasn't been touched.

"Plainly, what I am saying is, I will make it worth your while to convince Tessa to return the Carpenter Collection. I don't care how you do it."

Slowly he pulled a thick envelope out of the drawer and opened it. Onto the desk fell several stacks of crisp one-hundred dollar bills.

"There's ten thousand dollars. If you agree, all of it will be yours."

Chapter

6

FOR A MOMENT the Hardys just stared at the stacks of money in front of them. Then Frank spoke up.

"Let me get this straight, Mr. Ruppenthal. For ten thousand dollars, you would like the two of us to talk to our friend, wine her and dine her if necessary—and somehow convince her to give back the collection."

"We'd be like spies, in other words," Joe said.

"If you like," Ruppenthal said with a smile.

"And we'd be accepting a bribe," Joe went on.

"Well, I prefer to think of it as payment for services rendered," Ruppenthal replied.

Frank and Joe both leaned back in their seats.

"Are you thinking what I'm thinking?" Joe asked his brother.

Frank nodded seriously. "I think so."

Ruppenthal looked nervous. "There's a lot that a couple of young men can buy with ten thousand dollars,'' he said, eagerly looking from Frank to Joe. "I'd jump at this if I were your age!''

"Well, we're not the jumping type, Mr. Ruppenthal,'' Frank said. "No deal.''

"Don't tell me—you don't think it's enough, right?'' Ruppenthal's face became red with anger. He slapped his hand on his desk. "Greed! You're just like that spoiled little friend of yours. This is a *museum*, not a bank. I have no more to give—''

"You missed the point,'' Joe said. "It's plenty of money. But you're bribing us to do something illegal. That's not the way we operate.''

"Let me tell you about illegal,'' Ruppenthal said, pointing a finger at Joe. "What Tessa Carpenter has done to me—*that's* illegal!''

"We understand what you're saying, Mr. Ruppenthal,'' Frank said. "We understand that the museum needs the Carpenter Collection—much more than Tessa does. And I really hope you do find that agreement. If not, I'm afraid the best thing you can do is take your case to court—''

Ruppenthal bolted up from his chair. "Out!'' he shouted, pointing to the door. "Take yourselves out of my office! If you think I'm going to spend months in court while that girl destroys everything I've ever worked for, you're crazy!''

Frank and Joe got up and walked toward the door. The slam of Ruppenthal's door echoed like a gunshot as the brothers exited into the hallway.

* * *

"I guess we won't get any information from him," Joe said as he and Frank walked out of the museum, past a row of newspaper vending machines. "Imagine him trying to bribe us. He must be pretty desperate." He sighed. "That *was* a lot of money, though . . ."

"Do I hear some second thoughts?" Frank asked as he put some change into the *Bayport Times* machine and pulled out a Sunday paper. "All I can say is, Ruppenthal is sleazy."

"Yeah, but sleazy enough to try to kill Tessa? And do it by ruining a priceless statue? You saw the look on his face when he saw the thing was shattered, didn't you?"

"It may have been an act, Joe. A sacrifice to remove himself from suspicion. He may either be trying to scare Tessa into giving it all back, or—"

"If there's no more Tessa, the art would have to go back to the museum!"

"Exactly. I think we ought to get home and see if we can dig up anything about Ruppenthal in the crime data base."

They jumped into the van, and Joe steered out of the parking lot. Frank settled in his seat and picked up the newspaper. Instantly his eyes lit on the headline.

"Listen to this, Joe," he said. "It's the lead article: 'Curse or Coincidence? Carpenter Heiress Narrowly Misses Death After Touching Legendary Dagger.' "

"I love a juicy story," Joe said. "Read it to me."

" 'The cream of the area's chic younger set was witness to a bizarre turn of events last night at the Carpenter mansion in the Cliffside Heights section of Bayport. It happened at approximately eleven P.M., under the full moon, and no one who was there is likely to forget . . .' "

"Oh boy, they're really milking it," said Joe.

"Let's see—'Several guests left, convinced that the horrible curse had indeed been brought to life. This opinion was echoed by a distraught Miss Carpenter, who was heard to say, "Am I going to have to live with the threat of death for the rest of my life?" Miss Carpenter agreed to grant the *Times* an exclusive interview today at the Cliffside Country Club—' "

"That wasn't too smart," Joe interrupted. "We've got to convince her to stay away from the press. All we need are reporters tagging along on our investigation!"

"Right," answered Frank. "And if there's a lot of publicity about this Borgia dagger nonsense, who knows what kinds of creeps will be after her—playing tricks, trying to 'cure' the curse, claiming to be descendants of the Borgias—"

"One thing seems a little strange to me. You'd think Tessa would want to keep this whole thing quiet. I mean, for someone so—so—*social,* this kind of thing could make her very unpopular."

Frank thought about that for a minute. "Maybe

so. But I don't think she's the kind of person ever to say no to her name in print.''

Joe drove up to the Hardys' rambling old Victorian house on a quiet street lined with maple trees in south Bayport. They parked and ran inside to their computerized crime lab, which also doubled as Frank's bedroom

The sleek computer took up very little space, but it contained the most sophisticated crime-fighting software available.

Frank flicked it on, and Joe pulled up a chair beside him. "Let's see . . ." Frank murmured, "Rubin . . . Ruck . . . Ruggiero . . . Ruppert.''

"Nothing,'' Joe said.

"Well, Ruppenthal's clean—at least so far. Let's try Squinder.'' He punched a few more keys. "Spivak . . . Spode . . . Squantz . . . ah! Here we are—Squinder!''

Frank and Joe stared intensely at the screen as a short list of information appeared.

Joe read parts of the list out loud: "Shoplifting a can of tuna fish, twenty years ago . . . disturbing the peace with loud speechmaking, eleven years ago . . . assaulting tow-truck operator who tried to remove limo from no-parking zone, two years ago. That's it.''

"Doesn't exactly seem like a candidate for murderers' row,'' Frank said.

Just then their eyes were drawn to the window by the slam of a car door. They looked out to see Fenton Hardy running toward the front door.

"What's up with Dad?" Joe asked.

Within seconds, Fenton was up the stairs and at the door of Frank's room.

"Turn off the computer, boys," he said, breathless. "I just got a police report. I'm on a case myself, but I think *you* might be interested in this one. The report is from the Cliffside Country Club."

"Something about Tessa Carpenter?" Frank asked.

"You'd better get over there right away. She's been shot."

Chapter

7

FRANK AND JOE bolted outside and into the van. With a screech of tires, they sped eastward.

Just past the Entering Cliffside Heights sign, the neighborhood changed dramatically. Neat, suburban houses gave way to a heavily wooded area. Joe hugged the road as it curved sharply.

"I have a feeling this road was built for people who have no reason to hurry," Joe grumbled.

Before long they saw a small, hand-painted sign that said CCC. It pointed up a dirt road to the left.

"Not very flashy, are they?" Joe said as he turned.

"Well, it *is* one of the most exclusive clubs in the state," Frank replied. "I guess they have no need to advertise."

Just up the dirt road was a clearing and a circular driveway. As they approached, a smiling man in a brown uniform stood in their path.

Joe jammed on the brake and the man went around to the driver's side.

"Easy, there," he said. "You're guests of . . . ?"

"Tessa Carpenter," Joe said quickly and gunned the van past the guard. He skidded to a stop in front of the clubhouse, a three-story stone mansion surrounded by lavish flower gardens.

As they parked and jumped out, they heard the guard's voice behind them: "Wait! You can't visit her now! Come back here!"

The brothers heard voices and followed them around the building to a large, open meadow surrounded by trees. In the middle of the field was a crowd of people, some of them police officers. Near this group a jittery horse was being calmed by a man in jeans. And circling around the crowd, taking notes, was the same society columnist they had seen at Tessa's party.

"Excuse us," Frank said repeatedly as he and Joe worked their way to the center of the crowd. There they saw Tessa, lying on the ground and sobbing. Kneeling beside her, Dr. Lansdale and Harley were swabbing her bloody forehead with a damp cloth.

"Is she all right?" Joe asked.

Harley barely looked up; he said nothing. But Dr. Lansdale smiled cheerfully. "Ah, hello, Frank and Joe! I had no idea you were members," she said. "I'm afraid Tessa had a rather scary fall. Nothing more than a scraped forehead, fortunately.''

"There's more to the story than that," Harley said. "Somebody tried to kill her."

"I don't know what happened," Tessa said, speaking with the loud, shaky voice of someone who has just had the scare of a lifetime. "I was j-just riding my horse—th-that interview had gotten me so upset and I needed to relax—and—and then I heard it—the shot."

"Were you hit?" asked Frank.

"N-no, but my horse got so upset he—he reared up on his hind legs and threw me off!"

"Could you see who did it?" Joe asked.

"No! I told the police—"

Tessa was interrupted by a scream in the distance.

All eyes turned toward a commotion in the woods. Three police officers, two men and a woman, were emerging. One of the men carried a silver-plated revolver. The other two officers were dragging a kicking teenager.

"It's Callie!" Joe said.

"Impossible," whispered Frank, frozen in disbelief.

"Get those handcuffs away from me!" they heard her scream. "Don't you understand? I'm on *your* side!"

"Sure, kid," answered the policewoman. "You just happened to be illegally trespassing in the woods with a gun when it went off, right? And now you can't help but resist arrest.''

Callie's eyes lit up when she saw Frank and Joe.

"Tell them who I am, Frank!"

The policewoman did a double-take. "Well, if it isn't the Hardy brothers," she said, smirking. "Is this one of your strange detective methods?''

"It's okay, Officer Novack. She's—uh, part of our investigation team," Frank said.

"That's what she told us," the policewoman said as Callie defiantly threw aside the two officers' arms and brushed herself off.

Suddenly two country club guards pushed their way through the crowd. "There they are!" one of them yelled. "They just drove past me! Seize them, officers!"

By now the crowd was buzzing with confusion. "All right, let's go back to our businesses," Officer Novack said, loudly. "Ms. Carpenter is unhurt, and these three young people are private detectives.''

One by one, the club members began to drift away. "Thanks, Officer Novack," Frank said a little while later.

"Well, we've gotten our report. Ms. Shaw claims that she found the gun in the woods while keeping an eye on Ms. Carpenter. At this point all we can do is take the gun to headquarters for analysis. But you can be sure we'll be in touch— especially with you, young lady.'' She shot a look at Callie. "If your story doesn't hold up, you'll be brought in for questioning."

As the officers walked toward their squad cars in the parking lot, Frank leaned down to Tessa. "All right, now you know who we really are. We'd like to help you out, since it looks as though one or two people are after your life—"

Tessa flung her arms around Frank. "Oh, I *knew* you were in some line of work like this. I'm so glad."

Frank uneasily pulled himself away and said, "We'll need access to your house, first of all—"

"I have a perfect solution," Tessa answered. "Be my bodyguards, both of you." Frank and Joe were silent. "I have the money to pay you. Don't you see? I need protection, and this way the two of you can pick up all kinds of clues. You'll live on the mansion grounds, in the servants' cottage!"

At that suggestion, Callie looked as if she could kill.

"Uh—we'll think about it," Frank said.

"The only thing to worry about now is how to get you inside to my office so I can take care of you," Dr. Lansdale said.

Joe, Harley, and Dr. Lansdale helped Tessa up and supported her as she walked toward the clubhouse. Frank and Callie followed a few yards behind.

"She won't stop at anything to get her hands on you," Callie said to Frank.

"Wait a minute! First things first," Frank said. "Just what *were* you doing in the woods, anyway?"

Callie looked away. "After you and Joe left for the museum, I got a paper and read that Tessa was going to be here today. So I decided to tail her and—well, investigate!"

"Investigate? Look, Callie—Joe and I are the pros. You can't do this on your own!"

"Well, I don't agree! After all, there should be *someone* on this case who isn't in love with Tessa!" She gave Frank an accusing look. "Anyway, I sneaked over a fence and into the woods. As I was looking for the clubhouse, I heard a horse galloping along a dirt pathway. Sure enough, it was Tessa. I watched her ride into the field, when all of a sudden there was this gunshot. I could tell Tessa wasn't hit, because the shot had come from farther down in the woods. But by the time I got there, there was no one—only that silver-plated revolver."

"Just like the one in Squinder's old cottage," Frank said.

By now they had caught up to the others. Dr. Lansdale was pointing to a spot in one of the gardens. A large patch of soil had been turned over, and hoses, bottles, and seed packets littered the ground.

"I think the arsenic has finally gotten rid of the weeds, Tessa," she said. "And I may actually plant some tomatoes this year!"

"That's great, Aunt Harriet, but I really need to lie down!" Tessa whined.

They continued walking into the clubhouse. Dr. Lansdale led them into her ground-floor office, a modest room with a sink, a chair, a desk, a cot, and several shelves full of supplies.

Tessa moaned as she was set down on the cot. "Oh! My head is killing me!"

"Well, you should have picked a softer place to land, sweetheart!" Dr. Lansdale said with a small laugh. "Here, let me get you a mild pain-killer."

Dr. Lansdale reached for a clear plastic bottle on one of the shelves.

"That's it, just relax," she said, not looking as she took a couple of pills out. "These will do the trick temporarily. Harley, be a dear and get a glass of water for Tessa."

Joe looked around the room. Harley was filling a huge glass of water. Frank was propping pillows behind her head. And Callie seemed disgusted with the whole situation.

Just then something caught Joe's eye. Just as Tessa was about to put the pills in her mouth, he picked up the bottle.

His eyes popped open as he read the label: Arsenic!

Chapter

8

THERE WAS NO time for words. Joe leapt across the room and swiped at Tessa's arm. The pills went flying into the air and fell harmlessly to the ground.

Tessa shrieked as Joe hit her arm. Instantly Joe felt a hand at the back of his collar.

"Just what do you think you're doing, pal?" Harley said. He drew back a fist.

"Saving her life," Joe said. He held out the arsenic for everyone to see.

The room fell silent, except for a gasp from Tessa.

"I don't believe it," she said finally, her face as white as the sheet on her cot.

"Oh, my word!" Dr. Lansdale exclaimed, taking the bottle from Joe. "How could I have done this?"

"What's a bottle of arsenic doing in here anyway?" Frank asked.

"My goodness, my goodness, what indeed?" Dr. Lansdale said, shaking her head. "I have told myself time and again that something like this might happen. I buy these from a drug company and then dissolve them in water to use as a weed-killer. I sometimes store them in here. And with my eyesight the way it's gotten these days . . . Oh, honey, how can you ever forgive me?"

"I-it's not you, Aunt Harriet," Tessa said, with tears welling in her eyes. "There's something else in control here, something bigger than all of us."

"Whatever do you mean, sweetheart?" Dr. Lansdale said.

"It's the Borgia curse, I know it!" Tessa was practically screaming by now. "I'm doomed! There's no place I can be safe!"

"Shh, it's all going to be okay," said Frank. "It was a simple accident. There are no such things as ancient curses. This is the twentieth century."

"The boy is right, darling," Dr. Lansdale said. "I'm so, so sorry. From now on I will never make such a careless mistake. I think the best thing for your nerves right now would be a nice, long nap."

She delicately helped Tessa lie back and popped a pillow under her head. "Tha-a-t's it. Harley and I will be here to watch over you, while I ask our guests to leave, okay?"

Almost immediately Tessa's eyes began to flutter shut from nervous exhaustion. Frank, Joe, and Callie tiptoed out the office door, waving goodbye to Dr. Lansdale and Harley.

"I'm sorry, I just don't trust her," Callie said as they walked out of the clubhouse. "The old-lady routine is too convenient. After all, she's a *professional*—a doctor would never do anything like that!"

"I don't know, Callie," Joe said. "She seemed so upset. Besides, she must be pushing seventy or seventy-five. I really think she's a little forgetful and careless."

"Besides," Frank added, "if she were really after Tessa, wouldn't it be a little obvious to knock her off in front of four witnesses?"

"I guess you're right," Callie said with a pout. "After all, *you're* the detectives. Well, now I've got to go rescue my car from its hiding place. I didn't have the *skill* to just drive right up like you did."

As she turned away, Frank could tell that she was only half joking. It seemed to him that Callie was not only jealous, but determined to crack this case herself. Joe and he could certainly use her sharp instincts; if only they could all work together.

"Listen," said Joe, interrupting his brother's thoughts. "What do you think of this bodyguard idea? It seems perfect to me."

Frank nodded. "I'm afraid I agree with you this time, Joe. We're going to need a lot of close contact—"

"I heard that!" came a voice from around a corner of the clubhouse. Callie came storming back toward them. "Close contact? I *know* what kind of close contact you want! I can't believe you're actually falling for her offer!"

Frank exhaled with frustration. "And I can't believe you were actually eavesdropping. Besides, you yourself said it was a fascinating case!"

"It's the victim who's fascinating to you, Frank—the poor little glamorous redhead! You're going to become her slaves, just like Squinder! And, by the way," Callie added, her eyes blazing, "I wasn't eavesdropping; I came back to see what time we were going to the movies tonight. But you can forget that now!" With that, she stalked away.

"Do I detect a note of anger?" Joe said with a wry grin. "Maybe you should drop the case. Then Callie will go to the movies with you tonight, and *I'll* be Tessa's bodyguard."

Frank raised an eyebrow at his brother. "All I can say is, if I manage to crack this case *and* keep my girlfriend, I'll take you both out to the movies—every day for a month."

Frank and Joe lurched to the left as the van took a sharp curve at forty miles an hour.

"Hasn't she learned her lesson yet?" said Frank. "She's going to ruin *that* car too!"

Joe kept the little blue convertible within his

sight as it raced along Cliffside Road. A long mane of scarlet hair billowed back from the driver's seat.

"Can you believe that incredible machine is her *second* car, Frank?"

"Well, I hope her third is a Model T. They only go twenty miles an hour." Frank reached out to steady himself as the van sped over a bump in the road. "We could have offered to drive her home from the club."

"I know, but when I called her from our house, she insisted she was well enough to drive!"

The setting sun washed the woods in an orange glow as the two vehicles approached the Carpenter mansion. In a cloud of dust, the convertible stormed up the winding dirt driveway and skidded to a stop in front of the four-car garage.

Covered with a thin film of dirt, the Hardy van followed slowly behind, its windshield washer squirting away.

"Mom and Dad have Tessa's phone number—right, Joe?"

"Yeah," Joe replied. "And if they need to find us, it shouldn't be hard. Tessa's mansion has been mentioned in all the newspapers this week."

"How did I ever let you sucker me into this bodyguard idea, anyway?" Frank asked as they pulled up behind Tessa's car.

"Me? Wait a minute—"

"Welcome home!" Tessa chirped, standing beside her car.

"Uh, Tessa—" Frank began.

"I can't believe how much better I feel after that nice, long nap!" Tessa went on. "Now, do you need help getting settled in the cottage?" They shook their heads.

She pulled open the van door and skipped away toward the house.

"Amazing how fast she bounces back," Frank said as he and Joe stepped out of the van.

They wandered through the mansion, until they found Tessa rewinding a cassette in a telephone answering machine in the sitting room.

"I love these things," she said. "So much better than secretaries. They don't make mistakes or take lunch breaks—and they're much cheaper."

Beep. There was only one message: "Hello, Miss Carpenter. Albert Ruppenthal here. Just wanted to let you know, the staff in our upstate warehouse has located your grandfather's agreement. It was buried in some files that had been transferred there after the museum fire. I'm expecting it to be brought here late tomorrow, and I expect you to be home Tuesday when we pick up the collection. You will, of course, be responsible for the cost of the Greek statue. Have a pleasant day."

Tessa sank into a leather armchair. Her rosy complexion had quickly become chalky white.

"This was bound to happen," Joe said gently.

He felt sorry for her; she looked more upset than he had expected.

"Bound to happen! That's easy for you to say!" Tessa snapped.

"Sorry, Tessa," Joe answered. "I didn't mean it to sound—"

"I know, I know," Tessa said with a sigh. "Maybe it's just as well anyway. This stupid art collection has caused me nothing but trouble." She looked around at the paintings on the sitting-room wall. "Besides, most of the paintings don't even go with the wallpaper."

"Even when you return the collection, there's still the small matter of our investigation," Frank said.

Tessa snapped out of her gloom. "Right!" she said, looking at Frank with adoring eyes. "What comes next?"

"Well, I will have to check out the parlor, and Joe—"

"No!" Tessa interrupted.

"What's the matter?" Frank said.

Tessa's bottom lip jutted out in a pout. She gave Frank a hurt look and said, "You're not going to leave me alone, Frank? I thought you were my bodyguard."

"Uh—yeah, Tessa. That's right." He looked at Joe and shrugged. "I guess that leaves you to search the house for clues."

"I guess so," Joe said listlessly. He nodded

slowly, walking out the door. "Only who's going to guard you from her?" he muttered.

"What?" Frank called out.

"Never mind," Joe answered as he went through the door.

The Borgia dagger was in its glass case on top of the broken sideboard still. Joe lifted the glass case carefully and saw the carved-oak wall through the case. Was there anything unusual? he wondered—any electrical switches, bugging devices? . . .

He opened the case, lifted the dagger, and peeked under the satin cushion. Nothing. He put it down and then looked in the corner where the statue had been. No mechanical tripping devices.

Maybe there was something in the room he wasn't seeing—a box of circuit breakers, a hidden TV camera—

He stood in the corner and leaned back against the oak wall, surveying the room. His elbow bumped against one of the intricate carvings— and it moved!

He sprang forward. The carving popped back to its original position.

Creeeak! A sudden vibration at his side caught Joe's attention. As he watched in surprise, one entire section of the bookcase swung slowly out of the wall, sending several books toppling onto the floor.

He grabbed the bookcase and pulled it out

farther into the room. Behind it was nothing but pitch-darkness.

A secret room, Joe thought. Just like the old movies. Now we're getting someplace.

With great caution, he took one step into the unknown—and fell straight down through broken cobwebs into a black abyss.

Chapter

9

HE HIT THE cement floor hard. For a moment he lay there, the wind knocked out of him. He flexed his arms and legs. Nothing broken.

Gradually his eyes adjusted to the darkness. He looked around him. A weak shaft of light spilled in from the opening he'd just fallen through. All it enabled him to see was the large, empty room he was in. On the far wall there was a low, open doorway.

He picked himself up and cautiously walked to this other doorway. To enter it, he had to stoop. Stepping carefully, he passed through. He reached out with both hands and felt rough plaster walls on either side of him. The ceiling scraped against his head. The absolute blackness in the tunnel gave him no clue as to his destination—except that he was moving on a sharp downward slope.

Guiding himself with his hands, he groped

THE HARDY BOYS CASEFILES

along, slowly at first and then picked up speed. This has to lead to something, he thought. A storage room, a boiler room . . .

Thunk. Before he could finish his thought, Joe had crashed into something. He rubbed his forehead where it had made contact with the object. With his other hand, he reached out and felt a wooden door that had blocked his path. He found the doorknob and pushed the door open.

Another dark room. Joe stepped inside—onto a small object that rolled out from beneath him.

"Who-o-oa!" he called out, clutching at the doorjamb, next to which he felt the cool metal plate of a light switch.

He flicked on the switch. The room was flooded with fluorescent light. As Joe's eyes adjusted, he saw trunks, boxes, garden equipment, and a floor cluttered with small objects, including the metal roller skate that he had just tripped over.

On the near wall was something he had hoped to find—a metal panel of circuit breakers. He opened the front of the metal box, and saw about twenty switches. He read the labels beneath each one: Kitchen, Sitting Room, Parlor . . . Below them all was a large, main switch. "Now we're cooking," he said to himself. This was the place where all the lights in the mansion could have been blacked out.

On the far wall were a few rickety wooden stairs that led up to two overhead cellar doors. Now Joe knew where he was. The tunnel had gradually led him down to the basement. He turned back and closed the circuit breaker box, climbed two of the four stairs, and pushed up to open one of the bulkhead doors.

The smell of fresh flowers wafted down to him. Joe stuck his head out into the sunlight.

He looked up and behind him to see the side of the Carpenter mansion. A flower garden stretched to the ends of the house on either side of him, and directly in front of him was a well-worn dirt path.

A dirt path that led directly to the servants' cottage.

A smile flickered across Joe's face. He jumped outside and ran around to the front of the mansion.

As he passed under the window of the sitting room, he heard Tessa's voice:

"Why don't you let me give you a massage, Frank. It will loosen you up. Being my bodyguard hasn't exactly been relaxing so far."

Joe looked through the window to see Frank sitting nervously on the edge of the couch. Tessa was standing behind him and reaching for his neck.

Frank shot up off the couch as Tessa's fingers made contact. "Uh, how about a walk in the— Joe!" he .cried, spotting his brother outside. "What are you doing out there?"

"I hope I'm not interrupting anything," Joe replied.

"No, no, come on in!"

Joe trotted around to the front door and then into the sitting room.

"Where have you been?" Frank asked. "We missed you!"

Out of the corner of his eye, Joe caught a glimpse of Tessa, slumped in an armchair, pouting.

"Well, at least one of you did," Joe said under his breath. "But never mind. I think we may have a breakthrough in the case. Tessa, do you have a flashlight?"

"Sure. Do you want me to get it for you?" Joe nodded. Barely hiding her annoyed look, she left the room and quickly returned with a large green flashlight.

"Okay, follow me!" Joe said. He led Frank and Tessa into the parlor. Tessa's jaw dropped as Joe walked over to the section of the bookcase that was swung away from the wall.

"There's a room down here," Joe explained. He pointed the flashlight into the void. "But you have to jump a couple of steps to get to it."

He circled the flashlight around, examining the dark room. Off to the side of the opening, a short metal ladder was leaning against the wall.

"It all makes sense now," Joe said. "There's a tunnel that leads down from this room into a storage area that houses the circuit breakers. Whoever tried to kill Tessa could have used that route to come up here"—he turned toward the

corner of the parlor at their immediate right—
"and then walked two steps into that corner to
shove the statue over."

"Amazing," Tessa said.

Frank nodded his head thoughtfully. "It could
have been only one person then, instead of two."

"Yeah, a real speed demon," Joe said. "He'd
have had to kill the lights, run through the basement in the dark, climb up the ladder, push the
bookcase back into place, topple the statue, and
then go back to turn on the lights again."

"Someone who knows the house backward and
forward—"

"And in the dark," Joe added. He turned to
Tessa. "You knew nothing about this fake bookcase?"

She folded her arms in front of her. "If I did,
don't you think I would have said something,
Joe?"

Joe gave her an embarrassed look. "Well, it is
your house, Tessa."

"This whole thing is giving me the creeps,"
Tessa said. "Secret passageways, moving book-
cases—I feel like I'm in a haunted house! Tomorrow I'm going to call someone to put a wall up
behind that bookcase. I've had enough—"

Frank touched Tessa's arm. "There's nothing
to worry about," he said. "I'd prefer it if you just
left it all alone for a while. We may pick up more
clues."

Tessa backed down instantly when she heard

Frank's voice. "Well, all right, if you say so," she said softly. Just then her eyelids drooped and she raised her hand to her mouth, trying to stifle a yawn.

"You look exhausted," Frank said. "Why don't we continue this tomorrow?"

Tessa nodded. "You're right, Frank. I think I'd better turn in. Sorry, guys. There should be some towels and sheets in the cottage. See you in the morning."

As Tessa went upstairs, Frank and Joe made sure all of the first-floor windows were locked shut. Then they went outside and secured the locks to all the house's entrances and then got their bags out of the van.

"How do you do it, Frank?" Joe asked as they walked toward the cottage. "She listens to every word you say and treats me like Jack the Ripper."

Frank rolled his eyes. "Don't get hung up on her, Joe. She's already got a boyfriend, remember? Besides we're here to solve a case."

"Yeah, you're right, as usual," Joe said with a sigh. Then his eyes narrowed. "Anyway, I think I have an idea who did it."

"I guess we can rule out both Ruppenthal and Lansdale, since they were actually in the parlor the whole time the attempt occurred."

"Not necessarily." Joe stopped in front of the cottage and looked back at the mansion. "Do you see what I see?"

Frank scratched his head. "A dirt pathway that goes from the cottage to the house. So?"

"Who did we see sneaking around the cottage after the party?"

"Of course—Squinder! Squinder might have tripped the lights to help anyone inside the room. Like Ruppenthal or Dr. Lansdale—"

"Or both." Joe gave his brother a knowing look as he opened the front door of the cottage. "Looks like we'll have to pay Edwin a visit tomorrow."

Eighty-five degrees. Joe had to rub his eyes twice before he believed the temperature on the outdoor thermometer.

"It's only eight in the morning!" he said. "Today will be a scorcher."

The Hardys quickly put on shorts and T-shirts, then headed for the mansion. By the time they got there, Tessa was already heading out, dressed in a white terrycloth robe.

"Good morning!" she sang. "I was just coming out to ask if you wanted to join me in a morning swim!"

"Swim?" Joe said. "Uh—we didn't bring—"

"Bathing suits? Don't worry. The room on the side of the cottage is a changing room. We keep extra suits there for guests."

"Thanks," Frank said, "but I think we'd better continue—"

"Sure we'll join you!" Joe interrupted, nudging Frank in the ribs.

"Great!" Tessa said. "You go ahead and change while I call Harley. He loves to swim in the morning."

As Tessa went inside to call, Frank and Joe headed back toward the cottage. They were passing beside the sitting room window when a sharpness in Tessa's voice made them halt in their tracks.

"Don't be a child, Harley! . . . Of course not. . . . I can't believe you're being so jealous. . . . Well, I'm calling *you*, aren't I?"

Frank and Joe glanced at each other. "I think we're creating a problem," Frank said.

Joe nodded, then shrugged his shoulders. "We could use Harley on our side, but it looks as though it's a little late for that. Come on, I'll race you to the changing room." The brothers dashed back to the cottage. "Last one in has to interrogate Squinder!" Joe said, already slipping out of his clothes.

But it was Frank who emerged first, running for the diving board. Joe followed behind him in a pair of baggy plaid trunks, trying to pull the drawstring tight.

Frank ran down the diving board and took a jump. Bouncing down onto the board, he prepared for the dive.

It was in that split-second he saw the thin

electrical wire on the bottom of the pool. Instantly his eyes followed it to an outdoor socket.

With every ounce of muscular control he had, he stopped himself from diving and jumped back down onto the board. Behind him was the sound of Joe's feet slapping the outdoor tiles.

He shouted in a voice so loud he thought his lungs would rip, *"Joe! Don't jump!"*

But it was too late. With horror, he watched his brother plunge into the clear blue water.

Chapter

10

THHHHHWOPP! STILL CLUTCHING the drawstring on his shorts, Joe did a belly-flop into the pool.

That image froze in Frank's mind—it would be the final image he had of his brother.

"NOOOOOOO!" Feeling more helpless than he had ever felt in his life, Frank let out a cry from the bottom of his soul. It seemed as though his mouth was the only part of his body that could move.

There were a few seconds of eerie silence as Joe floated to the surface. Frank couldn't help but turn away from the pool. He had seen some gruesome things in his life, but the sight of his brother's electrocuted body would be too much to bear.

"What? Too much glare from the water? Come on in!"

Was it a hallucination? The voice sounded exactly like Joe's. Frank spun around and looked into the pool, as a sheet of water hit him squarely in the face.

Frank did a double take. There, treading water, was Joe.

"Don't look so shocked. It was only a belly-flop!" he called out.

Frank's face broke into a broad grin. Immediately he ran around to the side and pulled the wire out of the pool—and out of the socket.

"Pretty lucky, huh?" Joe called out. "It must be dead."

"I have a feeling whoever put this here had something else in mind," said Frank.

Just then Tessa scampered down to the pool area in a bright red- and orange-striped one-piece bathing suit. "Hey, why didn't you wait for me?"

Joe shielded his eyes. "I didn't want to be blinded by the suit before I went in!"

"Very funny." Tessa gasped as she saw Frank. "Frank, what are you doing with that wire?"

"It was in the pool. It must have been put in overnight."

Tessa's face turned white. "By someone who knew I take morning swims." She swallowed nervously and steadied herself against a pool chair, her arms shaking. "I—I can't believe this. Why would anyone want to do this to me?"

"Well, we don't know that, Tessa. But we think Squinder may be a major player here."

Suddenly Tessa grabbed Frank's hand. "Are

you all right?" she said. "You didn't get a shock or anything, did you?"

What about me? Joe thought. I'm the one who jumped in.

"Fortunately, no," Frank said. "Even though it was plugged into that outlet." He pointed to the socket by the side of the pool.

"Aren't you lucky!" Tessa exclaimed with a sigh of relief. "That hasn't worked in years. Thank goodness my dad never had it fixed!"

"I think we'd better take a rain check on this swim," said Frank. "We've got to start tailing Squinder."

Tessa shook her head. "I just can't believe it. I know he hates me, but he'd *never* do anything like this."

"Maybe you'd like to come with us and confront him."

"No way! I don't want to go near him anymore."

"In that case," Joe said, climbing out of the pool, "why don't I stay here to guard Tessa while you go, Frank?"

"Yeah, good idea, Joe," Frank said. "In fact, I think I'll call Callie. She can help me follow Squinder."

Joe disappeared into the changing room as Frank went to the cottage to call Callie. After she agreed to meet him at Squinder's house, he reminded her of the address, and he threw on his clothes and jogged out to the driveway.

"So long, Tessa!" Frank yelled as he jumped into the van.

"Oh! Just a minute!" she called out. Tessa ran toward Frank with her arms outstretched. Frank leaned out the window, and she gave him a loud kiss on the cheek.

"I just wanted to thank you for caring about me so much. Good luck." With that, she wrapped her arms around his neck.

Frank sighed with relief as she let go. Then he became aware of a car pulling up behind him. He turned to look. A feeling of dread washed over him when the car pulled up beside him.

Staring at him through the passenger window was an angry Harley Welles.

"Um, morning, Harley," Frank said. "Sure is a hot one, huh?"

With a wave of his hand, he sped down the driveway.

Squinder lived in a section of Bayport only four miles from Cliffside Heights, but it seemed light-years away. Old two-family houses stood side by side with run-down apartment buildings. Tiny front lawns had become nothing but dirt with stray patches of weeds. Except for the squeals of children and the barking of stray dogs, everything was silent and still in the hot summer air. On porches and in open windows, people stared into the distance, lazily fanning themselves. As Frank drove by, they gave him hard unseeing looks.

He made a right up Lakeview Avenue and looked for number 94. Up the street about half a block was a row of attached houses. Callie's car was parked in front of the last one. As Frank approached, Callie jumped out of her car, waving to him.

He parked his car and hopped out. "What took you so long?" she said. "I don't like waiting."

"I had a longer drive than you," Frank answered.

"How's Tessa?" Callie asked, raising an eyebrow.

"I'm sure she's in her glory right now. She's got both Harley and Joe fighting for her attention."

"Good! That leaves you and me to bust this case wide open!" She grabbed Frank's hand and pulled him toward the house marked 94.

"Hey, just a minute. You have to promise me you won't go sneaking off on your own again just to show us up."

Callie put an innocent look on her face. "Me? I wouldn't *dream* of it! Scout's honor!" She raised three fingers.

"Okay, partner, let's go."

Ninety-four Lakeview Avenue was a small, brown house in dire need of a paint job. Just below the roof, some of the siding had fallen off. A battered cyclone fence enclosed the tiny front yard, which hadn't seen grass in years.

Hanging on the fence was a rusted metal sign. Frank squatted down next to it.

"Can you read it?" asked Callie as she pushed open the front gate.

"Not really. It's all covered with graffiti. No, wait a second, I can make out—"

"Never mind, Frank. Look, there's a note taped to Squinder's door!"

"Bo—ware—No, that's beware—of—"

"Beware of what?" asked Callie, halfway to the front door.

"D-dog! *Dog!* Look out, Callie!"

Callie froze as she heard a deep growling and a rhythmic jingling sound. Before she could react, a huge black animal came barreling around the house.

Thinking fast, Frank picked up a stick from the ground. He ran through the gate and stopped in front of Callie, holding the stick high over his head.

"Don't even try it!" Frank shouted. The dog stopped short, baring its huge white teeth.

Frank slowly approached the dog, threatening it with the stick. The dog barked furiously as it backed away.

"Go ahead, Callie! I'll hold him off while you try the front door!"

"Are you sure?"

"No problem! I've got him in control!" Frank hoped he was telling the truth.

Timidly, Callie walked toward the door. As she moved, though, the dog lunged.

Whack! Frank slammed the stick down in the dog's path. The dog backed off, and Frank lifted the stick into the air again. The dog's eyes followed the stick, and it braced itself as if to run.

This is interesting, Frank thought. He began waving the stick slowly in the air. The dog's tail began to wag. Then Frank jerked the stick suddenly to one side, and the dog practically leapt off the ground in the same direction.

"Careful, Frank!" Callie called to him. "It might be part Doberman, or German shepherd—"

"Or retriever!" Frank shouted. He flung the branch clear across the street. Like a shot, the dog darted across after it.

Frank ran to the gate and slammed it shut. He turned to Callie and wiped his hands. "Luckily, that dog is all teeth and no brains!"

Together, Frank and Callie read the scrawled handwriting on the yellow sheet taped to the door:

Dear Simon,
Am at mall, fourth floor. There may actually be a shooting today. See you at 6.
T. G.

"This guy is stupider than I thought," Frank said. "How could he leave a more obvious clue?"

"Come on! Let's catch him before he kills somebody!" Callie raced to the front gate, only to stop short.

Waiting on the other side of the gate, the branch clenched between its teeth, was the black dog. "Uh, why don't you go first, Frank? It seems to like you more," Callie suggested.

Frank opened the gate and let the dog in. Quickly Callie scooted out to her car. Then Frank pulled the branch from the dog's mouth and tossed it up to the front door of the house. As the dog tore away, Frank shut the gate and jumped into the van.

Callie followed Frank to the Bayport Mall. They parked in the indoor lot and ran toward the mall elevator, just as the door was about to close on a tightly packed group of people.

"Excuse us!" Frank said as he pulled open the doors. He and Callie jammed inside, drawing a carful of dirty looks.

"Four, please," Callie said pleasantly. A skinny, sour-faced man grumbled and pushed four.

The trip to the top seemed to take forever. On each floor, the elevator stopped to let off someone from the back.

Frank and Callie leaned forward as the doors finally opened on the fourth floor. But a bearded man held out his hand, preventing them from getting off the elevator.

At the same time two gunshots rang out. Behind the bearded man, a man in a dark blue suit was running as if his life depended on it.

Chasing after him, with an automatic pistol, was Edwin Squinder.

Chapter
11

"STOP HIM!" CALLIE screamed. She lunged forward.

"No, Callie! He's got a gun!" Frank yelled.

Ignoring Frank, and pushing aside the bearded man, Callie ran straight for Squinder.

Shoppers screamed and hit the floor as Squinder ran past them. His face was twisted with grim determination, his eyes focused on the man in the blue suit. He didn't even see Callie as she stuck out her foot in his path.

"Wh-o-o-oa!" Squinder let out a helpless yelp as he stumbled against Callie's foot. He tumbled onto the floor, and his gun went flying into the air. Huddled against the store windows, the shoppers gasped in horror.

"Cut!" a voice rang out. "Who's the girl?"

"I don't know, Jerry!" the bearded man by the elevator said. "She ran right past me!"

Callie looked around. Bright white lights shone

down on her from all corners of the mall. Snaking along the floor were thick electrical cords, and groups of people laughed at her from behind TV cameras. One of them screamed out, "I think we should keep it, Jerry! She's great!"

"Okay, break!" the first voice said impatiently. "Clear the area, will you? We'll shoot again in ten."

Murmuring and snickering, the shoppers got up from the floor and walked over to a tableful of snacks and soft drinks.

Callie gulped. Her face turned red as the bearded man approached her. "Okay, kid, you just broke up our scene and made me look like a fool. When are you people going to realize this is no way to get yourself on TV?"

"Sorry, sir, but I thought—I thought—"

"Never mind! Just don't let me see you here after the break, okay?"

As the bearded man stormed off, Callie turned to Frank at her side. He patted her shoulder. "Anyone could have made the same mistake, Callie. If you hadn't reacted so quickly, I would have been the one to disrupt the shooting."

At once they became aware of Squinder standing behind them. "Still you hound me!" he said, his voice edged with fury.

Frank turned around calmly and said, "It was a mistake, Mr. Squinder. You see—"

"I see plainly enough!" Squinder said between clenched teeth. "First of all, it's *Grant* around here—Tyrone Grant. But revealing my real name is part of it, I'm sure. Part of your master plan to ruin my career!"

"I wouldn't throw accusations around if I were you, Squinder," Frank said. "Not before we find out why you conspired to kill Tessa Carpenter at her party the other night!"

At that, Squinder's eyes bulged open. He clutched his chest with one hand and staggered back. "You vile, evil juvenile delinquent! How *dare* you accuse me—"

"After all, who did we find lurking around the side of the mansion with a revolver after the lights went out? Lurking near the pathway that leads to the circuit breakers in the basement, I might add!"

"Circuit breaker? What?"

"Not to mention finding your little silver-plated revolver in the woods of the Cliffside Country Club yesterday, just after Tessa was shot at!"

"Young man, you wound me to the quick! If my professional pride weren't at stake, I'd—I'd give you a sound thrashing! As for the country club, I was here all day—yes, I know it was Sunday, but they had to make up for a rainy day—waiting for a turn to play my meager role." He grabbed a sheet of paper from a nearby table. "Here, for your information, is yesterday's attendance sheet."

Frank read, "Grant, Tyrone. In: 7:30 A.M. Out: 6:35 P.M."

"I don't know why I should even dignify your other complaint, but I most certainly was *not* in the Carpenter mansion on the night of that depraved party!"

"You just happened to stop by that night, right? And despite all the people around, you thought you might get away with sneaking into the servants' cottage for your gun—"

"A loud party would be the best cover for my entry into that cottage, sir."

"Five minutes, everybody! Five minutes!" a voice called out.

Squinder looked at his watch and groaned. "I'm wasting much too much time with you two. Now will you please excuse me? You've already destroyed an otherwise marvelous day."

Without waiting for an answer, Squinder walked toward the refreshment table.

"I still don't trust him," Frank said.

"Frank, let's get out of here," Callie replied. "I don't think Squinder's about to give us any more information."

The elevator door *whooshed* open behind them, and they stepped inside. This time they were all alone.

"Okay," Frank said. "Here's the plan. I need to follow up some other leads today, but I think someone had better keep an eye on Squinder. Would you do that?"

Callie nodded eagerly.

"Keep track of everything—phone calls, meetings, any strange behavior. Follow him to his house. But make sure he doesn't recognize you."

"How can I do that?"

The elevator opened on the parking lot. Frank went to the van and opened the sliding door. He looked both ways, then lifted up a floor panel. Underneath was a hold, jam-packed with equipment. He pushed aside a small camera, a lap-top computer, a box of diskettes containing a crime data base, a cellular mobile phone, and some magnetic metal disguise panels for the van.

"Ah, here it is," he said. He opened a box and pulled out a pale green uniform.

"Here's a worker's coverall. It'll be big, but if you put it on and cover your head with this"—he pulled out a beat-up baseball cap—"I think you'll be all right. You can collect papers and trash." He gave her a heavy-duty plastic bag.

"I've always loved high fashion," Callie said. She took the clothes and walked toward a nearby women's room. "Wait here while I change."

When Callie emerged from the women's room, the sleeves and legs of the uniform rolled up twice, Frank had to stifle a laugh. "You'd better watch out," he said. "The TV director may hire you for comic relief."

"Just what I need, encouragement!" Callie said. She tossed Frank her bundle of clothes and headed for the elevator.

Frank drove out of the lot, in the direction of the Bayport Museum. At the top of Cobb's Hill in the center of town, he stopped for a red light. His mind wouldn't stop racing. Now that Callie was taking care of Squinder, he began to think about Ruppenthal. There were too many loose ends—there *had* to be a way to get him to answer questions.

He was almost too involved to see a familiar car parked just beyond the top of the hill. A fiery red Lamborghini.

Frank pulled up behind it, just as someone came out of a nearby convenience store, carrying a huge stack of newspapers.

Thump. The newspapers were dropped by the side of the car, revealing Harley.

Frank gave a couple of taps on his horn and climbed out of the van. "Hi!"

Harley looked at him without expression. "I was driving by and saw Tessa's car," Frank continued. "I guess it's fixed!"

"Yes, they fixed it Saturday actually. Surprisingly it needed very little work. She wanted to go out and get it herself, but her 'bodyguard' thought she should stay in." Harley sneered at the word *bodyguard*.

"That's an awfully quick body shop!"

"The best. You get what you pay for, you know."

"What's with all these newspapers?"

"What's with all these questions? Tessa's on the front page again today, so she wanted a few copies, all right?" Harley opened the car door and tossed the keys on the dashboard.

Frank chuckled and tried to make a joke. "Wow, she's demanding. I guess she wants one for every room in the house, huh?"

Harley stood up and came face to face with Frank. "Well, *you* don't seem to mind it when she demands your attention."

"Hey, I was just kidding, Harley. Here, let me help you with the newspapers." Frank leaned over and began to load papers into the car.

"Get your head out of Tessa's car," Harley snapped. "I don't need your help."

"Easy, Harley, I didn't mean anything—"

"That does it! I've had enough of you." He gave Frank a push—a push that normally would have only rocked him back on his heels. But pressed up against the Lamborghini, he lost his balance and fell into the front seat.

Harley dove in after him, fists flying. Frank tried to swing back, but there was no room to maneuver between the dashboard and the backs of the bucket seats. He grabbed Harley's arms and thrust him backward against the steering wheel. The car horn squawked as Harley's back caught the edge of the wheel. His dark eyes blazing, Harley tried to pull Frank up and jam him against the opposite door.

But Frank yanked an arm loose and put a headlock around Harley. Trying to squirm free,

Harley jammed his knee against the emergency brake. With a click, the brake released.

As Frank and Harley fought inside, they were too busy to notice that the car was beginning to roll down the hill.

Too busy to notice it was heading straight for a gas tanker stopped at a red light below!

Chapter

12

STRUGGLING TO BREAK free, Harley fell off the front seat onto the floor. It was in that moment that Frank finally noticed the tanker.

"What the—we're moving!" Taking advantage of the distraction, Harley grabbed at Frank's collar.

"Get over it quick, buddy," Frank said as he wrenched himself free of Harley, "we're in *big* trouble."

Heooonk! Heooonk! By now the truck driver was blowing his horn, trying desperately to avoid the accident he saw coming in his rearview mirror.

The front of the Lamborghini was a tangle of arms and legs. There was no chance Frank could sit up and put on the foot brake in time. The tanker loomed larger and larger through the windshield. Frank yanked up on the emergency brake.

SCCCRRREEEEEEK! The car jerked violently, throwing Harley and Frank into the dashboard. But then it continued rolling, as if nothing had happened.

"We burned out the hand brake!" Frank said. The tanker was now fifteen feet away, still stuck at the red light. Both of its doors flew open. Screaming, the driver and his partner ran for the sidewalk.

There was only one chance. Frank reached behind him and grabbed the steering wheel. He pushed hard to the left.

The wheel moved a few inches, then clicked and stopped. The car swerved only slightly.

"It locks when there's no key in the ignition!" Harley shouted, sweat pouring from his brow. He reached down on the floor for the brake.

But it was too late for the brake. Frank felt his hair starting to stand on end as the car sped toward the tanker's left side. Then he remembered the keys on the dashboard. He grabbed them as Harley reached for the door handle. "Get off me!" he cried. "Let me jump!"

Frank jammed the key in and closed his eyes. He didn't want to see this.

A shudder pulsed through the car as he turned the key. It was still moving. Frank shoved his body against the wheel and opened his eyes. Through the right window he saw the side of the tanker *whooshing* safely by, maybe two inches away.

Harley lifted his head. Together, he and Frank

looked in the rearview mirror. The car had sailed past the intersection just as the light turned green. Peeking out from the side of a brick storefront were the tanker's driver and passenger.

With plenty of time to step on the brake now, Frank brought the car to a stop in the left lane.

"D-drive us to the side of the s-street, okay?" Harley said, unable to stop his voice from shaking.

Harley fanned himself with a newspaper as Frank pulled up to the curb. "Thanks," he said quietly.

"It's the least I could do, after the new body work," said Frank. "You may want to replace the emergency brake, though."

Harley smiled weakly. "You saved my life. How can I ever—"

"Repay me?" said Frank with a smile. "Well, you can start by being a little more friendly. We're in this together, you know."

Harley sighed. "Sorry, Frank. I guess I've been letting my jealousy show. But it seems that every time I turn around some guy is falling madly in love with my girlfriend."

"Look, Harley, I'm not in love with Tessa; I already have a girlfriend. And besides, the most important thing now is that someone is trying to kill her. If you really care that much for her, why don't you help us out?"

Harley looked stunned. "I'm *trying* to, by keeping an eye on Tessa."

"That's my brother's job. And I wouldn't worry about him. He gets that way with a lot of girls, and he's given up on Tessa by now."

"So what else do you want me to do?"

"Follow me to the Bayport Museum and help me pin down Ruppenthal. I could use some support."

Before Harley could answer, Frank hopped out of the car and ran back up the hill to his van. He passed the tanker and glanced up at the driver, who looked as if he wanted to kill him.

"Got to get those brakes fixed!" said Frank with a cheerful wave. He continued to run, without looking back.

Harley nervously fingered his hair as he followed Frank into the museum. "Look, Frank, I'm no detective, but I really think we ought to get back to the mansion. Tessa needs us. Besides, she's probably worrying about where I am."

"This won't take long," Frank answered. "We're just going to ask Ruppenthal a few more questions. Keep the heat on him."

"Personally, I don't think a wimp like Ruppenthal is very dangerous. Besides, he says he's found his agreement."

"Look, Harley, let me do the detective work. All you have to do is look menacing. Try hard."

With that he turned and walked through the museum door. Harley scowled as he followed behind.

Frank led him through the main hallway and into the outer office. The receptionist looked up from his computer. "Here to see Mr. Ruppenthal?" he asked, adjusting his glasses.

"Yes," Frank said, bluffing. "I'm Frank Hardy. I have an appointment."

The man turned back to his keyboard. "Why don't you take a seat in his office? He had an appointment, but I'm expecting him shortly."

Harley followed Frank into the empty office, where they both sat down.

"The museum looks ridiculous without that artwork, doesn't it?" Frank said.

Harley nodded absentmindedly. Beads of sweat were forming on his forehead, and he clenched and unclenched his fingers.

Finally he threw his hands in the air and stood up. "He's probably gone for the day. This is a total waste of time." He loosened his collar, looking around. "Let's go. This whole thing gives me the creeps."

Just then the silence was broken by the sounds of a door opening and footsteps in the hallway. The receptionist's voice chimed out, "First door on the left."

Harley spun around anxiously to face the door. "It's not Ruppenthal," he said.

The footsteps stopped. Two very large men in drab brown suits filled the doorway.

"We were just leaving," Harley said in a

choked voice, staring up into a broad, craggy face with a stubbly beard.

Without saying a word, the man stepped forward and grabbed Harley by the collar.

"No! No!" Harley sputtered as the man picked him up and threw him against Ruppenthal's desk. Harley let out a yell and fell onto the floor.

Instantly Frank sprang up from his chair into a karate stance. The hulking man faced him with a sinister grimace—and reached into his jacket.

"Hey, hey!" the other man called out to his partner. "What are you doing, stupid? Neither of these guys is Ruppenthal. They're way too young!"

The first man grunted and put his arm down. "Where's the big guy, punk?" he said to Frank.

"It looks as though he's left for the day."

The man lifted a clenched fist. "I'm not sure I believe you," he growled. But his partner grabbed him by the shoulder and said, "Come on, don't waste your time on this peach-fuzz! We were given bum information—let's get out of here!"

The men turned around and strode out of the doorway, leaving the scent of stale cigarette smoke in the room.

"Are you all right?" Frank asked.

Harley rose to his feet, one hand massaging his ribs. "Is this a normal day in your line of work?" he asked with a pained look on his face.

"More or less," Frank answered, his mind

already racing on to other things. "Ruppenthal's obviously in trouble with somebody—but who?"

"I couldn't even guess. Do you know what that goon was reaching for in his jacket?" Harley asked. "It wasn't—"

"A gun?" Frank smiled. "Why else would someone like that be reaching for his armpit? I don't think he was putting on deodorant."

"Look, Frank, I really don't think we should hang around here. What if they come back?"

Frank looked at this watch. "You're right. It's four-thirty anyway—Ruppenthal probably *has* gone home by now." He looked around on Ruppenthal's desk and pulled an envelope out from a stack of papers. "Here's his home address, in Short Neck. That's the next town over, just past the Carpenter mansion."

Harley shook his head violently. "I will absolutely not go with you to this man's house. I'll drive with you in that direction, but I plan to turn up Tessa's driveway—and don't try to talk me out of it!"

"Fine," said Frank with a shrug of the shoulders. "I'll follow you. Maybe my brother will change places with you for a little while."

Frank quickly copied down Ruppenthal's address, then he and Harley whisked out of the office, past a bewildered receptionist.

Within minutes the van and the Lamborghini . were on their way to the Carpenter mansion.

As Frank drove up the driveway, the first thing he noticed was a black car parked at the top. He pulled up behind it and saw the MD license plate.

"Hello, boys! Where's Tessa?"

Frank turned to see Dr. Lansdale waving from the front door of the mansion.

Harley parked the Lamborghini and jumped out. "She was with Joe when I left. They were supposed to stay here."

Dr. Lansdale looked puzzled. "Well, the front door was open when I arrived, but I can't find them."

Frank and Harley gave each other a surprised look. "Why don't I check the grounds while you cover the house," Frank suggested. Harley agreed, and Frank went over to the garage.

All four doors were open. Lawn equipment and a collection of barbecue grills were scattered across half the garage. The other half was totally empty.

They must have taken the other car, Frank thought. He ran back toward the mansion, only to see Harley rushing out the front door.

"The dagger! The dagger!" he blurted out.

"What?" said Frank. "What happened to it?"

Harley's eyes were wide open in fear. "It's gone!"

Chapter

13

FRANK RUSHED PAST Harley into the parlor. The bookcase had been pushed back into place, and all the paintings hung untouched. He went straight to the sideboard. The glass case lay there, its top open, its satin cushion rumpled. But the Borgia dagger was nowhere to be seen. He turned to Harley and Dr. Lansdale, who stood dumbfounded in the doorway.

"Harley, check upstairs. Dr. Lansdale, look in the hallway and the sitting room. If we're lucky, Joe has just hidden it somewhere for safekeeping."

Frank scoured the parlor. He looked in drawers, checked under the rug, shook books down from the bookcase.

Nothing.

Soon Harley and Dr. Lansdale appeared in the doorway again. They both shook their heads.

"What do you think happened to it?" asked Harley. "You think someone kidnapped Tessa?"

"There's no ransom note, and the other car is gone. I've got to assume she and Joe went somewhere in a hurry, maybe taking the dagger with them for some reason. Any ideas where they might be?"

"The country club!" Harley said immediately.

"Or the mall," Dr. Lansdale suggested.

"Well, I guess those leads are as good as any. Dr. Lansdale, you and I will go to the club in my van. Harley, you check out the mall."

"Right!" Harley eagerly hopped into the Lamborghini. Frank helped Dr. Lansdale into the passenger seat of the van and then climbed in on the other side.

The two cars took off down the winding driveway, leaving a trail of dust. As they reached the bottom, Frank suddenly jammed on the brakes. Harley skidded to a stop behind him, barely missing the rear bumper of the van.

In front of them, trudging wearily up the road, was Joe.

"Hey, what's all the excitement about? I could use a little lift," he said.

"Joe! What are you doing here?" Frank called out from inside the van. "Where's Tessa?"

Joe shrugged his shoulders and said, "Off floating through the countryside somewhere, far away from the dark terror of Joe Hardy."

"You lost her!" Frank said.

"Well, it's more complicated than that," Joe answered. "You know, a guy tries to be on his best behavior, tries to be the ideal bodyguard, right? He keeps quiet, does his job, and then decides to make conversation—asks a dumb, innocent, friendly question—"

Frank crossed his arms. "What did you ask her, Joe?"

"Well, I was reading *Personality* magazine and I got to thinking about the actors in the movies—you know, the ones who have to do those kisses in close-up? Well, I realized these people probably don't even really know each other—"

"I don't believe this," Frank said, rolling his eyes. "Get to the point, Joe!"

Joe lowered his head. "All I did was ask how she would feel kissing a perfect stranger—"

"What?" Harley bellowed.

Joe protested, "She didn't even give me a chance to—"

"Cool it, you guys," Frank said. "Go on, Joe, what did she do after this 'innocent, friendly' question?"

"Well, she gave me a look, ran outside, and drove away. I tried to run after her. I even ran all the way into town, hoping she just stopped at an ice-cream store or something, but no luck."

"Did she take the dagger with her for any reason?"

"I don't think so. Why?"

"It's gone, Joe. The front door of the mansion was open, and the dagger was gone."

"Well, Tessa *was* storming around the house this afternoon. It's possible—"

"My guess is that someone else has it—someone who wants to use it—"

Joe finished the sentence. "On Tessa!"

Dr. Lansdale gasped. "Oh, my poor little girl!"

"Look, chances are it's nothing serious," Frank said. "She's probably at the club or driving around blowing off steam. Why don't you and Harley comb the town for her, while I take Dr. Lansdale and look for Ruppenthal. I've *got* to track him down—"

"Hold it a minute, Frank," Joe said. "You want *me* to go with Harley? Uh, I hate to say it, but that doesn't sound like the best combination."

They both glanced over at Harley pacing back and forth, his hands curled into fists. "Right," Frank said. He gave Joe the piece of paper with Ruppenthal's address. "Okay, you go with Dr. Lansdale. Try to get Ruppenthal to talk." He reached into the van. "I'll take one of the mobile phones and call you when we find Tessa."

As Frank stepped into Harley's car, Joe gunned the van down the road toward Short Neck.

"Please, Joe, I'm a little slow at this sort of thing," said Dr. Lansdale. "Why are we looking for Albert Ruppenthal?"

"Sorry, Dr. Lansdale. Frank and I can't help thinking Ruppenthal's up to something. He and Squinder are the only ones who seem to have clear motives for wanting to harm Tessa."

Dr. Lansdale stared out the window distract-edly. "I still can't believe this is happening. Why would *anyone* want to murder Tessa Carpenter?"

"We're not sure. That's why we've got to follow every lead."

"And you think Mr. Ruppenthal might be behind this?"

"Possibly. The only thing that puzzles me is that he says he now has the agreement that gives the collection back to the museum."

"A bluff, perhaps?" Dr. Lansdale suggested.

"Maybe, but why?"

She shrugged her shoulders. "Well, he may know that you and Frank are guarding her. If he gets you to believe he has the agreement, then you'll think the Carpenter Collection legally belongs in the museum."

"And we'd stop guarding her if we thought she was doing something illegal."

"Precisely. This could be a means of luring you two away from her so he can attack."

Joe smiled. "You're not 'a little slow at this sort of thing' at all, Dr. Lansdale."

"Not when my Tessa's life is at stake!"

"All right, then!" Joe reached into his pocket and gave Dr. Lansdale the paper on which Frank had written Ruppenthal's address. "Let's find him."

Before long they left Cliffside Heights. Dr. Lansdale directed Joe through Short Neck and onto a road of small houses and towering maple trees. House after house looked almost identical: white shingles, freshly cut lawns, and flower gardens. But one was completely hidden by enormous green hedges.

"That's it," said Dr. Lansdale. "I must say," she added as Joe pulled up in front, "it looks sort of creepy and overgrown."

"I don't see a car in the driveway," Joe said. "We may have to wait for him."

"How do you expect to involve me in this?" Dr. Lansdale asked.

"Wait here and watch carefully while I check around. As soon as Ruppenthal lets me in, I'll sit him down and question him. I have a feeling he'll be offering me a bribe I've already refused. If he does, I'll somehow get him to offer it to me in the front room."

Joe opened the van's secret floor compartment and pulled out a small camera. "I'm setting this zoom lens for you. All you have to do is press this button and film the exchange of money. We'll build a case on Ruppenthal."

Dr. Lansdale grabbed the camera with excitement. "I'll do anything to help put this awful fellow behind bars."

"Just keep the windows up. They're tinted, so he won't be able to tell anyone's in here."

Joe walked up the empty driveway. He noticed large plastic bags of trash by the side of the house. To anyone else, it would not have seemed unusual, but Joe noticed none of the other houses had put their trash out yet.

He walked to the front door and rang the bell. No answer. He tried another time, then went over to the front windows.

One peek was all it took. Joe ran back to the van and yanked open the front door. "Quick, Dr. Lansdale, move over!"

"What is it? He's not home?"

"Not only that! There are sheets over all his furniture, and the trash is out early. He's gone all right—and it's a good bet he's on the run!"

Beeeep. Beeeep. Dr. Lansdale was startled by the sound of the mobile phone.

Joe picked it up. "Yeah, Frank . . . You did? . . . Is she okay? . . . A *what?* . . . Location? . . . We'll be right there!"

Joe threw the van into gear. The tires left a black double curve as he made a squealing U-turn.

"They've found Tessa," he said.

"What is it, Joe? Is she all right?"

Joe tightened his grip on the steering wheel. He didn't quite know how to say this. "They don't know. She's lying in a ditch by Fairground Road."

Chapter

14

DR. LANSDALE CLUTCHED the dashboard as Joe zoomed back into Cliffside Heights. The tree branches alongside the road bent in the wind as the van went by.

Fairground Road was a sharp right about a half mile past the Carpenter mansion. The van teetered sharply to the left as Joe made the turn.

The numbers on the digital speedometer changed in rapid succession. Finally Joe caught sight of two cars off to the side of the road.

"There they are!" cried Dr. Lansdale.

Joe drove onto the shoulder and stopped behind Harley's car. To their right, on the grass by the side of the road, Harley was cradling a woozy Tessa in his arms. Frank was kneeling nearby.

Dr. Lansdale threw open the van door and rushed out to Tessa, with Joe close behind.

"What happened?" Joe called out.

"We found her in the woods, almost unconscious," Frank said. "We never got to the mall."

"Why were you going on this road?" Joe said. "The mall's much closer to town."

"Harley knew about some sort of shortcut. And it's a lucky thing we came this way, or we'd never have found her."

"Is she hurt?"

"Doesn't seem so. There's practically no sign of struggle. But there is something very weird—"

Frank was interrupted by a muffled cry from Dr. Lansdale.

All eyes looked down. Dr. Lansdale was quickly brushing away hair from Tessa's forehead. Underneath was a red mark that looked like a huge, jagged scar.

Frank bent down and immediately realized it wasn't a scar at all. Shaped like a twisted lightning bolt, the mark had been drawn onto Tessa's forehead with bright lipstick.

Frank stared at it, bewildered. "It's a letter *B*," he said.

The color had drained out of Dr. Lansdale's face. "Yes," she said, nodding gravely. "It's the ancient symbol of the Borgia family."

Immediately they all fell silent.

"What are you all staring at? Tell me!" Tessa cried out. Now fully awake, she glanced from face to face with terror in her eyes.

Realizing where everyone was looking, she

shot her hand up to her forehead. With a sweep of her fingers, she wiped away some of the lipstick.

"What is this—some sort of joke? What's happening to me?"

"Everything's okay now," said Harley with a reassuring smile. "Just lie back and take it easy for a few minutes."

He rocked her in his arms, but her eyes were on Frank. "Frank, I'm scared," she said, her voice quivering. "I never should have gone off alone. But your brother—"

Frank sat down across from her. "I know. From now on, there are going to be some changes." He gave Joe a sharp, quick glance. "The three of us will stick together at all times— and Harley and Dr. Lansdale will help us. Now, tell me what you remember."

"Well, I wasn't really watching the road. All of a sudden, this big blue sedan honked its horn." Tessa choked back a sob. "I thought it was trying to pass, so I moved over. Then it pulled up alongside me and came closer and closer. I had to drive off the road."

"Did you see who was in the car?" Frank asked.

"No, I don't remember anything from that point on," she said. "I must have hit my head or something—it's all a blank."

"Nothing in the rearview mirror? Was it one or two people?"

Tessa looked confused. "Two, I think."

"Male?"

"I think so."

"Wearing business suits?"

"I don't know—maybe. Why? Do you know who it might be?"

"I have a feeling Harley and I may have run into them earlier." Frank got up and began pacing around. "But why all this Borgia hocus-pocus? We've got to put these pieces together. Tessa, we'll take you back to the house, and Dr. Lansdale can take a look at—"

"No," Tessa said sharply. "I'm too frightened to go back there. Whoever's trying to kill me can easily find me at home."

Dr. Lansdale stood up and took Frank by the arm. She led him away from the other three. "Just a minute, Frank," she said softly. "Tessa's right. Going back to the mansion isn't such a good idea, especially since the dagger has disappeared. We can't be sure the thief isn't still on the premises."

"That's true," he answered. "But don't you think Tessa's head should be looked at?"

"She seems fine, aside from being shaken up. Let's go to a diner or something for a couple of hours, where she can at least calm down. That's what she needs most."

"If you say so, Doctor. Actually, a restaurant might be a good place to sort out all the clues."

Frank turned back to Joe. "Callie's been tailing Squinder for a while. I'll go pick her up to join us. Why don't we meet you at the Argo for dinner?" Then he smiled at Tessa. "It may not be the kind of restaurant you're used to, Tessa, but it's safe, and it'll be more comfortable than sitting here!"

Callie broke into a grin when she heard the Hardys' van pull up behind her car. She was parked a block away from Squinder's house.

Frank walked over to the car and leaned in the driver's window. "I came to relieve you from watch duty."

"Good. I was starting to get bored. I tailed Squinder home from work, and he hasn't left since then."

"Did you see anything suspicious?" Frank asked.

"Not really. He reshot his scene a couple of times at the mall, then sat around watching them shoot another scene, and finally went home a couple hours ago."

"Any visitors?"

"One guy, sort of short and greasy-looking. He had on a jacket and bow tie, wore tortoise-shell glasses. He may have been the 'Simon' whom Squinder was going to see at six o'clock."

"Is he still inside?" Frank asked.

"No, he left alone shortly after he arrived."

"Good work, Callie. How about taking a dinner break?"

Callie's face lit up. "Great! I was wondering when you'd ask! Where are we going?"

"Actually," Frank called over his shoulder as he walked back to the van, "we're meeting Joe and the others at the Argo."

"Joe and the others! Just a minute, Frank, I thought *we* were going out!"

"Come on, Callie! Wait till you hear what happened!" With that, Frank started the van and rolled away from the curb.

Steaming, Callie followed him.

Frank and Callie pulled into the parking lot, just underneath broken neon letters that said TH A GO REST URANT. For a Monday night, the Argo was pretty busy. Several cars were there, and a lively clanking of plates resounded from the dining room.

In a large booth at the far corner of the dining room, Tessa, Dr. Lansdale, Harley, and Joe sat glumly reading their menus. Behind them, four teenagers were casting quick looks at Tessa and giggling.

"What took you so long?" Joe asked. "We're starving!"

Callie sat on the edge of her seat next to Tessa, and Frank sat across from them. "Looks like you're creating a little stir here," Frank remarked, referring to the table behind them.

"They must have read the paper today," Tessa said.

"It's that front-page article I was telling you about," Harley said to Frank.

"After the interview with me," Tessa continued, "that society columnist happened to stick around long enough to see the whole thing happen. And voilà—the news story of his lifetime, probably."

"And more celebrity for you," Frank said.

"As if I needed it," Tessa answered with a laugh.

As Frank and Callie opened their menus, Tessa took out a compact and freshened her makeup.

"Uh, excuse me, are you by any chance Tessa Carpenter?" They all looked up to see a middle-aged woman with a grinning man and two children.

Tessa smiled sweetly. "Why, yes. Do I know you?"

The woman and man laughed. "Oh, no! We've been reading all about you in the papers and magazines," the woman said. "My children have never met anyone famous. I just wondered—could you—I mean, would it be too much to ask you to—"

"Sign an autograph? Of course!" Tessa answered.

The woman turned to the little boy behind her. "JASON! GET MY MENU—AND ASK THE WAITER FOR A PEN! ON THE DOUBLE!" She faced Tessa again and said, "Thank you. You have no idea how much this means to him."

While they ordered and began eating their food, several other people began to drift over to the table to ask for autographs. Tessa greeted each one cheerfully.

"It's almost as if she enjoys it," Frank muttered to Joe. Callie leaned over to listen to the brothers as menus, placemats, and napkins were being signed over her head.

"Look at this," Joe answered. "They're lining up. Every single table in this restaurant!"

"Except for that nerdy-looking guy over there. He's just watching the whole thing," Frank said.

Joe and Callie turned to look at a balding man with spectacles, a bow tie, and a navy blue blazer.

Callie did a double-take and spun around, her eyes wide with excitement. "That's the guy!" she whispered.

"That's what guy?" Frank asked.

"Simon! The one who visited Squinder this evening."

Frank and Joe kept a careful eye on the man while they finished eating. Before long the autograph seekers thinned out, and soon the only people in the room were the ones at their table— and the balding man.

"Why is he just staring at our table with that weird smile?" Joe said under his breath.

"I don't know," Frank answered.

Suddenly Tessa let out a big sigh. "I don't believe this. Is *this* what my life is going to be like from now on? Smiling and signing menus? Answering policemen? You know, they're still calling and asking questions about the shooting."

"That's one of the things I wanted to talk about," Frank said. "You've got to keep a distance from the press—"

"He's getting up," Joe said, interrupting.

Frank watched as the balding man rose from his table. He took out a wad of neatly folded and clipped dollar bills and put some on the table. Then he straightened out his blazer and made sure that a few long strands of black hair were in place over his bald spot.

Callie craned her neck around to see the man walk slowly over to their table. His eyes were focused on Tessa with a sinister glint. When they weren't looking at her, they were darting nervously from side to side.

The table fell silent as everyone realized what was happening. They all stared as the man approached.

He adjusted his collar after stopping beside their booth. Silently, he let his small eyes rove around the table, then he nodded.

With a strange half smile, he looked straight at Tessa. "Hello, Miss Carpenter," he said. "Edwin Squinder—or should I say, Tyrone Grant—has told me all about you."

Frank felt every muscle in his body tense as the man reached into his breast pocket and slowly withdrew a gleaming silver object!

Chapter

15

"It's a gun!" Tessa screamed. Silverware and saucers fell on the floor as Callie and Joe leapt up from the booth. Both lunged at the man with lightning-quick speed.

The man let out a frightened squawk as Callie reached him first, barreling headfirst into his stomach. He tumbled backward into a loaded tray of dirty plates, which flew across the room.

Joe immediately jumped on top of him and pinned his arms down as the man struggled desperately to protect his face. His glasses lay half on the floor, still dangling from one ear.

"Help! Help!" he cried in a high-pitched whine.

Callie bent down and pulled open his jacket to reach inside his inner pocket.

She looked down at the silver object in her hand. It was small, flat, and rectangular, with a clasp on one side.

"Are you crazy?" the man said. "It's not worth that much! Take it if you want it so badly."

Callie flipped the clasp. The top of the object sprang open. Inside, stacked neatly, was a pile of business cards. She read the top one:

SIMON LESTERMAN COMPANY
Talent Agency
Film, TV, Commercials
Phone: 555-STAR
New York   Bayport

Callie and Joe looked at each other numbly. Then Joe hopped off the man, his face quickly turning red with embarrassment. "We-we're *so* sorry, sir. *Please* forgive us. We thought you were a—a murderer."

The man sat up, his face puckered with anger and confusion. Long, thin strands of black hair hung down around his collar. "*Murderer?* Are you out of your—" As he put the silver case back in his jacket pocket, he stopped. He glanced down at his hand. Slowly he pulled the case back out. A trace of a smirk began to form on his face.

"I see—" he said slowly. "You thought my card case was a gun!" A low chuckle began to form in his throat. Nervously, Callie and Joe laughed along with him.

One by one, everyone at the table joined in laughing, as a confused busboy rushed over to clean up the damage.

"What a team, huh?" Joe said, catching his breath. "Let's check out that busboy—I think he has a bazooka!"

The busboy scrambled into the kitchen and Callie and Joe sank into their seats.

"You see, sir, Tessa Carpenter is with us," Frank explained to the man, "and there are so many—"

"Kooks after her," the man said with a toothy grin. "I understand; I've been reading the papers. Ordinarily I'd press charges, but these are special circumstances." He pulled his card case out again. "As a matter of fact, Tessa is the person I want to see."

He held out a card to her. "My name's Simon Lesterman. Talent agent. I represent Tyrone Grant. To be blunt, you're hot, Tessa. I mean that in a commercial sense. Just look at the way those people flocked after you. You've got the looks, the charm, the exotic background. You could make it big in films or TV."

Tessa looked at him with disbelief. "Is *that* why you interrupted our dinner? You just want to use my fame to make yourself a little money, don't you?"

"You wouldn't do badly yourself, sweetheart."

"*Sweetheart?*" Tessa fumed.

Lesterman shook his head with admiration and said, "Look at that. You're even gorgeous when you're mad!"

"Get him out of here!" Tessa muttered to Frank.

"All right, sir," Frank said. "We're all very tired now. Sorry for the confusion, but I think it's best Tessa's left alone now, okay?"

"Sure thing, young man," Lesterman said. Then he turned back to Tessa. "In case you want to talk, my number's on the card."

Smoothing his hair back into place, he walked out of the restaurant.

"Imagine the nerve of him," Tessa snapped. "Trying to leech onto me like that." She looked scornfully at Joe and Callie. "Thanks for saving my life from that dangerous murderer. I haven't laughed that hard since before this whole thing started."

Callie bit back the angry retort that was on the tip of her tongue. Tessa Carpenter made her furious. Tessa had been the one to shout "It's a gun!" even though Joe and she had been the ones to tackle Lesterman. And despite Tessa's big show of disgust at Lesterman's offer, Callie could see a glimmer in her eyes. The excited glimmer of someone who had just been flattered. She could easily tell that Tessa was thinking about TV fame.

Tessa put Lesterman's card in her pocketbook and looked around the room. "Check, please!" she called out to their waitress.

Frank leaned forward, finally able to ask a question that had been nagging at him. "Tessa, when you left the house today, did you know where the dagger was?"

"Of course," Tessa answered. "In the parlor."

Frank and Joe looked at each other. Dr. Lansdale and Harley exchanged a worried glance. "Uh—I think we have a new problem here," Joe added.

"What now?" Tessa said.

"The dagger is missing, and so is Ruppenthal."

Callie's eyes widened, and Tessa gasped. "This gets worse and worse!" Tessa said, burying her head in her hands. "Do you think *he* took it?"

"We're not sure," Frank said. "But don't worry, we'll find it."

"This dagger has caused me so much pain," Tessa moaned. "I'm sick of the whole situation—as soon as you get the stupid thing back, I'm going to auction it off!" She stood up from the table and walked toward the door.

Dr. Lansdale paid the bill, and they all went out to the cars.

"Please, won't you all come home with me?" Tessa pleaded. "I feel so keyed up and scared."

"I'll drive you," Harley said, putting an arm around her. He led her to the Lamborghini. "One of you can take my car."

They left the diner together—Frank in the van, Callie in her car, Harley and Tessa in the Lamborghini, and Joe and Dr. Lansdale in Harley's car.

The Lamborghini led the way—slowly, cautiously.

"All of a sudden Harley's a model driver," Frank said to himself.

Suddenly Harley's brake lights flashed. "What's he doing now?" Frank asked. "Oh, stopping for gas."

The Lamborghini slowed down and made a right turn into a gas station. The other three cars pulled over beside the curb.

Harley drove up right behind a white station wagon full of boxes and suitcases. With his back to the Lamborghini, a man was gassing up the station wagon. When he finished, he held the hose in one hand and fumbled around in his pockets with the other. Out came a set of keys and a matchbook—but no money. The man scratched his head, then opened his front door.

Honk! "Come on, move it up, will you?" Harley shouted. Annoyed, the man turned around.

"Hey, hold your hor—"

The face was instantly familiar.

Ruppenthal.

Immediately six doors slammed as everyone got out of a door.

"Stand back!" Ruppenthal screamed, a look of blind panic covering his face.

"Hello, Mr. Ruppenthal," Frank said. "You know, you're just the guy we want to see—"

"I'm warning you, don't take another step—anybody!" Ruppenthal said, holding the gas nozzle as if it were a gun. He looked at Tessa with savage eyes. "You couldn't give me a chance, could you? You couldn't at least wait until the day ended!"

Overcome with his own fury, Ruppenthal took two steps toward the Lamborghini and pressed the handle on the nozzle. A stream of clear gasoline splashed all over the car's hood. He squirted a trail of it along the ground up to his own car door.

Tessa and Harley shielded themselves and ducked away. "What are you doing, you fool?" Harley asked.

"We'll see who's the fool," Ruppenthal replied, dropping the hose onto the ground. He reached into his pocket and took out the book of matches. "All my life I've worked hard, lived by the rules. But you've changed me, Tessa Carpenter. You've turned me into a monster—a monster as ruthless as you are."

With a frantic ripping motion, he lit a match and held it poised over the gas-soaked car.

Chapter

16

"MURDERERS!" RUPPENTHAL SNARLED, as Harley and Tessa backed away. "Now toss me the keys to your cars—all of you!—or I'll blow you sky-high!"

"Has he lost his mind?" Callie whispered to Frank.

"I don't know," answered Frank. "But I don't think I want to ask him just now."

Quickly, Frank, Harley, Callie, and Joe reached into the cars, pulled out the keys, and tossed them onto the ground in front of Ruppenthal.

"Yeouch!" Ruppenthal cried as the match burned to his fingers. He threw it away from the car—and Joe sprinted toward him.

But instantly Ruppenthal lit another. "Back off," Ruppenthal said, with a maniacal grin. "It's not so easy. Thought I'd be a pushover, didn't you? Now, turn your backs."

Slowly, everyone obeyed him. Still holding the lit match, Ruppenthal climbed into his car. "Count to ten thousand, backward—and let me hear it!"

As they all started to mumble, Ruppenthal blew out the match and sped off, his tires screaming.

As soon as he heard that, Frank ran to the open door of the van. He jumped into the front seat and reached for a cigarette lighter next to the steering wheel. He pushed it in three times and then turned it twice to the right. With a jangling sound, a set of keys popped out.

He revved up the engine. "Callie, do you have extra keys?"

She shook her head no. "But my mom will bring me a set."

"Good. Drive everyone home. I'm going to get Ruppenthal."

He slammed the van into gear, made a noisy U-turn, and roared off into the street.

Looking left and right, he kept his eyes peeled for any sign of the white station wagon.

Suddenly Frank noticed something in the passenger-side mirror. A person—hanging on to the door for dear life.

He slowed down and stopped in the middle of the road. "What do you think you're doing?" he shouted.

Tessa's face popped into the window. "That was so exciting! I have *always* wanted to try that!"

"What, ride holding on to a van going sixty miles an hour?"

Tessa nodded, grinning.

"You must *like* to put your life in danger!" Frank shook his head. "Come on, get in—we're wasting time!"

She plopped into the front seat and Frank resumed the chase. He went to the end of the street, where it branched off to the center of town. He drove in the opposite direction, toward the parkway entrance. There he saw a line of cars, waiting to get on.

None of them was the white station wagon.

"We've lost him," said Frank. "He could be anywhere by now."

He spun back through the streets of Bayport, again seeing no sign of Ruppenthal. Dejected, he headed back toward the Carpenter mansion.

"That was fantastic, Frank! I felt like I was in a movie!"

"Yeah," said Frank dryly, "with one exception. Most movies have happy endings."

"Don't worry, maybe he's on his way to flee the country—and good riddance!"

"Tessa, what was he saying about 'waiting till the end of the day'?"

Tessa rolled her eyes. "Oh, how bizarre! Imagine, him calling *me* a murderer! I think this whole thing has cracked the poor man's mind!"

Soon they were climbing up the driveway to the

mansion. Frank flicked the ignition off sharply as he parked the van.

"Easy, Frank," said Tessa in a soothing voice. "I think you need to relax a bit."

"Uh—okay! Let's go inside and wait for the others!" Frank said and quickly slid out the door.

Tessa followed him into the mansion. He went straight into the sitting room and paced around.

"Well!" he said. "I have to admit, *nothing* seems to fit in this case. If Ruppenthal took the dagger, then—"

Tessa sidled up next to Frank and gently put her finger on his lips. "Shh," she whispered. "Let's forget about the case for a moment, okay?"

Frank took her hand and led her to the couch. Together they sat down. "I'm sorry, Tessa, I don't mean to hurt your feelings—but you *know* that Callie is my girlfriend. We're very happy together. This—what you're doing is not right."

"How can you say that, Frank? You're not *married* to her!"

"Tessa, don't you feel funny about all this? I mean, betraying Harley behind his back—"

Tessa looked shocked and hurt. "Harley has meant nothing to me—absolutely nothing, from the instant I met you, Frank. I can't help it!" For the first time, she moved her eyes away from Frank. "I—I love you."

Frank sank back in the couch. He watched the glistening outline of a tear form in Tessa's eye.

"I don't know what to say," he whispered.

Tessa wiped her eyes and sat up straight, a brave smile etched across her face. "Well," she said, "that's that, I guess." She fanned herself with her right hand and looked at the window.

"Imagine that," she continued. "We've been sitting here the whole time with the window shut. This room sure could use some air."

"Yes! Good idea!" Frank stood up and reached over Tessa for the front window behind the sofa. He gave a yank, but the window held fast. "Must be locked or something."

Tessa looked up from beneath him. "Oh, there's a special pin you have to pull. Here, let me help you." She reached up toward the center of the window as Frank continued to struggle.

The pin was just beyond her reach. She stood up, the back of her head practically brushing against Frank's face. There was a moment of tense stillness as Tessa tried to move the pin. Then, with a sudden movement, Tessa spun around and planted a kiss on Frank's lips.

At that exact instant the room was lit by the headlights of an oncoming car.

Frank and Tessa sprang away from each other. The sounds of slamming car doors burst the silence.

"Hey! What do you think you're doing?"

"Harley," Tessa muttered. "Perfect timing."

"Frank, is that you?"

132

"And Callie," Frank moaned. "We're both in luck."

The front door crashed open as Harley, Callie, and Joe entered the mansion. They had dropped the doctor off at home.

Harley's hulking form loomed in the doorway. Behind him stood Callie with a confused expression on her face. "You got what you wanted, didn't you, Tessa?" Harley shouted. "I've been in this with you all the way, risking my neck—"

"Harley, don't!" Tessa said.

"And now you think you can just toss me away like an old piece of clothing that you grew tired of!" Harley rushed forward, glaring at her with blazing eyes. "I've had enough," he growled. Then a deep laugh slowly welled up from within him.

Tessa's face blanched. She grabbed the edge of the sofa. "No—you wouldn't!"

"Really? Well, I've got news for you. You'll *never* get that dagger now!"

As Tessa froze in shock, Harley bolted outside.

"Go after him!" Tessa screamed. "He's going to spoil everything!" But Frank didn't move. He stood stock-still, head bowed, clenching and unclenching his fists. Joe stepped into the room, and he and Callie could do nothing but stare at Tessa in confusion and disbelief.

Suddenly Frank wheeled around and faced Tessa. He frowned, the face of a man furiously thinking—or just furious. "You know something about this, don't you?" he growled.

"I—what do you—me?" Tessa stammered. "How dare you accuse me—" But her protest was weak.

"Start talking, Tessa. I want to know everything," Frank demanded.

Tessa's lower lip began to quiver. She let her hair fall in front of her face as she collapsed onto the sofa. "I know who's been causing all of the murder attempts," she said in a thick voice.

"Who?" Joe burst in. "It's Squinder, isn't it?"

Tessa shook her head. "No, it's not Squinder. It's not Ruppenthal, either."

Her voice cracked as she let out a sudden sob. She raised her watery eyes toward Frank, searching for sympathy, understanding.

"Who is it, Tessa? You might as well come out with it," Frank said softly.

All at once, a rush of tears cascaded over her cheeks. She buried her head in her hands and wept. "It was Harley and me!" she blurted out. "We staged the whole thing."

She looked up to see everyone frozen in shock. The secret she'd held back could remain hidden no longer, and the words spilled out.

"Squinder was right. I did spend all the money my parents left me! How could I afford to keep up the house, let alone hired help—I *had* to fire them all. Even if I sell the mansion, it'll just be enough to pay back my loans and buy me a small house in Bayport—and then I'll have to get a job!

"That's why I took back the art collection," Tessa continued. "To sell it." Dark streaks of mascara smeared across her face as she wiped her eyes.

"Go on," Frank said. "What does this have to do with the Borgia dagger and the murder attempts?"

"The Borgia dagger was all a publicity stunt. Everything was set up by us—the shooting, the wire in the pool, the letter *B* on my forehead."

"Then why—"

"We thought if we could create a whole news event around the dagger, I'd get a fortune for it at an auction, and I'd never again worry about money. Harley has been my boyfriend since we were kids, and I promised him a cut of the auction money. But . . ." She glanced guiltily at Callie. "Then you came along, Frank. Harley could sense I was losing interest in him, that I didn't really love him, and—"

All of a sudden, she sat bolt upright and put her hand to her mouth. "Oh, no!" she gasped.

Frank, Joe, and Callie all rushed forward. "What is it?" Frank said.

"Harley—" she said, her voice catching. "Harley has the dagger. He hid it in the flower garden."

Joe looked at Frank. "Let's find him!" he said.

135

Immediately the brothers ran for the hallway. But before they got out of the room, they stopped in their tracks.

Silently, as if on cue, the room had been plunged into total darkness.

Chapter

17

"HARLEY! NO!" TESSA screamed at the top of her lungs. But she was answered by silence. "He's gone crazy, I know it!" she said. "All he wants is revenge!"

"And with that dagger, there's no telling what he'll do!" Joe added.

"Or where he is," Callie said.

Suddenly a shriek cut through the air. "Aaaaaaah!"

Frank tensed. "What's wrong?"

"Ow," Joe's voice answered. "Quiet, Tessa, it's only me! You just stomped on my foot!"

"Oh!" Tessa sighed. "I was looking for the flashlight. It's in—"

Thud. "Here." The eerie silence was broken by the sound of a drawer opening. Then a shaft of light cut through the sitting room.

"There are two flashlights here," Tessa said.

"Great! I'll take one," Joe said.

"Shh! Listen!" Callie whispered. A rhythmic *creak, creak, creak*. And then it abruptly stopped.

"Where's it coming from?" Tessa asked.

"I don't know," Joe said. "But I think we'd better deal with these lights right now, before we're dead ducks!"

Joe led them out the front and around the mansion to the cellar doors. Pulling one open, he climbed down into the room and flicked the master circuit breaker. That ought to do it, he said to himself, rushing back outside.

But the mansion just stared back at him, pitch-black.

"We're out of luck," Frank said. "He must have cut a power line."

"All right," said Joe. "If we're not going to get him to come out here, we'll just have to go in after him. Come on!"

Their flashlights blazing, all four scurried back in the front door. The hot dampness of the summer night made them feel as if everything were moving in slow motion. Musty smells of old wood and dusty carpets hung in the air as they went from room to room.

Thunk. Frank jerked his head upward at the noise above them. With a sprinter's quickness, he dashed into the hallway and up a stairway, followed close behind by Joe. At the top, he beamed the flashlight down the empty hallway.

"You're doing this all wrong, Harley," Frank

called out. "There are four of us, and one of you. It's useless. Come on out."

No response. "The noise was from the room on the right," Frank whispered. He and Joe edged down the hallway toward the room, their backs along the wall. They stopped inches from the room's doorway. It was closed. They froze for a long second.

In a burst of strength, Frank whipped around and kicked the door open. Immediately he ducked back against the wall.

The door rattled on its hinges, but no one came out. Frank held his flashlight into the room, then looked in. A four-poster bed stood neatly made, surrounded by dark wooden furniture. He stepped toward the closet and flung it open. Three lonely winter coats rocked back and forth with the updraft from the door's movement.

"Disappeared," Joe said.

Frank looked out into the hallway. "Where are Callie and Tessa?" he asked.

As if in answer, a piercing scream rang out from the other end of the floor.

Frank and Joe charged down the hallway in the direction of the noise. Out of one of the rooms came gasps of shock. They rushed inside, and Frank shone the light on a figure crumpled on the floor.

"Callie! Are you all right?" Frank asked, kneeling next to her.

"I—I think so," she answered, her left hand covering her ear.

"Let's see." Frank took her hand away and looked at her ear. "It's bleeding a bit, but doesn't look too bad."

"What are you doing here alone?" Joe asked.

"After you guys ran off, Tessa and I thought we'd take the back stairway. She went straight up to the third floor, but when I got to the second, I thought I heard a noise."

"So you came into this room, without a flashlight?" Frank said.

Callie nodded. "Anyway, the minute I walked in here, I heard someone call Tessa's name in a low voice behind me. I turned around and saw Harley's outline—then he nicked me with the dagger. When I screamed, I think he realized who I was, and he tried to pull back. Then he ran out of the room, cursing." She shuddered. "I think he's gone completely crazy."

"You're lucky he didn't get more than the ear," said Joe.

"We can't just stand here," Callie pleaded. "He's vicious! If I had been Tessa he would have killed me."

"We've got to get to Tessa!" Joe said. "She's alone!"

Suddenly from upstairs came another scream. Even as it echoed through the house, Frank, Joe, and Callie were flying up the back stairs. They ran into a large attic room.

There, beneath the sloping wood-beam ceiling, Tessa and Harley stood at opposite ends of an oak table.

"Get away from me, you beast!" Tessa shrieked. Harley stood poised with the Borgia dagger, faking from side to side, looking for a way to run around the table.

"Drop it, Harley!" Frank called out. Harley looked toward the door, into the glow of Frank's flashlight.

"*Yeeeeaaaaaggghh!*" Screaming, Harley hurled himself across the table. He caught Frank at stomach level and tackled him to the ground. The light zigzagged crazily around the room as the flashlight clattered to the floor. Frank grabbed for it, but it rolled out of his reach.

"How about a little taste of the Borgia curse?" Harley hissed as he raised the jeweled dagger.

Joe grabbed the flashlight off the floor and pointed it directly at Harley and Frank—in time to see Frank push Harley's arm back. The dagger flew against the corner wall.

All motion in the room followed it. Frank, Harley, Joe, Callie, and Tessa dove into the corner. A tangle of arms and fingers reached out toward the dagger, but only one person's hand closed around it.

"Get back! He's got it!" Frank yelled. He, Joe, and Callie fell away as Harley brandished the dagger over his head.

Then, with a sudden lunge, he pushed Tessa to

141

the ground. The dishes stored in the old break-front behind him rattled as he pulled her in front of him. She let out helpless sputtering sounds as Harley locked his elbow around her neck.

"*You're—ch-cho—king—me!*" she was able to say.

Frank and Joe rushed toward her.

"Stand back!" Harley barked, holding the dagger to Tessa's throat. The brothers stopped in their tracks.

"It had to come to this, Tessa, didn't it?" Harley said, his voice rising to a high-pitched frenzy. "We had it planned so perfectly. We both could have been so happy for the rest of our lives. But you destroyed it—you destroyed it with your greed. Admit it!"

"H-Harley, stop it!" Tessa said, struggling to breathe. "You're out of your mind!"

Harley tightened his grip. "Admit how you betrayed me. Admit that you were going to take all the auction money for yourself and leave me with nothing—that you pretended to fall in love with Frank Hardy as an excuse to break up with me!"

"No! Please!" Tessa cried.

With a choked cry, Harley pushed her violently against the cabinet.

Whock! The doors flew open. Harley shot a glance upward, just in time to see the shower of plates and silverware flying toward his head.

Tessa wrenched herself loose and hit the

ground. The sound of crashing metal and porcelain was like an explosion.

Joe turned off the flashlight, and pandemonium broke loose.

It was only a matter of seconds that the fight lasted, but it ended with a dull thud.

When Joe shone the flashlight again, he was standing over Harley, who lay rock-still on the floor, the dagger dangling from his right hand.

"Oops. I, uh, I guess his head got in the way of the flashlight," Joe said with a guilty grin. "Hope he's okay, though."

"He'll be all right," Frank said, pulling Tessa away.

"He almost killed me!" she cried between gasps.

"Well, he's not too dangerous now," Frank reassured her. "At least until he wakes up."

From outside came the sound of a car door closing.

"Who could *that* be?" Callie asked.

"If we're lucky, it's the police, checking out some clue," replied Joe.

Tessa fell against Frank, shaking and trying to swallow breaths. He put his arm around her, and with Joe's help, they sat her down away from the mess.

"Please forgive me, Frank," Tessa said. "Harley was wrong. I did everything out of love for you—a love that was foolish and selfish—"

"Just a minute!" Callie broke in, pointing her

flashlight at all three of them. "There's something missing here. Maybe Harley did fire the shot at the country club, and put the wire in the pool, knowing the socket didn't work. But it couldn't have been only Harley who pulled that stunt at the party. How could he have shut off the electricity *and* pushed the statue down?"

Frank and Joe looked at Tessa. The sound of footsteps on the back stairs were like muffled drumbeats.

"And," Callie went on, "how could Harley have hidden the dagger? Frank was with him the whole time when he found it was missing!"

Instead of answering, Tessa gazed tensely at the door. A dull light illuminated the hallway as the footsteps approached the room and stopped.

"Don't bother to get up. I'll only be a minute," a voice said.

Frank, Joe, and Callie swung their heads around as the room was lit in a soft, flickering glow. Holding a kerosene lantern in her left hand. Dr. Lansdale smiled evilly. In her right hand was a gun.

"Here, my friends," she said with a cold glint in her eye, "is your missing link."

Chapter

18

DR. LANSDALE SNICKERED. "Just think, for a few brief moments you'll have been the only other people on this earth who knew about my almost-perfect plan."

"You!" Callie said under her breath.

"What's the matter? Didn't think a doddering old lady doctor had any guts?" She shook her head and gave Tessa a disgusted look. "You really blew it, Tessa. Everything had been going like clockwork. I was hoping this wouldn't have to get messy."

"You wouldn't kill us," Joe said.

"Oh? The three of you—stand together near Harley," Dr. Lansdale ordered. "Tessa, you move away. This will look like Harley shot them and then put a gun to his own head." She chuckled. "I can see the *Times* now—'HEIRESS'S JILTED BOYFRIEND IN TRAGIC BLOODBATH OVER LOVE.'

It'll be just another saga in the long history of the Borgia curse.''

Slowly Frank, Joe, and Callie stood up and walked toward Harley.

"Please, Aunt Harriet, I never expected—"

"That's enough, Tessa! Now get over here. Stand right by me!"

As Dr. Lansdale pointed her gun at Frank, Tessa meekly got up. "I—I tried to protect you, Aunt Harriet. I was all set to take the rap and leave you out of it. No one would have gotten in any real trouble—"

"And you'd kiss my money goodbye as Ruppenthal took everything back, right?" Dr. Lansdale shook her head. "Sorry, my naïve little girl."

Frank and Joe surveyed the room with their eyes, looking for some distraction, some way of escape. . . .

"Hands high and eyes straight at me!" Dr. Lansdale said sharply. "I wasn't born yesterday, you know."

The three of them had no choice. Dr. Lansdale's lantern cast ghostly shadows on their faces as they silently obeyed. Slowly, they edged toward the motionless Harley, as Tessa shuffled closer to the door.

"Faster! What is this? Am I in a nursing home?" Dr. Lansdale said impatiently.

Tessa hung her head as she obediently approached Dr. Lansdale.

"I hope you're competent enough to hold this," Dr. Lansdale said. She handed Tessa the lantern and then placed both hands on the gun. With a strong, steady motion, she raised it—and aimed it between Frank's eyes.

"What a waste," she said with a sigh. "This is the smart one." Carefully, she cocked the gun.

From the deepest reaches of her soul, Callie unleashed a long, terrified wail. She pressed her eyes tightly shut.

It was hard to tell what happened next. The room got brighter. A shot rang out. There was a scream.

Callie opened her eyes. "Frank!" she yelled. She turned to look at her boyfriend. His body was still standing. His arms were still raised in the air. His mouth hung open in amazement.

Callie looked over to the door. Tessa had raised the flame in the lantern to full blast—and was holding it in front of Dr. Lansdale's face.

"Enough! Enough!" Tessa shrieked, pushing the lantern into Dr. Lansdale's face again and again. "This was your idea in the first place! You turned Harley into an animal, you ruined my life—and now I see you for what you really are—"

"You spoiled little twit!" With a slow but well-placed swing of her left arm, Dr. Lansdale ripped the lantern out of Tessa's hand. It flew through the air and smashed underneath the oak table.

"I really didn't want to have to do this," Dr. Lansdale snarled.

She swung the gun at Tessa.

Now there was no question—it was the right time. Callie leapt across the room. With a swift chop, she attacked Dr. Lansdale's arm. The gun crashed to the floor and slid across the room.

Howling desperately, Dr. Lansdale dove after it. She reached for it, only to find a foot had gotten there first. Callie's foot. She kicked the gun sharply toward the lantern.

All eyes followed the gun—and suddenly the room became dead still. The gun was circled by flames. Flames that the lantern had thrown onto the dry, old floor and table.

"Put it out! Somebody!" Tessa yelled.

"Where's the fire extinguisher?" Joe asked urgently.

"Fire extinguisher? I don't—"

That was all Frank and Joe needed to hear. "Come on! This place is going to catch like a pile of dried twigs!" Frank shouted. He grabbed Callie and ran out, pulling Dr. Lansdale. Joe lifted Harley and carried him into the hallway.

They shot down the stairs and barged out the front door.

On the lawn was a squad car. Two policemen emerged from it and sprinted toward the mansion.

"Here they come!" a voice called out in the muggy night air. "Two white males, age eighteen to twenty-one—hold it, it's Frank and Joe Hardy!"

Cursing and scratching, Dr. Lansdale struggled to wrench herself from Frank's grip. "Let go of me, you disrespectful young—"

Frank ignored her as they stumbled toward the squad car. "Officer Riley—the third floor is on fire!" he shouted.

"I've got eyes, Frank," Riley replied. "I've just called the fire department." He lowered his brows in a scowl. "I happen to have ears too. We heard a shot. Who's going to be the one to explain it?"

"Officer, look what this young hoodlum is doing to me—" Dr. Lansdale yelled.

"Hey, hey, now!" Officer Riley said. "Have you gotten carried away, Frank? Let her go, she's safe now!"

"Officer Riley," Frank said, "this woman fired the shot you heard. It was meant for me."

Riley looked from Frank to Joe with suspicion. "*This* woman?"

"Wait a second!" Joe interrupted. "Why did you come here?"

Officer Riley held up a silver-plated revolver in a clear plastic case. "Exhibit A, from the Cliffside Country Club shooting. Our ballistics experts traced this to the Carpenters. Officer Novack and I were coming here to ask Miss Carpenter a few questions."

"Yes, it's hers!" Dr. Lansdale cried out. "Ar-

149

rest her! It's the Borgia curse—it's still following her! Arrest them all!''

"Ah, it's all clear now," Riley said, sarcastically. "We've got an ancient curse, an elderly lady who shoots young men, and a girl who's shot at by a person using her own gun."

"And therein lies—" Joe began.

Riley rolled his eyes. "A long story, I know." He grabbed Tessa and Dr. Lansdale. "Come on, you're both coming to the station house. It's going to be a long night."

But Tessa's eyes were fixed in sheer horror at the smoke that was now billowing from the third floor. "I—can't—leave," she said, in almost a whisper.

"It's her house," Officer Novack said. "Let's at least wait till the fire department gets here."

"Fire department!" Dr. Lansdale cackled. "If they're anywhere near as bright as you fellas, we'll be here all night!"

Officer Novack gave Dr. Lansdale a long, hard glance. "You've got some explaining to do," she said.

Dr. Lansdale folded her arms as Officer Riley reached for his handcuffs. Orange flames began to dance from the rooftop of the mansion. From the bottom of the hill came the sound of sirens.

Behind Frank was a soft, sniffling sound. Frank turned to see Callie, sobbing.

"I-I'm just a little shook up," she said.

"With good reason," Frank said. He wrapped

his right arm around her and looked deep into her moist eyes. "*You're* the reason we're all alive."

Callie wiped away a tear and smiled. "Well, the Hardy family aren't the *only* good crime-fighters in Bayport!"

Together they watched the burning mansion with a bittersweet sadness.

Joe buttoned his leather jacket and rolled up the window of the van. "What kind do you want to get?" he asked.

"Now let's get this straight," Frank answered sharply. "This Halloween candy is only for kids who come to the house, okay? I don't want this to be like last year, when you finished it all off yourself!"

"Fine, fine," Joe said as Frank steered the van out of the brisk October air and into the shopping mall.

They were alone in the elevator as they took it up through the mall. Slowly it came to a stop at the third floor.

"Watch it, Joe!" Frank shouted. They both peeled to opposite walls as the door slid open to reveal a short, bald man with a machine gun.

"Trick or treat!" a voice squeaked from behind the mask.

"Honey, come on," a woman behind him said, urging him into the elevator. "These boys are shopping. Wait till we get home."

Frank and Joe chuckled as they walked through

151

the floor. "Looked a little like Albert Ruppenthal," Frank said.

"Yeah, except Ruppenthal's smiling a lot more since he got that court injunction to get the Carpenter collection back."

"Well, he'll be spending a lot more time in court, what with that suit against Tessa for destroying the Greek statue—"

"And the suit against Harley for hiring those two thugs to rough him up!"

Frank smiled. "What a day that was. You should have seen the look on Harley's face when he knew they were coming, and we were the only ones in Ruppenthal's office!"

"And little did you know Ruppenthal saw the whole thing through the window, walking back to the museum from lunch that day."

"Yeah, no wonder he wanted to get out of town so fast."

Motorized witch models flew around a replica of a haunted mansion in a toy store window they passed.

Joe looked at it briefly and turned to Frank. "I hear they've repaired the damage to the third floor of the Carpenter place. Has Tessa finally decided to get an apartment and turn the old house into a museum?"

"Those were the rumors a while back," Frank said with a shrug of his shoulders. "The last time I spoke to her was at Harley and Dr. Lansdale's sentencings. She said she had let the fire insurance policy lapse on the mansion, so the repairs had to come from her own pocket. Now she's more broke than ever. She's just lucky most of the artwork survived."

They stopped to watch a soap opera flickering from seven TV sets in a store window. A young blond man in a tuxedo was trying to comfort a woman in a mink coat. The woman was sobbing hysterically, her head buried in a sofa pillow.

"I wonder what ever happened to Tessa," Joe mused.

"Got some sort of job, I guess," Frank suggested.

"But what? What kind of job could someone like that possibly be qualified to do?"

They watched the soap opera quietly for a few more minutes. The blond guy stormed out, revealing a butler who was eavesdropping.

The brothers began to turn away. But suddenly their attention was drawn to the TV again. In a shrieking rage, the rich young woman burst up from the sofa and faced the butler.

Both Frank's and Joe's eyes popped open as they found themselves staring into seven images of Tessa Carpenter's face.

"I guess that answers my question," Joe said. "Looks like she must have turned to Simon Lesterman to help her."

Tessa stormed around the room, sometimes screaming and breaking furniture, sometimes pleading. The butler pleaded with her to stop.

"It's just like she is in real life," Frank said.

"And don't look now, but the butler is played by Edwin Squinder!"

As Joe watched Tessa and Squinder's furious overacting, his mouth slowly formed the trace of a smile. "You know," he said, "I think they're both finally where they belong."

The sound of Frank and Joe's laughter echoed through the mall, mixed with the muffled screaming from the TV set, as they raced each other to the candy store.